P9-CQZ-477

F. Rosanne Bittner
Tennessee Bride

POPULAR LIBRARY

An Imprint of Warner Books, Inc.

A Warner Communications Company

POPULAR LIBRARY EDITION

Popular Library® and the fanciful P design are registered
trademarks of Warner Books, Inc.

Cover illustration by John Ennis

Popular Library books are published by
Warner Books, Inc.
666 Fifth Avenue
New York, N.Y. 10103

 A Warner Communications Company

Printed in the United States of America

First Printing: June, 1988

10 9 8 7 6 5 4 3 2 1

I saw him the first time,
In the sweet green of spring.
My eyes fell upon him,
And I wanted to sing.

He was strong, and so handsome;
So wild and so free;
A man of the mountains,
In high Tennessee.

His arms drew me close,
And I melted away.
His lips warmed my own,
And together we lay...

In the soft mountain grasses,
Where he made me his bride.
And our love, through all hardships,
To the end shall abide.

—F. Rosanne Bittner

◊ *Author's Note* ◊

This story takes place in the state of Tennessee, between 1824 and 1827. The location is mostly along the Hiwassee River in the Smoky Mountains of eastern Tennessee.

Although the leading characters in this story are white, parts of my story involve Cherokee Indians. As in all my stories, I work diligently on historical accuracy, especially when writing about the American Indians, for whom I have a great respect. Therefore, you will find in this story a few references to the Cherokee fight through Congress and the courts to be allowed to stay in their homelands of Tennessee and Georgia. These particular references are based on fact, and there really was a Cherokee Indian leader named John Ross who led this legal fight all the way to the Supreme Court.

Although my story does not take the readers all the way through this legal battle, it might be of interest to you to know that the Cherokee won and the Supreme Court ruled that they could stay—at least in the state of Georgia. However, the state of Georgia defied the Supreme Court ruling and forced their Indians into Indian Territory (Oklahoma), along what has come to be called the infamous "Trail of Tears."

Although some real history is involved in this novel, major characters in this story, as well as the basic story line, are purely fictitious and a product of this author's imagination.

◇ *Prologue* ◇

He was called River Joe, and to most he remained a man of mystery, a topic for gossip over glasses of whiskey in the taverns, and over the clotheslines of the women in the mountain settlements. He was a white man, but raised by Cherokee Indians—"as mean at heart as those savages," some said.

Every spring River Joe came down from Indian settlements high in the Smokies to trade deerskins, handmade bearskin coats, and the like for food and supplies to take back to his people. He never said much, and even though his blood was white, he didn't trust most other white men. After all, the white settlers in this part of Tennessee had already chased the Cherokee to higher elevations, where they had found peace and safety from white raiders who burned their homes and crops and abused their women.

"Captured by the Cherokee," some said about River Joe. "Just a boy then. They say his pa was killed and his ma was killed, too, only she was raped first. That goes to show you the kind of people them Indians are. No matter how civilized they say they are, their men still pant after white women and their own women is loose as prostitutes. And that River Joe might be a white man, but his heart is Indian, and folks had better not trust him too far."

Such were the rumors fifteen-year-old Emma Simms had heard about the mysterious River Joe. Emma didn't know

1

much about the outside world, for she had never strayed far from the broken-down farm along the Hiwassee River where she lived with her mother and stepfather, Luke Simms. Luke was a hard, cruel man, who during drunken rages often beat Emma and her mother.

Emma stayed away from Luke as much as possible, which was why she often went for walks alone, especially to a special place along the Hiwassee where she had found an old raft caught in the rushes along the bank of the river. Emma considered the raft, the wildflowers, and mountain laurel that bloomed all around as her own secret retreat; the only place where she could go to dream a young girl's dreams, where she could hide away from her cruel stepfather and was free to wonder about the man called River Joe.

On a gentle day in spring 1823, Emma suddenly realized she was not alone in her secret hideaway. She felt someone watching her, and as she cautiously moved her eyes along the surrounding forest, she saw him—a tall man in buck-skins, his hair a dark brown but long like an Indian's, his eyes dark but showing no malice. And she knew in that moment that she saw him only because he had decided to allow himself to be seen.

Emma could only stare back at the intruder. But it was not fear that made her speechless. It was surprise, and total fas-cination. How many times had he watched her before, with-out her knowing it? He was the handsomest man she had ever seen, and surely the tallest. His shoulders were broad and powerful-looking, and a wonderful warmth flowed through her as his dark eyes moved over her. Then, as quickly as he had appeared, he vanished, and she realized she had not even been afraid of the stranger.

For the next three days, every time Emma went to the raft, the tall man in buckskins appeared, saying nothing, only watching her, then quickly disappearing. Emma made a secret vow not to tell Luke or even her mother about the stranger. Luke would probably try to shoot him, and her mother had enough problems of her own. Her mother would never understand Emma's fascination, her wonderful secret. She would tell Emma she must never return to the raft—the secret retreat that made her hard life bearable.

Emma had never had anything all her own—but now she had this, her own special hideaway, and a secret. She had seen the white Indian. She was sure it was he who had watched her, and the memory filled her dreams at night.

But then he stopped coming. Spring turned to a blistering, steamy summer, and then fall and winter. Gradually Emma forced herself to stop thinking about the stranger, for apparently he had left for good; the only excitement she had ever had in her short life was gone. Reality brought back hard work and cruel beatings, and her mother, who had lost several children, became pregnant again. Spring and the birth of the baby approached, but the tall man in buckskins did not return.

Emma stopped watching for him, thinking him gone for good. Little did she realize that those first glimpses of the white Indian were the beginning of a great love that would carry her to hell and back . . . back into the arms of a man called River Joe.

◊ *Chapter 1* ◊

It should have been a beautiful morning, that spring day in 1824. But sixteen-year-old Emma could not hear the birds singing. She did not see the blooming wildflowers or the lovely blue sky.

The only person who had come close to loving Emma Simms, who might have protected her from those who threatened and terrified her, lay in a grave at Emma's feet. Her mother, Betty Simms, was dead. After years of miscarriages, with Emma her only surviving child, Betty had finally carried a baby full-term, only to die giving birth. The baby had died soon after.

Emma had no doubt that the difficult birth and all the miscarriages before it were the fault of her stepfather, Luke Simms, whose name Emma had long ago been ordered to take as her own. Luke had worked both Emma and her mother like plow horses on his small farm along the Hiwassee, deep in the Smoky Mountains of Tennessee.

Life was hard, and the farm had never amounted to much, for Luke was lazy and liked his whiskey. While fences needed mending and sheds were falling down, Luke had begun selling off livestock. There were only a few pigs and cows left, and Emma wondered how they were going to survive much longer.

"Ashes to ashes," the preacher was saying now. He had come from a distant settlement, one Emma had never seen.

4

She had lived her whole life on this little farm, which her real father had owned. He had died when she was four years old. Her mother had then married Luke, a neighbor, who seemed friendly enough at the time, but who soon turned into a drunken tyrant, putting his "woman" and stepdaughter to work, using a hard hand on them when they "got lazy." He had never been kind to Emma, nor had he seemed to have any fatherly feelings for her. And after Emma's mother had had several miscarriages, Luke seemed to resent her more and more, accusing her of being a "useless woman" for not giving him any children of his own.

Now Betty Simms lay dead after trying to do just that. Twenty-nine. She was only twenty-nine. Compared to her mother, Emma was already an old maid at sixteen. Her mother had given birth to her at thirteen.

"Mountain girls get married young," Luke Simms was always complaining. *"Why ain't that daughter of yours married off yet? You know Tommy Decker wants to marry her."*

"She hates Tommy Decker," her mother would argue. *"Tommy would be cruel to her."*

"A man can treat a woman any way he pleases," Luke would answer, glowering.

Betty Simms always gave up the argument then, but at least she helped stave off any decision about Emma's marrying Tommy.

Emma's eyes stung with tears as she stared at the wooden box in the freshly dug hole behind the collapsing cabin where she would now live alone with her stepfather, a thought that made her feel ill. She had not known truly warm love and affection even from her mother in years, but she didn't blame the woman. Betty Simms was worn out and abused. She had turned hard; she had lost the ability to see beauty in life, the ability to love softly and gently.

But Emma struggled to hold these things in her own heart. In one tiny corner of her mind she knew by instinct that there were such things as peace and love and that the song of birds and the brilliance of spring flowers were things of beauty. In stolen quiet moments alone she had allowed the sweet air of the Tennessee mountains to renew her spirit; let the soft swish of the rushing waters of the Hiwassee River soothe her soul; let the sight of a bird in flight give her dreams of going away and finding a better life; and she had dared to dream of loving a man who would be kind and gentle, a man who would be nothing like her stepfather, or like Tommy Decker, who stood now on the other side of her mother's grave.

She refused to look at Tommy. Surely now that her mother was gone, Tommy would come for her, demand that her stepfather allow them to marry. Emma could think of nothing worse than being Tommy Decker's wife. To call herself a slave would be a more fitting description. And she shivered at the thought of how he would treat her in the night. He had told her several times, with an ugly, teasing grin, exactly what a man and woman did to get babies.

"And we're gonna have lots of babies, Emma Louise Simms, if you get my meanin'."

"I might be like my mother and not be able to have babies," Emma would reply.

"Well then, we'll have fun findin' out, won't we?"

Emma swallowed back a lump in her throat. She felt exposed now, vulnerable, unprotected. Her mother's objections had been the only barrier between herself and Tommy. Now she could feel his cold blue eyes on her. She guessed Tommy could be considered good-looking, if he were not so mean. He was twenty now, tall and strong, his hair red as fire and his skin peppered with freckles. If he smiled kindly, it might be a nice smile. She had struggled to find something about him to like but had never come up with even one commendable trait.

Tommy hadn't an ounce of kindness in his soul. Every time he came to visit her father, sometimes with his friend, Deek Malone, he took the opportunity to tease Emma with talk of bad things men and women did together, to threaten her physically. She had always stayed near the house, and she had always depended on her mother to protect her. But now her mother was gone, and she knew instinctively that Luke would never help her if Tommy chose to go through with any of his threats.

She glanced at her stepfather and saw no tears. The man stood staring at the wooden box as though he were angry at Betty Simms for dying and taking the baby with her, and he had always blamed Emma for her mother's birthing problems.

"If she hadn't had you so damned early in life, her insides wouldn't be all messed up," he would say. *"That first husband of hers should have kept himself from between her legs for a while, till she was older."*

The words rang in Emma's ears. Picturing what he meant, and remembering Tommy's descriptions of mating, made her positive she could never do such things. Even if she met a kind man, the thought of having babies terrified her now—not only the act of mating, but having seen her mother's pain and agony and now her death. Taking a man and having babies were surely humiliating, painful experiences, and she wanted no part of it, especially not with Tommy Decker.

She could not help letting out a whimper then, and her thin shoulders shook. So many things confused her, the contrasts between beauty and ugliness, peace and turmoil, smiles and tears, life and death. She had no one to console her, to talk to her, explain things to her—only Luke, Tommy, and his father, Jake, who were their closest neighbors, and the preacher. Emma wished she could talk to Mrs. Breckenridge, the traveling schoolteacher who had spent so much time with her a year ago. Mrs. Breckenridge and her husband were dedicated people who trudged through the Smokies, visiting mountain families and bringing formal schooling to children who would otherwise have none. The little bit of reading and writing and numbers Emma had learned had made her hungry for more, and her mind had begun to fill with curiosity about the outside world.

Mrs. Breckenridge had worn fine dresses and had told her about theaters and schools of higher learning, and big stores in big cities like Knoxville where a person could walk in and pick out anything she needed and buy it on the spot. Through Mrs. Breckenridge Emma had seen another kind of life, a gentler life, and most of all, she had seen love—real love between a man and a woman. Mr. Breckenridge was so good and considerate, with never a harsh word for his wife.

Then Luke Simms, in a drunken rage, had thrown both Mr. and Mrs. Breckenridge off his property, telling them never to come back.

"Quit fillin' my daughter with ideas about bein' somethin' special," he had shouted. *"She knows her place. She's right where she belongs, helpin' her ma and pa. Before long she'll be married off and busy puttin' out babies like a woman's meant to do. She don't need no education."*

The Breckenridges had left, fearing for their lives, and Luke Simms had burned the few books Mrs. Breckenridge had left behind. Emma would not forget that day for the rest of her life. She felt a prison door was closing on her. Now, with her mother dead, that door had been locked. She didn't know enough about the outside world to go into it alone. This little farm deep in the mountains had been her whole world. With no money, little education, and no experience in anything but feeding pigs, how could she go to the big cities Mrs. Breckenridge had told her about? Calhoun, Knoxville —they were downriver, far away. And they were places Emma knew next to nothing about.

The future seemed hopeless now. Instinct told her the Breckenridges would not return. They had deserted her, just as her mother had now deserted her in death.

Emma lifted her tear-filled blue eyes from the grave, trying to find some beauty in the day to keep her from wanting to die. Rhododendrons and azaleas bloomed wild here and there in the surrounding woods. Mockingbirds, robins, wood thrushes, and hundreds of other birds sang their songs, oblivious to the sorrow in Emma's heart. The hickory, oak, sycamore, poplar, and maple trees all burst with new green leaves; nuts were forming on a nearby walnut tree, their green skin hard and new.

She concentrated on the woods and the birds, not even hearing the rest of the preacher's words. She let her mind wander to less painful thoughts, remembering those four days last spring when she had seen the white Indian. He had never come back, but for a long time she had wondered about him, fantasized about him.

Somehow she sensed he was different from Luke and Tommy. He could have hurt her, could have done bad things to her, but he had not. And the look in his dark eyes still brought a wonderful warmth that moved deep inside her chest and belly, stirring a curiosity about men, making her wonder about things she had never dared to consider before.

And then, as though some powerful spirit had read her mind, her thoughts took form. The white Indian appeared in the trees just beyond where Luke and Tommy stood. Emma was unable to stifle a gasp, and it made everyone else turn.

He stood so still at first that one would hardly have noticed him, the way a deer would do to keep from being seen. Yes, Emma could see it was the same man, the same magnificent body and buckskin clothing! His nearly waist-length hair was tied to one side of his head and hung down his broad chest, nearly reaching the wide, leather weapons belt he wore. His skin was tanned dark, and even from a distance Emma could see he was as handsome as ever.

"My God! It's that white Indian," Jake Decker exclaimed.

"What!" Tommy Decker stared. "Hey you!" he shouted. "What the hell are you doin' there watchin' us?"

To Emma's disappointment, the stranger turned and disappeared. Her heart pounded with excitement, and suddenly she felt hot and sweaty. He had come back! It had been a whole year, and he was back again! Why? She had thought she would never see the white Indian again. How ironic that she should see him now, in this sad, dark moment of her life.

"You sure that was River Joe?" Luke asked Jake.

"Sure I'm sure! I seen him once—last year—tradin' with Hank Toole."

"Kind of gives you the shivers." Luke scowled.

"Probably sneakin' a look at Emma," Tommy said. Emma felt his eyes on her again. She refused to look back at him. "All that pretty blond hair probably fascinates him, after livin' around them savages all his life."

"Not all the Cherokee are savages, son," the preacher cut in. "Most are quite civilized."

Tommy looked darkly at the man. "You preachers and your missionaries are always on the side of people like that. But they're still savages as far as I'm concerned—me and most others around here. We've already chased them higher up into the mountains, and if we're lucky they'll get out of Tennessee altogether. The government is gonna make some laws that will chase all of them pesty buggers clean to Indian Territory where they belong."

The preacher breathed deeply, and Emma could see he was struggling to control his temper. "I do believe they were here first, Mr. Decker."

"Maybe they were, but this land is meant for us whites. We know what to do with it. They waste it." Tommy clenched his fists. "And I don't like that white Indian goin' around peekin' at my woman."

Emma felt her pride and anger rise quickly at the remark. "I'm not your woman!" she blurted, fighting her terror.

"You will be soon!"

"Mr. Decker, this is a funeral," the preacher interrupted. "This poor girl's mother has just died, and I have not finished the service yet."

"Then hurry up and finish," Tommy yelled. "I want to go find that River Joe and find out what the hell he was doin' around here!"

Emma burst into tears and dropped to her knees beside the grave.

"I'm sure he was just coming here to trade something or

look for a job. He has worked other places. He means no harm, Mr. Decker. I'm sure he left because he realized there was a funeral taking place."

"You calm yourself, Tommy," said Jake, the young man's father. "Let the preacher finish his service."

Emma sniffed and wiped at her eyes with a shaking hand. How she wished her mother would just wake up and come back to protect her. The preacher continued his little sermon, and soon it was time to shovel the dirt into the hole.

Emma wanted to scream. She wanted to tear at the box and pull her mother out. She almost hated Betty for leaving her now. Why had her mother not just left Luke? In her heart Emma knew the answer: remote mountain life was all the woman had ever known; she was afraid of the outside world.

Emma wondered then if her own fate would be the same. Would she end up abused all her life, married to a cruel man, finally dying young, never knowing anything else? She wept as Luke and Jake filled in the grave.

Tommy watched Emma, hungering for her. She was the prettiest girl in the mountains. Her blond hair was the color of cornsilk, her eyes big and blue. Over the past year her breasts had filled out to a roundness that made them seem too big for her tiny body. She was so small for her age that she always seemed too young to marry, even though she was older than most married mountain girls.

But Tommy wasn't really sure he wanted a wife at all. If he could have Emma Simms without marrying her, that would be even better, for he wasn't certain he wanted to settle in these mountains and be just a homesteader. He liked adventure, wanted to go to a big city like Knoxville. He liked riding with young men from other settlements, liked heading into the mountains to raid Cherokee settlements.

Tommy Decker was sure he knew all he needed to know about women. He had taken most of his own by force, finding the fight stimulating, convinced that they all actually enjoyed it. But he had not been able to conquer Emma, and it frustrated him. She was so stubborn and proud, and would hardly look at him. Other girls had fought him, but not with the same determination in their eyes. Most of the others had given up in the end, but something told him Emma would never give up, never submit to him willingly.

He wanted badly to break her down. It was becoming obvious that even if he married her, she would still not be willing. And for some reason Luke Simms still had not given his final permission to marry Emma. Tommy could not imagine why the man was putting him off, but it didn't matter anymore. Tommy didn't really want to be married and tied down. He had considered it only in order to get under Emma's skirts, but more and more he was determined to do that without the bonds of marriage.

Now that Emma's mother was dead, perhaps it would not be so difficult. Emma's mother had always gone along with Emma's refusal to marry Tommy. But now if Tommy took what he wanted without the legality of marriage, Luke probably wouldn't do a thing about it. Luke didn't care one whit about his stepdaughter.

That girl needs a good lesson, he thought. He was sure, with all his experience, that once he got inside her she would like it. She would probably wish she had given in sooner, and then he would get the ultimate revenge. He would break her down and then refuse to marry her, just as she had been refusing him. He smiled at the thought of it, almost laughed out loud.

Emma got to her feet, still sniffling, and walked toward the woods to pick a few wildflowers to put on her mother's grave. She wiped at her eyes, staring into the trees for a moment, wondering where the strange white Indian called River Joe had gone, and why he had finally made another appearance. For some reason, the vision of him would not leave her mind, and she almost hoped that he might be somewhere near, still watching her.

She turned and walked back to the grave, which was now completely covered, and laid the flowers on it.

"I'm gonna get on Smoke and see if I can find that River Joe," Tommy said then.

"You'd be better off leavin' him be," his father told him. "You don't know nothin' about that man. He might be dangerous."

"He isn't dangerous if he isn't pushed," the preacher told them.

"We'll see," Tommy answered, walking over to his "fine black." That was what he called his horse, a gelding called Smoke. Tommy was very proud of it, the only thing of value he had to call his own. But Emma hated the animal, which was as cocky and unpredictable as its owner. Tommy had deliberately chased her down once with the horse, and when she fell, he threatened to ride right over her.

He walked over to the animal now and mounted up. Emma was glad he was leaving.

"Ain't no white Indian can get the best of Tommy Decker," he announced, sitting straight and sure on his "fine black," trying to make an impression on Emma. "I've raided many a Cherokee settlement. They don't even fight back."

He rode off into the woods, and the preacher shook his head. "I wouldn't count on River Joe not fighting back," he commented. "But I doubt Mr. Decker will find him. River Joe is the kind of man who is found only if he wants to be."

Emma stared into the woods again, at the spot where River Joe had disappeared. She felt that seeing the white Indian had been some kind of sign, a vision that somehow consoled her.

"Give the girl some time," she heard the preacher say to her stepfather. "It is a great shock to a girl when she loses her mother. Don't force her to marry right away."

"It's time," Luke Simms answered. "The girl is sixteen years old. Tommy wants her. And with her ma gone, I'm thinkin' of sellin' this farm and gettin' out altogether. Got no future here. I been talkin' to Hank Toole about jobs in

Knoxville. Hank will be comin' by on his riverboat again soon and I'll have him tell folks up and down the river that my place is for sale. If I leave here, I ain't takin' that girl with me. I'm on my own then. And if Tommy don't want her, Hank says he's got some ideas for what I can do with her."

Emma didn't wait to hear the rest. Terror filled her heart. Her future was being decided for her, and there would be nothing she could do to change it. Why had Luke been talking to Hank Toole about her? Hank operated a riverboat called the *Jasmine*, running it up and down the Tennessee and Hiwassee rivers, trading with the mountain people and taking their wares and produce back to Knoxville where he sold them for a profit.

Hank came by about once a month. He had always been friendly to Emma, acting like a jolly friend, telling her tall tales about city life; but there had been something about his attitude the last couple of years that made Emma uneasy and almost afraid. She could not imagine what kind of "ideas" Hank could have for her if Tommy didn't want to marry her. Emma was curious about the world outside her farm but sometimes terrified of it, and now she wished the *Jasmine* would not come by this month at all.

She walked off in the opposite direction from that in which Tommy had ridden, wanting to be alone, to think, to decide what she could do to avoid having to marry Tommy, without having to go away with Hank Toole. Most of all, she wanted to think about seeing River Joe again.

She headed for her little hideaway, the raft that still lay lodged along the riverbank, wanting to get away from Luke and the depressing grave. As she stumbled and climbed over vines and fallen trees, someone watched, his dark eyes following her. He moved behind her then, his moccasined feet making no noise, the dancing fringes of his buckskins and his quick movements blurring into the background of quivering leaves. He studied the golden hair, her exquisite shape;

its perfect roundness obvious even under her loose cotton dress. She was older now, a budding young woman. And she was beautiful, the prettiest white girl River Joe had ever seen. He silently followed her to the raft.

◊ *Chapter 2* ◊

Emma wept. She had no idea how long she had been sitting on the old raft, but the tears of sorrow and terror would not stop. It felt good to cry, but so terribly lonely, for there was no one to care, no one to comfort her.

Finally she leaned over and reached into the water, splashing its cool refreshment onto her face and washing away the tears. She was afraid of the river's rushing waters and would not go in to swim. Luke was always talking about how many people had drowned in this river, and when she was smaller Tommy Decker had hung her upside down in the water so that he could see under her dress when it fell away from her. She would never forget the humiliating and terrifying moment as he held her legs and kept her under the water until she was sure her lungs would burst and she would drown. Nor would she forget the day she saw the body of a little boy who had drowned at a settlement farther upriver and had floated to shore at her farm.

But she felt safe on the raft. She could watch the river from it, and for years she had sat there to watch for the *Jasmine*, and Hank Toole, who always brought her some trinket from the big city. She no longer watched for Hank with much enthusiasm. Now she just wished she could stay in her little hideaway forever. But that was impossible, and she knew she must think hard now, plan; she must consider what she should do now that her mother was dead.

She could not run away on her own. She would most likely die in the mountains, for she did not have the slightest idea where to go or how to survive alone in the forest. A wild animal might eat her alive, or she might die from exposure and hunger. Even if she survived, what would she do when she got to a city? She had no skills, no money, and no knowledge of the ways of city people.

But Hank Toole did. Hank knew Knoxville well. A terrible helplessness swept over her when she realized Hank might be her only choice.

She stared downriver. He had always been friendly to her. In spite of the discomfort she felt in his presence, maybe he would be kind enough to take her on his riverboat to Knoxville, where Mrs. Breckenridge might be living now. Surely Hank would do at least that much for her. Then she could get a job in Knoxville and pay Hank back.

She felt almost sick at the few choices she had. Could she really trust Hank Toole? In his most recent visits, he had insisted on putting an arm around her, giving her squeezes, calling her "honey," and commenting on how Luke's "little girl" was getting all grown up. She wished she knew why Hank made her feel so afraid, wished she understood people better. Hank was the kind of man whose words and gestures were always friendly, but his dull blue eyes were hard to read. He wore fancy suits, but they never fitted his short frame quite right. His belly hung out over his pants, and he always needed a shave. Still, it wasn't his appearance as much as his eyes and his gestures that bothered her.

Maybe it would be best just to give Hank a letter to deliver to Mrs. Breckenridge. The woman would come for her then, Emma was sure. Mrs. Breckenridge would insist that Emma be allowed to go home with her and her husband. The only obstacle was that Hank was friendly with Luke. Emma wasn't sure the man would help her if it meant going against what Luke wanted.

As she picked a wildflower, her racing mind came up with yet another idea. She could sneak aboard the *Jasmine* and stow away until it was too late for Hank to turn back. Then, no matter what Luke wanted, Hank would have to take her on to Knoxville! Maybe her fear of the man was silly. After all, she had known Hank since she was a little girl. He certainly wouldn't hurt her. She took hope in the thought, and she decided that she would start packing her things into a gunnysack that very night so that she would be ready. It might be a week before Hank came, but then again it could be tomorrow.

She breathed deeply to keep from crying; she must be strong and brave now. Her mother was gone. There was no one to fight for Emma Simms but Emma Simms herself.

She fought the panic that kept trying to edge into her soul. Her mother was dead. None of it seemed real. She had just put flowers on the woman's grave, yet she expected to go home and find Betty Simms breaking open a jar of home-canned cherries or hoeing up a new spring garden.

She stood and turned to go back. She wanted to be alone beside her mother's grave. She did not look forward to the rest of the day. Tommy, his father, and Luke would probably all get dead drunk tonight, and she would have to cook for them and wait on them. Emma had to be nice to Luke's "guests," rude as they might be, or Luke would hit her. And she could only hope that Tommy would get so drunk that he would pass out. That was the only way he would leave her alone. Until he passed out, she would have to find ways to stay away from him.

She started off the raft, then stood still, watching, listening. She felt the presence again. Her heart pounded with curiosity and anticipation, a sixth sense telling her she was again being watched.

A moment later River Joe moved out of nearby trees that camouflaged him. For several long seconds they just looked at each other, and again Emma felt a pleasant warmth and a surprising absence of fear.

"*Siyu*," he greeted her.

Emma swallowed before speaking. "What do you want?" she asked, her voice squeaking from surprise and caution.

"I heard you crying. And I saw you on that old raft," he answered. "It is dangerous to stand on old, rotten wood."

His perfect English surprised her. His voice was calm and sure. She told herself she must be crazy to trust him, to be speaking to him. "You . . . you've got no right here. This is my private place. Nobody else has ever come here."

A faint smile passed over his full, finely etched lips, lighting a face so utterly handsome she could not help staring.

"Places like this do not belong to one person," he answered. "They come from *Esaugetuh Emissee*, the Maker of Breath, and they are for everyone."

"The Maker of Breath?"

He nodded. "God."

She studied the woods all around him. Could she get past this man if he meant her harm? He looked very powerful, and he wore a big knife at his waist, as well as a pistol.

"Well, I don't know about your Maker of Breath. All I know is I have to get back, and—"

Suddenly a board snapped, and she screamed as her right foot caved through the underside of the raft. The river was high from spring runoff, and Emma's struggles to get her foot free set the raft in motion. Before she could scream for him to help her, River Joe was there grabbing on to the raft as it began to float into the cold waters.

"Don't let go! Don't let go!" Emma yelled. "Don't let me go into the water!" She struggled vainly to get her foot loose from the splintered wood as River Joe fought against the strong current, trying to get the heavy raft back up onto shore.

"Sit still!" he told her. "Wait until I get this thing out of the water!"

She clung to the edge of the raft, watching him strain to pull it higher onto the shore. He tugged, dragging it up onto the bank with strong arms, then leaned close, breaking the boards with his bare hands to release her foot.

"I told you this thing was dangerous," he said.

She watched in surprise, amazed at his quick movement, his clear speech, and the strength of his big hands as he pulled her leg free of the boards. Then he reached around her waist and lifted her off the raft.

She noticed that he smelled of leather and fresh air, a wonderful, clean, spicy scent. She clung to his arm and looked up at him, feeling strangely warm when her eyes met his dark gaze. He held her close for a moment, and her heart pounded with a mixture of terror and fascination. For that one brief moment she forgot about her problems, felt comforted, protected. This was a wild, white Indian, a man she didn't know at all, and here she was letting him hold her.

"Why were you crying?" he asked, his strong arm still tight around her. "Who was in the grave?"

Her eyes filled again, reality returning. "My mother."

With genuine sympathy, he said, "I am sorry. Remember that death is only part of the great circle of life. It is not to be feared. Someday you will be with your mother again. In the meantime be glad that she has been freed of the hardships of this life."

Their eyes held a moment longer, and she felt comforted; she almost wished he would enfold her in both his arms and hold her even longer. How wonderful it would feel to be held! She began to redden then, realizing she was still pressed close to him and had not objected. "I think you should . . . put me down."

The faint smile returned and he gently released her. "Are you all right?"

She looked down at her leg and bent to feel her ankle. "I think so." She straightened, meeting his eyes again. "Thank you. I . . . I'm afraid of the water. I saw the dead body of a boy once who had drowned upriver." How could she tell him about the humiliating thing Tommy had done to her?

"You should not be afraid of the water. Or of anything."

"Aren't you ever afraid?"

An odd sadness darkened his eyes. "Only for my people, the Cherokee, and what is happening to them."

"Then you *are* the one they call the white Indian—River Joe?"

He nodded. "What are you called?"

"I'm Emma Simms."

His eyes moved over her, and she suddenly felt naked. She stepped back slightly. "If I scream real loud, Luke will hear me and come," she said defensively.

He grinned. "I will give you no reason to scream. Who is Luke?"

"My stepfather."

"And who is that boy who yelled at me?"

She guessed River Joe's age to be perhaps twenty-six to thirty. Tommy was younger, but it was more the difference in their personalities and conduct that made the age difference seem even greater. Yes, to River Joe someone like Tommy must be just a boy.

"Tommy Decker. His pa is a friend to my stepfather. They're from the MacBain settlement."

"You are Tommy's woman?"

Her face reddened and her eyes flamed. "Never! I hate him! He wants to marry me, but I won't do it."

His eyebrows arched and he grinned again. "Then whose woman are you?"

She could feel the crimson in her cheeks. The way he referred to her as someone's woman gave her wonderful, warm feelings, and an odd pressure deep inside that she had never felt before. "I . . . I'm nobody's woman."

His eyes moved over her again. He thought of Yellow Sky, dear, sweet Yellow Sky. But she had been dead a long time. "Most girls your age belong to a man," he told Emma.

She folded her arms in front of her self-consciously. "First a girl has to find a man she wants to be with. It really isn't your business, you know, whether I belong to anyone." She felt proud that she was actually talking boldly face to face with the white Indian everyone else feared. She saw the faint smile again, and she was annoyed. "Why do you always look at me? Why did you come here last year and then leave for so long a time?"

His eyes moved over her again. "You were not ready."

"Ready for what?"

He smiled more. "It does not matter. I will tell you this much. I came back because I wanted to see you again, see how you had grown. I traveled farther south last year than I usually do; and in my travels I came upon this place and caught sight of you. I liked what I saw, and all last winter back up in the mountains I thought about you, the girl with the cornsilk hair and eyes like the sky. I came to see if you were still here, and I am glad that you are."

Her cheeks felt hot. Was he saying she was pretty? Was she being too bold and taking a great risk standing here talking to him? "You shouldn't be here, you know," she told him. "And you shouldn't go around sneaking up on folks like that. You could get in a lot of trouble. Some people think you are bad."

He nodded, smiling sadly. "You go back now. It would not be good for us to be found here. I am considered Cherokee, even though I am white. Men like your father think a pretty white girl should not talk to an Indian."

She rubbed at the backs of her arms nervously, wishing his dark eyes would not make her feel so flustered and warm. "He's not my father. I told you, he's my stepfather. He's not a nice man, and I don't much care what he thinks about who I talk to." She looked around the woods. "Where did you come from?"

"I live much higher in the mountains. But for now I have a camp not far from here—my horse and a pack horse are there. I have brought deerskins to trade to Hank Toole."

"You know Hank?"

He nodded again. "I have traded many times with the man who travels the river." He stopped short then, listening. "Voices. They come looking for you. I must go, for your sake." He walked past her and she turned.

"River Joe!"

He stopped and turned.

"Thank you . . . for helping me."

He studied her beauty again, wishing he could carry her back with him, this lovely girl with the golden hair who had never known a man. For some reason it angered him to think of someone like the smart-mouthed Tommy Decker being her first. Would she be obligated to marry him, now that her mother was dead?

"Be strong, Emma Simms. I will pray to *Esaugetuk Emissee* and ask Him to give you strength and courage for the lonely days ahead. I know the feeling of losing a loved one through death. I have lost a mother . . . and a wife."

He turned and disappeared, as though he were no more than a spirit. She watched after him. A mother, and a wife! A wife! River Joe, the white Indian, had lost a wife to death. She had seen such loneliness in his eyes when he told her. And she felt such warmth at the memory of being held close to him. She found herself swept by an overwhelming disappointment that he had gone. Perhaps she would never see him again. Yet she still did not fully understand why he had come at all.

"Emma! Where the hell are you!"

"Here, Luke." She hurriedly left her secret hideaway, not wanting him to see it, and ran through the woods toward his voice.

When she reached him, he gave her a shove toward the cabin. "Where have you been, girl? We need some supper. Don't you realize we've got company?

"This ain't no time to be runnin' around in the woods alone," he fumed as they headed back. "That damned wild Indian is around here someplace. Tommy come back—said he couldn't find no sign of him. You watch yourself, girl, else that man will do somethin' to you worse than death."

Emma smiled to herself. "He's probably far away from here by now, Luke."

"Well, I wouldn't bet on it."

They passed Betty Simms's grave, and Emma stopped to fix the flowers, some of which had fallen away.

"Forget about that," Luke said. "Flowers ain't gonna do her no good now, girl."

Emma rose, staring at the man who was now in control of her life. "Didn't you love her at all, Luke?"

The man scowled. "Love? What's love? Just a stupid feelin'. A man marries a woman to satisfy his needs and to get sons. Your mother didn't do neither one for me. Now get on into the house and fix us somethin' to eat."

Emma turned, struggling against tears again, telling herself to be strong as River Joe had told her to be, wondering if the Maker of Breath knew about Emma Simms and would give her courage as River Joe had said He could. She forced herself to think about the white Indian, forgetting the horrible ache in her heart and considering how amusing it was that everyone was talking about River Joe, telling her to be careful going out alone.

She cherished her secret more than anything now. She had been with him. She had been with the one called River Joe, had spoken with him! She had actually been held close to him, totally at his mercy, and had not felt one ounce of fear. She hoped—no, she prayed to the Maker of Breath—that she would see River Joe again.

The man was handsome and wore an expensive suit, but something about his slick, dark eyes was chilling, especially when he was negotiating for yet another unsuspecting young girl.

"You sure she's worth this much?" he asked Hank Toole.

Toole smiled through teeth yellowed from too many cigars. "You'll see for yourself, Mr. Gates. That stepfather of hers is givin' you a real deal. She's worth twice this much."

Sam Gates grinned, his well-groomed appearance and firm build making him look younger than his forty-eight years. He handed Hank two hundred dollars, anticipating how delightful it would be breaking in the pretty little girl Hank was to bring back to him. Emma Simms was her name, and she was supposedly blond, blue-eyed, full-breasted, and beautiful—and most important of all, a complete innocent. Sam always felt his blood race a little hotter, his heart beat a little faster, at the thought of initiating a new girl. When he was through with them, they were ready and willing to work for him in the rooms above his saloon in Knoxville, where male customers could find whatever kind of sweet treat they hungered for.

"You'd better be right, Hank," the man told Toole. "You know I don't like to be disappointed."

"Have I ever disappointed you, Mr. Gates?"

Sam Gates studied the man intently, making Hank feel uncomfortable. Hank had heard stories of how cruel this man could be when he was angry or when someone crossed him. Some of the girls Hank had brought to the man had never been seen again. Hank had never asked questions. He only paid the money to whoever wanted to sell the girls, then made a profit on them from Sam Gates if the man was pleased.

"No, Hank, you have never disappointed me," Gates was saying. "I think you're too smart for that. You do have a good eye for women."

"Then you can trust me on this one, Mr. Gates. Ain't another girl up in them mountains as pretty as she is. I've watched her grow up. And she's the proud type, you know? Ain't no man been inside this one . . . yet."

Both men laughed. "I'll have to see what I can do to break that pride," Gates answered, his dark eyes glittering.

Nigger Jim, Hank Toole's black slave, walked by then, glancing at the money that changed hands. He knew what it was for, and he felt sorry for the poor little girl who would be the victim this time. He suspected it was Emma Simms, but men in his position had no power to help anyone else.

The man quietly went about his business, stoking the boiler of the *Jasmine* with wood, preparing to get the small steamer under way for its monthly trip up the Tennessee and the Hiwassee to trade with settlers in remote areas. He threw more wood into the boiler, wishing he could do the same to Hank Toole and the white man called Sam Gates, who bought and sold young girls the same as slaves. He guessed that few black slaves, men or women, had it as bad as some of the poor young girls who were sold to Sam Gates.

Emma lovingly planted more flowers around her mother's grave. For some reason, the past week since her mother's burial had been more bearable after spending that brief moment with the white Indian. His strength had had a calming effect on her; his words about the Maker of Breath were comforting. She had seen honest concern in his eyes, and had felt so warm and protected when he scooped her up in one strong arm and pulled her off the raft.

The more she had thought about it over the past week, the more she had realized that the man had literally saved her life. Why? And why had he even been there in the first place? Had he followed her there? Was he watching her, thinking about attacking her? Why had she felt so safe, so unafraid, when he held her so close?

For the first time in her young life she began to imagine a man being nice to her, imagined what it might be like to lie with a man and do what a woman did to get babies. She had never met a man who stirred something so deep inside her that it almost hurt. She found herself wishing River Joe would come back, wishing she could talk more with him, wondering if he really thought she was pretty.

Maybe he liked only Cherokee girls. Maybe he was teasing her, laughing about the silly white girl.

"What do you think, Mama?" She traced her finger over the grave. "Luke was so mean to you. Can a man be nice to a woman? I wish I could tell you about River Joe. I wish I could ask you about this funny feeling I have for him. I don't even know him. I only talked to him once, and I'll probably never see him again."

She sighed deeply. She was glad neither Tommy nor Luke was there. Both had left on hunting trips; Tommy with his father the day after the funeral. Now that he was not there to push her into marrying him, Emma had some time to think. Her dilemma about how to avoid Tommy had not changed, but she fantasized about River Joe helping her. Surely only a complete fool would expect any help from the white Indian! The man might not even come back. He might wait another whole year to return. She had to concentrate on the here and now and stop thinking about what might be. Luke should be back from hunting in a day or two, and when Tommy returned there might be no escape. Hank Toole still seemed the only answer. She had packed her things and could only hope Hank would come soon with the *Jasmine*. Somehow she would find a way to get on that boat.

She rose and drank in the sweet air, again letting nature soothe her soul. When Luke was gone it was like being out of prison. She could be free and happy, at peace. She looked at the sad, leaning cabin with its sagging roof. Mrs. Breckenridge had told her about fine, sturdy homes in the city. She had been embarrassed for the woman to see the sorry condition of the little two-room cabin she lived in. She did her best to keep it clean, but everything they owned was so dilapidated, and Luke was so messy, it was almost impossible to have a nice house.

She looked around the decaying farm. Everything seemed to be falling apart, and now her stepfather had threatened to sell everything and leave. She hated leaving her mother's grave behind, but somehow she had to get away, and the only thing she could think of so far was to find a way to sneak onto the *Jasmine* when Hank came with the supplies.

It was then that she heard the horse. She turned, surprised to see Tommy Decker riding in. Her heart pounded in panic as chickens scattered beneath the hooves of Tommy's "fine black," and a couple of pigs snorted and scurried away. Luke had let most of the fencing get so bad that animals wandered about freely.

Emma stood as if frozen. Tommy was supposed to be gone on a hunting trip. What was he doing here? She was alone! Now he rode his horse closer, positioning himself between Emma and the house.

"Hi, Emma, honey. You're lookin' mighty pretty today in that fine pink dress. You got anything pink underneath it?"

"You get off my place!"

"*Your* place? This is Luke Simms's place. And I know Luke ain't here, because we all run into each other up at the Sillsbury settlement. Luke went home with my pa. I told them I'd be along." He grinned, his blue eyes cold, his nostrils flaring with desire. "After a while."

Emma could think of nothing but getting to the cabin and the musket Luke had left behind. He had several guns and kept them all loaded, prepared to shoot a deer or a squirrel from the house if one happened to wander too close.

"You and me are gonna have us a good time, Emma Simms. I've waited for you long enough," Tommy said. "You might as well get them clothes off, else I'll do it for you."

Emma found her legs and darted toward the house, but Tommy swung around his "fine black" so that the animal's head slammed into her back, knocking her down. Emma screamed and scrambled back to her feet, heading for the house again. But Tommy dismounted and chased her down, plowing into her and knocking her down again near an old, broken fence.

They lay in the grass. The second fall had knocked Emma's breath away, and she lay helpless while Tommy spread himself on top of her, pinning her down. "No sense goin' into the house, is there? Might as well do it out here, where the sun's shinin' and I can see you real good. I don't mind the grass, honey."

Tommy's voice was gruff with excited lust, as Emma squirmed and screamed for help.

"Go ahead and scream, honey," Tommy growled. "You won't be for long. Your screams will turn to moans, and you'll be beggin' for more before I'm through with you!" He tried to kiss her, but she lifted her head and butted his mouth.

"Ouch! You damned, uppity bitch!"

Emma twisted savagely and spit at him, but then a big fist landed on her cheek, bringing on a black dizziness. She felt him ripping at her dress, ripping it down from the neck and exposing one breast and most of the other.

"Damn, you're the prettiest thing I ever did see, Emma Simms," she heard him say with a groan. "You'll be okay, Emma, honey. You'll find out how good it feels." She felt a wetness on one breast, and vomit rose into her throat. She couldn't let this happen! Not with Tommy Decker, and not this way!

"You got a lesson to learn, Emma Simms, and I'm gonna teach you," he said then, his voice gravelly, his mouth still lingering at her breasts. "A girl your age ought to be broke in by now." A hand moved up under her dress and groped at her bloomers. "You think you're too good to marry me, so I'll just take it for free, little girl."

His voice was husky with desire and he moved both hands inside her bloomers and under her bottom, feeling the soft flesh there, sure he had knocked her senseless enough to have his way with no trouble. Emma felt his mouth at her breasts again, and she grasped desperately for something to hit him with. Her hand felt something soft, and she thought it was dirt. With one quick, deliberate movement she pushed it into his eyes and he cried out, pulling up and rolling off of her.

"Damn you!" he screamed. "Cow shit! You rubbed cow shit in my face! You bitch! You bitch! I'll kill you, Emma Simms!"

Emma quickly crawled away, scrambled to her feet, and picked up a loose fence board. Tommy sat rubbing at his eyes, and Emma took advantage of the moment. She swung hard with the board, slamming it across the side of his head.

Tommy cried out and fell sideways, and in her desperate fear and anger Emma hit him twice more, cracking the board over his head and across his shoulders.

Tommy let out an odd groan and hunched over. Emma threw down the board and rushed into the cabin, slammed and bolted the door, then ran to the corner where the musket sat loaded. She pointed it out the window at Tommy.

"You get out of here, Tommy Decker, or I'll blow your brains out with this gun!" she yelled. "I mean it!"

He remained huddled and groaning, rocking back and forth, holding his head for several more minutes while Emma watched him. She kept the gun trained on him, hoping it was primed and ready to fire.

Tommy finally got to his knees. Emma's eyes widened at the sight of him. Blood poured from a huge cut near his temple, and already the side of his face was beginning to swell. He managed to get to his feet, stumbling around and holding his head, groaning in pain.

Emma was amazed that she could have done so much damage, but she didn't regret it. She fought the horrible panic that she might not have the courage actually to shoot him, telling herself that she had no choice if he came after her. She felt sick at the thought of his mouth at her breast, his hands fumbling at her bottom.

She wished River Joe were here right now; he would give Tommy Decker such a thrashing that he would never set foot near her again. Maybe he would even kill Tommy. She had no time to stop and wonder why she had suddenly thought of

River Joe, or why she thought he would help her. The thought simply came to mind naturally, as though she had always known the man and could depend on him for protection.

But at the moment she wondered if even River Joe could have done any worse damage than she had done with the board. With effort, Tommy straightened up and looked toward the house, blood streaming down his face and soaking the front of his checked shirt.

"You'll regret this, Emma Simms! I'll get you for this—someday—somehow! I'll strip you naked and tie you down and do things to you that you never even knew a man could do to a woman! I'll rip your insides out, that's what I'll do! You'll wish you would have let me do it today, the easy way!"

"You get off this land, Tommy Decker, or I'll use this gun!"

He stumbled toward his "fine black." "You damned bitch!" he almost wept. "You're gonna pay for this! You'll see!"

Emma watched him go to his horse, darting to another window so she could see him better. She shivered at the sight of his face. His left eye was beginning to swell shut and he spat blood from his mouth. He managed to climb up on the horse, then sat there panting. With one final curse, he rode off into the woods.

Emma watched after him for a long, long time, waiting to see if he would come back. When it seemed that he would not, she slowly set down the musket and slid to the floor. The terror and humiliation of the event had finally set in. She pulled her dress back over herself and huddled against the wall, weeping bitterly.

Never had she felt more alone and abandoned. Never had life looked so hopeless. She realized she was foolish to think River Joe was going to stand around in the woods and magically protect her. She had met him once and now he was gone. It was stupid to think of him as someone to rely on.

Now she was in a worse fix than ever. What would Tommy tell his father and Luke? If Luke thought Tommy had raped her, he would force a marriage for certain, saying it was the only proper thing to do. No matter what happened, this thing would come to a head soon, and now, more than ever, she could not bear the thought of marrying Tommy. He would push the issue even harder now, even if he didn't want to marry her. He would do it for spite, getting the last laugh.

She breathed deeply, leaning back against the wall and trying to gain control of herself. River Joe. What a stupid thought for her to have! After the encounter with Tommy, the thought of any man touching her now was ugly and hideous. Were all men the same when it came to these things? River Joe was a big, strong man, bigger than Tommy. And he had been raised by Indians. Maybe he was as mean and forceful as Tommy when it came to those things.

She sniffed, and rose to find a wash pan, feeling sick at the manure still left on her hand. She scrubbed her hands vigorously with strong lye soap. She hoped there was nothing in her hair, for she was not about to get undressed and take a bath tonight. She would have to be watchful all night.

When her hands were clean she reached under her little cot and pulled out the gunnysack that held her few clothes —clothes packed and ready to run away on the *Jasmine* when it came. She removed her torn dress and pushed it under the bed, then pulled on a clean, blue cotton one. It was wrinkled, and she cried again; it was the last straw— having to put it on wrinkled and rumpled. . . .

She felt the back of her hair, grateful that it seemed clean, except for some dirt she could brush out. As she pulled the brush through her hair, she looked into an old, yellowed mirror that hung over her scratched and faded dresser. A bruise was forming on her left cheek, and she wondered how she would explain it. Tommy might be too proud to admit what had happened. If he held his tongue, Emma could tell Luke she had fallen on the dock at the river and hit her face on a post. And if Tommy did tell, she would show Luke the torn dress and explain what had really happened. It was proof of how much she hated Tommy Decker. Maybe then he would give in and say she didn't have to marry him.

Her mind swirled with indecision, as she desperately tried to figure out what might happen to her now. Surely Hank Toole would be coming soon. She had to get away before Tommy Decker tried to hurt her again. She might not be lucky enough to get away from him the next time.

She picked up the musket again, walked to the table, and lit a lamp. It was getting dark. She hated the dark, the sounds in the surrounding forest. But she had never been as terrified as she was now. Would Tommy come back? She walked over to a rocker near the fireplace and sat down. If Luke was drinking with Jake Decker this late, he might not come back tonight. The man obviously cared little for her safety, giving no thought to the fact that her mother was dead and she was completely alone.

She began rocking, telling herself she must not fall asleep. Tommy Decker's leering, freckled face and prying hands haunted her.

Her heart jumped when an animal growled somewhere deep in the woods. Was it a bear? A wild pig? A bobcat? Moments later a wolf's howl pierced the air. She clamped her hands around the gun and sat frozen in the rocker. She prayed to the Maker of Breath for protection, but she was not certain just who River Joe's mysterious God was. She knew little about God, other than her mother telling her she had long ago stopped believing in one.

Darkness fell, and she wondered if wild animals would come and tear at the doors of the flimsy cabin until they gave way, then come inside and devour her. Or maybe Tommy would return with friends. She could only hope she had hurt him badly enough to keep him away. Even so, he would not stay away forever. He would come for her, just as he had said he would, so it was more important now than ever to get away. Tommy Decker would want his revenge.

Something creaked and she jumped again, wondering how she was going to get through the night. *He'll come back,* she thought, wishing she could die. *Tommy will come back and he'll do bad things to me and kill me!*

There was no one to help her.

◊   *Chapter 3*   ◊

Emma awoke to the sun beaming through a crack in the curtains. She sat up with a start, rubbing her eyes. Morning had come, and she had survived the night.

She rubbed her neck. It ached from sleeping sitting up in the rocker. She stretched and rose, set aside the musket, opened the door, and breathed deeply of the mountain air. Morning brought her renewed courage. Birds sang and flowers still bloomed, and the Hiwassee rippled and splashed in the distance.

After a quick breakfast of bread and honey, she brushed her hair and readied herself for the day. She felt some pride at having made it through the night, and now in the sunlight, some of the horror of Tommy's attack had faded from her mind.

She walked back to the door, carefully checking outside, then picked up the musket and went out. She walked over to where she had scuffled with Tommy the evening before and saw the board she had used. There was blood on the end of it. She shivered at the sight of it, again surprised at her strength and courage. No, it wasn't courage. It was just plain anger and pride.

She set aside the musket, picked up the bloody board, and put it inside the shed, hoping she wouldn't have to explain anything to Luke. She didn't want anyone to know. Not only would he make her marry Tommy, but she would be ashamed to have to explain what he had done. She hurried to start her chores: feeding the pigs and throwing out more feed for the cow. She wondered if Luke was going to get more feed when the *Jasmine* came; they were almost out, and Luke had not planted a corn crop last year. The feed that was left was from the year before.

Farming on the Simms place had dwindled to tending a small garden that supplied enough food for the family. She doubted that Luke had anything worth trading to Hank Toole for more supplies, and if he couldn't sell the farm right away, what would he do? She told herself not to worry about it. She would find a way to escape by then. It would be Luke's problem.

She glanced over at her mother's quiet grave, again feeling the pain of her loss, and the worse pain of realizing her mother had never known love or happiness. Would life be that way for Emma Simms?

She carried the musket to the garden behind the cabin and began hoeing, watching constantly for movement, worried that Tommy would return. But she saw nothing.

Noon came, and Luke still had not returned. Emma milked a cow and drank the milk, eating more bread and some cold boiled pork. She spent the rest of the afternoon hoeing more, trying to keep busy, to keep from thinking about Tommy's attack. But she was still terrified he would return.

Evening came, and while sweeping the back steps she saw a movement through the trees; she dropped her broom and picked up the musket, raised it, and moved toward the back door of the cabin. She put her foot on a step and moved up slightly. She watched, telling herself to be brave, telling herself if it was Tommy Decker she should shoot him even if she was hanged for it.

The figure came closer, emerging from the sharp shadows the sun made through the leafy trees. It was a big man, riding a horse and leading a pack horse. It was River Joe.

Emma held the musket steady as he rode closer on a big roan gelding. He halted the horse a few feet from her, staring down at the musket, then moving his dark eyes to meet her blue ones.

"I saved you from the river the other day. Now you hold a gun on me."

"After yesterday I hold this musket on anybody who comes by."

His eyes softened. "What happened to your face?"

She began to redden then. "I . . . fell."

He sighed deeply and shook his head. "Who hit you, Emma?"

Her eyes began to tear. "N-nobody."

He dismounted and tied his horse to a tree limb. The pack horse was tied to the lead horse and loaded down with deerskins. River Joe turned and faced her then. "If you are going to use that thing, you had better hurry up and do it." He stood still, studying her face and feeling a great anger at the thought of someone hitting her. "Put down the musket," he said. He did not shout the words. They were a simple, gentle command.

She lowered the gun, wondering why on earth she obeyed him so easily. He looked around the rundown farm.

"You are alone?"

"Yes, sir. But that doesn't give you license to use your fists on me or try to take advantage of me. I'll shoot you first." She reddened more, realizing she had blurted the words without even thinking. She thought she read some humor in his eyes then as he folded his arms, looking bigger than she had remembered him.

"You won't have to shoot me. Is that what happened to you yesterday? Somebody hit you with his fist?"

She turned away, sighing deeply and setting the musket against a sagging step railing. This River Joe was not a man easily fooled. She stood with her back to him, and a moment later he was behind her, standing one step below her but still taller than she. She felt a gentle hand on her shoulder, and just as it had at the river, all her fear of him vanished. He turned her but she kept her head down until he lifted her chin to study the bruise. She looked up at him almost defiantly.

"Tommy Decker?"

She sniffed and turned away again, more embarrassed over the feelings his touch and looking into his eyes had stirred in her than over what had happened with Tommy. Did he sense these wild emotions she felt when he was near?

"Yes," she answered quietly. "But he didn't . . ." She swallowed and wiped at her eyes. "I rubbed manure in his face." She whirled then, looking at him proudly. "I pushed it right into his face and eyes, and then I hit him with a fence board, three times. He's hurting a lot worse than I am right now! I showed him no man takes Emma Simms for free!"

Their eyes held for several long seconds. Could he read her mind? Did he know she was thinking right now of an ending to that statement? *No man but River Joe.*

He broke into a handsome grin, then laughed lightly. "Well, you are one hell of a woman, Emma Simms. Tommy Decker must be ready to crawl into a hole from embarrassment."

Now she smiled, too. "I expect so. You want to see the board I used? It still has blood on it."

He laughed more and shook his head. "No. I believe you." Their eyes held again and he sobered. "I am just sorry I was not around. I left to do more hunting. I have smoked a lot of deer meat for my family up in the mountains. I came back here to see if the *Jasmine* has shown up yet." He looked back, his eyes scanning the woods like a cunning animal. "Your pa due soon?"

"Hard to tell. When he goes off drinking with Jake Decker, sometimes he's gone for days at a time. I didn't used to mind. But now with my mama dead, I'm here all alone."

He looked at her again, his hands on the wooden railing, the upper portion of his body leaning close to her.

You're the most handsome man I ever saw in my whole life, she wanted to tell him. His face was chiseled perfectly, his eyes dark and set wide apart, with nice eyebrows over them and thick lashes surrounding them. His lips curved cleanly, and his nose was straight and finely shaped.

"Your stepfather is a fool to leave you alone." He touched the bruise on her cheek lightly with his fingers. "Tommy Decker should die for this," he said quietly. "One so small and pretty does not deserve to be treated this way."

She stared into his face, speechless, amazed that she had let this man touch her again. "Would you have killed him, River Joe?"

He studied the soft skin of her face—so fair, just a few freckles, the big, blue eyes. He saw her childlike curiosity, sensed her innocence and trust, and wanted her just as he had the first time he had seen her. Why had *Esaugetuh Emissee* led him to this white girl he could never have? Why did he feel this rage over her treatment or care at all what happened to her?

"I probably would have, out of anger. And I would hang for it. It is very bad for an Indian to kill a white man, and I am considered an Indian."

Her heart swelled with excitement. He would have risked his life for her! Surely she was right in looking at him as a protector. Still, he had not been there, nor could he always be there. And why should he?

"It isn't right," she said aloud, always concentrating on using "isn't" instead of "ain't," just as Mrs. Breckenridge had taught her. She wondered how it was that River Joe used such good speech. "They shouldn't judge you that way."

"They should not even judge the Cherokee that way. They are good people, Emma, kind and hardworking. They marry and have families just like your people, They love, and they grieve, and to them this land is home."

"I don't know much about them. All I hear is bad things. Tommy sometimes raids Cherokee settlements with other young boys. He brags about it."

She saw his eyes flash with anger. "This Tommy must be a coward, to attack young girls and Cherokee villages. I would like to meet this excuse of a man up close sometime."

Emma shivered at the look in River Joe's eyes, a sudden, wild look that reminded her that this man was an Indian at heart, a man of the mountains. Why was she standing here talking to him so casually, especially after the horror of Tommy's attack the day before?

"Come," he told her then. "Come sit by the river with me."

The questions in her mind vanished, as though he could cast a spell on her. What would her stepfather do if he caught her talking to this wild man? River Joe took her arm, and she did not resist. He led her around the cabin toward the river.

"Are you all right then?" he asked. "Are there any other bruises, any injuries?"

"I don't think so. I hit my head kind of hard when he tackled me. It knocked the breath out of me for a minute, but that's all. Soon as I got it back, I grabbed for something to hit him with." His hand was firm and warm on her arm. "I picked up what I thought was dirt and rubbed it in his face."

Pigs and chickens scattered as they walked to the riverbank.

River Joe stopped a moment, turning and looking down at her. "You are very brave and very smart." His eyes moved over her as though to look for injuries. "You are sure he did not hurt you? Did he touch you wrong?"

Her cheeks felt hot and she turned away. "He didn't get a chance to do anything really bad." She wondered why he cared. He had looked at her almost possessively. "He tore my dress and—" She pulled her arm away, crossing her arms in front of her, looking out at the river. "The river is still rising," she said then. "Look at the dock! We can't even sit there. The water is right up to the top of the boards. Must have been a lot of snow up north of us. The runoff is high this year."

She felt a gentle, reassuring hand at her shoulder, and River Joe nodded, sensing she wanted to change the subject. "One year, when I was small, the river came up as high as your stepfather's cabin, washed away a lot of settlements and killed a lot of people. I have a feeling this could be another bad year. There are rain clouds in the west. A good hard rain could mean a lot of trouble."

He led her to an old log, where they sat down.

"I've never seen a real big flood," she said. "The river always comes up in the spring, but it's never come close to the cabin. I don't know what I would do. Water scares me."

"You do not have to be afraid of water. Water is a friend, just like fire, and the animals—everything. The only thing you should fear is other people, and even then you should not fear them, just do not trust them."

She turned and looked at him then, frowning. "Then why should I trust you? All I've heard about you is bad things, and here I am talking to you like I've always known you."

He grinned. "That is what you call instinct. You feel the trust. You know by instinct that you can trust me, and the same instinct tells you that you cannot trust Tommy Decker. Animals have the best instincts. They know when they should run, and when they can walk up and eat out of your hand."

She smiled. "Have you fed wild animals out of your hand, River Joe?"

"I have, mostly deer and squirrels."

She sighed deeply and turned, straddling the log and keeping her dress pulled over her legs. "I never knew anybody like you before. You're nothing like others say, at least not when I talk to you like this. How did you get your name?"

He watched the wild river. "The Cherokee named me when they found me floating down the river on a raft all alone when I was about five. I have vague memories of what happened, but at that time I could not remember anything, except that my first name was Joe. Since they found me floating the river, they started calling me River Joe. I have always loved the river—and the mountains."

"And what do you remember? How did you get on that raft?"

He sighed deeply, reaching down and pulling at a weed. "After I got over my fear I began to remember. My parents were moving to another settlement. Outlaws attacked us, raped and killed my mother, murdered my father, and stole most of our belongings. They did not have any use for me, so they just set me on the raft and pushed it out, hoping I would drown, probably."

"That's terrible!" Her heart went out to him. "I'm so sorry. What an awful memory!"

He looked at her, smiling sadly. "You have some pretty bad ones of your own." He looked down at the weed again. "At least I was raised by a loving people. Of course, because of my parents being found dead and me missing and showing up later among the Cherokee, everybody figured it was the Indians that did it, that they kept me to raise as their own. But it was not the Cherokee who killed my parents. It was white men. I have always hoped I could find them, but it has been so many years ago now that I doubt I ever will."

"You talk good English, River Joe. You must have remembered a lot."

"Not so much from that as because of missionaries. There are a lot of white missionaries among the Cherokee."

She wanted to ask him about his wife but was afraid to bring it up. Maybe it hurt him too much to talk about it. She felt guilty that the thought of his having had a wife actually gave her jealous feelings. What was it like to be the wife of River Joe? Was it a duty only a Cherokee woman could perform? Had he been kind to his wife? Did she dare believe a man could be good to a woman?

"This is really strange, isn't it? Me sitting here talking to you like this," she said. "I never told Luke about seeing you at the river. He kept telling me to watch out for you, and I almost laughed."

He smiled then, turning and straddling the log so he could face her. He rested his elbows on his knees. "You are quite a girl, Emma Simms. It feels good talking to you. You are smarter than other white girls I have seen at other settlements, and braver—and nicer."

She couldn't hide the sudden jealousy that moved through her blue eyes. "Do you know a lot of white girls?"

He laughed lightly. "Several, but only from a distance. I think they all think I am going to eat them alive." He saw an odd disappointment in her eyes and he sobered. "But never have I met one as pretty as you, or been able to talk to one like I can talk to you. And never have I even cared to talk to one."

Her cheeks felt hot. "You really think I'm pretty? Nobody ever told me I was."

"You are not just pretty. You are beautiful."

She watched his eyes, wondering if she might faint and fall off the log. When this man was around, all her worries always left her, her grief disappeared, and her heart felt lighter.

"Isn't this the craziest thing?" she asked. "I never had something like this happen to me in all my life. I mean . . . you're the one they call the white Indian. You're supposed to be some kind of savage, mean, a killer. You're the last person in the world I should trust. And here you are. I mean, I can talk to you so easy. I feel like I've known you forever, and this is only the second time I've ever spoken with you. Don't you think that's strange, River Joe?"

He shrugged. "Maybe not. Many things in life cannot be explained, Emma. Every spring I come down here to hunt, to trade, to earn money to buy supplies to take back to my people. Raiders have chased them high into the mountains, where it is more difficult to grow food and there is less game. I roam the settlements, looking for jobs, trading bargains, spend most of the summer down here, then take the supplies back for the winter, which even in Tennessee can be very cold when you are high in the mountains."

His eyes moved over her then and she felt a wonderful warmth flow through her blood.

"For no logical reason I came lower last year," he continued, "to a different part of the Hiwassee. And then I saw you, and when I returned to my people I thought about you for many months. So this spring I came back again. I came to this farm, hoping you would still be here. And there you were, kneeling at a grave, looking very lost. I knew then that *Esaugetuk Emissee* had led me to your farm deliberately last spring. The Maker of Breath knew you would need me, so He showed me this young woman with hair like cornsilk, knowing I would not be able to forget her."

She felt hypnotized by the dark eyes, and she wondered at the strange fire within her.

"Yes, life is strange, *Agiya*, for since that day I pulled you from the raft I have not been able to stop thinking about you. I could have gone to any other settlement to meet up with the *Jasmine*. But I came here, so that I could look at you again; and so that I could find out if the beautiful white woman with the golden hair is still no one's woman, as she told me that day at the river. And now that I have learned what happened with Tommy Decker, I see that she is still a free woman."

Emma just stared back at him, feeling suddenly awkward, wishing she had on a nicer dress and that her hair was cleaner. How terrible she must look after a sleepless night, with a bruise on her face and her eyes probably still puffy from crying.

What was this man telling her? That he wanted her for himself? He hardly knew her! And after yesterday . . . Would this man be any different from Tommy? Was he kind, like

Mr. Breckenridge? She felt so ignorant and lost. This man was strong and sure, knew his purpose in life, knew about so many things. He had roamed the mountains and rivers, lived among the Cherokee, had even had a wife! So he surely knew all there was to know about women. Did he look at her as a woman then and not a child?

"I . . . I don't know much . . . about men and all." She looked down then. "I mean . . . except for them being mean, like my stepfather was to my mama, and like Tommy is to me. You . . . you've got me all mixed up, River Joe. How can you . . . talk to me like that . . . when you hardly know me?"

"I know all I need to know. I already told you about instinct. And I believe strongly in the Maker of Breath leading us to our destinies."

She met his eyes again, feeling suddenly weak, feeling a rush of emotions, the odd ache deep in her belly, her heart pounding so that her chest hurt, her whole body tingling strangely. "What did that word mean . . . *Agiya?*"

"It simply means woman—but is only used for a special woman, a beloved woman. The Creeks call a beloved woman *Amayi*."

"And what is the word for . . . for a beloved man?"

He smiled. *"Asgaya."*

Their eyes held again and she repeated the word softly. He leaned closer then, and she sat rigidly as he lightly kissed her bruised cheek.

"Somehow I must see more of you, *Agiya,*" he said.

She wondered what kind of fool she was, to let him kiss her cheek and to wish that he would kiss her mouth. Just looking at Tommy or thinking about him made her feel ill. And here was this stranger, kissing her on the cheek!

"My stepfather would never let you see me," she answered. "If they caught you with me now they would shoot you. They think you're dangerous and uncivilized."

He only grinned. "And what do you think?"

She studied the dark eyes. "I think maybe . . . maybe you

could be trying to fool me." Her eyes teared. "Don't fool me, River Joe. I . . . I have nice feelings when we talk." She looked down again. "Don't try to trick me. How do I know you aren't mean like Tommy?"

He reached out and took her hand. "If I were like Tommy, wouldn't you already know it?"

She swallowed, wanting to cry, wanting to ask him to hold her tight again, feeling the awful helplessness. "I guess I would, wouldn't I?"

He nodded. "You have suffered much. I saw your stepfather shoving you around that day after I left you at the river. He is cruel to you. And now Tommy has been cruel to you. You are afraid of men. Cruelty is all you have ever known. But it is not that way with all men, Emma."

He squeezed her hand and the almost painful yet wonderful ache came deep inside her again. She swallowed, wishing she were more experienced, wondering what Mrs. Breckenridge would tell her now.

"It's hard for me to believe a man can be good." She looked over at the rising river. His hand was so big around her own, yet so gentle. "My mother lies in her grave because of a cruel man." She looked back at him. "I was going to run away . . . sneak aboard the *Jasmine* when it came, and after we got far away I was going to have Hank Toole take me to Knoxville, to look for a woman teacher who used to come here. Her name was Mrs. Breckenridge, and she was real pretty and real nice. She taught me a lot of things . . . reading and writing and such . . . and about life. . . ." She reddened again, looking down and picking at some torn lace on her dress. ". . . And love. Her man was good to her. Anyway, I just figured if I could get away on the *Jasmine*, Hank would help me settle and maybe get a job, and I'd be away from here—away from Tommy."

He looked at her for a long time. "Do not go with Hank Toole," he said then. "I have traded with him, but I would not trust him, Emma. Do not leave with him."

She met his eyes again. "But what else can I do? Luke

hates me. He's going to sell the farm and hand me over to Tommy Decker, and now I'm scared he won't even care if Tommy marries me or not." She began to tremble. "Tommy will do bad things to me. He'll take me to his friends. I know him. I know what he'll do." Her voice began to shake with panic. "He'll want to hurt me bad now, after what I did to him."

He grasped her other hand. "Tommy will not hurt you. I promise."

"How can you promise? You can't be around all the time, River Joe, like yesterday. He'll come back!"

He squeezed her hands tighter. "What did I tell you about not being afraid? Wasn't the Maker of Breath with you yesterday. Did He not help you?"

She blinked back tears, wanting to show him how brave she was. "I don't know much about God—yours or mine."

"They are the same. There is one God, and He brought me here . . . to help you."

Their eyes held, and thunder boomed in the distance. A storm was coming. Emma felt a chill, as though the thunder were some kind of warning. She wondered if hitting her head the day before had made her lose her mind, for the dark, handsome man called River Joe was leaning closer, and in the next moment his mouth was on hers, moving in a slow, gentle kiss, her first real kiss. Yes, she must be crazy, for she was letting him do this! He gently forced her lips apart, tasting the inside of them with his tongue, while thunder pounded and echoed through the surrounding mountains.

She gripped his hands tightly as he left her mouth then, kissing her once more lightly before drawing back. She sat there, her hands almost hurting from squeezing his, her eyes closed, waiting in near terror to find out if he meant to do something worse. After a moment she opened her eyes to see him just sitting there watching her, a teasing grin on his mouth. She knew her face was turning crimson then, and she jerked her hands away.

"I shouldn't have done that."

"Why not? It was nice."

Her eyes teared in confusion and in fear that he was only toying with her. If she took his advice and didn't leave on the *Jasmine*, what would happen to her then?

"Why did you kiss me?"

He sobered, seeing her questions and fears. "Because I wanted to. And because I wanted to show you it can be nice." His eyes moved over her again, resting for a moment on her full breasts, breasts that made her feel self-conscious because they had grown so large. Was he like Tommy, always teasing her about her breasts, calling them other names, talking about all the different "sizes" he had seen and tasted. She felt a burst of wicked desire at the thought of River Joe tasting her breasts the way Tommy had tried to do the day before. Surely if he did that the way he had kissed her . . .

She jumped up from the log. "You've got me all confused now, River Joe." She walked a few feet away, folding her arms and rubbing her elbows nervously. "I don't know what to do. Maybe you're just joking with me, and even if you aren't, I hardly know you. I . . . I had enough problems deciding before . . . and now you come along and tell me not to go with Hank. But why shouldn't I?" She whirled and faced him. "What are you going to do to help me?"

He slowly rose, walking up to her. "I do not know yet. But I will think of something. If you will trust me, I will take you wherever it is you want to go. But I would have to talk to your stepfather first, or I would be accused of stealing you away."

She reddened more. "I can't go running off with a man I hardly know! And I . . . I have no way to pay you. I don't even know if I *can* trust you!" She looked away, touching her lips. "I shouldn't have let you kiss me. You'll think . . ." She wished she could crawl into a hole. "You think that because I let you kiss me—"

"Emma, I want to help you," he said gently. "I do not

expect anything back from you. I do it because the Maker of Breath led me to you to help you. Just let me come back when your stepfather is here. I will be here when the *Jasmine* comes. I have to get my trading done first. My family depends on me to bring them these things, so before I do anything, I must wait for the *Jasmine* and unload my deerskins. Just promise me you won't get on that steamboat. I will find a way to help you."

She wanted to run and hide. She had surely made a fool of herself, letting him kiss her so easily! He was probably laughing to himself at her right now. This whole thing was probably a joke to him.

"I don't know," she answered, almost in tears. "I . . . maybe . . ." She met his eyes. "Don't be fooling me. I'm all mixed up."

He nodded. "I know. I would not fool you, Emma. I do not lie and I do not break promises."

She sniffed. "Then if . . . if somehow I could . . . go with you . . . promise me you'll take me to Mrs. Breckenridge, if that's where I decide I want to go."

He nodded. "I promise."

The black clouds rolled in over a western ridge of mountains. Emma found it amazing how rapidly everything had changed for her, all starting with her mother's death. She felt the storm clouds coming into her life and heart as well as to the sky. She watched River Joe's dark eyes for a long time.

"You . . . you better go," she said. "Luke could come back anytime. It would be bad for him to find you here with me alone."

He nodded. "I will be around—close. I will not go away this time."

She told herself it was ridiculous to trust him, yet his words calmed her. "Watch out for Tommy Decker," she warned. "He sneaks around a lot."

The wild anger moved through his eyes again. "Men like Tommy Decker do not worry me. I hope he does come around."

Lightning blistered the western skies and Emma looked out at the approaching storm. "We're going to get that rain, like you said."

He nodded.

"The river will get higher, won't it?"

"Probably. Do not worry about the river, Emma. You just watch yourself, and trust me."

She wiped at tears and managed a smile. "I don't have a lot of choices, do I?" She shook her head. "I don't understand, River Joe."

He suddenly turned his head. "Someone comes," he whispered. He hurried up to the cabin and behind it to untie his horse. Emma quickly followed, wondering how on earth he knew anyone was coming. She saw and heard nothing but the approaching storm. He quickly mounted his horse, then looked down at her. "Remember what I said. Do not get on that boat."

"I'll remember."

He rode off into the trees, quickly disappearing. She wondered what he did when it stormed, how he stayed dry. And then as she stood watching after him, she wondered if he had really been there at all.

Her mind raced with confusion. She still felt warm and wonderful. He had said she was pretty, brave, nice to talk to, smarter than other white girls. He had held her hands, and . . . and he had put his mouth over hers and kissed her. The wild man River Joe had kissed her, and she had let him!

She put fingers to her lips again, still wondering if she had lost her mind. The thought of his doing other things to her brought an intense desire to every nerve in her body. Never had she felt so strange, so alive, so different, so withdrawn from all her other problems.

She heard a horse now and gasped. What if it was Tommy! She ran to the cabin, telling herself it was silly to worry, because River Joe was watching this time. But was he really? Or was he just toying with her in a different way from Tommy?

She reached the steps and turned to see it was Luke who was coming. She wondered if he had seen Tommy, if he knew. Would he be angry, force a marriage then and there? Knowing Luke, he would be angry not at Tommy but at Emma for not letting Tommy have his way. He would be angry that she had spurned a potential husband. Maybe he would even drag her to another settlement and offer her to any man there.

Emma had hated being alone, but she also dreaded Luke's return. Now that her mother was dead, there was no buffer between herself and her stepfather; and Luke was a man who enjoyed showing his authority. She hoped she could keep things peaceful for the next few days—until the *Jasmine* came . . . and River Joe.

Thunder and lightning ripped the sky as Luke rode his horse into a shed and unsaddled it. He came toward the cabin then, carrying his musket and supply pack. He stumbled slightly, and Emma felt sick. Luke was drunk.

$\Diamond$ *Chapter 4* $\Diamond$

"Curry that horse down for me, Emma," Luke grunted, not even asking first if everything was all right. "But go fix me somethin' to eat first."

He walked past her and into the tiny kitchen of the two-room cabin. Emma followed him inside, noticing that he reeked of corn liquor and tobacco. He sat down heavily in a chair, as though his legs would hold him no longer. Luke had gotten lazy and was gaining weight. He was a big man to begin with, tall and strong and menacing, with a shock of thick, dark hair and a heavy, dark beard. He took off his hat and threw it on the floor, and Emma hurriedly began cutting some bread.

"I would have come home yesterday," he said, his words slurred, "but Tommy come home last night a terrible mess. I helped Jake tend to him."

Emma felt a nervous heat come to her face and hands. "What do you mean? Did he get hurt?" she asked carefully.

"That damned black horse of his throwed him. Can you believe it?" The man chuckled then, and some of Emma's panic left her. "He's always braggin' on that animal," Luke continued, sniffing and wiping his nose on his shirtsleeve. Emma handed him some bread and honey. "His 'fine black' really landed him a good one," he went on, biting into the bread and continuing with his mouth full. "Like to killed the boy. Tommy hit his head on a post and then a rock when he landed—and to top it off he landed face down in manure." Luke hurriedly swallowed and then laughed louder, slapping his hand on the table. Crumbs were stuck in his black, curly beard. "Serves him right for always braggin' up that horse."

Emma smiled, realizing Tommy had lied about everything, too embarrassed to explain what had really happened. Now she had something on Tommy. If he bothered her again she could threaten to tell everyone it was not his horse but one small girl who had beat on him and given him his wounds. That was the last thing he would want his father and his friends to know.

She knew though that it was still only a matter of time before he found some way to get back at her. She still had to get away. Tommy's misfortunes had put Luke in a good mood, which was rare. She dared to take heart in his laughter, but in the next moment her relief quickly vanished as she handed him some hot coffee.

"Here, Luke." She gasped and let out a little scream when he suddenly grasped her wrist tightly, making hot coffee spill onto her hand. Her eyes quickly teared and she looked straight at him in surprise.

"What the hell happened to your face?" he growled.

She swallowed. "I . . . I fell . . . on the dock. The river water is so high that it's right up to the edge, Luke. The dock is slippery. I didn't think it would be that bad. I went out to see if the *Jasmine* might be coming, and I slipped and hit my face on a post."

He studied her for a moment, then let go of her. "Serves you right for bein' stupid enough to go out there." He continued to study her closely, and she struggled to keep from turning red or looking guilty. "You ain't seen that River Joe anywhere around, have you?"

Emma shook her head. "No, sir." She backed away and put a hand to her heart. *He was here, Luke,* she wanted to say. *He was here, and he kissed me, right on the lips. He's coming back for me.* How she wanted to say it, to throw it in his face! But Luke was drunk. And even sober, he would surely beat her for being with the white Indian. If she had any hope of Luke allowing River Joe to court her, this was not the time or place to bring it up.

"Well, you ever see him, you shoot first and ask questions later," Luke ordered. "Jake says that River Joe carved a man up pretty bad up at the Gillmore settlement. He don't watch out, he's gonna get himself hung."

Emma's eyes widened. "Carved a man up?" She could not imagine River Joe being that vicious, not the River Joe she had just been with.

Luke guzzled some coffee. "Knife fight. The way Jake tells it, that River Joe spoke to a white girl, and the man that was fixin' to wed her got all hot and pulled a knife on River Joe. I always heard no man pulls a knife on that white Indian and lives to tell about it. I guess maybe the story is true." He bit off another piece of bread and honey. "At any rate, Jake seen it all. It's lucky for River Joe that the other man pulled his knife first, but people are still talkin' about puttin' a noose around that white Indian's neck. Jake says River Joe put that knife into that man's gut and just moved it right up to his throat like he was slicin' open a hog for slaughter."

Emma put a hand to her stomach. River Joe? The man who had just touched her so gently? Kissed her so softly? The man who said he'd be watching out for her?

"I better never see him come around here or I'll shoot him on sight," Luke was saying. "I could do it and nobody would blame me."

Emma struggled not to cry. There had been little hope before that River Joe might be able to approach Luke about seeing her. Now there was no hope at all. In fact, he would be better off not even to try. But that left her right back where she had been before—with no future but to be handed over to Tommy Decker. And at the moment, she wondered how wise it would be to go running off with River Joe, if indeed he was truly serious about taking her away. She shivered at the picture of Joe ripping his knife through a man's insides, and she wondered if that was how she would end up if she went with him.

"By the way, when Hank Toole gets here on the *Jasmine*, I'm talkin' to him about spreadin' the word up- and downriver that I'm sellin' the farm, Emma." Luke burped loudly before continuing. "All I got to do is figure out what to do with you. I'll talk to Hank about it." He guzzled more coffee. "You've had your mournin' time. Your ma's dead and you're a woman now. Tommy's been after me for a long time to let him marry you. Your ma always fought it, but she ain't here to bitch at me for it now. So I reckon if Hank don't have any better ideas, Tommy can have you if he still wants you. Go on now and curry down that horse."

Emma moved toward the door, wanting to scream in desperation. She hesitated in the doorway, struggling to find a way to change his mind, again feeling prison doors closing around her. River Joe had slaughtered a man with his big knife. How could she let herself depend on such a man?

"Maybe . . . maybe I could go with Hank to Knoxville," she suggested carefully. "Find that Mrs. Breckenridge . . . get a job, Luke. Then I'd be gone and wouldn't be a burden to you."

He turned and looked her up and down. "I'll make the decisions, girl. And you ain't got the education, nor money nor anything else to be goin' off to the city like that. If you go with Hank, it will be for other reasons. I'll decide after I talk to him."

She felt fear creeping through her bones. "What do you mean . . . other reasons?"

Luke slammed down his coffeecup, making her jump and spilling coffee on the table. He got up and walked over to her, fists clenched, and Emma cringed against the door, staring up at his black beard and dark, bloodshot eyes.

"It ain't for you to wonder about, girl. You're my property now and I'll decide what to do with you."

"But . . . I got a right to know, Luke."

His hand came hard across her face, so hard that she fell against the door, a flimsy door that might as well not have been there, for the bottom of it was broken and hung loosely from the frame. The door swung open and Emma fell down the wooden steps to the ground.

"You got *no* rights, girl! Now go curry that horse like I told you! Do it quick or I'll come out there and lay into you some more!"

Emma scrambled to her feet and ran to the shed where Luke had left the horse. She grabbed a support post inside the shed and wept. Outside, clouds opened up from the now-dark sky, and rain began to pour down in a sudden torrent. Soon rain began dripping through a hole in the shed roof.

Emma cried from confused fear and the lingering pain of Luke's blow. She glanced at the cabin. Luke had lit a lantern, and through the window she saw him raise a bottle of whiskey. Rain dripped on her head, and she stumbled around the post to another stall, which she had cleaned out and filled with fresh hay just that morning. She fell sobbing into the hay, determined not to go back into the cabin that night for fear of a worse beating. She would wait. Luke would soon fall asleep from all the whiskey.

She had to think. She had to stop crying and decide what to do, to figure out what Luke meant about talking to Hank first. And most of all she had to decide if River Joe really would help her, and if she could really trust him after all.

She curled up into the hay, wondering if River Joe was out there, wondering how safe she was anywhere now.

Thunder rolled and lightning flashed, occasionally lighting the inside of the shed with its brilliance. Emma had fallen into a weary sleep, lying curled into a corner of the clean stall, unaware of the dark figure who moved to the back of the shed and looked through an open window. He saw her lying there when the lightning flashed again, then moved through the window like a silent shadow.

Thunder rumbled through the mountains and the horse whinnied. Emma stirred awake, sensing in her sleep that something was amiss. Her eyes blinked open, and she saw a talk dark figure looming over her in the darkness.

She gasped and started to rise, but a big, strong hand immediately covered her mouth. He came down close, and an arm moved around her shoulders. Broad shoulders hovered over her as he laid her back down in the hay.

She pushed against him in a fruitless effort to get away, momentarily confused, her first thoughts of Tommy.

"Don't scream," said a soft voice. "It's me. River Joe."

She stopped pushing, but she lay breathing in short gasps, wondering if she was any safer with this man than any other. Something she could not even explain kept her from screaming out when his big hand slowly moved off her mouth. In spite of what she had heard about this man, she could not bring herself to scream and risk Luke's coming out and shooting him.

He lay on top of her then, one leg sprawled over her own,

one hand under her back, the other hand at her neck. He moved it over her throat and to her cheek, touching it gently, his arm pressing against one breast.

"I saw him hit you . . . saw you fall," he whispered.

Thunder crashed and lightning flashed again, lighting up his face, which seemed even more handsome in the night, and yet wilder. His hair was brushed out long, and some of it fell lightly against the side of her face.

She knew she should be terrified, yet she felt no fear. For several long seconds they lay there, watching each other whenever the lightning made things brighter, and she wondered why she didn't fight him as she had fought Tommy. Then he came closer, his mouth covering her own, his tongue parting her lips and moving inside her mouth, his hand leaving her cheek and moving down, reaching under her hips as he pressed the kiss harder and moved himself directly on top of her.

She felt a swelling hardness push against her pelvis, and she whimpered in a mixture of fear and desire. She pushed at him then but he only held her tightly, leaving her mouth and moving his lips to her cheek.

"Don't fight it, *Agiya,*" he said softly. "I will make you my woman. I cannot let any other man be the first to do this."

"No, River Joe," she whispered. "I'm not ready. I hardly know you."

He kissed her eyes, and again she wondered why she didn't fight harder.

"You know all you need to know." He kissed her nose. "And I know the Maker of Breath brought me here to you and gave me these feelings."

He bit lightly at her lips, then invaded her mouth again. She wanted to protest, to stop his hand from moving around her hip and down to her knee, then slowly up her thigh under the leg of her bloomers; but the feel of his big hand touching the bare skin of her leg sent a fire through her blood that was too wonderful to stop.

His kiss was rich and warm until his lips left her mouth again, traveling over her throat and down her dress, kissing at her full breasts through the cloth.

"Please don't," she whimpered. "I'm scared."

His hands moved from under her dress to the buttons at the front. "What did I tell you about being scared, Emma?"

She wondered at the odd power he seemed to have over her. Never did she have more reason to fight this, yet none of the objections in her mind would culminate into a physical attempt to get away. He was unbuttoning her dress. Every touch was so gentle, every word whispered softly. If she was being forced, then it was being done magically, gently; and she knew in reality she was not being forced at all. She wanted him. She wanted to know what this was like, and she wanted this strange, wild but gentle man to be the one to show her.

Her dress came open. He gently pushed one side off her shoulder, exposing a breast, and she gasped when his big hand pushed her breast up full, cupping it gently. She could not stifle a whimper when his mouth came down to cover a nipple, and she shivered with a brand-new, wonderful passion when she felt the warm moistness of his mouth as he softly sucked at the fruit of her breast.

What a fool she must be, lying there in a shed with this wild, white Indian she hardly knew! What kind of power did this man wield, that he could so easily make her want this? He continued to taste her breast in a lovely, pulling motion, while his hand left her breast and moved back down under her dress, into the waistline of her bloomers, down over the hairs no man had ever touched, his fingers invading the most private part of her body.

She grasped at his hair, weakly whispering for him not to touch her there, but his fingers worked in a magical, circular motion that brought the wonderful ache to her insides and made her gasp for breath. He kept it up, bringing on the most wonderful, almost agonizing desire she had ever felt. Tommy had never made her feel this way. Surely this was exactly what he had tried to do to her, and yet it was nothing like this.

"What are you doing?" she whimpered.

He left her breast and moved his lips over her throat to her mouth. "Hush, *Agiya*. This is only the beginning." He moved one finger deeper inside her, making her gasp and whimper. "Someday I will taste you here, where my hand touches you. I will taste the sweet nectar of my woman."

His mouth covered hers again, and she felt a wonderful, warm pulsation deep inside, a pulsation that turned to an almost aching throb, while the thought of what he was telling her made her arch up, pushing against his hand, wanting his fingers to move inside of her.

Tommy had made similar remarks, but in a sneering, threatening way, as though she were an animal. But River Joe didn't make her feel that way at all. She felt like a beautiful woman, and it excited her to know she was pleasing this virile man. He was pulling at her bloomers now, moving them down over her hips. He sat up and pushed the front of her dress up to her waist, then gently pulled the bloomers down over her legs and her old leather shoes.

She lay naked from the waist down but was not afraid. Lightning lit the stall again, and he groaned something in the Cherokee tongue. He lightly stroked her secret place and rubbed her flat belly.

"I was right, *Agiya*," he said. "The hairs of your love nest are also the color of cornsilk. You are magic. You make me feel weak, yet when I put my life in you I will feel a new power."

Her heart beat wildly at the knowledge of what he was telling her. He would mate with her. She should stop him, yet she seemed to have lost all control over herself. He grasped her knees and pushed her legs apart, and they felt almost numb. He stood up, unlacing his buckskin pants and stepping out of them. He untied his loincloth and let it fall, and in the light of the storm she looked upon man, able to see only a dark spot at first.

He knelt between her legs, and the lightning flashed brighter. She saw him better then, and to her he looked huge, much too big to mate with her.

"Wait!" she squeaked, putting her hands against his powerful chest as he came closer again. He only grasped the hand and squeezed it.

"There can be no waiting now," he said. "It must be done."

She shook her head, her breath coming harder, yet still she could not move. He reached down and grasped the bottom of his buckskin shirt, pulling it up over his head so that he was naked. He came down closer, pulling her up against him. Her bare breast touched his skin, and she grasped his powerful upper arms. Her fingers dug into his muscles.

"Will it hurt?" she whimpered.

He kissed her gently, his great swelling pressing against her belly. "Only the first time," he whispered. "I will be quick, *Agiya*, and it will be done. From then on it will get better, and you will come to your *Asgaya*, asking him to come to your bed."

He covered her mouth again, drowning out all other objections. She felt his hand reach down to guide himself into her, and then it came, the sudden thrust that made her scream with pain. Her scream was stifled by his own mouth, which pushed harder against her as he invaded her, taking her virginity in one push, bringing on a pain that made her dig her nails deep into his flesh.

He left her mouth, and she gasped in pain, burying her face against his shoulder as his big, sure hands grasped her under the hips and he pushed himself rhythmically, groaning her name softly.

"Hang on, *Agiya*," he told her softly, kissing her hair.

Moments later she felt a throbbing deep inside herself. He groaned with great passion, then seemed to relax. After a few more seconds he pulled himself out of her and held her close, and she could not stop the tears that came then from the realization of what had just happened to her.

"Do not cry, *Agiya*. I am sorry if I hurt you. The hurt will go away. This I promise."

Her tears came in bitter sobs, tears over more than the fact that she had just let this near stranger invade her body and rob her of her virginity. She wept over her mother, wept over her terror of what could happen to her if she stayed with Luke, wept over the fact that she had no idea if she could trust this man who held her, if he truly cared for her and would take her away, or if he had just used her. She was so ignorant of men and mating.

Had she just been raped without even knowing it? Were there ways to force a woman without physically beating her? Would River Joe do that to her? Would he leave her now and never come back? Luke had said that River Joe had gotten in trouble over another white girl. Had he done this to others, only to go on his merry way and laugh about it?

He was petting her hair, kissing her forehead now. "Please stop crying, Emma. It will be all right now. You are my wife now. By Cherokee custom I have only to lie with you and be one with you, and you are mine."

Her heart took hope at the words. She breathed deeply to stop her tears, wiping at her nose and eyes with her dress.

"Do you mean it? I'm your wife?" She leaned her head back, watching his eyes when the lightning came again. She saw love there, saw a gentle smile on his face. Rain fell gently now, the earlier torrent letting up.

"I would not have done this if I did not want you for my woman. Now it is done. It cannot be changed."

Thunder boomed again, and their eyes held. He leaned close and kissed her again, several times over on the mouth, then the throat, then moving to her breast again, kissing her nipple.

"Someday my sons will suckle at your breasts," he said softly.

He gently pulled her dress back over her shoulder and breast then, kissing her lips once more.

"You don't think . . . I'm bad?" she whimpered.

He smiled. "No. I do not think you are bad. I think you are a good woman, and the most beautiful woman I have ever seen. I think the Maker of Breath brought me here so that I would find the woman who can help ease the pain of the loss of my Yellow Sky and help me learn to love again."

Her heart soared. "Do you love me, River Joe?"

His hand moved over her chest and belly. "I have just told you that I do."

"I love you, too," she whispered.

He gently massaged her belly. "The hurt will go away."

She was glad it was dark so that he could not see her blush. She found it hard to believe what had just happened. She felt light, happy, beautiful.

"What will we do now?" she asked.

He moved his hand up to stroke her hair. "We will wait for the *Jasmine*. I must get my trading done. Then I will come for you and speak to your stepfather."

"No!" She looked up at him again. "He said tonight that he would shoot you on sight if he saw you around. He said you killed a man up at the Gillmore settlement."

He rose, resting on one elbow. "Did he say why?"

She wiped at her eyes more as the rain came down harder again. "He said it was over a white girl."

He let out a disgusted laugh. "That stupid girl followed me everywhere. She was trying to make trouble and she found it. I finally told her to stay away from me. She ran back to her husband-to-be, told him I spoke to her—called her pretty. She wanted to make him jealous. With her watching, he wanted to show what a big man he was. He came after me with a pistol. I was not even wearing one at the time. He shot at me while my back was turned and ended up killing a horse I had just bought." He sighed, sitting up and pulling on his buckskin shirt.

"Luke never mentioned that."

"They seldom mention the truth. Men like Tommy and Luke and the others do all they can to make the Cherokee look bad, and I am considered Cherokee." He tied the laces of the shirt, then stood up and tied on his loincloth and pulled on his buckskin pants. She could see him now and again as the lightning flashed, studied his magnificent physique, and found it incredible that this wild man of the mountains had just made love to her, had turned her from girl to woman.

"They only tell the parts that make me look bad," he continued. "When the man missed with his pistol, another man threw him a knife. With the girl watching and his own jealousy raging, he had no choice but to try to kill me with it. But no man comes after me with a knife and lives to tell about it. I am better with a knife than anything." He moved to lie down beside her again, rubbing a hand over her arm. "You are cold." He pulled her close to warm her. "When I thought about that dead horse, I could not stop myself from ripping him open once I sank my blade into him."

She felt a great relief that the girl meant nothing to him.

"Luke says he's going to let Tommy marry me. But he said he'll wait for Hank first. I don't know what for. At least that means I don't have to worry about Tommy till the *Jasmine* comes. Besides, Luke says Tommy is laid up bad. He told his pa that his horse threw him."

River Joe grinned. "He did, did he?" He leaned over her again. "Sometimes I wonder what you would have done to me if you had decided to fight me."

She ran her hands over his powerful arms. "I doubt I could have stopped you. But I didn't want to. Some folks would say it was a real bad thing I did."

He put a big hand to the side of her face. "Not my people. There is nothing bad in doing what comes naturally, Emma, what is right in the heart."

The rain came down harder and he sat up, pulling her up with him. "You should be inside."

"Luke was drunk. I could probably go in now. He'll sleep hard till late morning." She grasped his arms. "You can't come here, River. He'll try to shoot you."

"Not when he is sober. I will be careful. The *Jasmine* will come soon. The river is still rising. Hank will have to get back downriver as soon as he can, before the river gets too dangerous. He will come before Tommy can give you any more trouble. I must leave you now."

"But where will you go?"

"I have a place not far. There are a lot of caves along the banks of the river."

"If we go away, where will you take me?"

"It depends on whether they let you come with me willingly, or if I must steal you away. We must try to do it the right way if we can, so there is no trouble."

He stood up, helping her up with him.'

"Will you be all right?" he asked.

"I think so." She hugged him around the middle. "Am I really your wife now, River?"

He grasped her arms, pulling her back and looking down at her. "Yes. It is the Cherokee way." He put a hand to her face. "You call me just River, not River Joe."

"River Joe is what everybody else calls you. I like just River. It's a nice name, one that only I will call you." She hugged him again. "I never thought something like this would happen to me, River. I never felt special before, and I never knew a man could really care about a woman. I never had anybody say 'I love you' to me before. Not even my mama told me that. But it's all so scary, to think of going off with you. You won't change, will you? You won't be like Tommy or Luke?"

His heart ached for her, his own emotions mixed. How quickly she had gotten into his blood. He had given in to his blazing desire for her. Now this young woman with the cornsilk hair belonged to him. She was depending on him. *Esaugetuh Emissee* had given him a great challenge, bringing him this far and letting him set eyes on Emma Simms.

"I am going up to the MacBain village to catch the *Jasmine* and get my trading done. It is only the next settlement upriver, so I can get back here before the *Jasmine* does. When I get here, I will have my trading done and be ready to go. The first thing we must do is take the supplies I came here for to my family."

She looked up at him. "Indians! You'll take me to the Cherokee?"

He smiled at her childlike surprise. "You will like them. You say you have never known love. There you will find much love, more than you know is possible after living with Luke Simms all your life. And you will be with me. Why should you be afraid? I am like one of them. Is there anything so different about me?"

She put her head against his chest and breathed deeply of the scent of leather. "I don't even know yet for sure. I'm taking a big chance, River."

"Not as big as the chance you take by staying here."

Her heart pounded with anticipation and excitement. No matter what happened, she would at least be away from this dying farm and from Luke Simms and Tommy Decker.

"I know. Come back for me, River. If you don't come back, I'll die. I'll just die!"

"I will come back. This I promise. I have just made you my woman, Emma Simms. And I intend to be one with you again, as soon as I can. Watch for the *Jasmine*. When you see it, I will be close."

"I love you, River," she whimpered. "I might be crazy in the head, but I love you."

He sighed deeply. "I am probably crazy myself. I have a way of finding trouble without even trying. I will pray to the Maker of Breath that I can have you without a fight." He pulled away. "Go inside now. You will want to wash. Try to get some sleep before your stepfather wakes in the morning. It will be only two or three days at the most now."

"I wish I could go with you."

"I would take you away with me right now, but people would see us together when I trade with the *Jasmine*, as I must do. I cannot let my family down, Emma. Hank Toole pays well for my deerskins. To take you now without permission would bring us much trouble."

"I know." She turned and saw her bloomers as the lightning lit up the shed. She reached down and began pulling them on, blushing again. Her insides ached, but she believed his promise that the hurt would go away. In spite of what they had done, it made her blush and feel weak to think of doing it again. And the thought of doing the more intimate things he had whispered, the thought of his seeing her naked in full light, made every nerve tingle and made her cheeks fiery hot.

"I will go now," he said. "I will be back soon." He led her to the stall entrance and she grasped his arm.

"River!"

He pulled her close.

"Don't let me down," she whimpered, reaching up around his neck. "Don't leave me here."

He kissed her neck. "I will not let you down. Remember not to be afraid, *Agiya.*"

The rain had again turned to a gentle drizzle, but more thunder boomed in the distance. His lips found hers and she was lost in his sweet kiss as he massaged her bottom with one hand. In spite of her pain, she felt an urgent desire to let him make love to her again. So, this was love, so sweet and wonderful that she wanted him even though she knew it would hurt.

"God be with you, *Agiya,*" he said softly, kissing her on the cheek.

"And with you. What was that word again, for beloved man?"

"*Asgaya.*"

She touched his cheek. "*Asgaya.* I will wait for you."

He let go of her and dashed out into the dark rain. She watched after him, the bright lightning lighting up the surroundings, but already he was gone. She stood alone, wondering if perhaps she had only dreamed all that had just happened to her. But then she felt the delicious ache deep inside.

She put a hand to her stomach. No. It had not been a

dream. River Joe had mated with her. She was his woman now, his wife according to Cherokee custom. River Joe had said it was so, and she believed him. River Joe had promised to come back for her, and she believed that, too. If he didn't come, there would be nothing left to live for.

◊ *Chapter 5* ◊

Emma stayed inside the cabin this time when the *Jasmine* came by. She didn't want to be around Hank Toole, afraid that her presence might somehow make her more vulnerable to whatever Hank wanted of her. She thought that perhaps if she stayed out of sight, Hank and Luke would forget all about her and not even discuss what to do with her.

Hank had come by on the *Jasmine* the second day after River Joe had left. He was on his way upriver to the Macbain settlement. She could hear him shouting now to Luke about the problems he was having because of the high river. Trying to go against the current was putting him behind.

"The trip back will be great," he yelled as he threw a rope to Luke. "Won't hardly have to fire the boiler at all. The current will carry us damned fast."

Emma watched from a window in the loft of the cabin, which was her sleeping quarters. She moved back from the window and flopped back down on the feather mattress of her bed, feeling the wonderful fire in her blood at the thought of being with River Joe soon, of letting him make love to her again.

The next time would surely be even more wonderful, perhaps in the light of day. She would lie beneath him, and he would do things to her, work his magic with his lips and his touch. It would be all right because she belonged to him now. He had said so, and she believed everything River Joe said. After all, he loved her. He really, really loved her.

She was a woman now—River Joe's woman. Who could ever have dreamed this could happen to her? All her feelings of helplessness and a hopeless future were gone now. She wasn't afraid anymore. River would come for her. It would be only two or three more days before he would come. If Luke would not give his permission for her to go away with River Joe, then she would simply defy the man and go anyway. How was a man like Luke going to stop a man like River Joe? River was the kind of man who took whatever he wanted.

She breathed deeply, feeling as beautiful as River had told her she was. She could still taste his lips, feel the pressure of his strong arms around her, feel his bare skin against her bare breast. She even liked remembering the pain, the piercing yet beautiful pain that told her she was no longer her own woman now—the pain that told her she had been claimed. In all her years of growing up around Luke Simms, having to cover her head with a pillow or run out when he beat her mother and took his pleasure with her, Emma never dreamed that lying with a man could be this beautiful. She loved River so much that she felt almost sick with it, and ever since that night River came to her she had hardly been able to eat.

She closed her eyes to dream of River, while outside Hank Toole handed Luke Simms a leather pouch full of money. Hank grinned through yellow teeth, then quickly spat out some tobacco juice. "Two hundred dollars, just like Mr. Gates promised," he said to Luke.

Luke nodded. "Good. I was hopin' the man would want her. I'd let Tommy marry her, but I don't think he cares that much, and he sure can't give me this kind of money. Gates will be pleased when he sees how pretty she is."

Hank rubbed at his privates. "That he will. I've been eyein' that pretty stepdaughter of yours for years now. She sure has filled out this past year."

Luke shoved the money pouch into his pants pocket. "I don't give a damn what you do with her. You want her now or later?"

"She's a fighter, I'm thinkin'. No sense takin' on trouble any sooner than I have to. I'll stop and pick her up on the way back. The river is runnin' fast in that direction, so the return trip won't be long. You have her ready to go in a couple of days."

"She'll be ready. I really can't do much—don't want her to know what's goin' on till she absolutely has to. You're right. She can be pretty stubborn. If she gives me too much trouble, I'll knock some sense into her."

Hank chuckled. "Just don't mess up that pretty face of hers." He turned and picked up a case of whiskey. "I'll be bringin' you food and whiskey for as long as you need it, just like we agreed—at least till you get this farm sold."

Luke took the case and Hank rubbed his hands on the sides of his pants. "You're sure she's a virgin? You ain't messed with her, have you?"

"Hell no. I never could when Betty was alive, and after we talked last month when you came by, and I found out how much more valuable she is untouched, I left her alone. I've been gone a lot. That helped."

Hank nodded. "Must have been hard, sleepin' in the same little house with a pretty thing like that."

Luke laughed, turning and carrying the whiskey to shore and setting it down. "You'd best be on your way, Hank. We've already unloaded all the food. I'm glad you talked this Mr. Gates into buyin' her."

Hank tucked dirty thumbs into the pockets of his fancy vest. "Sam Gates is always lookin' for somethin' like Emma. He owns a real fancy place in Knoxville. It's pretty well known he's got whores upstairs, but he likes to keep it kind of quiet—especially about buyin' some of the girls and bringin' them there against their will. He don't like too many people to know that, if you get my meanin'. Could get him in some trouble."

"Sure, I understand." Luke scratched at his curly, black hair. "Only one who knows about this is Jake Decker, and he knows better than to say much. I expect him and Tommy would have liked a turn at her first, but I promised you a virgin, and that's what you're gettin'."

Hank nodded. "I been waitin' a long time for this. My little girl sure turned into some kind of woman, didn't she? All these years I been bringin' her toys and trinkets, and all of a sudden she ain't a kid no more." The man breathed deeply, glancing around the farm. "Where is she, anyway?"

"I think she's in the house. It's just as well this time around."

"I expect so. You take good care of my little girl now, you hear? I'll be back for her in a couple of days."

Luke grinned and shook Hank's hand. "She'll be here."

Hank boarded the *Jasmine* again, and Luke untied the mooring rope and threw it on deck. He stood on the bank and waved as Hank got the steamboat under way. The man pulled a rope and tooted his steam whistle.

Emma got up off the bed at the sound and went to the loft window again. She looked out and saw that Hank was leaving. She felt relieved. No one had come for her. Apparently what Hank had in mind for her had not worked out.

Luke turned and started carrying a couple of crates toward the cabin, yelling at her to come and help. She wondered how he had paid for the supplies.

River Joe waited as the *Jasmine* docked at the MacBain settlement. The rain had stopped, but the river was so high now that the dock had washed away and the *Jasmine* moored right along shore.

It was four days since River Joe had left Emma. It had taken only a day and a half to get to the settlement, but the rising river had apparently given Hank Toole some trouble. He had arrived late, and River Joe felt apprehensive. He didn't like leaving Emma for so long, and with the river so high, the trip back downriver would be much swifter for the *Jasmine*. He would have to leave as soon as his trading was done in order to get to Emma before Hank Toole did.

River Joe was surprised at how lonely he felt since leaving Emma. He had not been this lonely since losing Yellow Sky. He thought he had gotten used to being alone, never thought he would want another woman the way he had loved and wanted Yellow Sky. But now there was Emma. She was not only beautiful, she had all the qualities he loved, strength and courage and pride, and a lot of spirit.

He had not meant to make love to her that night in the shed, but he had seen Luke Simms knock her down the steps and seen her run into the shed. And against all wisdom he had gone to her. His intention was only to hold her, to keep her warm. But the moment he wrapped her in his arms, sensed her vulnerability and sweet trust, all common sense had left him.

He realized now that he had been foolish from the first moment he had set eyes on Emma Simms, a whole year earlier. He never should have gone back there. It was when he decided over the long winter that he would go back to that place and see her again, rather than leave that first time and never go back. Now he had no choice but to take her away with him. He had promised he would come for her, and now that he had invaded her, owned her, remembered the ecstasy of being inside her, he was willing to risk all danger to keep her forever to himself. She trusted him now. He would do whatever he had to do to protect her and be with her.

He watched Hank Toole shout orders to the people who

gathered around with wagons and pack horses, ready to trade.

"Careful now! The river's dangerous," the man yelled. "Hurry it up! I gotta get back to Knoxville before this damned river gets any worse."

He waved to some of them, people he had traded with for years. As always, he sported his "city clothes," as he called them. "Latest fashion," he always bragged.

Hank Toole liked to put on a show of being the successful businessman; he was always full of stories for the mountain people about what was happening in the "outside" world. He liked nice clothes but did not have the class for them. They didn't fit his pudgy figure well, and with his face always showing a two- or three-day stubble, his teeth yellow from constant smoking and chewing, his hands never clean, the finest clothes were wasted on him.

River Joe kept his eyes on the man, wondering why Emma's father would want to talk to Hank before deciding whether to let Tommy marry her. What would Hank Toole have to do with it? Whatever it was, it was nothing good, of that River Joe was sure. He had never trusted Hank Toole, even though the man was usually fair in his trading.

What River Joe didn't like was the way Hank bragged about cities, exaggerating stories, especially when trying to impress the pretty young girls. He was always extra friendly with the women, and once River Joe had seen a frightened-looking young woman with Hank on the riverboat. River Joe could not help wondering at the time why the girl was with Hank, for she certainly did not look willing. River Joe suspected her fate, but he had never been to Knoxville to see for certain. Calhoun was the biggest town he had visited. Such places were dangerous for him, just as this little settlement could be dangerous if he wasn't careful.

He had a feeling it was important to get back to Emma before Hank Toole did. It seemed incredible to him that a man could sell off one of his own, but any man who knocked around his young stepdaughter the way Luke

Simms did was capable of such a deed. If Luke Simms tried to sell Emma, her fate would be even worse than having to go with Tommy Decker.

River Joe moved his pack horse closer, pulling a sledlike device behind it piled high with various kinds of skins. People were dickering with Hank now, everyone trying to hurry, some afraid to go aboard the *Jasmine* because of the fast-flowing Hiwassee River. A few people, especially women, moved away from River Joe when they saw him, looking at him as though he might come down on them with a hatchet at any moment.

"Get away from there. That's the white Indian," one man told his daughter, giving her a jerk.

River Joe did not look at them. After his experience at the last settlement, he was not about to set eyes on a white girl when he was in the middle of a settlement.

"I thought they hung him," someone else said in the distance.

"River Joe!" This time it was Hank calling out to him. "I wondered when I'd see you."

River Joe moved closer and others backed away. "Well, now, Indian, what brings you so far south again this time?" Hank asked. "You're a hell of a long way from your people."

"No game up there," River Joe answered. "Even down here it was scarce. I had to come farther south to gather enough skins. I have brought many, mostly deer, a couple of bearskins and some beaver and squirrel. Still, it was not a very good hunt this time."

"Well, now, let's see what you've got."

Hank walked behind the pack horse and examined the pile of skins. "You sure know how to clean these skins, River Joe." He shook his head. "I'm sorry, but I can't give you as much as last time, though. The demand isn't as high this year. As it is I could be gettin' myself in trouble. Folks in the cities is hollerin' about gettin' the Cherokee out of Tennessee altogether. Somebody like me trades with you—that means you've got supplies for them people that will help keep them right here. That makes me an enemy to my own people and I lose business. You understand?"

River Joe studied the man's dull blue eyes and bloated face. "No," he answered bluntly. "We bother no one. My people are very high in the mountains now. What harm can they do?"

"Well, now, you know it don't make much difference to me, River Joe. But I gotta watch out for myself, that's all. I have to give you about half what I give you last time."

River Joe felt his temper rising. "Half! I cannot buy enough supplies with only half."

"Now, watch that temper, River Joe. I hear tell you ain't too popular around here right now. You're walkin' on eggs, if you know what I mean."

Hank smiled, but River Joe saw right through it. Hank Toole had heard that there had been trouble. He knew he could cheat River Joe this time, knew he didn't dare argue or raise his voice or put up any kind of fuss. Hank had control over how much he paid, and there was nothing River Joe could do about it. He would pay him half of what the skins were worth and make a fine profit in Knoxville.

"You better keep an eye open, Hank," someone in the crowd spoke up. "River Joe got a taste of blood up at the Gillmore settlement a few days ago."

"Oh, River Joe here and I go back a long way," Hank answered, reaching out and patting River Joe's arm, the grin still on his face. "Right, River Joe?"

River Joe just stared at him, unsmiling.

Hank's smile faded. "Well? Is it a deal or not?"

"Apparently you leave me no choice," River Joe answered, his voice even and cool. He yanked out his big knife and people gasped. Hank stepped back, wide-eyed. Everyone breathed easier when River Joe bent down and sliced through the rawhide strips that held the skins to the sled. He jammed the knife back into its sheath and picked up the skins, throwing them at Hank's feet. "I will take my money now," he said then.

Hank eyed the man darkly. He walked past River Joe and onto the small steamer. It was more like a barge with a small cabin built onto it for living quarters, and the boat was loaded with goods to take back to Knoxville. River Joe wondered if Emma was intended to be part of Hank's baggage. Hank disappeared into the little cabin, emerging moments later with a small leather pouch of coins. He paraded up to River Joe and plunked them into his outstretched hand.

"Watch your step, River Joe," he bellowed, enjoying facing up to the big white Indian in front of others. "Wouldn't take much to get you hung right now, you know."

River Joe half-smiled, turning to shove the coin pouch into a parfleche that hung over his pack horse. He eyed Hank Toole carefully then. "Always before you have been fair with me," he said. "Today you have proven you are just like all other white men—a thief."

Hank's face reddened and his eyes suddenly seemed bloodshot. "You watch your mouth in these parts, River Joe," he warned in a low growl.

"I always speak the truth," River Joe said calmly.

He was preparing to leave, when someone shouted out to him, "Hey, Cherokee!" River Joe turned to see a group of young men from the settlement walking toward him, one of them with bright red hair and a bruised, swollen face. "You makin' trouble, Indian?" the red-haired one sneered as he swaggered closer.

River Joe said nothing. He picked up the reins of his pack horse and stood facing them.

"I know you," the redhead goaded. "You was pokin' around Betty Simms's grave a couple weeks ago. What the hell were you doin' hangin' around there? You like to scared poor Emma Simms to death. Was you lookin' at that little white girl with the idea of gettin' inside her ass? We already know you like little white girls."

River Joe told himself to stay calm. This was the red-haired young man who had been at Emma's mother's funeral—Tommy Decker. The thought of the young man raking over Emma and trying to force her and beat her made his anger rage inside, calmed only by the young man's swollen, battered face. So, this was what Emma had done to him.

He could not help loving her all the more as he looked at Tommy now. Emma had done considerable damage to the young man, and River Joe could not resist rubbing it in.

"What happened to your face?" he asked, deliberately grinning.

Tommy Decker's blue eyes turned to ice. "None of your goddamned business, Indian! I asked you a question. What was you doin' sniffin' around the Simms place?"

His words were not all formed correctly, and it was obvious his jaw was slightly dislocated and giving him a lot of pain. River Joe wanted to laugh at the sight, realizing that little Emma had done this to the man. It made him proud of Emma Simms. She was right. No man took her unless she wanted him to. How he wished he could tell Tommy Decker that River Joe had won the prize, that Emma Simms was his woman now.

"We seen you," Tommy was sneering. "Me, my pa, Luke Simms, even the preacher. You'd best stay away from Emma Simms. She's mine."

"Are you married to her?"

Tommy frowned. "Hell no."

"Then she is not yours." River Joe turned to lead his horse away, but Tommy grasped his arm, pushing him back around.

"You better answer my question, Indian!"

River Joe jerked his arm away, fire in his eyes. "Do not touch me, white scum!" he seethed, wanting very much to feel his blade sink into the soft flesh of Tommy Decker's belly.

"You be careful, Tommy. You're in no condition to fight that big bastard," one of the other boys spoke up.

"You stay out of this, Deek!"

One of the men of the settlement walked closer, carrying a musket. "What's this, Tommy? You sayin' River Joe was caught hangin' around the Simms place?"

"Yeah. And everybody knows what happened up at the Gillmore settlement. Looks to me like the white Indian here has turned to his own kind when it comes to females, and I say he's been prowlin' around like a male dog lookin' for a bitch in heat."

Women gasped and reddened, and more men gathered around, while River Joe calmly watched Tommy Decker, hoping the day would come when he could break his neck and watch him die.

"Ain't none of the white women safe around here with him hangin' around," Tommy added, holding his chin up confidently. "He must have got tired of them dark-skinned Cherokee girls. I bet that's why he came farther south this time, lookin' for a white girl to take back with him."

The man with the musket raised the gun. "You better come with me, River Joe."

River Joe casually rested his hand on his knife. "Where? I have done nothing wrong."

The man eyed the knife warily. "Maybe. Maybe not. But you've caused a few problems the last few days, and some of us don't like the way you looked at Hank over there. All I want you to do is come sit in a shed for a while—just till Hank is well on his way. Hank will leave yet today, and these people here will go on back to their homes and the women will be back inside. You'll have time to calm yourself and I'll send these here troublemakin' boys home."

A crowd gathered, a few more men holding muskets. Tommy stood grinning, a crooked grin because of his injuries.

"I have no interest in your weak women, and I must leave right away," River Joe told the man with the musket. Emma! He could not let Hank Toole get to her first! "Just let me go and you will hear no more from me."

"Come on now, River Joe," the man answered. "I don't want to shoot you. Neither do these other men here. You don't come this far south often, and we've never had cause before to hold guns on you. But that incident the other day up at Gillmore has folks a little wary. Why not cooperate? Might save yourself a lot of trouble—maybe even save your life. Some folks are still talkin' about hangin' you."

"Sounds like a good idea to me," Tommy sneered. "I wouldn't mine hangin' every Cherokee man and boy in Tennessee. We can keep the women and pretty young ones for more pleasurable things."

He and his friends laughed, but their smiles faded when River Joe's dark eyes moved to bore into Tommy's blue ones. "I will remember what you have said," he told the boy. He made a vow then and there that someday Tommy Decker would die at his hands, more for what he had done to Emma than for what he had said.

"You hear that?" Tommy accused, pointing at River Joe. "He threatened me. You all heard it."

"Why do you make trouble for me?" River Joe asked. "I have done nothing to you."

"You set your eyes on Emma Simms," Tommy answered. He put a hand to his sore face as a dull throbbing pain returned.

River Joe turned to the man with the musket, realizing that at the moment he couldn't fight everyone who stood there ready to take him on or shoot at him. He had little choice at the moment but to do what these men asked. He could not help Emma at all if he was dead.

"I will go with you," he told the man. "But I want my horse and my pack horse tied near me where I can watch them."

The man nodded. "All right. Bring the pack horse along. Where is your ridin' horse?"

River Joe nodded toward the distant trees. "Tied there— the big red one."

"Ain't nothin' compared to my 'fine black,'" Tommy bragged.

River Joe moved his dark eyes to the young man. "At least mine does not throw me off," he answered. "But then perhaps I am just a better rider."

Tommy's eyes widened as his friends burst out laughing. Tommy's face turned so red that his freckles didn't even show. He stepped closer to River Joe, fists clenched, standing nearly as tall as the white Indian. "How did you know that?" he growled.

"People talk," River Joe replied, smiling.

"You son of a bitch!" Tommy pulled back a big right fist, but River Joe instantly grabbed Tommy's right wrist just as the young man made ready to hit him. At the same time River Joe grabbed Tommy's left wrist also, pushing back as Tommy pushed in return. Both men stood there pushing against each other for a moment until River Joe outmuscled Tommy and shoved harder, sending the young man sprawling onto his rear end.

Tommy's friends laughed more, as did some of those in the crowd. The man with the musket stepped between River Joe and Tommy. "Let's go, River Joe, before this turns into somethin' ugly. We got no law around here but our own. Come with me now and you and Tommy can both cool off."

Several men led River Joe away, while Tommy's friends grabbed him and held him back when he started to charge toward River Joe again.

"Leave him be!" one of Tommy's friends warned. "You heard what he did to Dave Moore with his knife. You lookin' to get gutted out?"

"He's a goddamned Cherokee, even if their blood don't run in his veins! And I won't have no Indian best me in front of everybody!"

"Save it, Tommy! There will be a better time."

Tommy jerked away, watching the men lead River Joe to a shed behind a tavern.

"I'll get that bastard!" He put a hand to his sore face.

There was someone else he would get, too, as soon as the swelling went down in his face. He was not about to let Emma Simms see him this way and know how much damage she had done. But he vowed she would pay dearly for his pain and humiliation.

River Joe walked into the shed, fighting an urge to bolt and run. How could he sit here while the *Jasmine* left? What would Emma think when Hank Toole showed up but River Joe didn't? Still, he would never show up at all if he tried to get away from these men now.

Two days. If they held him here overnight, it would be two whole days before he could get back down to Emma's. Hank Toole would most certainly reach her first. The only way to hope to catch up would be to find a way to escape after dark.

In the distance Hank Toole hurried people along, anxious to get to the rest of the settlements before the river got any higher. None of them knew he was even more anxious to get to Emma Simms. The trip back to Knoxville was going to be a pleasant one, and Sam Gates would be very happy with the pretty blond-haired merchandise Hank was bringing along on his return trip.

Darkness fell, and the small MacBain settlement quieted. The one and only tavern in town was full of men discussing the possibilities of their fellow Tennessee native, Andrew Jackson, running for president, and what he might do to help get rid of the Cherokee. Arguments turned from the presidency to whether the river would crest before it washed away the whole settlement, and Tommy Decker drank with his father and several friends, bragging about facing up to River Joe.

Outside, rain came down steadily again, and the streets ran with mud.

"River's risin' even more," one of River Joe's guards spoke up. A man stood at each corner of the shed where River Joe was being held, local settlers watching him in shifts. His weapons had been taken away and put with his gear.

"I don't like it," the second man answered. "This whole village is gonna get washed away. Seems like it's just one storm after another."

"Why don't you let me go?" River Joe said then. "The *Jasmine* left hours ago. I can't get far in this rain anyway, and I did nothing wrong in the first place. Let me leave now. You men should be watching your homes and families. That river is going to get higher than it has in years."

"Sorry, River Joe, but we all decided," one of them answered.

Laughter and shouts could be heard then, as four young men came stumbling out of the tavern and through the rain toward the shed.

"It's that damned Tommy Decker again," one of the men complained. "I can tell by his laugh. That boy's gettin' to drinkin' too much. That's probably why he got throwed from that horse of his."

The two men laughed, and River Joe was immediately alert, rising from the bench he had been sitting on.

"Just relax there, River Joe. We'll send him on his way. He's probably pretty drunk by now—been over there drinkin' with his pa and friends."

Tommy stumbled into the light of a lamp then, wearing a cape and hood against the rain, holding a bottle of whiskey in his hand. "How you doin' there, Ben? Keepin' a good eye on the bastard Indian there?"

He and his buddies all laughed, the other three not wearing anything against the rain. They stood with their hair dripping wet, all of them staring at River Joe.

"Why don't you get out of here, Tommy?" said the one called Ben. "You'll just make more trouble."

"Tell him! Tell him, Tommy!" said one of the other boys. They all laughed again, pushing Tommy toward River Joe.

River Joe watched him carefully, wishing he could kill the boy right then and there with his bare hands. Tommy swallowed some whiskey and stood on wavering legs, leering at River Joe.

"Hey, Indian," he sneered, leaning closer. "I got somethin' to tell you that's gonna make you laugh."

They all snickered again and the two guards pushed at the other three. "Come on, Tommy, get out of here," Ben repeated.

"You shut up!" Tommy whirled, fists clenched. "I gotta talk to River Joe here. I got somethin' to tell him, Ben. You owe my pa money, so shut up!"

Ben reddened some and just stared back at the young man, keeping his musket steady on River Joe. The other boys snickered more and Tommy turned to River Joe.

"Guess what my pa told me tonight, Indian!"

River Joe said nothing, waiting for Tommy to continue, ready to defend himself if the boy tried anything.

"I found out that I can go down to Knoxville in a few weeks," Tommy continued, speaking more clearly now that the whiskey had dulled the pain in his jaw. "And I can get into Emma Simms anytime I want—for the right price! All of us can!"

The other boys laughed hard then, one making lewd gestures and howling.

"Let me at her!" another yelled.

Never in his life had River Joe had to struggle so mightily to stay in control and look unconcerned. "I do not know what you mean," he said carefully, "nor do I care."

Tommy snickered. "The hell you don't. You wanted to get into that pretty blond girl's pants yourself. Only my pa says Luke has plans to sell her—to a man in Knoxville who buys pretty little mountain girls to use at his, uh, tavern. Only they do more than serve drinks."

Another young man howled and swallowed some whiskey, and River Joe felt desperate to get out of that place fast. Emma! Was Tommy telling the truth? Of course he was. It all made too much sense. That was why Luke wanted to see Hank Toole once more before deciding what to do with Emma. He folded his arms, gauging the situation, continuing to look unconcerned.

"Luke is her stepfather," Tommy went on. He turned to the two guards. "Can you believe it? I done told Luke I lost my interest in Emma for a wife. She's too damned uppity and independent. So ol' Luke up and sold her. Hank Toole has the pleasant job of pickin' her up and takin' her to Sam Gates—that's the man's name down in Knoxville." He laughed again, taking a slug of whiskey. "Ol' Sam will break her, and she won't be so uppity anymore. Then me and my friends are goin' down to Knoxville and have us the best time we've had in years. I can't wait to see the look on Emma's face when she sees me walk in and tell her to strip down."

They all laughed, and the two guards looked at each other. "I don't believe it. Would Luke really do that?" Ben asked.

"Sure he would!" Tommy answered. "He's sellin' the farm, and he ain't got no use for the girl. Why not get a little money out of her?" He turned to River Joe. "And I bet ol' Hank Toole will give her a try on the way there. That big braggart is always lookin' at the women."

River Joe's dark eyes drilled into him. "If you have to go to Knoxville to get into bed with Emma Simms, after she has been beaten and probably drugged, it does not say much for you as a man, does it?"

The others quieted and Tommy straightened. "What did you say, Indian?"

"You heard me. You could never get her any other way."

Tommy gripped the whiskey bottle tightly. "How would you know?"

A faint grin moved over River Joe's mouth. "I know more

than you think. I even know what really happened to your face."

Tommy stared back at him in surprise, hesitant at first, trying to figure out what this man knew.

"What's he talkin' about, Tommy?" one of his buddies asked.

Tommy began literally to shake. "What are you sayin', Indian? You been talkin' to Emma Simms? You been with that girl?"

"All I'm saying is that you are a coward, Tommy Decker. A coward and a liar! You aren't even man enough for the whores, let alone decent women."

"You bastard!" Tommy growled. He swung the whiskey bottle, but River Joe deflected the swing with his arm, at the same time bending a knee and kicking hard into Tommy's privates. The young man cried out in agony, bending over, and River Joe's left fist came up hard under his jaw, landing a blow that made a snapping sound and jerked Tommy backward. He fell into Ben, knocking the musket sideways just as it went off. The musket ball went astray and lodged in a piece of wood, the shot muffled by a loud clap of thunder so that people inside nearby buildings heard nothing.

In what seemed a split second, River Joe pulled the knife he kept hidden in his knee-high moccasins, and he was waving it at the others.

"Shoot that musket if you want," he said to the other guard. "But I guarantee I will throw this knife directly into your heart before I go down!"

The man hesitated, and the other boys just stared, then bolted and ran. Tommy lay seemingly unconscious at Ben's feet, blood pouring from around several broken teeth in his mouth and a badly bitten tongue.

"Both of you know I have done nothing wrong, and I have hurt neither of you," River Joe said to the guards. "Now let me go!"

Ben and the other guard stared, and the second one finally

lowered his rifle. "I ain't takin' on the likes of you," he said to River Joe. "Get goin'. We'll tell them Tommy started it. It's stormin' too bad out tonight for anybody to care about chasin' after you anyway, but you better never show up here again, Indian."

Joe moved cautiously past the man, still waving his knife. He backed over to his horse, which was tied with his pack horse next to the shed. He eased up onto the big roan gelding and turned it, taking up the reins of his pack horse and shoving his knife back into his moccasin, then rode off into the darkness.

Ben and the other guard looked at each other and breathed a sigh of relief.

"I could just about feel that blade movin' into my gut," Ben said.

"Me, too."

"Let's get Tommy over to the doc. The dumb kid deserves what he got."

Both men bent down to pick up Tommy.

"What do you suppose River Joe meant when he said he knows how Tommy's face really got hurt?"

The second man shrugged. "Who knows?"

"You think it's true—about Luke sellin' that pretty little stepdaughter of his to Sam Gates?"

"I wouldn't be surprised."

"Poor girl."

The second man grunted. "This boy is right heavy, ain't he?"

They carried Tommy out into the rain and down the street to a doctor, while River Joe rode hard. The *Jasmine* would reach Luke's place by morning. Even at a hard ride, River Joe would be lucky to get there by midafternoon. Every moment counted, and now he could only pray the *Jasmine* would somehow be forced to slow down. Emma! He had to get to her!

◊ *Chapter 6* ◊

Emma hurriedly finished her chores so that she could clean up and be ready. Every day she made sure she was clean, her hair washed and combed, for River could come for her at any moment.

Four days had gone by, four very long, lonely days. This was the morning of the fifth day. It had rained almost constantly the last two days, and as she ducked about now in yet another storm to do her chores she watched the trees for River. She had spent her nights curled up into her pillow, thinking of nothing but that night in the shed, a night that somehow didn't even seem real. But the spot of blood on her bloomers had been real. To Emma it was only a symbol that she was now River's woman.

The bleeding had quickly stopped, and she wondered how easy it was for a man's seed to turn into a baby. That part scared her. She had seen her mother lose so many babies, then die when she finally had one. Would that happen to her if she got a baby in her belly? And if she lost babies like her mother had done, would River still love her? Maybe he would be angry with her and turn ugly like Luke had done. Maybe he would grow to hate her.

She stopped scattering chicken feed and stared over at her mother's grave, the flowers she had put there all wilted now. She put a hand to her belly, realizing suddenly that more than anything on earth she wanted to give River a baby, be the wife he needed, do all she could to make up for the wife he had lost. But having a baby brought terror to her soul. She decided she would have to pray to the Maker of Breath that she could carry a child and would live to nurse it and raise it, for she would love that baby more than anything on earth.

Now that she had known love, real love, had felt this wonderful feeling, had been held gently in the arms of one who cared, she realized how much love she had deep inside herself to give. Love was so beautiful! Now she knew why Mrs. Breckenridge always seemed so happy. There was nothing in the whole world more wonderful than being loved, and to have someone to love in return!

She walked over to a large sow that lay in the mud nursing new babies, so many that there were not enough teets for them all. It had stopped raining again for the moment, and Emma took time to bend down and pick up one of the babies, feeling how fat and soft it was, wondering what it must be like to hold a real human baby to her breast, a baby who was her very own, River's child, planted in her belly and coming back out of her. Her eyes teared at the thought of how awful it would be to lose a baby.

She rubbed the little pig's belly, wondering what River's first wife had been like. Was she beautiful? She must have been very dark. Did he like Emma's own light skin? But of course he did. He had said so. He had admired her golden hair.

She felt a flush of warmth at the memory of the way he had gently caressed the hairs between her legs, saying that they too were the color of cornsilk. She could hardly believe she had let him touch her in the ways he had, let him look at her. Thrilling desire rushed through her at the thought of it.

She set down the piglet and turned to finish feeding the chickens, so glad that at least during this time while River was away, Tommy had not come by. Luke had not even mentioned the young man. And Luke had decided to mend a few fences and straighten things up as best he could in order to try to sell the farm. That kept him busy and away from her. She had not felt his fist at all these last four days.

She was not afraid now of Luke's threats to sell the farm and hand her over to Tommy. She was afraid of nothing now that River had made her his woman and promised to come back. He would never let anything bad happen to her.

Thunder rolled in the distance. Another storm was coming. She turned and watched the river, which had never been so high. It was nearly halfway up to the cabin now. All the animals had moved up with it, and sometimes Emma saw a washtub or a piece of fencing and occasionally a drowned animal go floating by.

The river was still her biggest remaining fear. The waters were high and rushing fast now. Luke said he wasn't worried at all. "That river would never reach this cabin," he kept assuring her. "I've lived here a long time, Emma, and I ain't never seen that happen."

She looked up at the black clouds. It seemed as though it rained every day lately. And it rained so much that the water could not soak into the ground; it simply ran off the top, into the rivers. Everything was damp, even inside the cabin. The animals didn't seem to mind, especially the pigs, who rolled and played in the mud in sheer ecstasy.

The river made a roaring sound now, rather than its usual gentle murmur. How much more could it rain without the river coming right up to their doorstep? If it got any higher, whole settlements were going to be washed away.

Her heart tightened. River! What if there was a tremendous flood, and River got caught in it. What if something happened that he could not get to her after all?

She set down the pan full of seed, and several chickens gathered around it, clucking and pecking at their food. Emma watched the trees again. This fifth day was the first time she had begun to feel doubt. It seemed impossible that River could have been fooling her, could have tricked her in order to lie with her. Had he done what Tommy wanted to do, only used kindness to get it instead of brutality?

No. River would never do that. He was too honest and open. His eyes, his touch, his kiss, his wonderful warm embrace, all were too filled with sweet love. She would have known. She would have sensed if he didn't really love her, wouldn't she? But what did she know about men? Nothing! Nothing but brutality and trickery. River had come in the night, stolen what he wanted, then left, with promises to come back.

The thunder came again, and she fought a building panic, telling herself it was simply the rushing river and oncoming storm, and all the horror and loss she had suffered lately, that were bringing on these feelings of doubt and fear. She told herself to remember love, to remember the Maker of Breath and all the things River had told her about not being afraid. He would come. He had promised.

She heard several toots then, and her heart leaped. The *Jasmine*! It was coming! River had said he would come when the *Jasmine* came, or soon after! She ran to the cabin to wash her face and change her dress. She must be ready! Her gunnysack was all packed, shoved under the cot.

"Emma, go get yourself prettied up," Luke shouted to her. "I want you to look nice when Hank gets here."

She stopped and stared at him a moment. He stood grinning by a fence he had been nailing. She frowned, an unexplainable fear creeping into her heart. Luke had never told her to get "prettied up" for Hank before. And why was he grinning like that?

She looked around the surrounding trees again. River. Where was River? Surely he would come anytime now. He had told her that he loved her. She would trust in that love.

The *Jasmine* tooted its whistle again, and she went inside to wash while more black storm clouds gathered and the rain began to fall lightly. She hurriedly washed her hands and face and changed her dress, then brushed out her hair. Luke would ask Hank in for bread and honey and coffee, like always. She would give Hank some fresh wild strawberries she had found. Hank and Luke would get some trading done, and Hank would leave.

But no! Hank had already stopped and let off some supplies. With the river so high and dangerous, why would he bother stopping again just for casual conversation and bread and honey? An ugly fear that she could not even name weighed heavily in her chest. She told herself to relax. River would come. He would show up anytime now.

She watched out the window then, waiting inside because of the returning rain. She wondered if there had ever been a year when it rained this much. How could the ground take any more? Surely the Hiwassee would swell even more, but River would come soon and take her to higher ground, where it would be safer.

It took nearly another half-hour for the *Jasmine* to maneuver to shore. She watched Luke and Hank running around in the rain trying to tie the steamboat in waters that were now well above the pier. The two men ran up to the cabin then, barging inside. Emma felt uncomfortable when Hank looked at her, and the odd fear over why he was here at all crept over her again.

"Well, well, how's my girl?" the man asked, grinning. "Why, you're no girl anymore, are you, Emma, honey? You're a woman, and that's a fact." He came close beside her and patted her bottom. Emma moved away, and Hank's eyes moved over her slowly, the same hunger in them as she had seen in Tommy's eyes the day he attacked her. "Yes, ma'am, you are probably the prettiest girl in these here mountains," he added.

It all seemed so much more clear now, after Tommy's attack, and after being with River Joe. Yes, she was a woman, and she knew why men looked at her the way they did. But when River Joe looked at her, touched her, it was with respect and love. Hank was hardly different from Tommy, just more cunning. It was incredible how much she had learned in only a few days, how enlightened she had become.

"I gathered some strawberries for you, Hank," she said, moving to the other side of the table. She filled two bowls and set them down for the men, noticing Hank and Luke exchange a look that said they knew something she did not. Emma's heart pounded harder. She said nothing, not wanting to believe the ugly thought that was beginning to creep into her mind. River was coming. She should not be afraid.

She set bread and honey in front of the two men and they ate, Luke breaking open a new bottle of homemade whiskey. Emma eased her way over to a rocker, hoping they would both go outside soon and she could use the moment to run away. Surely if she ran into the woods, River would find her. She didn't care about the rain. It might even help her hide. She didn't care about anything now but getting away, not even sure why she should run, only sensing a sudden danger.

River. Surely he was close by. Why didn't he come? Was he waiting for the *Jasmine* to leave? She got up and moved to a window, staring out, watching for him. All her hopes and dreams were centered now on River Joe. She had loved him fiercely. He had promised to come. Again she fought the horrible possibility that he had not meant any of it. Maybe he was well on his way back to his people, laughing about the stupid mountain girl he had gently raped. Was that what had happened to her?

"I don't know how much longer I can hold out on this river, Luke," Hank was saying. "This is about as bad as I've ever seen it, and now more rain is comin'. You better get yourself to higher ground."

Luke waved him off. "This river don't scare me. She'll never get this high."

"Well, now, I wouldn't be too sure about that." Hank took a swallow of whiskey. "Say, I seen River Joe up at the Mac-Bain settlement. I never knew him to come this far south before."

Emma stiffened, casually walking back over to the rocker,

somewhat relieved to know River had gone where he said he would go.

"Lots of people around here have seen him. We even seen him once," Luke told the man. "The day we buried Betty. He come walkin' right out of the trees, then disappeared again."

"He's like that. I guess there was some trouble with him up at the Gillmore settlement, and then he give me a little trouble over not gettin' enough for his skins, so they held him up there."

Emma felt a sickness in her stomach.

"I mean to tell you, I was relieved," Hank went on. "He was in a piss poor mood over them skins, and then that Tommy Decker come along and tried to start somethin' with him. Say, what the hell happened to Tommy's face anyway?"

"Horse throwed him."

Hank chuckled. Emma struggled against tears. Where was River?

"Well, anyway, I'll be well on my way before they let River Joe loose. I wouldn't be surprised if they didn't hang him after they think about it awhile. People would sleep better nights knowin' he was dead."

Emma felt a pressure growing in her head, felt suddenly removed from everything else. Hang him! Not River! He was coming for her. He was her only hope. She loved him. She had lain with River Joe, taken him inside herself. It couldn't end this way!

"Why would they hang him, Hank?" she blurted, walking closer to the table.

Hank turned, his eyes moving over her again. "Oh, just to get rid of a nuisance. After what he did up at the Gillmore place . . ." He kept moving his eyes from her breasts to her belly. "They figure he's got a yen now for pretty little white girls, like you." The man reached out and grabbed her hand before she could back away. He rubbed the back of it with his thumb. "But don't you worry, little one. I'd never let that white Indian hurt you. You're goin' to Knoxville with ol' Hank. Did your pa tell you about that?"

Her cheeks felt warm and she pulled her hand away. "No." She looked at Luke. "Are you . . . are you going to let Hank help me find Mrs. Breckenridge?"

Luke looked at Hank and they both chuckled. "Not exactly, girl," he answered. "You'll meet some women, but they won't be anything like Mrs. Breckenridge."

Emma moved farther back, watching them both carefully. "I don't want to go."

"Come on now, honey." Hank rose. "For years I been tellin' you about Knoxville and other places, and you been askin' about it, sayin' how you'd like to see them places. Well, now I'm gonna take you, and you'll meet somebody who's gonna put pretty clothes on you, like you always wanted. Why, when we get through with you, you won't recognize yourself when you look in the mirror. You'll be the prettiest girl in Knoxville."

She looked at Luke. "I want to stay here."

Luke rose also. "You can't. I'm leavin' myself after a while. And since you object to marryin' Tommy Decker, I'm doin' what I got a right to do, Emma. Now Hank here has give me good money for you from a man in Knoxville who will make a real pretty lady out of you."

She felt even sicker. "Money? Luke, that's like . . . that's like selling me. You've got no right selling me like a . . . like a cow or a pig."

His dark eyes flashed the look she had seen many times before, usually before he hit her. "I got all the rights, Emma Simms. And I ain't goin' back on no deals with a man of Sam Gates's position. So you just get your things together and go with Hank."

"Sam Gates? Who is Sam Gates?"

"A very wealthy man in Knoxville who is anxious to meet you," Hank answered. He stepped a little closer. "Come on now, honey, I got to get the *Jasmine* back into the river and get goin'."

She watched them both carefully, then bolted to the right, heading for the back door. But Hank was ready, catching her around the waist and dragging her back, reaching around her breasts with his other arm to pull her. Emma tugged and kicked, grabbing a pan to reach back and hit him with in the head, but Luke grabbed her wrist and yanked the pan from her hand. He jerked her away from Hank and slammed her across the side of the face with the back of his hand, knocking her sideways into an old iron cookstove.

"She's a stubborn thing. You better tie her, Hank," she heard Luke saying.

Before the dizziness left her and she could rise again, someone rolled her onto her stomach and pulled her wrists behind her. "Get me somethin' to do it with," Hank was saying.

Emma began struggling wildly again, and Hank pushed her arms up high so that it brought her pain. He sat on her hips, leaving her helpless.

"Luke, don't do this," she screamed. "Let me stay here! Please, Luke. River's coming! River Joe is coming for me! He'll pay you if he has to!"

Someone began tying her wrists, and someone else grasped her hair painfully. "What'd you say girl?"

The tears came then. "River Joe is coming for me."

He pulled her hair harder. "You been with him? You been with that white Indian?"

She grimaced in pain, not answering. Someone jerked her to her feet then, her wrists tied tightly behind her.

"I asked you a question, girl! You been with River Joe? You been sneakin' around lettin' trash like that get under your dress?"

She jerked in a sob. "He loves me. And I love him! Just let me go with him, Luke, please!"

He landed her another blow, and she was unable to ward off her fall with her arms. Blackness moved in to take over when her head hit the floor, and she could think of nothing but River, holding her in his strong arms, making love to her, bringing her the beautiful pain, making her his woman. He had said he would come. Had they hurt him? Maybe he was dead. Who was going to come and help her now? And if River was dead, what difference did it really make what happened to her? She would simply find a way to kill herself.

"Sam Gates paid good money for a virgin," she heard Hank say.

"I know. I had no idea, Hank. River Joe of all men! Good God!"

"I don't like it. This makes things more dangerous for me."

"He can't get to you in the middle of that ragin' river, and you said yourself they detained him at the MacBain place. Besides, him comin' for her is probably all in her head. No wild man like that is gonna worry about one stupid white girl who spread her legs for him. There's probably others just as stupid in some of the other settlements. He'll go back to his people and mate up with some Cherokee girl. Don't pay no attention to what she said."

"Well, Sam Gates ain't gonna like this."

"Well, it ain't my fault, and I ain't givin' back none of the money."

Someone picked her up and slung her over his shoulder. She felt a hand rub over her hips and heard Hank's voice close. "Well, since she ain't so fresh anymore, I expect I got a right to have at her myself at least."

"Do what you want. I don't give a damn, especially since she laid with that white Indian!"

"By the time Sam's customers get through with her, she'll forget all about him. She'll tame down and learn to like it in time."

Emma felt herself being carried then, felt wind and rain, heard the raging waters. The river! Hank was taking her on the *Jasmine* and she would be in those black, swirling waters! She could never get away then. She was terrified of the water.

River! If only he would come. He would kill these men for what they were doing! He would swim the swirling waters to get to her, she just knew it.

Now the water was very close. Someone lowered her. She fell onto something hard and sensed darkness. A door closed, and she felt a rocking motion. She was on the boat, but she couldn't move or think straight. Everything hurt. Because of the wind and rain and the raging river, she couldn't hear the voices clearly now.

She slipped down, resting her head against what felt like a sack of potatoes, her last thought of River kissing her, promising to come back.

When Emma awoke, she was not sure how much time had passed. Everything hurt terribly, and her hands felt half-asleep. Her head was throbbing as she managed to sit up. Everything was total darkness. She slipped sideways, dizziness overcoming her, then just let her head rest again on the sack of potatoes. After a few minutes her eyes adjusted, and she could barely make out a very small room, probably one of the tiny storerooms above the deck of the *Jasmine*.

She knew this boat. Hank had let her explore it many times, when she was an innocent child who thought him simply the friendly man from Knoxville who owned a pretty yellow steamboat and traded supplies with settlers. There were a couple of tiny storerooms above deck, and an area below deck for more storage. Many supplies were stacked above deck, and she wondered how they were going to stay put in the midst of the storm that was tossing the *Jasmine* wildly now.

As her head became more clear she realized the kind of business Hank Toole was really in, and she wondered how many other women he had purchased and taken back to the city with him. All these years he had been waiting for her to grow up, and Luke had been waiting for the chance to sell her. How glad she was that her mother was not alive to know about this.

She tried to sit up again, groaning with the pain in her head. Where was River? Who was there to help her now? Everything was gone—the only place she had been able to call home, her mother . . . River. River. How wonderful it would be to feel his arms around her at this moment, hear him telling her not to be afraid, feel him lift her and carry her away, off this horrible little boat and away from the terrifying river.

But he probably would not come. He might even be dead. And if he wasn't, maybe he had never meant to keep his promise in the first place. Maybe she really was just a stupid mountain girl, one of many he had charmed with his gentle hands and sweet words, winning them over with that warm, beautiful smile, that utterly handsome face and powerful build. He was a man of mystery, who probably made lots of girls curious and excited and knew the power he had over them.

The helpless tears came then. What was she to do? What kind of fate awaited her in Knoxville? She didn't know much about those things, other than to be sure it was something bad, something that would involve men using her.

The *Jasmine* creaked and groaned, and Emma curled up, sure that at any moment the small steamer would break apart and she would be swallowed up into the black waters. At least drowning would be better than going to Knoxville. The day had started out so full of hope. How could such happiness turn into such horror so quickly?

She heard footsteps then, and the door was flung open. Someone came inside the tiny storeroom, and she could tell it was dark and raining outside.

"Let's go, honey," she heard Hank say. "We're tied up here for the night. Been here quite a while. The river's too dangerous to go any farther. Lots of trees down, pieces of junk floatin' all over the place." He grasped her arm. "You awake now?"

"Hank, please take me back," she begged. "You used to be my friend."

"That was when you was little, honey. You ain't little no more."

She tried to jerk away but he pulled her back, much too strong now for her to struggle against. "No, ma'am, you ain't little no more, and I been waitin' a long time for this. I reckon' the *Jasmine* will hold up while I make use of my cabin for a while."

She tried to get away again and he grabbed her around the throat. "I got a nigger down below feedin' the boiler," he growled. "You be real nice to me, Emma, or I'll let him come up and have his own turn at you. That what you want, a nigger havin' at you?"

He pulled her outside in the rain and then led her stumbling along beside him to his little cabin. He shoved her inside and closed the door. The tiny room reeked of tobacco and whiskey, and a urine pot sat in the corner. She thought how the room was like Hank, painted pretty outside but dirty inside, just like Hank was smelly inside the nice suits. The only furnishings were a cot, a dresser, a table, and a chair.

Hank pushed her onto the cot and raised the wick on a lantern so that the room was brighter.

"Well, now, ain't this cozy?"

She could see him better now, saw that he was dripping wet. His hair was matted and his teeth looked yellower by the lamplight.

"Hank, please don't," she asked. "It's bad out there. You . . . you should be watching the boat. It's making all kinds of noises, Hank. It's going to break up and we'll all die!"

The man chuckled. "Not the *Jasmine.*" The boat lurched and he grabbed the bed rail to stay on his feet. "Somethin' about a captain keepin' his ship goin' in a storm that brings all the juices up, you know what I mean, honey?" He took off his coat and threw it aside, then unbuttoned his shirt. "Now that the white Indian done broke you in, this shouldn't be too bad. You might even enjoy it. I'll get to see what I been wantin' to see for a long, long time—and you'll take a man on the wild river. Don't it kind of excite you, just thinkin' about it?"

She had to think. Her only hope was to have her hands free. She swallowed, forcing a smile. "You'll be nice to me?"

He grinned back, taking off his shirt and unbuttoning his pants. "Ain't I always nice to you, honey?"

"Will you untie my hands? Please? They're asleep, Hank. I promise not to fight you. I'm scared of the river. Where would I go?"

He came closer, dropping his pants and sitting down on the cot, removing his boots. The *Jasmine* lurched suddenly and he fell over her legs. He kicked off his pants then and crawled up onto the cot, hovering over her.

"Okay. I reckon you've tamed down some by now. Roll over."

She scooted back, feeling sick at the look in his eyes. "I'll . . . I'll turn around."

Hank chuckled. "Sure. We'll do this more than once. Once you learn to like it, we can try it other ways. You promise to be a good girl? I don't want to have to hit you again. You're already all black and blue from Luke knockin' you around."

"I promise. I'm so sore, Hank. Surely we're good enough friends that you don't want to see me hurting."

He watched her carefully, then moved to the table, picking up a knife. "Sit real still now." He slit the ties on her wrists and pulled them off. She brought her arms around in front of her, rubbing her blistered wrists with cold, sleepy hands, then shivered against the dampness of her dress.

"Let's take these wet clothes off of you, honey," Hank said then, leaning up close behind her and unbuttoning her dress.

She sat very still, telling herself to wait until the moment was right, waiting for the life to come back to her hands.

Hank opened her dress, pulling it down over her shoulders. He turned her, gazing at her breasts like a hungry cat.

"Well, well. Ain't you just about the prettiest thing ol' Hank ever set eyes on." He rubbed at his privates, then leaned close, pushing her down to the cot and putting his full weight on her. His breath reeked of tobacco, and she kept her lips tightly closed as he tried to kiss her. She waited then until he turned his head to try to move down to put his mouth over her breast. She raised her head up then, grasping his hair as though eager, then jerked his head close and bit his ear as hard as she could, drawing blood.

Hank screamed in pain, sitting up and holding his ear.

"You bitch!" He backhanded her hard, and she reached up and gouged hard at his eyes and face, drawing more blood, realizing she had to fight hard now or he might get hold of her wrists again and tie her.

Hank screamed out again, trying to grab her arms. She wiggled free, falling off the cot and scrambling for the door, but she had not done quite enough damage to stop him, and he leaped off the bed and grabbed her away from the door, all the while cursing at her.

The *Jasmine* lurched again and they fell, Emma hitting her head on the dresser. She struggled against the awful dizziness, her head already screaming with pain from Luke's blows. She felt Hank turning her over, felt her dress being pulled up and her bloomers ripped.

Suddenly the cabin door burst open. She felt wind and rain, felt another presence. Hank got up off her legs then. "Jesus Christ!" she heard him gasp. "River Joe!"

◇ *Chapter 7* ◇

"You stay away from me, River Joe!"

Hank backed away, and Emma rolled to a sitting position, regaining her senses in time to see River Joe grab Hank Toole's head with his bare hands and shove the man hard against a wall several times.

"Wait! Wait!" Hank was screaming, grasping at River Joe's powerful arms fruitlessly. "River Joe, use your head! You'll hang! You'll hang!"

Emma watched in wide-eyed shock, her head swimming with pain and confusion; her heart swelled with joy that River had come, but at the same time she was horrified at his powerful violence. At the moment he seemed hardly aware of her presence, his eyes wild, his whole attention directed at Hank Toole.

"God damn you!" Hank screamed. "You're killin' me . . . you stupid bastard!"

Emma backed up against the dresser as River Joe jerked Hank around by the head and threw him toward the door. He had not said a word, but Hank was still screaming obscenities and warnings, gasping for breath then as River Joe stood watching him, fists still clenched.

"Look, I . . . paid good . . . money for her, River Joe!" Hank panted. "She belongs to Sam Gates! You'll . . . be sorry for this!" He crawled toward the foot of the bed, where a pistol hung in a belt over the rail. Blood ran from his ear and face, where Emma had bitten and scratched him.

"She belongs to me!" River Joe answered in his low, commanding voice. "You had no right taking her against her will!"

"All right! All right! Take her!" Hank said. "Take her, and I won't say nothin'. Just . . . take her . . . and get off my boat! Just don't . . . kill me!"

"River, don't kill him," Emma pleaded. "They'll . . . hang you!"

His eyes moved to Emma then, as though he was seeing her for the first time. She pulled self-consciously at the front of her dress, and her face was still bruised from Luke's earlier blows. Her dress was torn in places, and one lip was swollen. Her nose bled slightly, and she could not control her tears of horror and pain.

"Don't kill him." She began to weep. "I . . . don't want you to die, River."

"You . . . you listen to her, River Joe," Hank said, moving closer to the pistol. "She's right, you know. They'll hunt you down."

There was a moment of indecision, while the *Jasmine* heaved and groaned in the wind, straining against its mooring ropes while the river raged at an all-time high, seemingly intent on sweeping the *Jasmine* away along with settlements, animals, and people.

River Joe was drawn to Emma, his heart torn at her condition and her tears. He had failed her. He had promised to come sooner. He looked over at Hank. "This is your lucky day," he growled. "I will not kill you. But you *deserve* to die, Hank Toole! You cheated me, and you took this innocent girl against her will! A man who would buy a young girl like a hog is a coward! You are worth less than the lizards who crawl in the swamps!"

He turned and leaned over Emma. "Let's get out of here." He helped her up, and it was then she saw Hank go for the pistol.

"River!" she screamed.

Everything seemed to happen at the same time. River Joe pushed her, and she heard the pistol fire. Emma landed against the doorjamb, at the same time seeing River Joe whirl and stumble. His big knife came out of its sheath; and the thudding sound of the knife landing in Hank Toole's chest seemed to come within a fraction of a second of the flash of Hank's pistol.

Emma stared in horror as blood spurted from Hank's chest for a brief second, then stopped flowing. Hank, his eyes bulging as he stared at River Joe, looked down at the knife, then fell backward in death, his eyes still staring.

River Joe stumbled over to the man, yanking out his knife and wiping it off on the man's long underwear. He shoved it back into its sheath. It was only then that he and Emma both realized someone else stood in the doorway. River Joe's eyes widened and he stood hesitant, looking toward the door.

Emma turned to see Nigger Jim watching. He wore an old soiled blue shirt and drooping cotton pants. His eyes were wide with terror, their whites standing out bright, lit by the lantern.

"I . . . I won't say nuthin'!" the man squeaked then, apparently thinking River Joe might use the knife on him, too.

River Joe moved toward him to explain, but the man turned and ran. River Joe ran out after him, and Emma heard a scream, then only the sound of the *Jasmine* groaning and shifting, its cargo beginning to crash to the deck, more supplies falling around in the hold below.

Rain and wind blew through the door, which banged back and forth against the wall. Emma stared at Hank's dead body, feeling sick to her stomach. A moment later River Joe appeared in the doorway, then she felt him lifting her, drawing her into his arms.

"*Agiya*," he whispered.

"River!" she wept, putting her arms around his neck. "Hank said . . . you were hanged . . . back at MacBain's."

"I got away. What did he do to you? Tell me he did not rape you!"

"No. You came . . ." She felt the warm wetness against her arm and leaned back, gasping at the sight of blood along the top of his left shoulder. "River, he shot you!"

"It is all right. It is just the flesh."

She couldn't stop the tears, hugging him tightly then, relishing the glorious comfort of being held in River Joe's arms. He had come! He had come for her! Nothing else in the whole world mattered at the moment!

"Are you hurt bad?" he asked her.

"I . . . don't even know. Luke . . . hit me . . . and then Hank knocked me down and . . . twice I hit my head. My head aches bad, River."

"Where are your things? We must get off the *Jasmine*. She is breaking loose and will be carried downriver any moment. If we do not get off this thing we will be killed. With this much rain, a wall of water and mud could come down from the mountains and wipe out everything."

"I don't . . . have anything. They didn't let me bring my clothes."

"Come then. We have to get back to land. My horses are waiting."

"River, the Negro slave! Jim! He saw you!"

"He slipped and fell into the river when I chased him. I tried to grab on to him, but he disappeared in the waters. He will drown. I am sorry for him."

"But what if he doesn't drown!"

"We cannot worry about that now. We must get to safety ourselves."

He lowered her, keeping one strong arm around her. "You must be strong for a little while longer, *Agiya*. You must hang on to me while I carry you through the waters to land."

She clung to his waist as he led her outside, where wind and rain lashed at her. It seemed that all heaven had opened up and she wondered if it would ever stop raining. The river roared beneath the groaning *Jasmine*. River Joe helped her to the edge of the deck, where a rope was stretched tightly, the only thing holding the *Jasmine* to a stump on shore.

"I hope this rope stays tied a little longer," River Joe shouted. "If it lets go, we will be swept downriver! Hang on to me. I got on this way, I will get off this way!"

She clung to the railing, staring into the dark, swirling waters as River Joe climbed over the railing and grasped the rope. Emma held her breath as he jumped into the threatening, roaring river, disappearing for a moment into the darkness. She wondered how he would be able to hang on against the current, with the bleeding shoulder wound surely hurting him.

"Come on, Emma!" he yelled through the rain and thunder. "Grab on to me around the neck!"

She didn't want to disappoint him, wanted to show him how brave and strong she was. And there was so little time! She climbed over the railing but all her courage left her as her terror of the roaring waters overwhelmed her.

"I can't!" she screamed.

"What did I tell you about being afraid!" he yelled back. "*Esaugetuh Emissee* is with you, *Agiya*. Climb onto my back! Hurry!"

"I'll drown!" she screamed.

"Emma, I can't hang on forever. You will drown for sure if you stay on that boat!"

He managed to rise slightly so that the rope was under his right armpit and he could wrap his right arm around it and hang on better. He reached up then with his left hand. "Trust me, *Agiya!* The Maker of Breath is with us. He helped me find you in time. He did not do that so that I could stand and watch you die! Now grab on!"

She stared at him another moment. This was River Joe. River Joe had come for her. He loved her. He had killed for her. She reached down, grabbing on to his powerful wrist and jumping into the water. She screamed as the current immediately pulled wildly at her, yanking her away from River Joe. River Joe hung on to her tiny wrist with a big, strong hand, and she felt her dress being literally torn the rest of the way off her body. She felt River Joe pulling, wondering where he got such amazing strength.

She herself fought then, turning against the current and helping him pull. She managed to get one leg hooked around his waist, then grabbed hold of his buckskin shirt and pulled more. It seemed an hour rather than minutes before she finally managed to get around to the front of him, wrapping her legs around his waist and her arms around his neck.

"Good girl!" he shouted. "Hang on to me, Emma! We will make it!"

Now he had hold of the rope with both hands. There was a loud crashing sound on the *Jasmine*, and then the sound of something cracking and groaning. The lanterns that hung in various places around the outside began flickering out, and the rope River Joe clung to began vibrating. He pulled steadily along it, saying nothing, while Emma clung to him in terror, wondering how in God's name he managed to hang on, especially with his wounded shoulder. Something large floated past them, and then Emma felt something bump her, scraping her leg and going on. It was too dark to see what strange things were floating by, and she wondered if some of those things were dead bodies. She clung fiercely to River Joe, sure the river would tear them apart any moment.

They finally made it to shore, coughing and panting. They collapsed to the ground, where River Joe lay taking deep breaths to regain his strength.

There was a loud snapping sound then, and instantly River Joe threw himself on top of Emma. The ground shook a moment later as a huge tree came crashing down nearby. River Joe held her a moment, still panting, then drew her closer.

"Emma," he said softly.

For a brief moment the storm seemed not to matter. He had come for her, just like he promised! He kissed her cheek, her eyes, pulling her close, realizing only then that her clothes had been torn away.

"My God, Emma! You will be sick!"

"I'm . . . all right . . . now that you came, River," she said, her teeth chattering.

He sat up, removing his buckskin shirt, grimacing against the pain in his shoulder. "Here. It is wet, but it is better than nothing at all."

Lightning flashed and he could see her fair skin, the full breasts he ached to taste again. But for now neither of them had any thought but to escape the river and the storm, to be dry and warm and somehow survive this awful night. "I know where we can go until the storm is over," he said. "Put this on and come with me. My horses are not far away."

"Joe, now you don't have a shirt. Now you'll be sick. And you're wounded."

"I have lived with the elements many years. Do not worry about me." He slipped the shirt over her head and she put her arms through the sleeves. It was far too big for her, but having the buckskin around her to break the wind felt much better.

They heard a loud snap just as he helped her up, and there were more creaking and groaning sounds from the *Jasmine*. In the almost constant lightning they could both see that the riverboat had finally broken loose. It turned wildly then, and was torn downriver by the wild current. It disappeared quickly into the darkness, carried by the roaring waters, and they could hear crashing sounds as the *Jasmine* bashed against the trees and rocks, floating free and untended, slowly breaking into pieces until Emma and River Joe heard nothing then but the sound of the roaring waters.

Emma wondered what had happened to Hank Toole's body, and if the Negro slave had really drowned.

"Can you walk?" River Joe was asking her.

Her head ached fiercely. "I . . . think so."

He took her arm and led her through the dark, rainy forest. She had no idea where they were, how far downriver they were from Luke's small farm. She whimpered in sorrow at the thought that maybe her mother's grave would be washed away, and she realized that if not for River Joe she would be utterly terrified at this moment. But he seemed to know exactly where he was going. She stumbled and fell, and he helped her up again. Then she stepped on a jagged stump and cried out.

River Joe stopped, grasping her around the waist.

"River, I lost my shoes!"

He picked her up then. How he could carry her after all he had been through, she could not imagine. "River, I can walk. It's all right."

"No. It is too dangerous."

Her head felt as though it was twice its normal size. She struggled to stay conscious, resting against his shoulder, wanting to cry with relief that he had come, that he really did love her. She was his woman. She was River Joe's woman, and as soon as they were safe and dry and warm, they would make love again. He cared so much for her that he had risked his life for her, and risked a hanging. She tried not to think about what the consequences of this night could be. She didn't dare think of anything right now but survival.

She heard him say something in the Cherokee tongue then and realized they had reached the horses. He set her on one, then climbed up behind her, holding her in one arm while he picked up the reins with the other hand. The rain came down even harder. She felt the horse turn, sensed that they were climbing. She had no idea where he was taking her and didn't care. Her head lolled back against his chest and she thanked the Maker of Breath that they had gotten off the *Jasmine* safely, and that this man was so strong and sure.

She slipped in and out of consciousness, unaware of just how much time passed or in what direction they were going.

"There will be a bad flood," she heard him say. "It will be many days before the *Jasmine* is found and anyone begins to figure out what might have happened to Hank, if his body is even found. And it will be even longer before people can organize themselves to come and find us. By then we will be well on our way higher into the mountains, and most whites do not like to come where we are going. Right now we have to worry about getting high enough not to be touched if the really big waters come! A wall of water and mud could come through and wipe out everything along the Hiwassee from the upper mountains all the way down the Tennessee River."

Those were the last words she remembered hearing that night. The pain in her head was finally obliterated by blessed unconsciousness.

Farther downriver the Negro slave Jim clung desperately to a piece of wood, while he screamed to God to save him from the raging waters. In his thirty-two years of life, all spent in slavery, he had never known this kind of terror. He finally managed to grab on to a tree branch and pull himself up, wrapping his ankles around the branch so that he hung above the water. He inched his way along the branch to the tree trunk, then slowly lowered himself, relieved to realize he was finally on dry ground.

He ran then, higher, deeper into the woods, his mind whirling with what he should do now. He belonged to Hank Toole. But Hank Toole was dead, and he had seen the big white Indian pull a knife out of Hank's chest. The Indian had taken the white girl and run off with her, or maybe they had both drowned by now.

What would people think when they found Nigger Jim? Would they think he had killed his master himself and had raped and drowned the white girl? Maybe they wouldn't believe his story about the big Indian. No one ever believed a Negro slave. They would think he had killed Hank in an effort to run away and be free.

His heart pounded with fear. What was he to do now? Where should he go? Should he tell what he had seen, or should he just say the flooding river destroyed the *Jasmine* and killed Hank Toole? Maybe he should try to get to Sam

Gates in Knoxville. Master Sam might believe him. After
all, it was Master Sam who had told Hank to buy the girl.
Jim had heard the whole conversation.

Yes. Maybe his only hope was to get to Master Sam. But
would he believe Jim's story about the Indian taking the girl?
Maybe even Master Sam would think Jim himself had killed
Hank so he could rape the white girl. White men were
always ready to believe things like that. How strange that
they thought nothing of raping Indian girls and Negro girls,
and sometimes even their own kind, and of buying and selling pretty, innocent girls like that Emma Simms. And yet if
they thought Jim had touched her, they would torture and
hang him.

He ran until his breath left him, then plunked down on an
old log, putting his head in his hands and trying to decide
what to do. Maybe if he headed north he would find help.
Maybe God had brought the flood so that he could escape!

Yes! Surely this was a sign from God. But where was
north? He was not at all positive where he was. He would
have to wait till morning, wait till there was some sunshine
so he could get his bearings. Surely with a flood this bad it
would be a long time before anyone bothered to look for
him. Besides, they probably thought he was drowned. He
would never have a better opportunity to get away. And he
secretly hoped the poor white girl Emma Simms would also
escape, and never have to go to Sam Gates.

Tommy groaned awake, unsure of the time, aware only
that it was very dark and that it was still raining. He stirred,
his head swimming from too much whiskey. He had awakened that morning in agony from sore privates and an aching
mouth from River Joe's blows the night before. His new
wounds only activated the pain he still suffered from
Emma's beating with the board.

He had lain in bed most of this day, listening to the river

roar as it rose more. Then he had drunk more whiskey to kill his pain, plotting how he could get even with River Joe and with Emma. He would go to Knoxville and pay whatever it cost to sleep with Emma Simms. The thought of the horror she would suffer when she was "trained" by Sam Gates brought a smile to his sore mouth; and then she would soon learn that Tommy Decker would be one of her first customers!

River Joe was another story. Tommy wasn't quite sure what to do about the man, but somehow he had to get his revenge. Twice the white Indian had made him look bad in front of his friends, and now he was almost certain River Joe had been with Emma. How else would the man know about how Tommy's face and head had been injured? Now the man had escaped. Tommy vowed he would find him eventually, even if he had to go to the top of the mountains. First he would go to Luke's place and make sure Emma had gotten on that boat with Hank Toole.

He groaned again as he attempted to sit up, wishing he had not drunk quite so much whiskey again tonight. But his pain had made it necessary. He wondered how many teeth he would lose from River Joe's blow, and he realized that if he was ever to get back at the man, it probably couldn't be with fists. He was strong, but River Joe was stronger. Somehow he had to find a way to make the man squirm, to make him suffer slowly, the way Emma would suffer when he got on top of her and did every ugly thing to her that he could think of.

He felt a terrible thirst and sat up on the edge of his bed, running his hands through his tousled red hair. It seemed too dark, and he squinted, hearing then the dull rumble. It took him a moment to realize what it was. The river!

He got up and walked to the window of the cabin he shared with his father. It sat on a rise at the outskirts of the MacBain settlement. He looked toward the little town, where lighted lanterns usually hung outside the buildings. But he could see nothing. As water began to trickle around his feet, he realized he couldn't see the settlement because it was under water! He heard a louder rumble and he knew in an instant what was happening.

"Pa!" He screamed the word, running through the darkness to his father's cot. "Pa, the river! We're gonna drown!"

Already the water was around his ankles. The rumbling grew louder. "Pa, mud's comin'! Get up! Get up!"

He shook Jake Decker wildly, but the man had drunk even more whiskey than Tommy had. He groaned and turned over, telling Tommy to leave him alone. In seconds the water was around Tommy's knees.

"Pa!" he screamed again, tears coming to his eyes.

An end wall of the cabin suddenly gave way with a mighty crack, and water roared around Tommy then, washing him over the top of his father's cot, flinging him, helplessly, into the darkness. He grabbed on to a small tree that floated by and hung on for dear life as the water tossed him about. The roar was almost deafening, and he wondered what had happened to all the other people. He wanted to cry over his father, but there was no time for that. There was time only to think about surviving. His father had surely drowned under that first rush of water.

"Smoke!" he screamed, remembering his horse. What had happened to his fine black horse? The thought of Smoke drowning hurt almost as much as his father's drowning.

He felt himself being tossed for what seemed miles, until finally his feet suddenly touched ground. Lightning flashed and he could see that he was on the side of a hill. He took advantage of the moment and began crawling uphill, hoping he could stay above the water. The Hiwassee continued to roar below him, and he climbed fast, so scared that it gave him the strength to clamber up the hill in spite of the ordeal he had just been through. He whimpered and called for Smoke all the way up, finally reaching the muddy crest of the hill.

He turned, looking down, waiting for lightning to flash. When it did, he saw nothing but water below.

"My God," he groaned. He clung to another tree, ready to climb it if necessary, staring at the waters below every time lightning flashed. He had never seen anything like this. He hoped the raging flood would find River Joe and bury him. Maybe it would even get to the *Jasmine*, break it up, and throw Emma Simms into its swirling waters.

He stood there panting, grinning at the thought of Emma struggling through the raging waters. It would serve her right. He remembered when she was smaller, when he held her by the ankles and dangled her headfirst into the river so that her dress fell upside down and he could look at her bloomers. He remembered how she had almost drowned, how terrified she had been, how she had cried. She had been afraid of the river ever since.

He laughed then but felt like crying, too. Smoke was surely gone, and his father drowned, too, and maybe all his friends. He realized how lucky the Cherokee were at this moment, living high up in the mountains. It wasn't fair, his father and friends dying, while the Cherokee would not be touched.

In his twisted mind he blamed all this on River Joe and Emma. If Emma had not hurt him and turned him away, he would not even have been here these last couple of days. And if River Joe had not hit him, he would not have had to drink so much whiskey to ward off the pain. Maybe he would have awakened sooner and rescued his horse and his father.

How he hoped both Emma and River Joe were dead! And if he ever found out they weren't . . . He clenched his fists, feeling frustrated at being defeated first by Emma, then River Joe, now the river. He clung to the tree, crying like a child.

Farther downriver the wall of mud and water continued on its destructive path, moving on to the Simms farm, swelling over cattle and pigs, sagging sheds and broken fences, swallowing up the dilapidated cabin and taking Luke Simms with it. The rocks and flowers and all markings around the grave of Betty Simms were washed away, along with the remains of an old, broken raft in that secret place along the normally quiet river, where Emma Simms had first spoken to a man called River Joe.

◊   *Chapter 8*   ◊

Emma awoke to the sound of birds singing. A shaft of sunlight warmed her face and she stirred awake, feeling comfortable and warm under several blankets. At first her mind was blank. She remembered nothing of the day and night before as she lay there trying to get her bearings. She stared at what appeared to be the entrance to a cave, and outside the leaves looked bright green and the sun shone brightly. It seemed so long since she had last seen the sun shine.

A fire crackled near the entrance, its smoke wafting into dark recesses above, pulled by a draft from some unknown source. She snuggled deeper, smelling the sweet odor of clean hides and realizing that beneath the animal skins that covered her, she was naked.

Slowly the memories returned. Hank, pawing over her, her hands tied behind her, the storm, the raging river. The river. River! River had come and saved her. He had killed Hank Toole, and he had struggled through the horrible rising flood and the black woods in the midst of a terrible storm, taking her with him. Where were they now? What about the river? How high had it risen?

Her heart tightened then when a horse whinnied, and a

tall, commanding figure appeared at the cave entrance, ducking inside and glancing at her.

"You finally awake?"

"River?" She held the cover up around her as he came closer, and at first she felt a lingering fear. A magnificent, powerful man, River wore nothing but a loincloth. She had seen that power the night before when he killed Hank, had felt it when he managed to hang on to her after she jumped into the river. Now they were alone. No one else could have put her naked body under these blankets but River. Had he slept with her under the blankets? Where was he taking her? Would his attitude toward her change now that he had her alone? Surely not. He had come for her, saved her, risked his life for her. But she had also seen his vicious side. Now she would be totally dependent on him. Would he turn mean as Luke and Tommy and Hank had?

He knelt beside her. "I have been worried about you. You have some kind of head injury. You better lie still all day today. I do not think we should keep going just yet."

She felt the tears coming. "I'm so mixed up," she whimpered. "And scared."

He smiled the smile that always made her feel better. "There you go again. How many times do I have to tell you not to be afraid of things? You are not afraid of me, are you, after all I have been through for you? You are my wife, remember?"

Her body jerked in a pitiful sob, and he came around behind her, sitting down on the other side of the bedroll and pulling her into his arms, gathering the covers around her. "Do not cry, *Agiya*. I know you have endured so much the last couple of weeks, and especially yesterday and last night." He held her close, rocking her lightly, kissing her hair. "I do not want you to be afraid of anything anymore. Hank is dead, and Tommy and Luke may also have drowned. You are not going to Knoxville. You are going high up in the mountains with me, to the Cherokee where you will find a whole new life. I will take care of you. You are my woman now."

She had half-expected him to rip away her covering and demand to have his way with her again. Lovemaking was the last thing she wanted right now, even with River. That first night he took her now seemed like a dream. Everything was different now, new and strange. He seemed to sense her confusion.

"How do you feel?" he asked.

"My head hurts bad." She turned and noticed that the deep, open wound on the top of his left shoulder was scabbed but oozing. "What about you?" She moved back a little to look at the wound, touching the front of his chest lightly as she examined it.

"I will survive."

Their eyes met then, and she noticed the small bruise under his left eye.

"I am sorry, Emma. They held me at the MacBain settlement. I could not leave."

"I know. I'm just glad they didn't hang you."

"I am glad I got to you when I did, or you would be swallowed up in that river. I have never seen anything like it, Emma. The big one came, just like I said it would. For a while this morning only the tops of trees that used to grow tall on the riverbank showed above the water. There cannot be much left. The flood is starting to recede a little now. But people are going to be too busy trying to salvage their homes and belongings to wonder about what might have happened to Hank and to you."

She studied the dark eyes, the handsome face. River Joe had claimed her, and he had come back for her. She was his woman now. Luke's farm was surely gone, and all those who would harm her were dead. "Are you really here, River? Maybe I'm still unconscious and I'm just thinking all this in my mind."

"No. You are awake. I am really here, and I love you, *Agiya*."

She had so many questions. What would they do now? Where would they go? A quick, penetrating pain tore through her head as she lifted it, and she cried out. River eased her back into the crook of his arm.

"Do not move around too much. I do not know much about head injuries, Emma, but I made an herbal tea that might help the pain." He carefully laid her back down, leaning over her then and bending down to kiss her forehead. "We will not go anywhere today. No one is going to come looking for us this soon. But tomorrow we must leave. If you still feel dizzy and weak, I will make up a travois for you to lie on."

"Where are we going?"

"I told you. To the Cherokee."

She blinked, putting a hand to her head. "Oh, yes. They . . . they won't hurt me, will they, River?"

He smiled again. "No, they will not hurt you."

She felt a tear slip down the side of her face. "River, I have to go . . . you know. Where . . . ?"

He got to his knees and lifted her carefully, then stood up. "Try to keep your head still while I carry you into the woods." He carried her outside. "There are nice, fresh sassafras leaves here to clean yourself with afterward," he said. He lowered her carefully to her feet. "I had better stay and hang on to you."

"No!"

"It is all right, Emma. If I let go of you, you will fall."

"No, I won't." Her head screamed, and the moment he released her the whole world swam and spun in front of her. She felt herself fainting, felt a strong arm catch her. By then she was too dizzy and in too much pain to care. He pulled up the blankets and held her, but she knew she couldn't do it right, and she felt a wetness on her leg. She started to cry and he held her close again.

Somewhere in the distant blackness she heard him saying not to worry about it, that he would take care of things. Then she was back inside the cave, grateful for a chance to sleep. She felt the covers pushed aside, felt something warm gently wipe her leg and her most private place. He was washing her but he wasn't doing anything bad to her. She felt the covers being drawn over her again, and then there was nothing until a gentle arm slid under her neck and lifted her slightly.

"Try to drink some of this," said a deep, tender voice. "You will feel better. And you need to get something in your stomach, *Agiya*."

She sipped a sweet and aromatic drink. Dimly she wished she could help him, too. He was injured. She wanted desperately to get up and move around, but the pain was too great. How could this man who had sliced another man up the middle with his big knife, had fought Hank Toole and struck that same knife into Hank's heart, be so gentle with her? How could someone so powerful have made love to her so sweetly?

She took several swallows of the brew.

"I am going to let you sleep now," he said, "while I try to kill a rabbit or a squirrel. I have some smoked meat in my supplies, but I want to save it for my family if I can. I will hunt for fresh meat for us." She felt him laying her back down. "I did not get to buy what I needed at the MacBain settlement; I will have to chance stopping at another settlement higher up. I doubt anybody that far away will have heard anything about you and me." He kissed her cheek lightly. "You rest, Emma. I will be back soon and make you something very good to eat. Do not be afraid if you wake up and find me gone. Do you hear me, Emma?"

"Yes," someone said in a distant voice. Was it she who spoke?

"Egasinee," he said softly.

She drifted off. Her mind floated, and it was night. She was lying in straw, and River Joe was hovering over her, his broad shoulders and long hair shielding her from anything beyond his body. His mouth was over hers, exploring, tasting, taking her to wonderful heights of ecstasy as his fingers touched her magically.

How sweet was the dream. They were one, his hands grasping her hips and his body mating with hers, claiming her as his wife. Yes, she was his wife. No one could hurt her now. River Joe would protect her, love her. How wonderful it was to be loved.

Then nightmares replaced the dream. A man was walking toward her. He was dirty and needed a shave, but he wore a fine suit. She backed away. The dream was changing. It was Hank, grinning. She stood there naked and he was coming for her. To her right she could see Luke. He was grinning, too. He made a fist, and it got bigger and bigger and turned into a rock. He was going to hit her with it. To her left a red-haired young man approached, riding a shiny black horse. He smiled, too. His blue eyes shot fire, and he dismounted. All three of them came closer now, leering at her naked body, threatening to beat her, telling her ugly things they would do to her. Hank reached out for her and she screamed and began flailing at him, pushing, scratching! Where was the board? She had to hit at them with the board!

Someone grasped her arms. No! They would tie her wrists, and she would feel the pain between her legs. But whoever grabbed her only pushed her arms to her sides and then managed to pull her close. She was screaming, but this man was not hurting her. He held her in strong arms, rocked her.

"Hush, *Agiya*. It is all right now. They will not hurt you again."

She could smell the scent of leather and fresh air, and a sweet scent like sassafras and leaves. She rested her head against something very soft, then opened her eyes and realized it was the velvety softness of finely cleaned and treated deerskin. Someone's long hair brushed her face.

"River," she sobbed.

"You have been sleeping a very long time," he told her. "That is good. But you have had a bad dream. Think only of me, *Agiya*, and nice things, the wildflowers and the sunshine."

"Don't go away."

"I will go nowhere now. The rabbit is all cooked. That is how long you have slept. Sleep more, if you wish. I have eaten, but I think it is more important for you to sleep than to eat, if that is what your body wants to do. I will hold you this time."

She felt him move in beside her naked body. He pulled the covers over both of them. He was apparently dressed now. She nestled into his shoulder, and he began massaging her bare back and her hips.

"*Egasinee*," he told her again. She wanted to ask if that meant "sleep" in Cherokee, but she could not form the words. She breathed deeply of his wonderful scent. She could go back to sleep. River was holding her. The bad dreams could not return as long as she was in these arms.

Emma opened her eyes to blue skies, looking up at a few puffy clouds and feeling herself bouncing lightly along on a sledlike device that was apparently dragging her. When she stirred she realized she was actually bound to whatever she was riding on, but her arms were free. She touched her head, trying to think, remembering the cave and River Joe. She turned her head and saw that a horse was pulling her, a big roan gelding. A black mare plodded beside it, packed down with supplies. She couldn't turn far enough to see if River was riding the roan, and she panicked at first. Was he still with her?

"River!" she called out.

She felt the sled come to a halt, heard a deep voice say "Whoa." A moment later he was bending over her. "It is about time," he said, kneeling down beside her. "You scared the hell out of me, Emma. It has been two days since we left the cave."

"Two days!" She looked around the surrounding forest. "Where are we?"

"Still heading up. I had to get going, so I tied you to this thing. I have been praying the bouncy ride would not make you worse. That must be some head injury Luke gave you."

"I . . . I want to try to sit up."

He reached over and began untying some straps. Her feet rested against poles stretched across the bottom of the device so she wouldn't slide down. He reached under her shoulders, helping her sit up. "How's that? Your head hurt?"

She put a hand to her hair. "No. Not so bad." Her hair felt flat and matted and she looked away from him. "I must look terrible."

"You look beautiful to me. Just to see you sitting up without as much pain, and hear you talking, seeing you conscious, that is all I need."

She looked down at herself, seeing that she wore one of his buckskin shirts. "Can I . . . can I clean up when we make camp?"

He put a hand to the side of her face. "If you feel well enough. But I will help you. Do not move around too much. You are back with me now and I want you to stay that way." He took her hand. "I thought I was going to lose you, Emma Rivers."

She stared at the big hand that enclosed her own. It was tanned dark, and so strong. This man had nursed her the last three or four days, had put up with her helplessness, kept her bathed and warm. He was all she had now. Her whole world had changed. She met his dark eyes. "What did you call me?"

"Emma Rivers. That is your name now. You are my wife, remember? On government records I am Joe Rivers. That makes you Emma Rivers."

She frowned. "Will I be recorded that way?"

He grinned. "Someday. But where we are going records are not kept. We must go someplace where we will not be found for a while, until things quiet down. I just hope my people are still camped where I left them. They move around a lot because of the raiders, which makes it hard to keep enough food. That is why I go south to trade skins for supplies, but that is going to be impossible now."

This was the first chance she had had in a long time to really study his face in full light, realize how beautiful he was. "I'm... truly your wife?"

"Yes, you are. Cherokee custom is as good as any. The Maker of Breath knows we belong together. That is good enough for me."

"That night in the shed...," she said, remembering. "It seems like it never really happened, River. But then I realize it did, and—" Her heart beat harder, and her throat felt tight. "And it was the most... the most wonderful thing that ever happened to me in my life. And I love you, River." She swallowed back a lump in her throat. "I love you more than anything I ever loved in my life—if anybody can say there ever was love in my life at all." A tear slipped down her cheek. "And for a while... I thought maybe you'd think I was bad, or maybe you were just laughing about it and wouldn't come...."

Her voice broke and he squeezed her hand gently. "I would not have done that to you, Emma Rivers. I love you, too. You have brought joy to a man who has been very lonely for a lot of years, ever since I lost Yellow Sky." He touched her chin, making her look at him. "I truly consider you my wife, Emma. And you must let it be real for you. Look right into my eyes and say it. Say, 'You are my husband, Joe Rivers.'"

Her eyes teared more and she swallowed, smiling bashfully then. "You... you are my husband... Joe Rivers."

He smiled. "And you are my new bride. I am taking you home, and I guarantee my people will love you and you will love them."

She broke into more tears, reaching out and hugging him. "I've never been really happy before, River. I never had anybody care about me like you do—or take care of me like this. I'll go anywhere with you. I'll be a good wife to you, I promise."

"I know you will." He kissed her neck. "Thank God you are better." His lips moved to her cheek, tasting salty tears. In the next moment his mouth covered hers, so sweetly, so gently, lightly exploring, refreshing her memory of that magical night when he invaded her body, when he moved over her so expertly as she lay helpless beneath him. She didn't have to be afraid. When he took her again, he would be just as gentle as he had the first time. She would simply lie in his arms and let him show her all the wonderful ways of being a woman, and it would be nothing like Tommy or Hank.

Hank. He had killed Hank! He left her mouth and she hugged him tighter. "Oh, River, what will happen if they come after you?"

"Do not worry about it right now. We have some time. That was a bad flood, Emma. There might not even be anyone left who knows enough to put this all together."

"Luke would! And Tommy would!"

"Hush, *Agiya*. Do not think about it right now. Just think about getting well. I know a good place to make camp. We will heat some water and wash you up and wash your hair and put a dress on you."

She sniffed and pulled away, wiping at her eyes. "I don't have any dresses with me," she answered, her body jerking in a sob.

"I have a couple along you can wear. They will probably fit you just fine."

She frowned. "Why would you have dresses along?"

He smiled sadly. "They belong to Yellow Sky. I have always kept some of her things with me. She often wore white woman's dresses. She would be very happy for you to have them."

Emma felt a terrible jealousy, combined with pity for him. Yellow Sky. What had she been like? She wanted to know so many things about her. When had he married her? When had she died? Had he loved Yellow Sky more than he loved her?

But River had already turned away, as though telling her he did not yet want to talk about it.

"In a couple more days I will go into a settlement for supplies," he said. He checked the horses' hooves, then turned back to her. "You lie back down now. Do you want anything before we go on?"

She shook her head. "Not if it won't be long before we make camp. Just hold me once more, River."

He came back to her and knelt beside the travois, reaching out and hugging her tightly. "Everything will be all right, Emma. And I can read your thoughts. No, I did not love her more—just different." He kissed her cheek. "We will talk about it another time. You just get well. I want to make love to you again. I ache for you, Emma."

She felt the strange fire move through her blood at the words. He kissed her lightly and laid her down again. "It will not be long," he said then. He mounted his horse and got under way again. She felt under the blankets and realized he had wrapped something around her bottom as if she were a baby. She reddened at the thought of it. He had looked at her again without her even knowing it. And how amazing that he could be so wild, so vicious when necessary, yet could care for her so lovingly. She had a lot to learn about this white Indian who had already claimed her. After all, he was her husband now.

They took shelter in an old, deserted cabin. Only three walls and part of the roof were left standing, but it was enough to protect them from the wind and give them privacy, although they were so deep in the woods that privacy made little difference.

River Joe insisted that Emma lie still on the bedroll that he laid out for her while he built a fire just outside the little shelter and carried a bucket to a nearby creek. Emma listened to the soft rush of water, thinking how quiet and peaceful it sounded compared to the raging river of a few nights ago. She wondered if Luke was alive or had drowned, and she wondered about Tommy Decker. She knew it was bad to wish such things, but she found herself hoping both of them had been lost in the flood.

River Joe returned, setting a small kettle over the fire and pouring some of the bucket water into it. "I will help you take a bath and wash your hair," he said. "In the morning you can put on a real dress. By tomorrow afternoon we will be at the Hicks settlement. You will have to wait for me in hilding while I get supplies. We should not be seen together yet."

Reaching into the parfleche on his pack horse, he pulled out a pale blue dress covered with tiny yellow flowers. He held it up. "This will fit you, I think. Do you like it?"

She studied the garment, which was neatly sewn, with short cap sleeves and a high, prim neckline, and a full skirt trimmed with delicate white lace. Again she felt a rush of jealousy, combined with an uncomfortable self-consciousness.

"I . . . I couldn't wear it," she answered. "It's so pretty. But . . . it wouldn't be right, River."

He walked closer, laying it across the bedroll. "Of course it would be right. Yellow Sky would have liked you very much, and I know her spirit is with us right now, glad that I have found someone who can make me happy again."

Her cheeks warmed, and she looked down at the dress, touching it lightly. "It's so pretty," she said almost absently. "I've never had a dress this pretty." She frowned. "Do all Cherokee women wear dresses like this? I mean, I thought they would wear deerskin dresses."

He grinned. "Those are called tunics. But many wear the white woman's dress. My people are not so different, Emma. In New Echota they have brick homes, big farms; they have schools and live just as well or better than many of their white neighbors."

"New Echota?"

"A city the Cherokee have built in northern Georgia. Many of them live there now. And there is another big settlement at the mouth of the Tennessee River, called Ross's Landing, a trading post run by one of our leaders, John Ross. Someday we will be able to have our own state and live peacefully."

She studied the flowers on the dress. "I've heard Luke and Jake and Tommy Decker talk about that." She met his eyes. "That kind of talk only makes Indian haters madder, River. The Cherokee must know that."

He frowned. "Of course they know it. But it is their right. All this land was once theirs. What is wrong with claiming what little is left and making it a state that no one can take away from us?"

"There's nothing wrong with that. But white men like Luke and Tommy don't want you to claim any of it. They want you out of this land altogether. They want you to go to Indian Territory."

"Many Cherokee have already gone there. Most do not like it. My own family insists on staying, and waiting for it all to work out. They will not go west, nor have they decided whether to go to New Echota. They love it high in the mountains right here in Tennessee." He picked up the dress. "Now please wear the dress when we wake up in the morning. Wear it for me. You need a dress, and I have one. Yellow Sky would want you to wear it."

She watched his dark eyes. "What was she like? You told me once she was very young."

The sadness came to his eyes again. He looked at the dress, fingering it lightly. "She was fifteen and I was twenty when we married. She had trouble taking my seed. She wanted to give me a baby but could not conceive, and three years after we married she died of cholera." He let go of the dress and rose, walking over to check the water. "Cholera is a damned poor way to go—a terrible death."

"I have heard others talk about it. I'm sorry, River."

He looked over at her, watching her quietly for a moment.

"I love you just as much as I loved her, Emma. If I did not have the same feelings of love and honor, I would not let you wear that dress. You are not second. You are equal, and I need you. Do not let Yellow Sky come between us. For me her memory is good and sweet, but she is gone, and meeting you has helped me realize that. You are my wife now. I have no other wife, and I will not have our bed shared by a memory."

She carefully set the dress aside. "I will wear it."

She looked back at him and he smiled sadly. "You will feel a lot better after I wash your hair. I will put some deer meat on the fire after the water is hot enough." She thought she saw tears in his eyes. "Thank you for understanding about Yellow Sky."

Her heart went out to him, and she felt a new surge of desire for him, actually wishing she would hurry and heal so that she could make love with him. She had a strange new freedom now—being free of Tommy and Luke, going to a brand-new life—yet in a way she was still a captive. But it was a pleasant captivity, for her captor was River Joe. He came to her with soap and water, dipping a rag into the water.

"Take off your tunic and the cloth I wrapped around you."

A nervous shiver ran through her blood. "Undress?"

He grinned. "Emma, I have done this several times already when you did not even know it. I have already seen all I need to see, and I am very pleased with my wife."

Her eyes widened and she turned crimson, her mouth falling open. "River! I . . . I can't just sit here naked in front of you!"

"Why not? I have already seen you that way, and I have already made you my woman."

"But it was dark when we did that!"

"Not when I bathed you. Come on, now, Emma, I am just going to wash you, and wash your hair. You said you wanted to fix it, feel prettier." He leaned up and kissed her mouth lightly, then gave her a smile as he unlaced the buckskin shirt she wore, helping lift it over her head, amused when she folded her arms over her breasts. He leaned down and kissed her milky shoulders, then handed her the rag, smiling. "Here. You can do it if you would rather. I will get something started to eat. I will help you with your hair when you are ready."

She took the rag. "You'll stay turned around?"

He laughed lightly, shaking his head. "I will stay turned around until you tell me. Are you sure you are strong enough?"

"I think so."

He sighed deeply, rising. "You tell me if you feel too weak."

He turned and walked back to put some meat in a pan over the fire. Emma loved him all the more because he did not look back once. She had to get used to this, learn to let River look upon her nakedness.

She washed, removing the soft cloth he had wrapped around her bottom, relieved to realize it was dry. She pulled on the dress, which seemed to fit very well. She buttoned up the front, then stood up on bare feet and shook down the skirt.

"You can look now. I need you to help me wash my hair."

River Joe turned, staring at her quietly, absolute love shining from his eyes. "It looks beautiful on you," he said. "I knew it would."

She smoothed the skirt. "It's a little wrinkled. You'll have to hang it over something so it can straighten out a little overnight. I'll put the shirt back on for sleeping. I just wanted you to see the dress."

He nodded. "Every day I realize more and more that I have done the right thing." He walked closer, putting his hands on her shoulders. "You are so beautiful, *Agiya*. We will have a good life together."

She smiled and he pulled her close. She breathed deeply of his sweet scent and he kept his strong arms around her.

"Don't ever take me back there, River. If you should ever decide you don't want me, don't take me back there."

"I would never do that," he said in a near whisper.

She looked up at him and their lips met. This time he kissed her harder than before, exploring deeper, reminding her of that first sweet, wonderful night, awakening a fever-ish passion in her soul and making her alive with curiosity about being taken by him again. It was not bad to want him that way. This beautiful man, this strong, brave, wonderful man, was her husband. She prayed fervently to the Maker of Breath that if Hank Toole's body was ever found, no one would guess River had killed him.

He left her lips and she hugged him tightly. "Let's hurry and climb higher, River. I'm afraid someone will follow. I don't want anything ever, ever to happen to you, or to part us. I would die if I had to be apart from you now."

He kissed her hair. "We will not be separated, *Agiya*. I will keep us together always."

◇ *Chapter 9* ◇

Jim awakened to a sharp blow against his left shoulder.

"What are you doin' here, nigger?" someone sneered. "You a runaway?"

Jim scrambled to a sitting position, leaning against a tree and staring up wide-eyed at three men, all dressed poorly, and all carrying muskets pointed at him.

"I ain't never seen him around, Bates," said one of them.

"You runnin' from your master?" Bates asked.

Jim rubbed at his sore shoulder, his heart pounding with fear. "N-no, suh, I'm . . . I'm just lost."

"Niggers don't get lost 'less they're runnin' away," the third man said.

"I didn't know where to go, mistuh. The flood! My mastuh, he done got killed in the flood."

The three men looked at one another, then Bates scowled at Jim. "Get up, nigger!"

Jim slowly rose, watching them warily.

"Who's your master? Who owns you?" Bates asked.

"Mastuh Toole. Hank Toole," Jim answered, his voice squeaking with fear. "He runs the supply boat . . . the *Jasmine*. It got wrecked in the flood, and I think he—" Jim looked around in the woods, debating whether to tell the truth about the big Indian and the white girl. Maybe they wouldn't believe any of it, and if they didn't, they would say he had killed Hank Toole. Maybe Hank's body would be so battered by the flood when it was found that no one would realize he had been stabbed. Maybe the body wouldn't even be recognizable. "I think he must be dead," he continued. "The flood, it was a terrible thing! It throwed me right off the *Jasmine*—I worked the boilers for Mastuh Toole. I got throwed into the river, and next thing I know, the *Jasmine* she's rippin' loose from her ties and crashin' downriver."

Bates stepped closer. He raised his musket sideways and rammed it against Jim, shoving him back against a tree. Jim grunted from the blow, his breathing coming quicker from fear and pain.

"How are we supposed to know you're tellin' the truth, nigger?"

Jim swallowed, searching the white man's eyes. "You check," he said, near tears. "You go on back there. You'll find out the *Jasmine* is all wrecked! The Good Lord only knows what happened to my mastuh! I'm tellin' the truth, mistuh! I didn't know what to do after that. I been scared somebody would find me and think I was runnin', just like you is thinkin'. But I ain't runnin', mistuh. I jist didn't know where to go or who would believe me! Ain't nobody gonna believe a slave! You go see! You go see!"

"The river is miles from here," another spoke up. "How long ago this happen?"

"Don't know for shuh," Jim answered. "Three . . . four days. Bad flood."

"Three or four days? How you been eatin', nigger? You been stealin' off our farms?"

Jim's eyes widened again. "No! No, I done lived on berries and such, mistuh. I didn't steal off you people, I swear! And I wasn't runnin' away! I was just afraid to go to a white man's house and try to explain."

"Sure," Bates said, nodding. "And I suppose you would have conveniently avoided every settlement along the way for that very reason—all the way *north!*"

"No! No, suh!"

Bates sighed, stepping back. "We better check out his story. We either got a runaway here, whose master should know—or he's tellin' the truth, which means we gotta figure out what to do with him."

"I ain't got time to go runnin' south to see what's happened with the Hiwassee or this nigger's owner," the second man answered. "Lord knows I ain't got the money to be ownin' nigger slaves, so I don't much care about the affairs of them rich folks who do."

"Well, you should care," Bates answered, looking Jim over and grinning. "Might be a tidy reward for bringin' this nigger back. Them slave owners put a lot of store in their property."

"I never thought of that," the third man put in. He poked around Jim's arms and shoulders. "This nigger looks healthy and well fed. He ain't been abused. Maybe he has one of them owners that pays for the best and pays good for them that's returned to him."

"I tol' you, suh, my mastuh is dead! They ain't no place to take me."

Bates rammed his gun butt into Jim's ribs, causing the slave to sink to his knees. "You're talkin' out-of-place, nigger!" He looked at the other two. "What if he's tellin' the truth?"

The third man shrugged. "Well, maybe somebody else would know. If we take him to some big plantation and tell them about it. Maybe we'd still get some kind of reward, or they'd buy him from us."

"What did you say your master's name was, boy?" Bates asked.

Jim held his ribs, sucking in his breath. "Hank . . . Toole. He done . . . owned a steamboat . . . called the *Jasmine*. He run it . . . up and down the Hiwassee . . . tradin' supplies with mountain folks. They was . . . a big flood. You'll see if you go there. Folks up here, they'll . . . hear about it soon enough. I got . . . washed ashore. The *Jasmine* . . . it was wrecked. I . . . I seen my mastuh go down," he lied, praying Hank Toole would be thought drowned and there would be no more explaining to do.

"Probably right about the flood, Bates," the third man said. "We've had so much rain the crops are about ruined."

Bates nodded, studying the black man before him. "Where did the *Jasmine* hail from?" he asked. "This Hank Toole, he must have called someplace home."

Jim slowly got to his feet. "Knoxville. He . . . docked there a lot. I done lived . . . on the boat. I never went into that big town with Mastuh Toole. I dunno who he go see when he go on shore."

"Knoxville." Bates rubbed his chin. "That's a long ways away."

"Not an easy trip if there's been a bad flood," the first man put in. "Count me out. I got my farm to think about."

"Well, all that rain just about ruined me," Bates answered. "You can stay and try to save that mess, Chadwick, but I think our best chance for makin' any money this year is maybe gettin' paid for returnin' this nigger here."

"I'm for that," the third man added.

"Come on, nigger," Bates told Jim. He waved his musket. "You come with us."

Jim shook with fear and hunger. "Where you takin' me?"

"Back to where we live. Got to stock up on supplies before we go."

"Watch him, Bates," Chadwick told the man. "He's built pretty good."

"His hands will be tied the whole way," Bates answered. "You'd best be tellin' the truth, nigger, else you'll be in a powerful lot of trouble," he said louder to Jim.

Jim breathed deeply to quell his fears. What if people figured out Hank had been stabbed? Who was left who knew Hank had a white girl along? Even if all of that worked out, where would he be taken? Hank had been decent to him, and he had liked working the river. He could end up with a much crueler master, working in the blazing heat of a cotton field.

Tommy picked through what was left of the cabin he had shared with his father. Where the man's body had been swept to was anyone's guess. Smoke was gone, too. The few surviving settlers of the now-vanished MacBain settlement straggled back to see what they could save. Some bodies were found nearby, some found snagged in trees and brush, some with hands or feet sticking out of the mud.

Tommy realized with irritation that he might have to spend the next few days helping the survivors find loved ones and getting them buried. New supply boats would surely be along soon, coming in from other villages and from bigger cities farther downriver that might have been spared. He hoped more help would come soon, for he was already getting sick of the mess and the smell of death all around.

As soon as he could, he would get enough supplies together and find a horse so that he could ride away from this place. There had been little enough here before to interest a young man of his energies. Now there was even less. His father had been one of the few reasons for staying in the little settlement. Now it was time to do something more exciting.

"Tommy!"

The young man turned to see one of his friends approaching. "Deek! Deek, I thought you were drowned."

Deek was nineteen, a lanky but strong young man who had ridden with Tommy on many Cherokee raids. He greeted Tommy with a wide grin, standing even taller than Tommy when he reached him to embrace him for a moment. "Hell, I'm too damn tall to drown!" the young man answered.

Tommy laughed, letting go and standing back to look him over. Deek's sloppily cut, shaggy blond hair lay in jagged hunks about his head and face.

"Pa and me both made it," he said. "Ain't this a hell of a mess, Tommy? I bet you never thought anything this wild would happen to us. Did Smoke get through it all right?"

Tommy's smile had faded. "No, Deek. My pa didn't, neither."

Deek sobered. "Sorry, Tommy." He glanced over at a distant rise where the houses showed the signs of high water but were not washed away. "We saved our house and some food and things. Come on home with me. We'll put you up."

Tommy looked out over the ruined town. "Well, maybe for a while. But I'm headin' for Knoxville soon as I get things together. You want to come along, Deek? There ain't nothin' left here for us now."

"Knoxville?" Deek frowned. "Why Knoxville?"

Tommy turned, grinning. "For the excitement, you dunce. And for Emma Simms."

"Emma?"

Tommy rolled his eyes. "Don't you remember? Hank Toole bought her and took her there—at least that was what my pa said he was supposed to do when he went back downriver from here. If she's there, I'm gonna go and pay the price to sleep with that uppity brat! If you got any brains, you'll come with me. There ain't nothin' left here for us, Deek. We gotta go where we can have us a good time."

Deek looked out over the devastated settlement. "It's a thought. I kind of hate to leave Pa right now, though, with all this mess. These people are gonna need help, Tommy."

"Let them help themselves. Riverboats will come along with new supplies. We can't stay here forever like they have, Deek. Look at them—been here all their lives and their mas and pas before that. And this is what they get for it, everything they worked for washed away." He looked into the trees to his left. "My own pa is there somewhere. His payment for stayin' around here was death."

"You'll want to come back, too, Tommy."

"Maybe." He sighed deeply and shook his head. "I sure miss Smoke, poor thing."

Deek stared at him, wondering that he didn't even mention missing his father. "How did you save yourself, Tommy?"

"I don't even know. I remember hangin' on to things, then touchin' ground. Then I just started crawlin', up and up."

Deek looked out over the ruined settlement, watching people wander about, picking up things here and there. He could hear women crying softly.

"Ain't it somethin' how fast the water goes back down, Tommy? What's it been, five, maybe six days? Where you been, anyway?"

Tommy ran a hand through his hair. "I kept goin' that night—run upon another settlement. Some folks gave me some clothes, food. I stayed on there. Couldn't bring myself to come back right away and see all this, maybe find Smoke layin' all dead and bloated. Some people put me up." He pointed. "That's them down there. The man and his son, they came back with a wagonload of supplies to see if they could help."

Tommy thought about the man's daughter. He had raped her in their barn, telling her that if she screamed, he would tell them she had invited him there. His threats had been enough to keep her quiet and make her obliging. He had hurt her, he could tell. He liked the power he had to hurt women, liked the glory of conquering them. And he was sure that after a bit she had liked it. Emma would learn to like it, too. He smiled and turned to Deek.

"Come to Knoxville with me, Deek. We'll look up that Tennessee Belle saloon and put down some money for Emma Simms. She's the prettiest girl ever lived in these mountains and you know it. Wouldn't you like a turn at her? And wouldn't you like to see Knoxville?"

Deek shrugged. "I reckon. But how do you know she even made it? That was a bad flood, Tommy. The *Jasmine* might have been wrecked. That girl might be dead."

"Well, we'll find out, won't we? On the way downriver we can check around. It will give us somethin' to do."

Deek kept watching the activity below. People trudged through ankle-deep mud, and someone was dragging a dead body to a spot where others had been stacked for burial. It would be a long time before this settlement was back to normal, if it ever would be. And what would there be to do in the meantime? The spring planting was ruined and the ground was still too wet to replant.

"Okay," Deek answered. "Maybe my pa will want me to get some things for him in Knoxville. We saved our horses from the flood. You can borrow one if you want. I don't really look forward to hangin' around here and listenin' to women cry and smellin' death. You think Knoxville was hit, too?"

"Could be. But it's a lot bigger. The flood couldn't have got all of it. I always did want to see somethin' bigger than Calhoun."

"Me, too."

Tommy turned and they shook hands. "From backwoods Cherokee girls to the painted women in Knoxville," Tommy said. "I wonder if the whiskey there tastes any better?"

"Or if the girls feel any better?"

They both laughed, heading for Deek's father's cabin.

"I wonder if Emma really made it to Knoxville," Deek said, walking in long strides on stringy legs, his blond hair flopping over his eyes. "I can't picture her bein' willin' about goin' there."

Tommy chuckled. "Me neither. Either Hank spun her a good tale, or he had one hell of a fight on his hands. I never could talk that girl into lettin' me under her skirts. Pissed me off."

"Hey, Tommy." Deek stopped walking. "What do you think happened to that River Joe? You think he survived the flood?"

Tommy's blue eyes turned to ice. "Let's hope not. But if he did, I'd sure like to run into him again."

Deek noticed Tommy's chin was still black underneath his stubble, and when he smiled there were purple marks on his gums. "What do you think about him and Emma? You think he really knew her? Talked to her?"

The look in Tommy's eyes gave Deek the chills. "Maybe more than that. He had that look on his face that night, you know? Like he had some kind of victory over me."

"Would you face him down if he ever came back around here?" Deek asked.

"Sure I would."

"He's awful big and strong, Tommy."

Tommy turned, grabbing Deek's arm and shoving him around. "Well, so am I!" His eyes were wild and he gritted his teeth. "I was just drunk that night. That's why he got the better of me!"

"All right! All right! What's wrong with a friend lookin' out for a friend? And don't forget that big knife of his."

"I ain't forgettin' nothin'—'specially not him talkin' about Emma. He had no right talkin' familiar about her. Only trouble is, he probably won't ever come around here again, after what happened."

"Well? He lives up in the mountains with them Cherokee, don't he? Maybe we'll have to do some raidin' again up there sometime. Got to do our duty riddin' Tennessee of them bastards, don't we? Maybe we'll run into him that way." Deek rubbed at his arm where Tommy had let go of it.

Tommy grinned again, and Deek marveled at how quickly Tommy Decker's mood could change. "Maybe," Tommy answered. "And then we could tell him about Emma Simms, how she's doin' in Knoxville. And if there's enough of us, we could teach that River Joe a right good lesson."

Deek grinned then. "Come on. Let's get the hell out of this stinkin' mud and away from all this death. Let's go to Knoxville. Your idea sounds better all the time, Tommy."

They headed for Deek's place, Tommy again lamenting the loss of Smoke. Just a few feet from the foundation of Tommy's cabin, Jake Decker's hand protruded from the mud, sticking up as though to beckon his son to come back and give him a proper burial. Tommy did not notice. There was no time for any more searching. He was anxious to get to Knoxville, and to Emma Simms.

The Hicks settlement was bustling with activity when River Joe led his pack horse down the muddy street lined with log buildings. A few wagons lumbered past him, heavily loaded with food and other goods. Their drivers seemed to be in a hurry, but they could not go very fast because of the mud. The heavy rains had taken their toll even on villages that were not near the river.

River Joe headed up to a supply store, dismounted, and tied his roan gelding. A few people looked at him cautiously and moved away, but one man hollered out to him, "Joe! River Joe!"

River Joe turned to see the man who owned the local livery. The Hicks settlement was bigger than most villages this deep in the mountains, with a livery, blacksmith, two supply stores, several saloons, a clothing store, and a little church that also served as a school. River Joe had come through here many times, discovering the people to be somewhat friendlier than at most settlements but still sensing a good deal of animosity in most of the citizens.

"You hear about the flood?" the livery owner asked, panting after running to catch up with him. "It was terrible!"

River Joe frowned. "No," he lied calmly. "I heard of no flood. I have come from the settlements along the Hiwassee, though. The river was getting very high."

"Well, you must have left just in time. A few days ago the Hiwassee flooded somethin' awful. Most folks in the other settlements in these parts don't even know about it yet, although with all the rain we had, we suspected. Some kid from a farm down along the Hiwassee managed to ride up here and tell us so's we could get some help down there fast." He nodded toward the disappearing wagons. "Them wagons is headed down to help. It was awful bad, I hear— whole settlements wiped out. We sent riders to some of the other settlements to tell them to go down and see what they can do, too."

River Joe wondered about Luke Simms and Tommy Decker. It would be no great loss if they had died in the flood. He nodded to the man. "No surprise, with all this rain. You think there are any supplies left here for those who need them?"

"Hard to say. They're gettin' low. You sure are lucky you left when you did. You headin' back up to your people?"

River Joe watched his eyes. No. This man knew nothing

about his scuffle at the Gillmore settlement or the trouble at the MacBain village.

"In time. I am in no hurry. The hunting was not so good this spring. I am going to do more before I go back."

"Well, good luck to you. I just wanted to find out if you knew anything more about the flood. I reckon I'll go down myself and see what I can do for those good people."

River Joe shook the man's hand and headed into the supply store. He still felt anger over being cheated by Hank Toole. He would not have much to bring to his sisters and brother and father this time. He would be short on flour, material, sugar, coffee, everything. There simply was not enough money this time to buy what was needed.

And now he had the additional worry of another mouth to feed—his new wife's. Still, the thought made him smile. He was bringing a surprise back to his family, that was sure.

He was grateful to *Esaugetuh Emissee* that Emma was better. They had been camped for two days now at the deserted cabin, and there had been no sign of her recurring blackouts. There was better color in her soft cheeks, and she was doing everything for herself. His desire was building, but he wanted to be sure she was well enough to make love with him. Perhaps tonight, when he returned.

He looked up into the hills in the direction of the spot where he had left her and prayed that she would be all right. He did not like leaving her alone, but for now he had no choice. They dared not risk being seen together.

Emma scrubbed towels and some soiled cotton shirts River had given her upon her insistence that she wanted to do something useful. It was late afternoon, and River had been gone since early that morning. Already she missed him, realizing how important he had already become to her life. She knelt at the creek, rubbing lye soap into soiled spots, then rubbing them against a big rock and rinsing them in the creek water. River had cautioned her not to do too much, but she felt so much stronger. The headaches had not returned, and just the respite from pain gave her new energy.

Life was going to be good! They were far away from the river now, and probably Tommy and Luke and anyone else who might give them trouble were dead. No one would connect River to anything. Surely the Maker of Breath would make it be so.

For the first time in her life she felt happy and free. River was kinder to her than anyone had ever been. What a wonderful feeling to be truly loved by a good man. She knew that soon River would want to mate with her again, and she was surprised that she looked forward to it. She was not afraid, even though she remembered the pain. River had promised it would get better, and she believed him. The thought of lying with him again sent shivers of passion through her blood, and brought the delicious ache to her insides.

She finished washing the clothes and towels and piled them up on the rock, picking them up one by one then and carrying them to low tree branches, where she hung them to dry; then she went back to put more wood on the campfire.

What would River want to eat when he returned? Maybe he would bring back enough flour for her to make a berry pie for him. Without a real oven it would be difficult, but she could make do with a dutch oven over the fire. She forced back a gnawing fear that River might not get back before dark. He had promised that he would. He had never yet broken a promise.

She put on a little more wood, then straightened when she heard an odd snorting sound. Her heart pounded. There were all kinds of wild animals in these mountains. When she was with River she gave no thought to them. But alone she was not so brave. River had left his musket for her, primed and loaded, as well as an extra hand pistol.

Emma stood still and listened. The sound came again, and she cocked her head, surprised that it sounded very much like the pigs on Luke's farm. She breathed easier for just a moment. She was used to pigs, had no fear of them. But then it dawned on her that there were no settlements near enough for domesticated pigs to be wandering about.

She felt ice move through her blood at the only other possibility—a wild boar! Few animals were as vicious as a wild boar could be, not even a bear. She eased her way toward the musket. She was not the best shot, and she realized that if she had to use the gun, she would have to make its one shot count; there might not be a second chance for her. If a boar charged, there would be no time for reloading.

She swallowed, feeling sweaty all over as she reached for the musket and raised it. The pistol rested on a stump beside the musket. She backed against one of the remaining walls of the old cabin, waiting, struggling not to breathe too hard even though her heart pounded wildly. She prayed that whatever was just outside the wall, it would wander off. She gripped the musket, watching right and left, for the animal could come from any direction, as the entire end of the cabin was gone.

She heard the snorting again, this time louder and lasting longer. Where was River? If only he were here! He would know what to do.

Finally, sniffing the ground as it moved around the collapsed wall to her left, a huge male boar appeared. It stopped, just then seeing her, and lifted its head, wiggling its huge, pink nose and sniffing hard. She raised the musket. The boar came a little closer, then snorted loudly. Her vision blurred by tears, Emma aimed the musket at its head and pulled the trigger. Fire shot out the end of the long barrel.

In the distance River Joe halted his horse, looking with surprise in the direction of the gunshot. Emma! He kicked his horse into a hard run, pulling the pack horse along behind.

◇ *Chapter 10* ◇

River Joe's horse was lathered by the time he reached camp. At first he saw only the clothes hanging about in the trees. The campfire crackled and a pan of hot water sat on a grate above the fire.

River Joe was dismounted before his horse even came to a full halt. He pulled his musket from its boot. "Emma!" he shouted.

She peered around the end of one of the half-missing walls, holding a huge knife in her hand that was covered with blood, as was the old, cotton shirt she had put on in place of the pretty dress. His heart froze at the sight of her, and he hurried on long legs to where she stood.

"Emma, what in God's name—"

He reached out for her but she backed away. "Don't touch me, River. You'll get blood all over you. I just wanted to be sure it was you that was coming before I called back." She grinned then. "Look! I got us some meat!"

She pointed to a pile of leaves, where the boar lay gutted out. River Joe frowned, setting aside his musket and walking closer. He looked from the wild pig back to Emma, astonishment on his face.

"You killed a wild boar?"

She nodded, her pride and excitement showing. "With the musket. It only took one shot. He'd make good meat for us, wouldn't he, River? Luke used to make me help butcher hogs back on the farm. So I thought I'd go ahead and start on him. I didn't know when you might come back." She looked down at the old shirt, holding out her arms. "I took off the dress so I wouldn't get any blood on it. I hope you don't care too much about this old shirt."

He just stared at her for a moment, his alarm changing to surprise, then pride, then an aching desire. After he had rescued her she was left with no bloomers. The shirt hung to just above her knees, but he knew that under it she wore nothing. Her legs were slim and shapely, and seeing her that way, really looking well for the first time since he had rescued her, brought a wave of fresh desire that swept through him as though someone had put something extra-warm in his blood.

"No, I don't mind," he said rather absently.

Emma felt the same warmth flow through her blood at the way his dark eyes moved over her. It would happen again. She wanted it to happen, but she wasn't sure what she should do, if she should tell him or say nothing. Was he waiting for her to say she was well enough? She still knew so little about men, at least men like River.

"If . . . if you can help me cut it up, River, we can smoke some, and pack some in lard. Did you bring lard?"

He nodded. At the moment he wasn't giving much thought to the dead boar. He folded his arms. "Well, aren't you something?" He looked down at the dead pig again, then grinned and laughed lightly. "I'll be damned." He looked back at her. "When did you learn to shoot that good?"

She shrugged. "I really can't. I just prayed to the Maker of Breath that the first shot would be good, because I knew I wouldn't have time for a second. I just aimed, and pulled the trigger, and down he went." She was smiling, but her eyes suddenly teared. "Actually . . . I was scared to death," she said, her voice breaking, even though she was still smiling. "There's nothing meaner than a wild pig, I always heard. And it was getting dark and I didn't know if you'd get back before the sun went down. And . . . well . . . anyway I didn't have any choice, because he was going to come after me. I could see it in those mean eyes." She swallowed and blinked back tears, sniffing and keeping a smile. "Are you proud of me, River? I got us some meat."

He grinned more, the sweet, warm smile that made her love him all the more. "Of course I am proud of you. And so will my people be proud when I tell them. You did well today, *Agiya*." His eyes moved over her again, and she read the desire there. He walked closer and grasped her arms, leaning down and kissing the top of her head. "I will help you butcher the boar and we will eat well tonight. Tomorrow we must be on our way again."

He stepped away and removed his weapons belt and buckskin shirt. She stared at the broad shoulders and powerful arms as he removed his knife from its sheath on the weapons belt and walked over to the boar. She watched him for a moment, somewhat overwhelmed by his size, truly looking at him for the first time since her injuries. To her relief, his wound seemed healed. She watched his big blade slice through the boar easily, and remembered that same knife slicing into Hank Toole's heart.

Hank Toole. If only the man's death were not there constantly to haunt her. River Joe had killed him. If people figured it out . . . How could she ever live without him now? It would be impossible. She would rather die.

She walked over to help him with the boar, and for the next hour they sliced off and skinned the best pieces.

"We do not have time to prepare this thing like we should. Some parts will have to go to waste," he said. "We will pack most of it in lard until we get even farther away where we can make a more permanent camp again and take a few days to smoke it. The folks at the settlement know about the flood below and they are sending people down with supplies. That means it cannot be long before the *Jasmine* is found, along with Hank's body. We still have plenty of time, I am sure. By the time he is found we will be even farther into the mountains. Once we reach my people, we will be almost impossible to find. We will just lie low awhile and wait."

She didn't say anything, but he noticed her slicing almost savagely into the meat. He glanced at her face and saw tears on her cheeks. He stopped his cutting and grasped her wrist.

"Do not get upset, Emma. You have been sick. Nothing is going to happen. I promise."

"You can't promise that," she said quietly, sniffing and wiping at her eyes with her shoulder.

"Emma, most likely when that body is found, it will be quickly buried like all the others, maybe in a mass grave. It will be so bloated no one will notice the knife wound. They will take it for granted he drowned."

"What about Hank's slave?" she sniffed.

He sighed deeply, returning to his cutting. "He most likely drowned, too. He fell into the river, remember?"

"But what if he lived, River? What if?"

River Joe frowned, setting aside some meaty ribs. "He would be too scared to say anything. They might not believe him. They might think he killed Hank himself. Who is going to believe a slave? I am sorry to put it that way. But it is a fact that no white man is going to take the word of a Negro; they have no more use for them than for the Indians."

She set aside a piece of meat and sat back on her ankles. He glanced at her thighs, already sure he would never get through this night without making love to her. He was so proud of what she had done, so happy she was getting well, so enraptured by her slender beauty.

"Why are people like that, River? What makes the color of somebody's skin mean they're not as good as the next man?"

"Nothing. It is all in the mind. Somewhere back in time the white man decided that if a man's skin was darker, he was somehow inferior. And they think the same about other whites who care about dark men, or live with them, like me. Because I was brought up by the Cherokee, I am considered just as bad as they are, although I am not sure what that is supposed to mean."

They finished the boar and put some of the meat on a spit over the fire. Emma added some wood to the fire while River Joe went for the soap and a cloth to wash with. "Let's go wash off this blood while that meat cooks," he told her. "We will pack the rest of it in lard later. I have to unload the horses, too, for the night."

She walked barefoot with him to the creek, where they both knelt down and scrubbed their hands and arms.

"Oh, River, this shirt is covered with blood."

He grinned. "Take it off and wash it then." He wiped his hands and chest with the cloth, then handed it to her, a smile on his lips. Her face was crimson as she took the cloth.

"I . . . I didn't bring my dress with me."

His smiled faded, every bone in his body aching for her. "You do not need the dress."

Their eyes held. She felt the same commanding power she had felt that night in the shed. She knew her cheeks were red and hot, knew she was trembling at the way he looked at her. She wanted this, yet felt so inexperienced, so helpless. He reached out and began unbuttoning the shirt, and she did not stop him, nor did she want to.

He stood up, grasping her arms and pulling her up with him. As he opened the shirt and pushed it off her shoulders, she let it drop to the ground. He pulled her close, pressing her breasts against the skin of his bare chest, and she felt almost faint with desire and anticipation.

Quietly he ran his hands over her back, down over her bottom, reaching down between her legs and pulling up with big, strong hands so that she came up and wrapped her legs around his hips. He encircled her in his powerful arms then, kissing at her shoulder, her neck, moving to her mouth. He kissed her hard, deep, groaning lightly. Her long, silken hair caressed the backs of his hands.

He moved his mouth from hers, running it along her cheek, lightly licking her skin, biting at her ear. She wrapped her arms around his neck and he walked with her, carrying her back to camp and to the bedroll, still holding her as he kissed her hair, her eyes.

"I want you so bad, River," she whispered. "I just don't know what to do."

"You do not have to know." He kissed her eyes again. "I told you that before."

He kissed her hard again, holding her tight against him with one arm while he ran his other hand down over the center of her bottom, his fingers reaching under her to probe at the sweet moistness there that told him she was ready to try this again. She whimpered and gasped at the touch, fire ripping through every bone and every nerve.

"It will be good," he told her, his voice husky with desire. He grasped her around the waist then, pulling her away and lowering her, breathing deeply at the sight of her standing there naked, desire setting him afire. He unlaced his buckskin pants and removed them along with his moccasins, then removed his loincloth. He stood there in all his manly glory, and for the first time in full light she looked upon her man. He took her hands gently in his own and moved them to touch that mysterious part of him that she had wondered about.

She almost felt like crying with the wonder of it. He was so soft, yet what she knew he would put inside of her seemed too huge to fit. No wonder it had hurt that first time. Was he really right in telling her it would hurt less and less?

"Don't ever be afraid to touch me, Emma," he said, "or afraid that I would hurt you."

He placed his hands on her hips and slowly lowered himself, kissing at her lips, her shoulders. He rested on his knees and caressed her breasts, then pulled one into his soft, warm mouth, making her whimper with desire. He moved to the other breast, drawing all her desires toward him as he sucked on its sweet fruit.

His lips moved over her belly then, lightly kissing at the blond hair that hid that which he desired most. She remembered his words, about tasting more than her breasts. She never dreamed it would be possible for her to let a man do more, yet even now he was coaxing her down to the bedroll while he still kissed at her.

He explored her intimately, and the ecstasy of it made her cry out his name in helpless abandon. How thrilling it was to please this beautiful, tender man. A lovely explosion rippled through her belly and made her cry out, and his mouth moved back up again from her belly to her breasts, her neck, while he moved between her slender legs, and that most glorious part of him quickly pushed.

She cried out. Yes, the pain was still there. But he was right. It was not as bad as the first time. And a yearning deep in her belly made her want him inside her, made her arch up to him and cry out with the ecstasy of taking him inside herself.

"*Agiya*," he whispered, groaning then, moving rhythmically, grasping her under the hips and pushing deeply, over and over until she wondered if she would die from the thrill of it. He whispered more words in the Cherokee tongue, words she did not understand but knew were words of love.

She grasped at his arms, rising up to him, her blond hair hanging down to the ground as she kissed at his chest and shoulders. Their lips met then, his tongue invading her mouth just as he invaded her elsewhere. She could not get enough of him, nor he of her. They moved in the thrilling rhythm for several minutes, his thrusts deep and hard, the pain disappearing and ecstasy replacing it.

She lay back and he rose then, grasping her hips in his big hands and actually pulling her to him as he watched the invasion, fire ripping through his loins at the sight of her flat belly and full, firm breasts, her closed eyes and the look of joy on her beautiful young face.

He changed his thrusts to circular motions, and his eyes were glassy with pleasure when she gasped at the new movement. She grasped at his forearms, then groaned his name when his life spilled inside of her. She could feel the added swelling, the throbbing release.

Tiny fears of getting pregnant flashed through her mind, for her mother had suffered so much from miscarriages and had died giving birth. But she told herself to ignore her fears. She didn't want River to know she was afraid of anything. And after all, it couldn't be that easy, and surely one didn't always get a baby this way.

He was whispering her name now, coming down to hold her close, kissing her face.

"Oh, that was so wonderful," he murmured, kissing her hair. "It was even more wonderful than the first time, because I could see you . . ." he kissed her several times over, "and taste you." He kissed her again, a deep, probing kiss. "And I knew this time it felt good to you," he said softly.

"River!" she whispered, her eyes closed.

"We will do it again . . . so many times, *Agiya*. I am so happy you are well now."

"I love you so much, River. I never knew I could feel like this."

He caressed her hair, smiling as he rose on one elbow. "My little hunter. You have provided the meat this time. Maybe I should send you on the hunts instead of going myself."

She smiled then, reaching up and touching his face. "I think we would end up very hungry."

He laughed lightly, running a hand over her belly and massaging it lightly. "We should turn the meat over the fire, and pack the rest. And I have to unload the horses."

"I know."

Their eyes held for several long seconds. She lifted herself to hug him. "I want to do it again, River. Is that bad?"

He kissed her neck, moving a hand around and under her left leg, lifting it and bending it toward her body as he moved on top of her again.

"No, it is not bad," he whispered. He pressed his mouth to hers and she tasted her own sweetness on his lips as she felt him swelling against her belly. He slid his other arm under her other leg, bending both of them up so that she would be helpless if he wanted her to be. There would be no fighting his power. But she did not want to fight him. In the next moment he invaded her again, while the meat over the fire, unattended, began to blacken, and while the horses grazed, their heavy loads still packed on their backs.

It took several men with ropes and horses to haul in what was left of the *Jasmine*. The wreckage was caught along the south bank of the Hiwassee, some of its cargo salvageable, much of it ruined.

"Easy now!" a settler named Ned Stewart yelled out. A tree branch being sawed to free the upper deck came crashing down. The man in the tree who had been working at the job all morning cheered, and horses tied to the creaking, broken boat pulled the rest of the wreckage onto shore.

"Somebody is going to have to figure out a way to get the usable stuff down to Knoxville," Stewart said to the others. "Somebody there ought to know what to do about it. It must belong to someone. Hank always went on to the Tennessee River and on to Knoxville to pick up more cargo."

"It's a shame," the other man answered. "Hank's been runnin' this river for a long time. I wonder who's going to bring us our supplies now."

"Oh, I expect there's plenty of other people been waitin' to move in on Hank's business."

Men swarmed over the remains of the boat then to determine what could be saved. The *Jasmine* had been carried miles downriver before catching along the bank, bits and pieces of it left scattered up the Hiwassee to where it had first begun breaking up, only a few miles east of Luke Simms's farm.

All along the Hiwassee people were trying to put their lives back together. Rebuilding had already begun, by strong, determined settlers who refused to let the river defeat them. Graves were dug, some single, some for mass burials. When Jake Decker was finally found, Tommy had already left with Deek for Knoxville. He was not present at the MacBain settlement for his father's funeral.

The MacBains, the first to settle there and for whom the settlement had been named, were all dead—the old grandparents, a son and daughters, and both the children's families. But the MacBain settlement would rise again, as would the Gillmore settlement and all the others that had been devastated by the flood.

For the moment neither village knew the fate of the *Jasmine*, which had floated nearly to the town of Calhoun. Wagons were brought up on which cargo that could be saved would be loaded. No one had a boat big enough to take what was left to Knoxville. The slower trip by horse and wagon would have to be made.

"Hey, Ned!" someone shouted down from the cabin. "He's here! Hank Toole is still on the boat—at least I think it's him."

Ned Stewart and several others hurried to the wreckage, as a man came out of the cabin holding his nose. "Goddamn, what a smell!" He leaned over and vomited. The odor made Stewart and the others move back again.

"We have to get him off of there and bury him," Ned told the others.

They all pondered how to get the bloated body off the boat. "Why not saw around the floor under him and put ropes under it and lift him out right on the boards," one of them put in. "Then we don't have to touch the body. Take a hatchet and chop through the floor at the four corners so's somebody can stand underneath and know where to saw."

"Not a bad idea. Get some hatchets," Stewart told the man. He looked at the man who had found the body. "You okay, Danny?"

The man nodded, blinking back tears. "I think so. This sure is a mess, ain't it?"

"It's a mess for a lot of people. I hear it's worse upriver."

Danny looked at Ned Stewart, keeping a hand to his stomach. "Somethin' ain't right about this one, Ned. Far as I can see, the cabin area was never under water. I don't think Hank Toole drowned."

Ned frowned, looking toward the cabin. "Maybe he got tossed around some, hit his head or something."

Danny ran a hand through his hair. "I could swear there's blood all over the front of him. And on his face, too, like somebody scratched him or somethin'. It's hard to tell, he's so swelled up. But I swear it don't look like natural injuries from no accident."

"I'll have a look." Ned folded his arm over his nose and mouth before going inside the cabin to see Hank's body lying flat on its back, swollen and blue. The man wore only the bottom half of long underwear, and the swelling and color from death did not hide the obvious dried blood all over his chest. There was an odd, gaping wound in the center of the chest, and the man's eyes were still open, as though staring in terror. There were lines of blood down his face, and more dried blood around one ear and down his neck.

Ned ducked out, choking and gagging. He breathed deeply of the fresh air. "You're right. We have to study it some more, Danny, in spite of his condition. If this is more than just an accident, we have to report it to somebody, at least in Calhoun, maybe in Knoxville."

Danny nodded. "What about his nigger? You think he could have done it?"

Ned shook his head. "I don't know. I can't believe any nigger would be that stupid."

"Well, he ain't been found. He might have thought he could use the flood to cover it. Maybe he decided to run off."

"If he did, he'll be found, and he'll have some explainin' to do."

Men returned with hatchets and saws. One wrapped a

cloth around his nose and mouth, tucked sassafras branches under it to prevent his smelling the odor of decay, then went into the cabin and chopped around the body, with a hatchet while another man went below deck to find the hatchet marks which told him where to begin sawing. The man with the hatchet came out gagging and pulled off the covering over his mouth.

"Ned! He looks like he's been stabbed."

Ned looked at Danny. "Ain't much doubt about it now." He sighed and shook his head. "Ain't this a strange twist of events? We got enough to do just cleanin' up this mess without havin' to figure out whether Hank Toole has been murdered and who could have done it."

"Murdered! You think he's been murdered?" the third man asked Ned.

"How the hell else would he get a stab wound, Davie?"

"He could have fell against somethin' sharp."

Ned shook his head. "No. He was in some kind of fight. There's blood and scratches around his head. And he wasn't even dressed."

The one called Davie looked back toward the cabin, making a face. "Maybe his nigger did it—waited till the man was sleepin'."

"Yeah, but why would Hank be sleepin' in the middle of a ragin' flood?" Danny put in. "That don't make sense. I just don't understand why he didn't have nothin' on but his underwear."

The three men stood pondering the situation while another man sawed around the body and more entered the cabin to rig ropes around the floorboards, preparing to lift the body once the man below had completed sawing around it.

Tommy Decker and Deek Malone rode through what was once Luke Simms's farm. Nothing looked familiar.

"I'll be damned," Tommy commented.

Deek whistled in wonder. "Ain't nothin' left at all."

Tommy curled his nose. "Sure stinks everywhere, don't it? We're gonna have to head a ways away from the river, Deek. Too many dead animals."

"And humans. You think Luke's around here someplace?"

"Most likely."

"Maybe Emma, too. Maybe Hank never stopped to pick her up on account of the storm."

Tommy studied the barren farm. The only thing remaining was a fence post and a few rocks that were once the foundation for the cabin.

"I don't think Hank would have missed his chance at that one," Tommy said. "He probably wanted a whack at her himself. I remember him looking at Emma once when I was there. Licked his lips like she was sugar."

They both grinned. "I wonder if Hank made it, Tommy," Deek said then.

"I sure hope so. I'm goin' to Knoxville for one thing, and that's to get a piece of Emma Simms."

"Well, let's get goin' and see if she's there," Deek answered with a wink.

They rode for several more yards, then saw the body sprawled in a bush.

"God damn!" Tommy made a face and backed his horse. He recognized the old cotton pants and the black beard. "It's him! It's Luke!"

"Damn." Deek stared. "Shouldn't we bury him?"

Tommy turned his horse. "Are you kidding? Let's get out of here." He headed up a hill. Deek stared at Luke's dead and bloated body for a moment longer, then turned and followed.

Chapter 11 ◇

Emma and River Joe had traveled for another week since leaving the campsite where she had killed the wild boar. That whole week she had known nothing but beauty, in the arms of River Joe. She had lost count of how many times they had made love, and just as he had promised, each time had been less painful, until now it was such ecstasy that it seemed almost sinful. But it wasn't sinful. River was her husband.

Her mother had told her that a woman was not supposed to enjoy mating. It was simply a duty one had to put up with to satisfy a man's needs and give him children. But River had taught her otherwise. Mating with the one you loved was as natural and right as breathing the air. Enjoying it was good, for the Maker of Breath wanted them to be together. And a baby conceived in love would be a healthy, beautiful child. She wondered if her mother had had so many miscarriages because none of the babies was conceived in joy and love. She felt very sorry that her mother had never known a man like River Joe.

A squirrel ran up a nearby hickory tree, and Emma felt the happiness returning to her soul when River held her in his arms. She breathed deeply of his now-familiar scent, kissing his neck.

"I love you, River."

He grinned, pulling back a little, kissing her forehead. "You are ready to go on?"

She nodded. "I'll get dressed and make us something to eat." She started to rise, but he reached under the long shirt she wore, pulling her back down to the bedroll, in one quick moment pushing up the shirt and moving on top of her. He had slept naked, as he usually did, and she felt him pressing against her belly.

"River! We just woke up."

"So? A woman looks more beautiful than ever in the morning, when her hair is loose and free and her body is still warm from sleep. There are no rules for when a man and woman should make love, *Agiya.*" He leaned closer, kissing her neck, and she could think of no reason to protest. The newness of their relationship was still thrilling, and she was sure in her heart it would always be this way.

She gasped as he slid into her, groaning with his own delight. She had already learned that doing this was never the same. Each time was different and wonderful in its own way. This time he had not even toyed with her first. He was simply inside her, and she felt wonderful sensations building, heightened by the fact that he wanted her so readily, and by the beauty of the sunny morning. He moved a little differently, rubbing that spot he sometimes teased with his fingers or tongue, and now the wonderful explosion came without his touching her that way at all.

Her insides ached with it, and she pulled at him fiercely then as she arched up to greet him. They moved wildly, rhythmically, and she lost all touch with the outside world. There was only River, his broad shoulders and long hair and strong arms, his big hands and warm lips. He fed her ecstasy for several minutes before finally releasing his own prolonged climax, pushing several times as his life spilled into her.

When he relaxed, they lay quietly, listening to the birds. "Of all the gifts from the Maker of Breath, this is the most wonderful," she said softly. "Giving my husband his pleasure, taking so much pleasure in return, making love under the warm sun with only the birds and the squirrels to see."

He kissed her neck. "I love you, *Agiya*. The desire was just so strong in me."

"I know. You didn't hear me argue for long, did you?"

He laughed lightly then, pulling away from her. "You lie still while I make a fire and heat some water so you can wash. Then we will eat and we must be on our way."

She watched him walk to a nearby creek, watched the muscles of his bare buttocks and strong thighs, sure that no more beautiful man could be found in all of Tennessee. She wasn't embarrassed to look at him anymore, and she gazed at him with delight as he returned with a bucket of water and knelt to light a fire with flint and steel.

"Will your people be hard to find, River?"

"Could be. I hope they are still where I left them. But if not, I'll have to track them down. Their main goal is to keep from being found by raiders. The place where they were camped when I left has been peaceful for quite some time now. But even this high up there are a few white settlements and enough Indian haters that the Cherokee have to be careful. If they are found, they will be harassed all over again and will have to move on. Some want to go to New Echota, where it is supposedly safer; but most consider this part of Tennessee their home and they do not want to go to Georgia, even though so many have settled there."

"Maybe we should go there."

"Maybe. But I consider Tennessee home, too. New Echota is quite advanced, they say—schools and all—and they are talking about starting a newspaper of their own, printed in both Cherokee and English. John Ross lives there part of the time."

"Tell me more about John Ross. You mentioned him once before. He must be an important man."

"He is one of the Cherokee's more educated leaders. He

has begun waging a court battle to allow the Cherokee in Tennessee and northern Georgia to be allowed to stay there, maybe even declare their own state, as I already told you." He watched the fire flicker and begin to burn. "John Ross feels the only hope the Cherokee have is to do everything legally, through the courts. That way no one can touch them. The secret is not to fight back when we are raided."

He looked over at her. She lay with a blanket pulled over her, watching him lovingly. How pretty she looked in the morning, her hair like a white halo spread about her.

"It is so hard for me not to fight back," he said then, turning back to the fire and adding some sticks. "I want to kill all of those bastards—slowly! But I refuse to make matters worse for the people who loved me and raised me as their own. I would have died if they had not found me and taken me in."

"But why can't you fight back, River? It's the natural thing to do. The raiders have no business doing what they do."

"I know. But the minute we raise a hand in defense, they will say we are at war, and then they will come in greater numbers and bring soldiers. They will say that because we have chosen war, we deserve no say before Congress or the courts, that we have no rights left at all. If we do everything just as legally and properly as we can, there is a chance we will win this thing. But this way is very hard on the Cherokee men, who take pride in protecting their own."

She sighed deeply. "It isn't fair."

He rose, setting the bucket of water over the fire and walking over to his supply sack. He took out a cloth and walked back to the water. "A lot of things are not fair," he answered. "Like the way you had to grow up." He dipped the cloth into the water. "And like me having to wash in this cold water so I can start getting our things together, while you get to wait until the water is warmer." He held the cold cloth to his privates and made a face, and Emma giggled.

"It was all your idea," she reminded him. "I don't feel sorry for you."

He washed himself and came back to his supply sack for a clean loincloth, made of softened doeskin. "Maybe it was my idea, maybe it was not. Women have a way of talking men into things without their realizing what is going on."

She reddened and snuggled into the blanket. "This time was different, and you know it. I was getting up to get dressed, remember?"

He finished tying the loincloth, grinning then. "I remember." He reached down and yanked away the blanket. She screamed and quickly pulled down her shirt, then giggled as he tickled her, curling up against the teasing fingers. He stopped then and bent down to kiss her.

"Thank you, Emma," he said softly. "I am such a happy man."

She reached up and touched his face. "Oh, River, I'm happy, too. Maybe things will work out after all. It's been almost two weeks since the flood. And if we can get up where we're hard to find, we can be happy and free, and in time people will forget about Hank Toole and River Joe. They probably think I drowned."

He patted her bottom. "No more talk about it. Get up and get washed, woman. We have some traveling to do."

As she dipped into the warming water to wash herself, River Joe dug some potatoes out of a leather supply bag. Happy as he was with Emma, he could not dispel his worries. Was there anyone left to link him to Hank, or who knew that Hank had had Emma with him? And what had happened to Hank's Negro slave?

He watched Emma again. How he loved her! How he prayed that nothing would happen to spoil this wonderful happiness he had found; nothing that would make him have to part from the beautiful young girl who made his heart sing with love again.

* * *

Tommy and Deek made their way slowly in a southeasterly direction. Neither of them had ever been to Knoxville, and their anticipation was keen. It felt good to be away from the small settlements where they had grown up, and, more than anything, Tommy looked forward to setting eyes on Emma Simms.

Never would he forget her beating him with the board and shunning his advances. His jaw had never been quite right since then, and it was painful to chew. He intended to settle that score somehow, someday. Tommy had always been proud of his smile, his white, even teeth. Now some of them were probably going to fall out, and his face had a crooked look to it. And it seemed at times he could still smell the manure Emma had shoved into his face.

His fists clenched at the memory. Being sold to Sam Gates to be a prostitute couldn't be a more fitting end for Emma. He wished he had been there to see her face when Luke handed her over to Hank Toole and she was told why. He laughed out loud at the thought of it.

"What are you laughin' about?" Deek asked, adjusting a weathered leather hat over his shaggy blond hair.

"Just thinkin' about Emma bein' at that place called the Tennessee Belle. Can't you just picture her dressed in a fancy red dress with half her tits hangin' out?"

They both laughed.

"I reckon she'll learn to like it," Deek answered. "Maybe she'll be right glad to see a couple of boys from home—give us a free turn."

They laughed more. Tommy slowed his horse then, pointing to smoke. "Looks like a campfire."

"Looks like."

"Let's go see. If they're friendly, maybe we can use their

fire for the night and not have to build one of our own. Maybe we'll even get a free meal."

"Well, be careful. We're gettin' far from familiar places, and we got money and supplies on us."

"Yeah. Yeah." Tommy pulled out his musket and laid it across his lap. Deek followed suit and they rode slowly through a sycamore grove, watching the shadows. They heard voices, smelled something cooking. Tommy put out his hand then, grabbing Deek's arm and making him stop. "Look there!" he said in a hoarse whisper.

Deek squinted to see through the trees, then saw a Negro man, his wrists in manacles and stretched over his head, chained to a tree limb. One of two white men near the campfire rose and walked over to the Negro man, a tin plate in his hand.

"Here you go, nigger," the white man said, dipping a spoon into the dish and holding something up for the Negro man to eat. "Chew fast. I ain't gonna stand here long. I'm tired."

The man shoveled food into the Negro man's mouth while he chewed and swallowed as fast as he could. Tommy stared at the Negro man a moment longer, then looked at Deek. "That looks like Nigger Jim, Hank Toole's nigger!"

Deek watched a moment longer. "Kind of does, doesn't it?"

"Let's go."

Deek started to object, but Tommy rode forward, hailing the white men near the campfire.

"Hello there! Friends comin' in." He held up his musket and the man feeding Jim dropped his plate and ran for his own musket, while the second white man rose from where he sat still eating, watching Tommy warily.

"Who are you?"

"Name's Tommy Decker, from up at the MacBain settlement. Headin' for Knoxville. Saw your campfire." He turned and nodded to Deek, who rode in cautiously behind him. "This here is my friend, Deek Malone."

The two men nodded to Tommy and Deek. "I'm Herman Bates," the man who had been feeding Jim answered. He was pudgy and soiled with a stubble of beard. "My friend here is John Williams. We're from Summerville." He noticed Tommy look over at Jim. "We found the nigger there in the woods near where we live—figure he's runnin' from his master. We was takin' him to the first big plantation we come across, see what we can find out about him, what to do with him."

Tommy dismounted, glaring at Jim. He walked closer to the man and prodded him painfully in the ribs with the end of his musket barrel. "Well, well. If it ain't Nigger Jim. How'd you get off the *Jasmine*, Jim? You run away from Hank?"

"No, suh! No! The *Jasmine*, she broke up in the flood! I got throwed in the river, and Mastuh Hank, he must have drowned."

"Hey, you know this nigger?" Bates asked Tommy.

Tommy turned, walking back to the fire, glancing again at Jim. "He's Nigger Jim—works for Hank Toole. Hank owned the *Jasmine*, a steamboat that run up and down the Hiwassee bringin' supplies to the settlements there."

Bates looked at Williams, who was a tall man dressed in baggy cotton pants and a blue shirt. He wore a weathered buckskin jacket and his hair needed cutting. Tommy guessed both men to be about the age of his own father. Their eyes were wary but friendly, and he lowered his musket.

"Sounds like this nigger's story might be true then," Bates said to Williams. He looked at Tommy, while Deek dismounted and tied both their horses. "He told us the same thing—said he worked for a man who owned a steamboat and that the boat had broke up in a big flood. You two know about the flood?"

Tommy nodded. "Real bad. I lost my pa. Our whole settlement was just about wiped out."

"Sorry to hear that. You two like some sassafras tea? A couple biscuits? We ain't got much left."

Tommy grinned, setting aside his musket. "Much obliged." He signaled Deek to join him and they both sat down on a log across the fire from Bates. Bates handed out a tin with biscuits on it, and Tommy took one and handed another to Deek.

"Me and John are farmers," Bates told them, pouring some sassafras tea into tin cups and handing them out. "The big rain ruined us. Then we come across this nigger here and figured maybe we'd make more money findin' his master and returnin' him than we would farmin'. Neither one of us has a woman—both dead. I ain't got nobody to run my farm, but there ain't nothin' left to run. John here has a couple of sons who can try to make somethin' out of what's left before the season is over. How bad is it then, along the Hiwassee?"

"Real bad," Deek answered. He finished swallowing a biscuit. "Lots of people dead, and lots of animals and crops lost. Whole settlements were washed away. Don't travel too close to the river. Everything stinks."

Bates nodded. "I expect so, with all that death."

Williams stood off to the side, saying little.

"So, you found Nigger Jim in the woods—pretty far from the river, I'll bet," Tommy said.

Bates nodded again. "He was sleepin'. Didn't have nothin' on him—no extra clothes or anything, I mean. Looked to me like he took a last-minute chance and started runnin'."

Tommy turned and looked at Jim again. "Where is she, Jim?"

Bates and Williams both frowned at the question, while Jim's eyes widened.

"Who . . . who you talkin' about, Mastuh Deckuh?"

Tommy laughed and shook his head. "You know goddamned well who I'm talkin' about. The white girl."

Jim swallowed. "I dunno who you mean, suh."

"What's goin' on here?" Bates broke in.

Tommy took a drink of the tea, then held out his cup.

"Ain't you got somethin' a little stronger to flavor this with, Bates? If you have some whiskey, I have some information that might be valuable to you."

Bates nodded at Williams, and he pulled a small bottle of whiskey out of a saddlebag while Jim watched in terror. Williams poured some into Tommy's cup, then into Deek's. Tommy took a swallow, then let out a long sigh.

"That's better," he said, glancing at Jim again, then back to Bates. "The man Nigger Jim worked for—he ran a riverboat up and down the Hiwassee deliverin' supplies, like I said," he told the man. "But sometimes he picked up mountain girls, some willin', some unwillin', but sold by their fathers or whoever owned them. Took them back to Knoxville with him to be turned over to a man called Sam Gates, who runs a saloon there called the Tennessee Belle. My pa told me all about it."

Bates leaned closer. "You mean, you think this Hank Toole had a girl along with him?"

"I don't think. I know. A real pretty thing—blond hair, blue eyes, big tits, and untouched, you know? I mean, this girl would make a nigger like Jim go wild with desire. You know how niggers are about white girls."

"It ain't true!" Jim protested, his eyes tearing. "There wasn't no girl along. If . . . if there was, I wouldn't be crazy enough to go near her, suh!"

Williams walked over to Jim, backhanding him hard across the side of the face. "You shut up till you're asked to speak!"

Jim shook with fear while Williams turned his attention back to Tommy.

"Her name was Emma Simms," Tommy said. "I knew her—a neighbor. My pa knew her steppa, Luke Simms. Her ma died and Luke wanted to get rid of her. Made a deal with Hank. The day before the big flood, Hank stopped at the MacBain settlement to do his tradin'. The Simms place is down from there. My pa told me that night that Hank was supposed to pick up Emma Simms when he went back up there and take her on to Knoxville with him."

He drank a little more of the spiked tea. "She's the kind of girl that makes a man crazy, you know? I been wantin' her a long time. When I found out, I decided to go to Knoxville myself. The girl was always too uppity before, always shunnin' me. I figured once this Sam Gates broke her in, I'd go have my turn at her. That's where me and Deek was headin' when we come across your camp." He looked at Jim again. "And now here's Nigger Jim, sayin' the *Jasmine* was wrecked and Hank was drowned." He rose, walking closer to Jim. "What happened to the girl, Nigger Jim? She drown, too?"

Jim shook his head. "I don't know 'bout no girl," he squeaked.

Tommy laughed, drinking a little more tea. "Sure you do, Nigger Jim. Why don't you just tell us the truth?" He suddenly kicked out, landing a booted foot into Jim's privates. The man cried out in pain. "You got all big down there for her, didn't you!" Tommy screamed at him. "You saw that pretty blond hair and you wanted to see if all her hair was blond!"

"No! No!" Jim screamed, tears stinging his eyes, nausea flooding him.

"You wanted her so bad I'll bet you killed Hank Toole yourself! You knew the *Jasmine* was in trouble! You grabbed that poor white girl and pulled her off the boat and raped her, you big, black buck! Then you held her in the water and drowned her so's everybody would think the flood did it! And you figured the flood would give you time to run off!"

Tommy landed a hard punch to Jim's ribs. The man groaned, hanging his head, in so much pain he couldn't find his voice. He struggled with his conscience. He had seen River Joe, knew the man from the times Hank had traded with him. Even though what he had seen the night of the killing had made Jim run, he was really only running from something he wished he had never witnessed. He wasn't genuinely afraid of River Joe. He would have turned and talked to him after all if he hadn't slipped into the water. He knew deep inside that River Joe was a good man, that he had probably only been trying to help the white girl.

And that poor girl surely never wanted to be with Hank. Surely River Joe had helped her. If he told these men the truth, they would chase after them and drag that poor girl back to Sam Gates. Jim had no doubts about what happened to the girls who went there. He had seen Emma Simms many times, practically watched her grow up. She wasn't that kind of girl. If he could just protect her a little longer, maybe she and the white Indian would get away.

"They wasn't . . . no girl along," he sobbed, finding his voice again.

"You're a liar, Nigger Jim!" Tommy yelled. "We got ways of makin' niggers talk, and you're gonna talk!" He walked over to the fire, taking out a stick that was red-hot on the end.

"Wait!" Bates jumped up, grabbing the stick away. "We found this nigger! You got no right comin' here and takin' over, Decker! Now you just wait up a minute! This nigger might be tellin' the truth!"

"I'm tellin' you there was a white girl with them!" Tommy answered.

"And I'm tellin' you this nigger is ours to do what we want with. We ain't gonna get near as much for him if we drag him back all beat up and injured!"

Tommy guzzled the rest of the tea and threw aside the cup. "And what do you suggest, mister?"

"I suggest first of all that if you want to share this camp and eat our food, you leave our nigger alone. And the other thing I suggest is that we wait and take him to Knoxville— to this Sam Gates you mentioned. If Hank Toole did business with him, maybe he'll know what to do. And maybe Hank Toole and the girl—if she was with him at all—survived. Maybe it's the way the nigger told it. If it is, he don't know for sure if this Hank Toole drowned at all. And maybe

he's just too scared to tell the truth about the girl bein'
along! Now I say we go to Knoxville and see if Hank Toole
and this girl ever showed up! If they did, Toole might pay
good money for us bringin' back his nigger! I don't expect
he'd be too happy about us bringin' the man back half-dead,
now, would he?"

Their eyes held challengingly, then Tommy sighed. He
shook his head and turned away. "You're gonna feel like a
fool when we get to Knoxville and find out Hank ain't
there," he told Bates. "I'm tellin' you that girl was along.
And if Nigger Jim is denyin' it, it only means there's some
foul play goin' on. And considerin' it involves that big nigger and a pretty, blond-haired white girl, there ain't too
many conclusions a man can come to!"

"Maybe not. But I ain't gonna maim this nigger when he
might be worth a lot of money! And if the girl belonged to
this Sam Gates, I say it's his business what to do about all
this. We'll take the nigger to Knoxville and you two are
welcome to come along, as long as you don't beat on him
anymore and you promise to pull your own load. Otherwise,
get out of this camp!"

Tommy stood there panting with rage, looking from Bates
to Williams to Jim, then to Deek. "What do you say, Deek?"

Deek pushed back his floppy hat and scratched his head.
"I think Bates there has a point, Tommy. Why not get some
money out of this if we can? A healthy nigger is worth a lot
more than one who's all broken up inside. If this Sam Gates
wants to set the whip to him to get the truth, let him do it.
We ain't got the right. And if Hank is still alive, he'd be
awful angry if we broke up his nigger's bones."

Jim closed his eyes and breathed deeply with relief, praying that Tommy would listen. Most of all he prayed that
Hank would be presumed drowned when he was found,
would be buried and his death reported as another flood ca-
sualty. If the girl got away with River Joe, no one would
ever know whether she really was on the boat. She, too,
would be presumed drowned in the flood. After all, her step-

father's farm had surely been swept away, as well as Luke Simms himself. Jim himself would be sold off to another master, and that would be that.

"I say it all stinks of a nigger rapin' a white girl and gettin' away with it," Tommy sneered. "But if you want to take him to Knoxville first, then that's what we'll do." He glared at Bates. "And don't accuse me of not pullin' my own load! Me and Deek will fend for ourselves. Only reason we'll stay on at all is because I intend to be there when you deliver Nigger Jim and see what kind of story he has for Sam Gates! And you can bet Hank Toole won't be in Knoxville waitin' for us!"

"Maybe he won't. But I ain't takin' that risk," Bates answered. He put out his hand. "Come on now, Decker. We got a lot of miles ahead of us yet. There could be money in this for all of us. No sense makin' the rest of this trip miserable. If you're right, I'll buy you a steak dinner and a round of drinks when we get to Knoxville. You ever been there?"

Tommy softened a little, deciding to shake the man's hand. But his eyes and hand were cold. "No."

They shook hands limply. "Hey, you'll like it," Bates said. "Two young men like yourselves will have a real good time there. Sit down now. I'll get you some more whiskey and we'll talk this all over, try to figure what could have happened. You're just all wound up from that flood and losin' your pa."

Tommy looked over at Jim again. "Maybe." He walked closer to the Negro, his eyes full of hatred. "We'll get the truth out of you, Nigger Jim! You only got till we get to Knoxville, and then you're gonna wish you was dead!"

Jim just stared at him, swallowing back his fear. He had not asked for any of this. If only Hank had not picked up that girl. And if only he had not seen River Joe standing over Hank's body, a knife in his hand. Right now he wished he himself had drowned that night in the river.

◊ *Chapter 12* ◊

Emma lay staring at the stars, which seemed to dance as the branches of trees swayed gently with a night breeze.

"How much farther, River?" She snuggled against him, and he kept a strong arm around her from behind.

"Another week, maybe. Depends if they're still where I left them."

"I sure never dreamed I'd ever live among Cherokoee Indians. Tell me again so I remember—the names of your family."

He grinned, kissing her hair. "My sister Mary is sixteen and Grace is twenty and married to Red Wolf. My brother, Peter, is eighteen. They are all Christian, like my Cherokee mother, who gave all of them their Christian names."

"Are you Christian, too?"

He sighed deeply, rubbing absently at her shoulder. "I am pretty much like my father, Gray Bear. I believe there is one God who rules the universe. Christians call Him the Christ. I call him *Esaugetuk Emissee*, Maker of Breath. The teachings of the missionaries who came to us were not so different from what we already believed, and the way the *Unega* conducts his life, I see very little Christianity sometimes in those who say they are Christian. At least the Cherokee practice what they believe. There are times when I wish I were not white at all."

"What is *Unega?*"

"White man."

She thought for a moment. "I don't know much about God and Christianity and all those things. Mrs. Breckenridge taught me some, and sometimes I close my eyes and I pray real hard to God. Since being with you I think of Him as the Maker of Breath, like you call Him. I think you're right. I think everybody has the same God. They just call Him by different names." She turned slightly, kissing his shoulder. "You really think of Mary and Grace and the others as your family, don't you?"

"They are all I remember. I have just a faint memory of my white parents, and I only remember my mother's voice when she was screaming, when those river pirates raped her."

She felt his grip tighten around her.

"Is that why you got so angry at Hank when he attacked me?"

He was quiet for several seconds. "Partly. And partly just because I wanted you myself. I knew you were a good person and he had no right hurting you."

"Did you cry, River—when the Cherokee found you and took you away, and you knew your parents were dead?"

He sighed deeply. "I no longer remember. All I know is Lily Gray Bear took me in and raised me, and then Grace and Mary and Peter were born and they were like brother and sisters. I learned to read and write from missionaries. By the time they came I had forgotten much of what I already knew, and wasn't even speaking English anymore. They tried to take me away from Lily once, but I put up such a fuss that they let me stay."

He rolled onto his back and stretched. "There have certainly been many times since to shed tears. I felt a great loss when Lily died of cholera . . . and then just a few days later Yellow Sky died." His voice dwindled. "No one avoids tears in such moments, not even grown men."

He lay there quietly for a long time, and she turned and lay snuggled into his shoulder. How she loved this man who was capable of feelings, capable of weeping when he mourned. At the moment she too felt like crying.

"Do you love me the same, River? Would you cry over me?"

He squeezed her closer, fingering her golden tresses with his other hand. "Oh, yes, *Agiya*, I would weep for you. I never want to feel that kind of loss again. You have no idea what went through my mind when I heard that gunshot when you killed that boar."

An owl hooted somewhere nearby, and she realized how frightened she would be if she were alone. But when lying next to River, she felt no fear. A campfire burned nearby, and occasionally the direction of the breeze would change and she would get a whiff of smoke.

"I wonder if the *Jasmine* has been found, River."

"I am sure it has by now."

Another moment of silence passed, and she felt his hold tighten again. Yes, he was worried, too. He just didn't want to talk about it.

"I hope Luke is dead. And Tommy, too. Do you think it's bad to wish somebody dead?"

"No," he answered firmly. "They were evil. Do not feel bad about their deaths, any more than I feel bad about killing Hank Toole. He deserved to die."

"I know. But if they figure it out, the authorities won't think that way."

"I do not care what they think. Besides, we will not be found where we are going, at least not right away. I have to get these supplies to my family. Then we will decide what to do. If it looks like there is going to be trouble, we will leave."

"But where would we go?"

"I do not know yet. Indian Territory, maybe. Maybe that new land called Texas where the Mexicans are allowing Americans to settle."

"Texas? I never heard of Texas."

"The Cherokee have. Some have already gone there and

to Indian Territory. They know that eventually there will be big trouble here. Those who do not leave voluntarily will have a hard time of it if they are forced out. They know how bad the white men can be."

"Why don't they all just go then?"

He sighed deeply, toying with her hair again. "That is where you have to let go of your white spirit and think like a Cherokee, Emma. The whites do not understand what this land means to my people. This land is their mother. You do not desert your mother. This land is sacred, and these mountains have been home to them for hundreds of years, maybe thousands. The Maker of Breath meant for the Cherokee to live in this land, not the white man. Most of them will fight to the death for it, only through John Ross they are carrying on that war through the courts. The only trouble is there probably will be death anyway. There already has been—at the hands of raiders. But there will be more if the Cherokee are forced out of this land. It will be a sad journey."

He turned over and kissed her cheek. *"Egasinee, Agiya,"* he said, telling her to go to sleep. "We have a long ride tomorrow."

She kissed his chest. "I don't ever want to be away from you, River. I would be so afraid if I weren't with you. I hope I never have to go back to the world I came from."

"You will not go back. And you will not be without me. Life will be good now."

She settled against him, quickly falling asleep, for she never doubted that she was safe in his arms.

People stared as four men rode into Knoxville with a Negro walking behind them, his hands tied behind his back and ropes tied around his waist.

"Must be a runaway," came the low voices.

"Hey, isn't that Nigger Jim?" someone said. "Maybe *he* killed Hank Toole."

Tommy slowed his horse and turned it, riding up to the man who had made the remark. "What did you say, mister?"

The man removed his hat. "Isn't that Nigger Jim, Hank Toole's man?"

"Sure is. Did you say Hank Toole's been murdered?"

The man nodded. "That's the rumor we heard. Most folks here in Knoxville knew Hank." The man looked over at Jim, who looked petrified at the words. "Course, we all knew Jim, too. I can't believe he'd kill Hank—seemed like a good nigger to me."

"There ain't no such thing as a good nigger or a good Indian," Tommy sneered. He looked over at Jim victoriously, then back at the man with whom he had spoken. "Them other men over there found the nigger tryin' to run away. We didn't know till now whether Hank Toole was alive or dead for sure. The nigger said he was drowned in the flood."

"Well, the way we heard it, the *Jasmine* was wrecked, all right. But when they found Hank's body, they determined someone had stabbed him to death—a pretty big wound in the chest. There were scratches on his face and he didn't have on any clothes."

Tommy's eyes lit up even more. "Scratches? Like the kind a woman would give a man who was tryin' to attack her?"

The man shrugged. "I don't know. Why don't you go talk to Sam Gates? Hank did a lot of work for the man. Sam owns a big supply store here in Knoxville, as well as a coal mine farther up in the mountains. You can usually find him over at the Tennessee Belle. He owns that, too. It's right up the street. You can see the sign from here. The sheriff has been talkin' to Sam about this whole thing." He looked over at Jim and shook his head. "Too bad. I reckon a man doesn't know who to trust anymore."

Tommy nodded to him and rode back to the others. "You hear that? I *told* you that nigger did it! And I told you there was a girl on that boat!"

Herman Bates sagged a little in defeat. "Well, we've got one question answered. Let's go talk to this Sam Gates."

Tommy looked back at Jim, grinning broadly. "I wouldn't doubt if your neck got stretched by tonight, nigger," he sneered. "You shouldn't have lied."

"But I . . . I didn't! I didn't know about no girl. And I didn't kill Mastuh Hank, I swear!"

Tommy just shook his head and turned his horse. "Let's go." They headed for the Tennessee Belle, as a few more people gathered and stared at Jim, who almost had to run to keep up. He looked worn and hungry as he staggered behind the four men down the dusty street dotted with horse dung.

Tommy took a good look around as they headed for the Belle. He had never been to a place as big as Knoxville. The town was a mixture of log buildings, a fort, and frame houses, some of them quite grand. To a young man from the mountains, this was an exciting place to be. Never had he seen so many people in one spot, or so many stores and liveries and churches and saloons. The town would be even more fun if he and the others got some money for returning Nigger Jim; he was already sure he didn't want to leave.

They approached the Tennessee Belle, a whitewashed building in good repair.

"Don't forget—we found him," Bates said as they dismounted and tied their horses.

"Well, if it wasn't for me and Deek, you wouldn't have known about Hank Toole and Sam Gates and all—or that a girl was along on that boat," Tommy answered. "We deserve a fair share of the reward, if there is one."

"I just want to get this over with and get home," John Williams grumbled.

"Home? Who would want to leave this place?" Deek asked.

"I would," Williams answered.

Tommy and Deek laughed, walking back to Jim and untying the ropes around his waist. "You've got some explainin' to do now, nigger," Tommy warned. "You better think about tellin' the truth now." He gave Jim a shove and the man half-stumbled up the wooden steps and onto the boardwalk. Tommy shoved him again as they all entered the saloon. Men sitting around card tables stared, and pretty women dressed in brightly colored taffeta and silk dresses whispered among themselves.

"We want to see Sam Gates," Tommy said haughtily. "We got somethin' for him."

One of the women looked at Jim disdainfully. "Get that nigger out of here, kid," she sneered. "Sam doesn't allow niggers in here."

"He'll allow this one. You tell him we've got Hank Toole's nigger here—caught him up in the mountains tryin' to run away."

The woman sauntered to a door at the back of the barroom. Tommy watched the sway of her hips, then moved his eyes to drink in the beauty of the others, already deciding this was the place to be. How he wished Emma Simms were here, but now there was the question of what had happened to her. Nigger Jim knew, and, by God, he would tell.

Jim stood near tears, his mind scrambling to think of what to say as a well-dressed man of perhaps his late forties emerged from the back room. His suit was perfectly cut; his vest and the scarf at his neck were silk. He was handsome for his age, with a neat mustache and dark brown eyes. He stuck his thumbs into the pockets of his vest as he approached, pushing back his suit jacket and revealing a gold watch. His black boots were spotless, and he eyed the four men with Jim warily, with the eyes of a man who had a lot of experience in dealing with people. Already he seemed to be measuring the worth of the men who had come to see him. He stepped up to Tommy, studying the bright red hair and the cold blue eyes.

His eyes moved then to the other three, and the air of importance about him kept them speechless, waiting for him to say the first word. The dark eyes moved then to Jim, looking the Negro up and down; then he stepped closer to the man and the room grew quiet with expectancy.

The rumor of Hank Toole's death had already spread through town, and many had been speculating on what could have happened. Sam Gates himself had wondered, especially about the young girl who was supposed to be with Hank on his return trip, the young girl for whom he had paid two hundred dollars.

"Well, Jim. At last we find someone who can help answer all our questions," Gates said then.

A tear trickled down Jim's cheek. He knew Sam Gates could be a cruel man, but he wanted to protect Emma Simms. "Mastuh Sam, I don't got no answers. All's I know is they was a bad flood. We was alone on that boat, I swear. The flood come, and I was washed right off the *Jasmine*, and I never knowed what happened to Mastuh Hank. I supposed he done drowned when the *Jasmine* broke up." The man sniffed. "I run on account of I didn't know what to do, where to go. I was scairt, Mastuh Sam, that's all. But these men, they done brought me back here, and I'll be glad to be you nigguh, Mastuh Sam, on account of I don't got no mastuh now. These men, they is expectin' a reward for bringin' me back."

Gates turned back to the four white men. "I am Sam Gates, as I am sure you have guessed by now. May I have your names?"

"I'm Tommy Decker, from the MacBain settlement up the Hiwassee," Tommy answered quickly, pride in his voice. "This here is my friend, Deek Malone."

Deek removed his hat, nodding his shaggy head. Sam Gates forced a vague smile and looked at the other two.

"I'm Herman Bates, and this is a friend of mine, John Williams. We're from Summersville. The heavy rains wiped us out. Then we found the nigger there sleepin' in the woods. We was gonna take him to a couple of plantations, see if they knew who he was. Then we run into these two young men here who said they knew him. They verified the nigger's story that he worked for a Hank Toole on a steamboat. But we aren't too sure the nigger is tellin' the truth about what happened to this Hank Toole. On our way through town we talked to a man who said Hank Toole was found murdered, not drowned. That true?"

Sam Gates turned and looked at Jim again. "It's true."

"Mr. Gates, there was supposed to be a white girl with Hank," Tommy put in eagerly. "Emma Simms. I knew her. My pa said Hank was pickin' her up on his return trip, which would have been before the *Jasmine* was wrecked. We've already been past her pa's farm and it's wiped out. We found Luke Simms's dead body but no sign of the girl. I think she was with Hank, but nobody has mentioned her, and the nigger says she wasn't on that boat. I think he's lyin', Mr. Gates. I think he raped that girl and maybe drowned her himself. She was a right pretty girl."

"No! No, I swear I didn't do that, Mastuh Gates!" Jim answered, his eyes pleading.

"It all makes sense, Mr. Gates," Tommy added. "They said Hank was found with scratches on him and no clothes on. My guess is he was havin' at it with the girl and she was fightin' him. Nigger Jim come upon them and got all excited seein' Hank layin' with a pretty white girl, so he killed Hank and finished the job himself, then drowned the girl. After a flood, bodies are hard to find. She's probably stuck in a tree someplace."

Sam Gates walked back to Jim, studying the man with cunning, perceptive eyes. "That true, Jim? You're already in trouble. You might as well tell us."

"No, suh. It ain't true."

"Hang him!" one of the men at the tables shouted. "If he messed with a white girl he ought to hang high, with no trial!"

"Cut off his privates first!" another put in.

Jim shook visibly as Sam Gates turned to the men in the room, putting up his hands. "Now, now, boys, we don't know if it's true Hank had a girl with him. But we do know

Hank was found murdered, and this nigger was found trying to run away. All of you enjoy yourselves. I'll take Nigger Jim back to my office and call for the sheriff. We'll get this straightened out."

Gates turned to Tommy and the others. "Come into my office and bring the nigger." He turned and walked ahead of them. The others followed, and Tommy grabbed Jim's arm and gave him a shove. Gates gave the piano player a signal and the man started clumping away on the keys again, picking up the mood in the room and distracting the customers from what was going on.

Men returned to drinking and cardplaying as Gates led the others through a door into a hallway, then through another door into a large office that contained a huge oak desk and red leather chairs. The men remained standing as Gates closed the door, then walked up close to Jim, his dark eyes showing his annoyance.

"Where is the girl, Jim?" he demanded, his voice calm but cold. "I know myself that Hank was picking her up. I paid good money for her and I want to know what happened to her. Did you get a yen for that white girl?"

"No! I done told you and told you. Hank didn't pick up no girl!"

Gates's face darkened with anger. He walked back to the door and called out to someone, and moments later a huge, well-built man came inside.

"Take this nigger to the shed out back, Stu. I want to know what happened to Emma Simms."

The man called Stu nodded, walking up to Jim and pulling at his arm.

"No! Wait, Mastuh Sam! Don't take me out there!"

"We've got to have the truth, Jim," Sam said, turning away and telling Stu to have drinks sent in for the four men who had brought Jim to town.

Tommy and the others stared as Jim was dragged outside. Moments later an auburn-haired young woman with painted green eyes brought in a tray of glasses filled with whiskey.

Everyone in the room stared at her billowing breasts as she served the drinks with a fetching smile.

"Thank you, Joanna, honey," Gates said.

Joanna smiled at the man and left. Tommy sipped the whiskey, noticing how smoothly it went down his throat. He had never tasted such good whiskey.

"I will pay all of you well," Sam said. "Jim is an important link to what happened. I believe you about the girl. I bought her myself." He looked slyly from one to the other. "To wait on tables and such."

Tommy grinned. "Sure. We know."

"No. You don't know anything," Sam replied, glaring at him warningly. He stepped closer. "Most men in town know what goes on here, Mr. Decker. It's accepted. But few of them know, including the sheriff, that I buy and sell women, like slaves. That could get me in a bit of trouble." He watched them all closely. "You men know now because of what just happened." He moved his dark eyes to Tommy again. "Since you knew this Emma Simms, you probably know that not all the women I purchase are exactly . . . willing."

Tommy snickered. "That's puttin' it mildly when you're referrin' to Emma Simms!" He swallowed a little more whiskey.

"What's gonna happen to Nigger Jim, Gates?" Williams asked.

Gates sighed deeply. "Oh, Stu has ways of getting the truth out of a man. We'll have the real story before long."

"Serves the nigger right," Tommy sneered.

"Shouldn't we tell the sheriff about this?" Herman Bates asked.

"In time," Gates answered. "We'll get a story out of Jim first." He walked around his desk and sipped his own drink. "You men have to understand that I have to be careful about this. I might have to convince everyone else that there was no white girl aboard the boat. If I can get Nigger Jim hanged for murdering Hank Toole, that will shut the whole thing up.

I will be out one pretty mountain girl, but I might be saving myself some trouble. The girl probably drowned anyway."

Tommy studied his whiskey, while Bates and Williams shifted nervously. There was an air of evil about Sam Gates that made a man uneasy.

"I think she's still alive and run off," Tommy said to Gates. "Emma is a pretty hardy girl." He rubbed absently at his jaw with his free hand. "She can take right good care of herself when she needs to."

Sam Gates shook his head. "No. Nigger Jim is too big of a man. If he raped her, he would have been too scared afterward to let her live. He would have killed her." He frowned. "I know Nigger Jim. Somehow I can't imagine him doing any of that. There is something he isn't telling us. But Stu will get it out of him."

Bates looked at Williams, feeling the ugly implications of the statement. Sam Gates would apparently use any means possible to get what he wanted, including torture. Both men wondered what kind of man they had become involved with, and both wished they had simply taken Nigger Jim to a plantation owner as they had first intended to do.

Bates felt a growing resentment for Tommy Decker. This was all his idea. There he sat, swallowing his whiskey, carrying on a conversation with Sam Gates as though he actually liked him, but in the few minutes he had been in the room with Gates, Bates had seen nothing to like or to trust. An almost cold evil seemed to emanate from Sam Gates, and he had sent Nigger Jim off to be tortured, without showing an ounce of feeling.

Bates didn't care a bit for Nigger Jim himself, but the strangely cold and threatening air about Sam Gates bothered him. What kind of man bought and sold young girls like slaves? What happened to those girls? Surely not all of them were willing in the beginning to do the kind of work Gates expected of them.

Stu finally returned, knocking on the door first, then darting inside and walking directly up to Gates. "He finally admitted there was a white girl on the boat," he said to Sam.

"I knew it!" Tommy sneered triumphantly. "Did he kill her?"

Stu sighed, keeping his eyes on Sam Gates. "It's a real strange story, sir. Nigger Jim says Hank attacked the girl. Jim heard her screamin' and all and then the *Jasmine* started breaking up. He went to Hank's cabin to ask him what to do, and he saw the girl lying on the floor, moving around, plenty alive all right. And he saw Hank, too, lying on his back, all covered with blood, already stabbed, it looked like. He says he's sure Hank went up there to rape the girl, and she must have fought him. But the strangest thing is, Nigger Jim says when he got there, there was a big man standing over Hank with a knife in his hand—called him the white Indian."

Tommy felt the chill of surprise and sudden awareness move through his blood. His eyes widened. "River Joe!" he exclaimed. He looked at Deek. "River Joe!" he repeated.

"We should've thought of that before!" Deek answered.

Sam Gates frowned. "I've heard of this River Joe—a white man raised by the Cherokee."

"He caused trouble up at the Gillmore settlement over a white girl," Deek said, his eyes lighting up.

"And more trouble at our place," Tommy added. He looked at Sam Gates. "The white Indian and Hank Toole argued over what Hank was gonna pay him for some skins, too! He must have gone after Hank—then decided to take not only Hank's money but the girl, too! He's got Emma! That goddamned River Joe killed Hank, and he has Emma!"

Sam Gates's eyes seemed almost black with rage. "Then he has stolen my property," the man almost growled. "And he killed one of my best suppliers." He startled them all when he turned and threw his whiskey glass against the wall, shattering it. "No one messes with Sam Gates like that," he snarled. "No one!"

* * *

"Are we going to climb forever, River?" Emma stopped to catch her breath. They had dismounted from the horses to relieve them of some of their weight. It seemed to Emma they had been climbing for days through colorful rocky canyons and thick groves of shady trees. "Seems like we're headed straight to heaven."

"In some ways we are," he called back.

She looked up to see he had reached a flat area and stood grinning down at her. "Come up here and look," he said. "We will rest here."

She put a hand to her pounding heart, taking a deep breath of the thinner air, and started upward again.

"We're lucky. The haze that usually hangs around the Smokies is gone today. You've got some view now, Emma."

She reached the top and turned. River Joe reached out and pulled her close, encircling her shoulders with one arm while he pointed with the other hand to what appeared as just an odd dot on the vast horizon below them. "Way out there . . . that's Knoxville."

Her eyes widened and her mouth fell open. Never in her young life had she seen anything like the sight before her now. She could not imagine how far she was seeing. The whole world was before her, and she shivered at the sight.

"Oh, River, it's beautiful! It's like . . . like we're close to God Himself."

"The Maker of Breath is very powerful here," he said reverently. "From here He watches over all of us. Here He is close to the birds and the heavens. The tops of the mountains are his throne. Up here my people are themselves stronger. They feel the peace of being closer to *Esaugetuh Emissee.*"

"Are we close to the village now?"

"Yes. Very close. Perhaps tomorrow we will be there."

She squeezed closer to him. "I hope they like me, River."

"I have no doubt they will love you."

She drew a deep breath, feeling like crying at the view. "How far can we see, River?"

"It is hard to say. Some claim that from this particular point one can see for hundreds of miles." He pointed again. "Way, way down there—perhaps forty or fifty miles—that is where your farm was, and the other settlements along the Hiwassee."

"I can see a little ribbon of water. Is that the river?"

"Yes. It is the Tennessee River."

"And that little spot is Knoxville?"

"Yes. It is maybe sixty or seventy miles, but not so far from where you once lived if you go by river. Through the mountains it is more difficult. No matter how one tries to get up here, it is difficult and dangerous. That is why the Cherokee have retreated so far. It is much safer up here."

"I wonder what is happening down there, River, and worrying. I wonder who is left alive. And I can't help wondering about Hank Toole—if they found him and all."

He gave her a squeeze. "We are not going to think about it for now. My people's village is very hard to find. Even if someone figures out what happened, it would be a long time before we were found. And we might even be gone from this place by then. For now we will go to my people and wait to see what happens. We are going to be happy, *Agiya*. This I promise."

She turned and hugged him fully. "Let's make camp right here, River. It's so beautiful."

He grinned, rubbing her shoulders. "All right. If that is what you want."

"It is." She looked up at him. "And I want to make love, right up here on top of the world, close to God and the clouds. Up here it's like we're the only two people in the whole world!"

His eyes looked sad as he smiled, for he, too, was wondering what had happened below. "How I sometimes wish that we were," he answered, coming down and meeting her mouth. How he loved her! How he prayed they would be left alone.

Sam Gates puffed quietly on an expensive cigar, eyeing Tommy and the others, who had waited for Gates's volatile temper to cool.

"I don't want this to go to the sheriff or to the public, because of the girl," Gates said finally.

"What are you going to do about Nigger Jim, sir?" Stu asked.

Gates sighed deeply. "He's going to hang for killing Hank Toole."

Tommy frowned. "But River Joe did it."

Gates nodded. "I want everything about the girl kept quiet. This is a lucrative business I have here, Mr. Decker." His eyes shifted to the other three. "If Nigger Jim talks, he might tell everyone Hank was bringing the girl to me, against her will. Nigger slavery is one thing. The slavery of young white girls is something else. I want Nigger Jim brought forward—gagged." He looked at his hired man. "Stu, I want you to stir up a crowd—tell them Nigger Jim killed Hank and confessed to it. I want him hanged by to-night. I will do my own investigating into what happened to the girl." His eyes darkened with revenge. "No one steals what belongs to Sam Gates," he sneered. "I paid good money for that girl, and I am going to find her, *and* this man called River Joe. I want him dead!"

"Let me find them for you, Mr. Gates!" Tommy blurted. "I've scoured the mountains a lot of times looking for the Cherokee. Me and Deek both have raided their settlements. If Emma Simms is with River Joe, it's a sure bet he took her back to the Cherokee with him!"

Gates watched him intently for a moment, then slowly nodded. "That might be a good idea. You know this Emma. You would recognize her."

Tommy's blue eyes lit up with hatred. "And I've got a score of my own to settle with River Joe," he added.

Sam laid his cigar in an ashtray and leaned forward on his desk, studying all four men. "I'm paying all of you for going to the trouble of bringing Nigger Jim to me. But only on the condition none of you tells the truth. All of you must go along with the story that Jim killed Hank. Whoever changes his story—I'll have his head on a platter. Understood?"

They all nodded.

"I just want to get my money and go back home," Herman Bates said. He didn't like this Sam Gates at all. He felt very uncomfortable in his presence, sure that if the man threatened to have his head on a platter if he talked, he meant every word—literally.

"Same here," Williams added.

"Not me!" Tommy put in. "I'm stayin' in Knoxville—except for leavin' to find River Joe and that girl."

"Do what you want," Bates replied. "I don't want none of it." He turned his attention to Sam Gates. "You got any idea the kind of man this boy is goin' up against? River Joe ain't somebody to mess with. Findin' Hank's dead body proves that. If he's involved in this, I aim to get out of it right now. If Tommy here wants to try to go after that man, he's welcome to it."

Sam shrugged. "Fine. Go outside and wait for me at the bar. I'll pay you in a few minutes."

Both Bates and Williams nodded and turned to leave. "You go after River Joe, you'll regret it, son," Bates stopped to tell Tommy on the way out.

Tommy almost shook with eagerness. "It's River Joe who's gonna regret somethin'!" he answered. "He'll regret he ever set eyes on Emma Simms!"

Bates just shook his head and went out with Williams, closing the door behind them.

Sam Gates turned his attention to Tommy. "You really think you can find this River Joe and the girl?"

"I know I can!" Tommy answered. He looked at Deek. "With me, Deek?"

Deek sighed, running a hand through his hair. "I reckon. Lord knows we've gone after the Cherokee enough times. But I don't know about goin' after River Joe in particular. Makes me a mite uneasy, Tommy."

Tommy's eyes smoldered. "Not me. I got too much hatred in me to worry about it." He looked back at Sam Gates. "How much does it pay, Mr. Gates?"

"Three hundred dollars each, plus a hundred dollars for bringing Nigger Jim to me, as well as all the supplies you need for your trip into the mountains."

"Whooeee!" Tommy whistled. Sam Gates smiled, realizing the money would sound like a king's ransom to a mountain boy like Tommy. He was getting off cheap. "That pretty little girl must mean a lot to you," Tommy observed. He leaned forward. "Truth is, Mr. Gates, you made a hell of a deal on that one. She's got everything you could want in a woman."

Gates turned to pace the room. "I don't care about that anymore, Decker. It's the principle of the thing now. This man called River Joe took something that belongs to me. I don't like that."

Tommy snickered. "I wouldn't like it either." He grasped the back of a chair. "When do you want us to leave, Mr. Gates?"

"Wait a day or two. Let this all blow over. The public will think Nigger Jim killed Hank Toole, and that will be that. Then you can leave. If you find this River Joe, you can leave him dead or bring him to me alive. Finding an alibi for killing him should certainly be easy enough. No one is going to care, since he might as well be Cherokee. And he sounds dangerous. On second thought, it might be best to kill him straight away. All I really want is that damned girl, and *definitely* alive. She'll learn not to run away from Sam Gates!" The whole room seemed to smolder with Gates's anger. "Be sure to bring her in quietly. I don't want anyone connecting her or River Joe with what has happened here today." He puffed on his cigar, staring at a picture of a naked woman on the wall. "I'll teach the little bitch one hell of a lesson."

Tommy grinned at the remark as Gates turned his eyes to the man called Stu. "Go get Nigger Jim. Gag him and tie him and take him out into the street. It won't take long to get a crowd up against him. Even the sheriff will agree he should be hanged."

He brushed at his satin vest, looking back at Tommy. "As of now, you work for me, Mr. Decker. But you do things the way I say."

Tommy nodded, grinning. "Yes, sir. Deek, too?"

Gates moved his eyes to Deek. "I suppose, if he can take orders and keep his mouth shut."

"Yes, sir, I can."

Gates looked at Tommy again. "How easy do you think it will be to find this River Joe and the girl? You think she's really still alive? Would she go with him willingly?"

Tommy remembered River Joe's words the night he was held prisoner at the MacBain settlement. "I got a feelin' she's *very* willin', sir. As far as findin' them, it might be easy, and then again it might not. Them Cherokee are real tricky, and they've gone higher up into the mountains."

Gates picked up his cigar again. "I am a patient man, Mr. Decker; I have a long memory and I hold grudges. If it took you three years, I would still want that girl. She belongs to me. By then she might not even be of any use to me, but I would want her anyway. I am very jealous and selfish of what is mine. There are uses even for women who are no longer . . . unspoiled, shall we say?"

Their eyes held; they were two men with equal disregard for human emotion or human rights. The only difference between them was age and wealth. Sam Gates needed someone just as unfeeling as he was, and he quickly discerned Tommy to be such a man. He put out his hand. "Good luck, Mr. Decker."

Tommy shook the man's hand, his eyes glittering with eagerness, his smile wide with anticipation. Now Emma Simms would *really* pay!

"Thank you, sir," he answered. "I'll find her. And it won't take no three years, I can promise you that!"

Gates nodded. "I hope you're right. Go on out and order yourself drinks on the house," he said. "I'll join you soon. And remember, keep your mouths shut."

Tommy grinned. "Yes, sir." He grabbed Deek's arm and left the room, excited to be working for an important man like Sam Gates, even happier over the prospect of hunting down Emma Simms.

Gates looked at Stu. "Those other two men who were with them. Pay them off and let them go. But once they're out of town, I want them killed. They know too much."

Stu nodded. "Yes, sir. I'll arrange it."

Stu left, and Sam Gates relit his cigar, staring again at the picture of the nude woman. His anger over someone else running off with Emma Simms smoldered in his gut as hot as the fiery tip of his cigar. If he ever got his hands on this Emma Simms, she would pay dearly for running off on him. And River Joe might as well consider himself a dead man.

◊ *Chapter 13* ◊

Emma drew in her breath when a dark man wearing a turban, buckskin pants, and a striped cotton shirt approached them. He carried a musket, and he called out to River Joe in a language Emma did not understand. But she had heard

enough sweet words from River Joe to recognize the Cherokee tongue, and to know that these were words of greeting.

River Joe answered, riding forward while Emma drew her
horse to a halt. The two men reached out for each other,
clasping wrists in a happy greeting. Emma realized the other
man was most certainly a Cherokee Indian, and also she
could see now that he was hardly any older than she. River
Joe finally turned to her, grinning. She reddened when the
young Indian grinned broadly, and she realized they were
discussing her. The younger man walked toward her, greeted
her in Cherokee, then put out his hand to her.

"I am Peter," he said in English. "And I am very happy to
know my brother has taken another wife. I do not think he
could have chosen a prettier young woman in all of Tennessee. I think I am jealous."

Emma reddened still more. "I guess I should say thank
you, Peter. I'm glad to meet you. River has told me so much
about you." She took his offered hand and he squeezed hers
lightly.

"River? This is what you call him?"

"Yes."

Peter laughed and released her hand. "It is nice. It makes
him special to you. That is good. Names are very important.
We all call him Joe. To you he is River."

Emma looked at River Joe, who was grinning proudly.
"The village is where I left it," he said to Emma. "We are
near it now. Peter was out hunting and scouting for raiders."
He looked at Peter. "There are no raiders nearby, Peter. We
have come all the way from the Hiwassee, and no one has
followed. There was a very bad flood down there—wiped
out a lot of villages. For a while people will be too busy to
think about hunting the Cherokee. They have enough on
their hands just surviving."

Peter nodded. "I would not wish such misfortune on anyone, but I cannot say I am not glad for the flood. Let us go
to the village then. Mary and Grace will be so happy to see

you! You have brought many supplies? We are very much in need of sugar."

"I brought what I could—plenty of sugar, I think. But I got cheated this year. The one called Hank Toole would not give me a fair price for the skins I brought him. So I could not buy as much." He sobered. "And I am afraid I am in some trouble, Peter. I will tell you about it later. If it brings trouble to the village, Emma and I will leave."

Peter scowled. "What have the white settlers done, Joe?"

River Joe looked at Emma and sighed deeply, moving his eyes back to Peter. "Let's go into the village first and get settled. My new wife is very tired. And she is nervous about meeting all of you. She has never been around the Cherokee before. She knows only the lies and half-truths she has been told by others."

Peter took the reins of Emma's horse. "Then she will soon learn the truth," he said to his white brother. He looked back at Emma. "You will find we are not the monsters the white man says we are," he said.

He walked off, leading her horse, and River Joe rode beside her. He reached out and squeezed her hand, then both of them ducked to avoid some low-hanging branches. River Joe let go of her hand when they broke through into a clearing where several small log houses sat in a row, with a few more scattered here and there. Men and women all seemed busy, either hoeing gardens, cleaning hides, chopping wood, or tending fires.

Emma's heart pounded with excitement, as dogs ran up to them, barking at the hooves of the horses. Nearly everyone stopped what they were doing and walked or ran toward them, some shouting to River Joe in English, some in Cherokee. Most of them stared at Emma, and many seemed to be asking River Joe questions. Peter made some kind of announcement, and there were gasps and "ooohs" and stares, and some pounded River Joe's horse or his leg as though congratulating him.

Emma was surprised at the neatness of the village. It was

laid out much like the villages she knew, and everything was tidy. The people who surrounded her were clean and handsome, many of them dressed the way any white man would dress except that most of the men wore turbans. Most of them offered bright, welcoming smiles, and when she recognized that there was no animosity on their part, her fears vanished. She seemed to be a sudden celebrity, and it felt so good compared to her obscure, brutal life on the farm.

"Joe, you are back!"

A young girl ran toward him then, a shapely, beautiful girl who could be no older than Emma herself. Her long, dark hair hung neatly to her waist, and River dismounted when she came close. He swept her up in his arms and hugged her, and Emma felt a fierce jealousy at the thought of Yellow Sky, the Cherokee girl he had loved and who must have been as beautiful as the young girl she was watching now.

She reminded herself that River Joe would hate it if she showed jealousy. She had to be mature enough now to avoid such silly feelings. After all, she was River Joe's wife, his chosen one. What was there to be jealous of? And her desire to be friends with these people whom River Joe loved overwhelmed any jealous feelings she might have.

Now River Joe was reaching up for her. She let him lift her down, and people gathered in a circle while River Joe kept one arm around the young Cherokee girl and the other around Emma.

"Emma, this is Mary, my sister. She is the same age as you are." He looked at Mary and spoke to her in Cherokee. Emma watched as Mary's brilliant smile faded slightly in curiosity, then returned.

"Wife! You are Joe's wife!" Her eyes moved over Emma appreciatively. "It is no wonder Joe picked you. You must be the most beautiful white girl in the valley. Emma? That is your name?"

Emma nodded. "Yes." She squeezed Mary's hands. "I am so happy to meet you, Mary. River has told me so much about all of you, and he kept telling me I would be welcome here. But I was afraid, until now."

"River?" Mary looked up at her brother, then back to Emma. "That is what you call him?"

Emma nodded. Mary breathed deeply and seemed to blinking back an urge to cry. "That is nice. You call him something different. That makes him special." She swallowed. "And he is . . . very special." She tossed her head. "Come!" She yanked at Emma then, running off with her. "We will be such good friends, Emma!"

Emma looked back at River Joe, who only smiled and shook his head. He took hold of both horses and followed, answering a barrage of questions from the others as Emma followed Mary breathlessly toward a tidy log cabin that had flowers growing all around it.

"The whole village will gather together to build a cabin just for you and Joe," Mary said. "For now you must live with Grace and Red Wolf, as I do. Peter, he stays here only part of the time. Mostly he sleeps outside, and our father, Gray Bear, he shares a cabin with another old widow man."

The girl charged though the door without knocking, and a pretty young woman looked up from kneading bread. "Grace, Joe is back!" Mary exclaimed. "And look what he has brought! A wife! And she is white!"

Grace just stared and blinked at first, then a look of surprise came over her face, followed by joy. "A wife!" Quickly, she wiped her hands on a towel and came around the table, a streak of flour showing at the temple against her black hair. "A wife!" she repeated. She looked Emma over. "Mary, look at her! Her hair is golden, and her skin . . ." The young woman put a dark finger to Emma's face. "So fair!" She clasped her hands. "You are very beautiful, wife of River Joe. What are you called?"

"I am Emma."

Grace smiled, and Emma was impressed by her warmth and beauty.

"My husband, Red Wolf, he is off hunting," Grace said.

"He will be back by nightfall." She put her hands to her face and looked around the cabin. "Oh, I wish I had known you were coming! I am not prepared!"

"It's all right, Grace. It's so good just being here. I'll help all I can. Please don't fuss or anything. River and I . . . we can sleep outside. In fact, we've been doing it for a couple of weeks now. I don't mind, really."

Grace looked at Mary. "Did you hear? A white girl who is willing to sleep under the stars!" She looked back at Emma. "You must be very brave and strong, besides being so beautiful. Joe would not have chosen a white girl if he did not see many strengths in her. What a lucky man, to find one who is also so beautiful!"

Emma blushed, feeling almost uncomfortable under the constant compliments. "Thank you, ma'am."

"Ma'am!" Grace looked at Mary again and they both laughed lightly. "A white girl who calls me, a Cherokee, ma'am!" They both laughed again.

Emma felt her cheeks going crimson. "Did I . . . did I say something wrong?"

"Oh, no! But we are not used to hearing respectful words from a white person, except for Joe; but he is like a Cherokee, so he does not count," Mary answered.

River Joe came inside then and Grace ran to him, throwing her arms around him. An older Indian man followed him inside, standing straight and somber near the doorway and carefully scrutinizing Emma.

"Joe, I am with child! I am finally with child!" Grace was telling River Joe. "Red Wolf is so happy."

"I am glad for you, Grace." They exchanged more words in Cherokee then, and Emma gathered he was telling her about the poor trading this trip. She felt awkward, aware of the old man at the door who continued to stare at her without smiling. He was tall and very wrinkled, but carried a lingering handsomeness and a hardness about his body that hinted he had been very strong in his youth. Finally River Joe turned to the old man and took his arm, bringing him forward and saying something to him in Cherokee and nodding to Emma. Then he said Emma's name.

"This is my Cherokee father, Gray Bear," he said to Emma. "He speaks very little English."

Suddenly the old man broke into a grin that soothed Emma's pounding heart. He put his hands on her shoulders and spoke to her in Cherokee, then leaned forward and touched each cheek with his own.

"Gray Bear welcomes you," River Joe said. "He says you are beloved because you are my chosen." Joe sensed her acute nervousness and moved to her side, putting a supportive arm around her. Proudly he made an announcement in Cherokee, to which they all responded with apparent admiration in their voices, and Gray Bear stuck out his chest and patted her shoulder.

"I told them that you killed a wild boar with one shot from my musket," River Joe said to Emma then.

Emma smiled, feeling better by the minute. River Joe asked that they all gather around one table for supper, so that he could tell them the whole story of how the Maker of Breath led him to Emma Simms and why he chose her for his wife. The little cabin seemed filled with excitement, and Mary grabbed Emma's hand and dragged her back outside to introduce her to others and to tell each person about Emma's killing a wild boar.

Never in her life had Emma Simms Rivers felt so welcome; nor had she ever felt so much love and attention. It was as though she had walked into a brand-new world, far from the ugliness she had known at the foot of the mountains. She had left a different Emma back there, an Emma full of fear and hopelessness, an Emma with no future. Here she had a whole new family, people who treated her as people should treat one another, and she had found gentleness in a man.

As Mary dragged her around, introducing her, all she could think about was the cabin Mary had said would be built for her and River, one she could fix up herself and keep tidy with no drunken Luke Simms to rant and rave and break things. A little cabin where she and River could be alone and make love whenever they felt like it, every morning and every night and maybe even in the middle of the day.

"Soon you will have a baby, yes?" Mary asked excitedly. "A child for Joe! He wants a child so much." She stopped and looked Emma over as though she were trying to determine what it must be like to be River Joe's woman. "You love him very, very much?"

Emma's eyes teared. "I love him more than my own life, Mary. I had a real unhappy life. River is the first person who has ever truly loved me and been kind to me. I just hope . . . I hope nothing bad comes of it for him."

Mary frowned. "Why should that be?"

"Just . . . I can't say. I have to let River tell you. But I do love him so; I would die without him now, just die!"

Mary smiled more. "I am happy to see your eyes when you speak of him."

"Mary! What are you doing?" Peter asked then, finding them together. "More people want to meet Emma! Come on!"

Mary pulled Emma away, and they were off again. Emma ignored the distant fear that always crept into her bones at the thought of becoming pregnant. River had mentioned it, and now Mary. Surely after all the times she and River had already mated, a baby would start growing in her belly. Would she die as her mother had?

Again she was surrounded by what seemed the entire village. She guessed the crowd to be perhaps a hundred or so people, and she wondered if there were more villages nearby. River had said they were scattered all over the Smokies. She was meeting people whose names she was sure she would never remember right away, when suddenly a strong arm came around her and pulled her away.

"Come on," River Joe said in his soft, commanding voice. He led her to another cabin and they went inside. "This is my father's cabin. He shares it with another old man. They are both outside. We can be alone for a minute." He turned her, gripping her arms and looking down at her. "You are okay?"

She drew a deep breath. "I think so. They're so . . . so full of questions and curiosity. I feel like a strange animal they've never seen before."

River Joe grinned and pulled her close. "I know. But they already like you, Emma. I just figured you needed a minute to catch your breath, and I know you are tired. Grace is fixing up Mary's bed in the loft and I want you to go up there and take a nap before we have supper. At supper you will really get to know the others, and I will tell them the rest—about Hank."

He felt her seem to collapse against his chest then. "Oh, River, they might hate me for bringing you trouble."

He petted her hair. "No, they won't. You did not bring the trouble, Emma, Hank did. They will understand."

"Hold me a minute, River. While we were alone, everything was so peaceful for us. All of a sudden we're surrounded by people."

"Things will quiet down once they have all met you and know the whole story. Soon they will have a cabin built for us and we can be alone again whenever we want to be."

She looked up at him, reaching around his neck. "I hope it doesn't take too long."

He met her mouth in a lingering, sweet kiss, pulling her off her feet and holding her tight against him. "In the meantime we can camp in the woods at night like we have been doing," he said in a near whisper, kissing her eyes. He kissed her once more, then released her so that her feet touched the floor again. "But for tonight I want you to sleep in a real bed in the loft. It has been a long, trying journey. I do not want my new wife getting sick." His dark eyes saddened, and he stroked her cheek with the back of his hand. "I intend to keep this wife for many years. I will not let death take you from me, Emma Rivers, nor anything else."

She smiled, turning her face to kiss the palm of his big

hand. "I'm fine, River, really. I never felt so much love." She met his eyes. "I think they really like me."

"Of course they do. I knew they would. Just be patient with all their questions for the next couple of days. They did not expect River Joe to come back with a wife, a white woman, no less."

He gave her a squeeze, then walked back outside with her amid teasing remarks from his Cherokee friends. Emma was amazed at their friendliness and at how most of them seemed to live very much like whites. River Joe led her back to Grace's cabin and inside where Grace and Mary were busily discussing what they should have for supper.

"Joe, the bed is all ready for her," Grace said.

"Oh, River, I should stay down here and help. I don't need to rest, really."

"You are my wife, and you will rest when I tell you to rest," he answered. "Now you climb straight up that ladder and lie down for a while."

"River, I'm too excited."

"Go." He led her to the loft ladder, and Grace and Mary grinned at each other as he ordered her up to the bed. Emma climbed up the ladder, and suddenly the bed looked very welcome. She pulled off her moccasins and lay down on it, her exhaustion and the strain of the past couple of weeks and all that had happened to her before that tumbling in upon her as she herself tumbled into a thick feather mattress.

Her last memory before sleep overcame her was hearing River Joe's fading words about her suffering a bad head injury from which he feared she might not yet be fully recovered.

Head injury . . . Yes, she still got an occasional headache. It was Luke's fault . . . maybe Hank's. Both of them had hit her. For a moment she remembered the ugliness at their hands, but then River Joe was holding her. Nothing could happen to her now. Nothing. Nothing . . .

* * *

Emma blinked open her eyes to what she was sure was morning sun coming through a tiny window in the loft. It took her a moment to remember where she was, and she turned to see River sleeping beside her. She frowned, rubbing at her eyes, sure she remembered going to sleep before supper. Surely she hadn't been sleeping ever since!

She pushed at River, whispering, "River, wake up."

He stirred, then turned toward her. She realized he was naked, but she still had on her dress.

"River, what time do you think it is? Have they had supper yet?"

He just lay there a moment, slowly opening his eyes, then grinning sleepily and moving closer to put an arm around her and move a leg over her own legs. "It is probably time for breakfast," he said softly.

"Breakfast!" She sat up. "River, you didn't let me sleep straight through!"

"Of course I did. Every time I came up here to check on you, you were sleeping so soundly I did not have the heart to wake you." He pulled her back down.

"Oh, but they'll think I'm weak—"

He laughed lightly, moving then to kiss her. "They know better," he said. "We all had a good talk over supper. They know what you have been through. You deserve a good rest."

She met his eyes, putting a hand to his chest. "They know about Hank, then?"

The joy left his eyes. "They have to know, so they can keep watch." He pushed some of her hair back from her face. "It is possible someone will come looking for us." He saw the panic in her eyes. "I just want you to realize it, Emma, that's all. It is just like I said before. It is possible no one is left who would even connect me to Hank's death, or who knew you would be on that boat. But if they do happen to figure it out, the first place they would look is among the Cherokee. My people keep scouts moving around all the time. If anyone is coming, they will know it, and they will hide us and swear we never came here. We will be all right. We have some time to think about whether we want to stay here or try to go away."

"To Texas?"

"I do not know yet."

"You don't really want to leave Mary and Grace and Peter or your father, do you?"

He sighed deeply, pulling her close. "Not really. But I will if I have to. They say this place called Texas is filling up fast, and so far the country of Mexico is letting more and more settlers go there. The Cherokee have claimed a considerable amount of territory there for themselves."

"A place far away—that would be best, wouldn't it, River? We would be safe there."

"From people here who might be hunting us—yes. But not especially safe. It is a wild, rugged land, Emma. I do not like the thought of taking you there. In such a remote, wild country, life is very hard, Emma, much harder even than here in the Smokies. And the land itself is completely different, hot and arid." He kissed her hair. "We need not go running off to Texas unless we are sure it is the only choice left to us."

She stared at the log beams of the ceiling. "I already like it here, River. I like your family, too. I felt surrounded by love right away. I've never known that before. And I always heard that Cherokee women were mean to newcomers, sometimes beating on them and chasing them away."

He grinned. "Under the old customs, perhaps, if the woman was a captive from another tribe. Most of these Cherokee are Christians, Emma. And you can already see they live very much like whites. No one is going to cast you out. Besides, they know that I love you, so they love you, too. You are a member of the family now."

She met his eyes. "It feels so strange—to have people care." She sat up again. "I'll not let breakfast go by without helping, River. It's bad enough that I missed supper last night." She stood up. "Where can I go take care of personal things?"

His eyes moved over her. "There is a place behind the cabin." He tugged at her dress. "Tonight we will camp in the woods out back and take care of some other personal things."

She smiled and reddened. "Maybe." She tossed her head and turned, and he grabbed her ankle. She let out a little scream and jerked at her foot. "River, let go! I've got to go!"

He laughed lightly and released her to search for her moccasins. They were light and soft, much nicer than her old leather shoes. River had made them for her. As she pulled them on, he lay watching her, the covers pushed down below his waist.

"Just maybe?" he asked.

She stood up, drinking in his masculine perfection. "You know better," she answered, giving him a sly grin. "I wish we were alone right now." She turned and climbed down the ladder, already looking forward to the night to come. They had traveled hard and fast the last few days, aware that they were close to their destination. They had been too tired to make love.

But now they were here. They were home. Already she felt the wonderful fire move through her at the thought of allowing River to take his pleasure with her again, and she was eager now to have their own cabin. Life was going to be good here. She was going to be happier than she had ever been.

◊ *Chapter 14* ◊

Emma felt as though she had been transplanted into a whole new world. She prayed every day and every night to the Maker of Breath that she and River could stay with these people whom she was quickly learning to love and to think of as her own family.

In only days a cabin was erected, and she could not get over the fact that she had a little home all her own. It mattered little to her that it had a dirt floor. The threat of having to pick up and move at any moment kept most of the Cherokee from going to the trouble of laying wood floors. But at least the floor was hard packed. She had a stone fireplace for cooking and warmth in the cold weather, but now in warm weather most of the cooking was done over an open fire outside.

The bed was homemade, the mattress stuffed with leaves and the softest trimmings from pine branches as well as feathers from ducks and geese. For the first time in her young life Emma was building memories that were happy. Mary and Grace had helped her sew and stuff the mattress, trimming branches, plucking fowl, and telling Emma stories throughout the chore, seeming never to mind the work. Stuffing the mattress was a time-consuming project, but Mary and Grace made it fun.

"Did you know that the possum used to have a bushy

tail?" Mary had asked Emma as she stuffed a handful of feathers into the mattress.

Emma frowned. "What? How would you know?"

"Oh, it is one of the many ancient stories of the Cherokee," Mary answered with a sly grin. "The possum once had a fine, beautiful tail and liked to brag about it. Then one day his friend, the rabbit, who was jealous of the possum's fine, long tail, came to invite the possum to a dance. The possum said he would go only if he had a special seat where no one would step on his tail and where everyone could admire it.

"The rabbit agreed, then went to the cricket's house. The cricket was a good barber. The cricket and the rabbit got together and plotted against the possum. The cricket went to the possum and offered to comb and trim his tail so that it would be the most beautiful tail at the dance. The possum agreed, and he lay down and closed his eyes and let the cricket groom his tail.

"Then the possum went to the dance, going out onto the dance floor and bragging about his tail, turning in circles and showing it off. He could not understand why the other animals gasped, then started laughing at him. Then he turned and saw that the cricket had not groomed his tail, but had shaved off all the hair! And he was so embarrassed that he turned over and lay helpless, grinning and speechless.

"That is why today the possum rolls over and lies still and grinning when taken by surprise. The possum's tail hair never grew back, nor did any hair grow on the tails of his descendants. So, to this day, possums have no hair on their tails."

Emma had listened like a child. Then she grinned. "Mary, you're playing a joke on me."

"Oh, no! The Cherokee really believe this! It is the work of the Maker of Breath. I can tell you about the race between the crane and the hummingbird, or about the magic lake, or about how the Milky Way was formed and why the buzzard's head is bare."

Emma giggled and Grace shook her head. "Mary, those

are Cherokee stories. Some we believe and some are for fun. You do not need to fill Emma's head with them."

"Oh, but I want to know. I want to know everything that I can," Emma answered. "Do both of you read? I saw some books in your cabin, Grace. I can read some. Perhaps we could read together and learn more. I want to read better."

"Yes, we read," Grace answered. "The missionaries taught us, in the days when we lived at the foot of the mountains instead of at the top like we do now. Some of our friends and relatives live at New Echota, where they are building schools. Someday we might go there. But this is home to us and for now we are content here."

She looked up from her sewing to meet Emma's eyes. "You are welcome to read the books, and if there are some things you do not understand, perhaps I can help. I am not sure I can read any better than you. We did not have many years to learn before we had to flee higher and leave our missionary teachers behind."

"I had a teacher for a while—a Mrs. Breckenridge. She was real nice," Emma said. "And real pretty. She and her husband used to come around to the settlements to teach the children. I liked her an awful lot. But my stepfather sent her away."

She stuffed in a handful of the soft pine needles into the mattress.

"Your stepfather was very cruel, Joe tells us," Grace answered.

Emma reddened. Had he told them Luke had sold her to Hank to be used like a harlot? "Yes. I don't miss anything back there, that's sure."

"And Joe is kind to you. He is a good man," Mary said. "Soon you and he will share this mattress. . . ." Her voice trailed off for a moment. "What is it like, Emma, to be with a man?"

"Mary!" Grace said chidingly, and Mary blushed, obvious in spite of her dark skin.

Emma felt the color coming to her own cheeks, and she

stared at the bright patchwork design of the material they had sewn together for the mattress.

"I don't mind," she answered softly. "I used to wonder, too." She swallowed. "It's . . . it's beautiful," she said. "I never thought it could be like that, but it is." She looked at Mary. "I hope you find somebody who makes it wonderful for you, Mary. You told me the boy Martin Crow wanted to court you. I bet he would be a good husband. I've noticed how he looks at you."

Mary smiled bashfully. "He wants to marry me."

"Mary! You have said nothing to us about this," Grace said.

Mary shrugged. "I was not sure what you would think."

"You know that we like Martin. You tell him that if he wishes to marry you he should be speaking to his aunt, who should then speak to me, since you have no aunt to whom she can go. Then we will set the bowl of hominy outside the cabin. It is up to you whether you give him permission to eat it when he comes by and asks."

"A bowl of hominy? What does that have to do with getting married?" Emma asked.

"The young man comes by and asks if he may eat of it," Grace answered. "If Mary tells him yes, it means she accepts his proposal of marriage. Then they begin living together. The man must prove his hunting abilities and the woman her cooking abilities. The man builds the woman a house, and she has one year to decide if she is happy being with him. After that she may leave him if she chooses, and the house is hers."

That had all been several days ago. Now the mattress was finished. Emma approached her new bed, leaning over and pushing on the mattress.

"Looks inviting," River said. He sat in a homemade chair at their pine table, smoking a corncob pipe.

Emma turned to him. "Did you know that by Cherokee custom, I could kick you out after a whole year, and this house would be mine and we wouldn't be married anymore?" she asked.

He grinned slyly. "I know. I just never bothered to tell you. Are you already thinking of getting rid of me?"

She folded her arms. "Oh, I don't know. I'll give you a little more time."

He set aside the pipe, then rose to sweep her up in his arms and hold her over the bed. "Well, while you're doing that, I'll take advantage of my husbandly rights."

She laughed as he dropped her on the bed. He raised her legs and pulled off her moccasins, running his hands up her legs and over her hips, grasping her bloomers and pulling them off. "We have to try out this fine bed," he said with a grin.

"River! It's the middle of the day. And I haven't even put blankets on the bed yet."

He only grinned more as he unbuckled his weapons belt and slung it over the pine bed rail, then unlaced his shirt and pulled it off. She watched as he finished undressing, not really objecting to his sudden desire. She knew he was as happy as she was about their new home.

Emma sat up and unbuttoned the front of her dress, pulling it off her shoulders, keeping her blue eyes on his dark ones as he sat down on the bed and reached behind her hair. He pulled out the combs that held it in a bun.

"I like your hair long and loose," he said. "Wear it free, like the Indian women."

He pulled a piece of it over the front of her shoulder, moving his hand down her hair until the back of his hand touched her breast.

"I am so happy, *Agiya*. Every day you grow more beautiful."

She felt her senses come alive. "'If I do, it's because of your love."

He bent down, kissing her shoulders, laying her back on

the new mattress. He tasted her breasts, pushing up on them first to bring out all their fullness. He lingered at each breast, pulling forth her deepest passions with gentle hands and tongue and lips until her breathing deepened and her eyes closed in pleasure. His hands massaged her belly, then he pulled the dress over her hips and legs and pushed it aside.

She reached up and moved her hands over the hard muscle of his arms. "I can't believe I'm really here, River—your wife, lying on our own bed in our own house. A few weeks ago I had no future and I had never known happiness. Now here I am, River Joe's woman. And Luke or Hank—nobody can hurt me anymore."

"That's right," he said softly, bending down and kissing her belly. She sucked in her breath as his lips moved to the tender crevices where her legs came together, only now they were parting, and she was still surprised that she could allow a man to be so intimate. But with River it seemed so right.

She moved into a world of ecstasy, where all talking ceased and all worries vanished. These were things that one should enjoy with every nerve and every inch of skin and breath and heartbeat. She wondered if she would ever get over the feeling that everything that had happened to her was just a sweet dream—if she would suddenly wake up to find she was still a prisoner on Hank Toole's boat, on her way to some strange man called Sam Gates.

The thought made her sit up toward River as he moved back up to her breasts. She embraced his head, kissing his hair, feeling a trembling desire at his strength and the knowledge of how he could use it against her, but did not. It seemed incredible that a man could be this kind.

"Don't ever go away, River, not ever," she whispered.

He kissed her shoulders, her neck, met her mouth, parting her lips and exploring with his tongue while he pushed her back down on the new bed and guided himself into her depths.

He needed no words to answer her, only this act. He

pushed deep and hard, commanding her passion, ruling her body, just as he had that first time in the shed on her farm. Always he seemed to know just the right touches and moves that sent her reeling into a whole new realm of existence, where one knew nothing but joy and ecstasy, where passion was almost painful and desire was overwhelming.

She felt the lovely pulsation building in her belly until again the wonderful, rippling climax swept over her, making her muscles contract responsively and tighten around her man so that she pulled at him, heightening his own passions and bringing a groan to his lips.

He moved deeper, harder, with a wonderful flowing rhythm that left her limp as he rose to his knees and grasped her under the hips, pushing into her at will, lost in his own world now, his hands clammy against her warm bottom, perspiration making his dark skin glisten.

He drew out the intercourse, bringing her the ultimate satisfaction. She didn't care if he kept it up for hours, it felt so wonderful. But finally his powerful thrusts came quicker, until on one last push he held tight, and she felt the swelling throbbing that told her his life was flowing into her again.

He breathed deeply then, staying inside her but relaxing as he ran big hands over her belly and came down to rest on his elbows, hovering over her. "You make me feel so good, *Agiya*." He kissed her breasts, her shoulders, her lips.

She ran her hands over his broad shoulders. "I'm so happy, River. I have a whole new family."

He grinned. "How does the mattress feel to you?"

She smiled in return, reddening. "I was comfortable."

"So was I. We will get much use out of it." He pulled away from her then and reached down to the foot of the bed, pulling a quilt over them both.

"River, it's too early to go to sleep."

"I know. We will just lie here awhile, enjoying our new bed."

She turned to face him. "River, did you know Martin

Crow wants to marry Mary? If Mary tells him yes, she has a whole year to decide if she wants to keep him."

He grinned, kissing her nose. "Yes, you reminded me of that a moment ago. So how did I do? Do I get to stay in your cabin awhile longer? Will you let me keep sleeping with you?"

She giggled then, reaching up to kiss his chest. "I'll keep you awhile longer. You're a fine-looking man. When I tire of you I'll let you know."

His huge frame hovered over her. "Then I had better take advantage of the time I have left with you, woman."

She traced delicate fingers around his nipples, leaning up then to kiss the hair of his chest. "I suppose you should," she answered. "I could change my mind anytime, you know."

"But I have not yet taught you all the ways to enjoy being with a man," he teased, grasping her hand and licking her palm.

"Teach me, then," she whispered, twisting her hand to clasp his tightly. "Teach me everything, River."

They dug the hiding place none too soon. Everyone joined in digging a hole that would be covered with boards and then chunks of dirt, grass, and branches, where River Joe and his wife could hide if anyone should come looking for them, and it was only a month later when the Cherokee scouts came to River and Emma's door. River was cleaning his musket, getting ready to go hunting, and Emma let the scout, Bear Paw, come inside.

"White men come—only two," he said to River Joe.

Emma put a hand to her stomach, and Joe set aside the musket. "How much time do we have?"

"Only a little."

"What do they look like?" Emma asked, her voice squeaking with worry.

Bear Paw shrugged. "Like white men, except even from a distance, I could see one had very red hair. I never seen such red hair on a man before."

Emma felt faint. "My God!" she whispered, turning her eyes to River. "Tommy! Who else could it be, River! He must still be alive! And they know! They must know."

River Joe rose. "You know the plan," he said to Bear Paw. "Emma and I will hide in the hole. Get my father over here, and an older widow woman who will pose as Gray Bear's wife. They will pretend this is their cabin. My horses are mixed in with the others, and there are two other roan geldings with the herd. They have no way of proving any of them belongs to me."

Bear Paw nodded. "Come. Hurry!" He left, and River Joe walked around to Emma, taking her arm.

"It is going to be all right, Emma," he assured her, feeling her tremble.

Tears came to her eyes. "I prayed so hard he was dead." She started to sob. "Was I bad to pray for that, River?"

"No. Come on now. What did I tell you about being afraid. I am here. Do you think I would ever let Tommy Decker touch you?" He put an arm around her, then grabbed up his weapons belt with pistol and knife before leading her outside to the hole, where Peter stood holding one board aside.

"Quick! Quick!" he said to them.

River Joe let Emma climb down the homemade ladder inside, then followed her. Peter put back the board, arranging more dirt and leaves around it so that nothing showed. Dirt fell through the cracks in the boards and River and Emma ducked their heads. River led her in the darkness to where they found a wooden bench that had been left for them to sit on.

"Sit down now and do not be afraid," River said. He moved his arms around her, realizing she was shivering. "Emma, stay calm." He pulled her close. "You might be pregnant, you know. I do not want you getting all upset and risk losing my baby as well as risking your own health."

She faced him, wishing she could see him better in the almost total darkness. "River! Why do you say I might be going to have a baby?"

He put a big hand to the side of her face. "Emma, we have been together over two months, and I have made love to you practically every day. I find it hard to believe my seed has not taken root in your pretty little belly, and I am perfectly aware that you have not had your time of month since I ran off with you."

A wave of emotion moved through her, and she was glad for the darkness then so he could not see her face. "You mean . . . when a woman doesn't have her time, it means she's going to have a baby?"

He grinned, pressing her head against his shoulder. "You did not know that?"

"No," she whispered.

He kissed her hair. "Sometimes I forget just how innocent you were when I took you away."

She pressed closer, gripping his forearm so tightly it almost hurt him. "River, I can't . . . I mean, I want to have babies for you, but . . . I don't really want to have one . . . inside me . . . I mean, to have to come out of me. What if I lose it, like my mama lost so many? Or what if . . . what if I die when I have it? Maybe I'm made just like mama and I'll die!"

He held her more firmly. "You will not die, Emma. I will not let you die. The Maker of Breath brought us together. He will not take you away from me that way."

They heard horses then, and voices. She clung tightly to him, curling up against his chest when she heard the familiar voice, catching only some of the words—"River Joe . . . white girl . . . came up here . . . my friend Deek . . ."

There were quiet answers from the Cherokee men. Emma covered her ears when she heard Tommy's raised voice, cursing the Indians, demanding to be allowed to search every cabin.

"It's him! It's him!" she squeaked. "It's Tommy and that Deek Malone! Deek is as bad as Tommy!"

"Hush, *Agiya*," River said, holding her tight and rocking her gently. "Think of the baby. Think only of having your own little baby."

How he wanted to break free and kill Tommy Decker! It would be so easy. But it was hard to say who had sent them. Perhaps they had come on their own; but if not, and they were killed, even more would come, looking for Tommy and Deek. That would mean big trouble for the Cherokee. They didn't need any more trouble than they already had.

Apparently for now only Tommy and Deek had come searching. River tried to determine why. To him it only confirmed his suspicion that someone else had sent them. They were sniffing things out, perhaps trying to keep it all quiet, probably for the sake of Sam Gates, who might not want other people to know that he bought and sold young women like slaves.

He could feel Emma's heart pounding against his chest, and it angered him that these men had come and upset her. He had no doubt that she was pregnant; and although he would say nothing to her, he too feared that her mother's problems might be visited upon her. He wanted a child badly, but more than that he wanted Emma alive and well.

They waited for what seemed hours, until finally Peter came and pulled away a board. "You can come up now. They have gone to search other villages. But none of our people has told anyone from other villages that you are here. If someone from another village comes here and finds out, we will tell them they must say nothing."

He stood back as Emma appeared at the top of the ladder. He reached down then and took her arm, helping her up and again admiring River Joe for the beautiful white woman he called his wife. "No Cherokee would betray River Joe," he said to her. "You do not need to be afraid."

Emma turned then, half-collapsing against River's chest and hugging him tightly. "Oh, River, they know! They're looking for us! They'll come back."

"And we will be ready for them, just as we were today," Peter said. "Do not worry, Emma."

She pulled away from River, blinking back tears. "I've brought you so much trouble. I know Tommy Decker. If he finds out, he'll come back and raid your village and do terrible things to you."

Peter tossed his head. "We have been raided many times. If it happens again it will not be your fault. I am not worried." He looked at River Joe and grinned. "It worked! You are safe. Our scouts have been watching. The red-haired one and his friend are moving on in search of another village."

"Did he say why he came? Was it for me and Emma?"

Peter sighed. "I am afraid so. They say you killed a man and stole a white girl who belongs to a man in Knoxville. The man wants her back. The red-haired one has promised to find her."

Emma let out a little groan but River kept an arm around her. "Let him try to get her back!" he growled. "She belongs to no man but me!"

River Joe led Emma back to their cabin, and Emma cried out when they went inside. Clothes had been torn from the homemade dresser. The table was overturned and several dishes were broken, dishes given to them by Grace, who had few to spare. The bed was torn apart, and the mattress that Emma and Grace and Mary had worked on so lovingly was slashed open, its feathers and leaves and branches strewn about.

"Oh, River! River!" Emma broke into tears, and River Joe felt a burning desire to follow Tommy Decker and murder him there and then. But he could not risk getting his Cherokee family in trouble. Instinct told him that Sam Gates was very powerful. Maybe Tommy would not come back. At any rate, he could not run after him, nor could he drag Emma off to Texas now, if she was pregnant.

Mary came inside then, her dark eyes flaming at the sight. She looked up at River Joe. "They did this to almost everybody," she said, hatred in her words. "They are bad!" She put a hand on Emma's shoulder. "Don't you worry, Emma. We will put the mattress all back together again. It will be fun," she said, trying to get some cheerfulness into the words. "We can tell more stories." She took Emma's arm. "Come on. Look! Most of the stuffing is still in the mattress." She pulled Emma over to the mattress and began picking up the stuffing material.

River Joe turned to Peter. "I know John Ross says you cannot fight back and kill white men when they attack us, or the government will say we are at war," he told his Indian brother. "But someday I must find a way to kill Tommy Decker. I need to kill him as sure as I need to breathe. And somehow I will find a way to do it without getting the rest of you in trouble, if I have to go all the way to Knoxville!"

"River, don't!" Emma said, rising from the floor. "Don't go there! You would be hanged!"

His eyes blazed. "It just might be worth it to watch Tommy Decker turn purple with my hands around his throat!"

Their eyes held, hers full of terror. She shook her head. "River," she whispered.

He walked closer and grasped her arms. "I told you not to ever worry about that redheaded bastard, and I meant it, Emma Rivers."

"But they know now! I was so sure they all were drowned, so sure we wouldn't have to worry."

"You let me do the worrying. You are my wife. All I want you to think about is having my baby, Emma."

"Baby! Are you going to have a baby, Emma?" Grace asked.

Emma blushed, for by then Gray Bear and Peter and Grace and her husband, Red Wolf, had all come into the cabin.

Emma wiped at her eyes. "I . . . I think so."

"Then tonight we will celebrate," Grace said calmly. "We will celebrate tricking the white men and the fact that Emma is with child." She put a hand to her own thickening waist. "Surely our children will not be born far apart, Emma."

Emma looked at her kind, smiling face, which was getting rounder as Grace grew more plump. "That's right. Aren't you scared, Grace?"

Grace smiled more. "No. And neither should you be afraid. Your baby was conceived in love. It will be a healthy baby, and you will be fine. I know in my heart the Maker of Breath wants our River Joe to have a son."

Emma looked up at River. "Promise me you won't go to Knoxville?"

She saw his jaw flex in a struggle to control his anger. His eyes finally began to lose their bitter hatred and return to their usual gentle brown. "I promise . . . as long as you are safe and here with me."

He pulled her close, looking at Peter then. "Keep a good watch. Make sure that bastard keeps going."

Peter nodded. "We will make sure."

◊ *Chapter 15* ◊

It was November 1824 when Grace gave birth to a baby boy. Helping with the difficult delivery only deepened Emma's fear over giving birth. Her belly was big, and the other women guessed that by the first of the year her child would be born. She could feel its movements, and was overwhelmed that something alive actually moved inside her, a baby fathered by River Joe.

She could only pray that Grace was right when she said that a baby conceived in love would surely turn out to be healthy and strong. River believed it too, and she tried to believe it in her heart. But she was still haunted by her mother's many painful miscarriages and death.

In watching Grace's agony, it was obvious to Emma that bearing a child had to be one of the most painful functions a woman could experience; but she swore to be brave about it for River wanted this child very much. Her biggest fear was that it would die or that something would be wrong with it, and she would disappoint River, who had been so good to her.

Grace recovered quickly, and Emma gained new hope when she saw that the child, named Jonathan, was healthy and handsome. He fed hungrily at his mother's breast, and Emma began to get excited over her own baby. A child would be the first thing she had ever had that would be all her own, that no one could take away from her. She could love it, and it would love her back. Emma's sense of womanly responsibility began to change her whole personality, so that much of her childishness began to vanish. River enjoyed watching the change, began loving her even more for the woman she was becoming.

Winter set in at the mountaintop with a deep chill that kept fireplaces burning and the women and children in heavy sweaters and thick stockings. Emma, Grace, and Mary spent a lot of time together, helping one another read, knitting, and talking about Martin Crow, who, it was rumored, intended to ask for her hand in marriage in the spring. It was wonderful food for gossip, and Mary secretly began sewing a marriage quilt.

Emma grew so big that doing anything was an effort. She wore tunics borrowed from some of the fatter Cherokee women, and just getting out of a chair and walking around seemed an accomplishment. River did many of her chores, treating her as though she were a piece of china about to break. He kept the fires going, determined she would not take a chill and get sick, and every night he lay beside her feeling her stomach, running his hands over it lovingly as though he were touching the baby, enjoying the kicks and rippling movements of the life inside her belly.

Lovemaking had ceased, and Emma missed it. Sometimes she wondered if he gave more than a passing thought to the still-slender Cherokee girls in the village, but he seemed not to mind her huge belly and the swollen look to the rest of her. He was so attentive that she seldom let her thoughts of his being attracted to someone else cause her much worry. River Joe loved her. She was carrying his baby, and after it was born they would finally have each other sexually again. All that mattered now was the baby.

It was early in January 1825 when the raiders came. Emma sat at the table in Grace's house reading a story to Grace, Peter, and Mary. Outside, a bitter wind blew, and everyone wore heavy jackets inside the cabin. River Joe came in first, followed by Red Wolf.

"We have to get into the hole, Emma," River said. "A lot of men are coming this time!"

"The hole!" Grace protested. "River, it is so cold outside."

"No choice. We are lucky the bad weather is slowing them down. These men look like the kind who would prefer to surprise the village and ride down hard on us. Get Mary and the other young girls into the hole with us."

He helped Emma get out of her chair, his heart aching for her. He grabbed one of Red Wolf's bearskin coats and threw it around her, helping her walk to the door, but then Emma cringed, grasping at her belly.

"River, I can't!" she cried out. She clung to his arm, unable to straighten up because of the pain. "Something . . . hurts bad!"

River Joe looked at Grace, his eyes full of fear. "The baby!"

"We have no choice," Grace said. "You must not be seen. The baby will come when it will. Being in the hole will not matter. It will just make it harder for Emma, but not as bad as if you were seen and taken away. You must hurry, Joe."

River Joe picked Emma up in his arms, and Grace ordered Mary to put on a warm coat and follow.

"River, no!" Emma protested. "I can't . . . have my baby . . . down there! It will die! It will die!"

"Our baby will be fine, *Agiya*," he said, holding her close. "Do not be afraid. I will be with you."

Emma was aware of others hurrying. Pain ripped through her again as cold air penetrated her nostrils. She felt River let go of her for a moment and she screamed for him not to leave her.

"I'm not going to leave you, Emma."

She was being lowered, and someone else was helping her as she tried to climb down the little ladder.

"I've got her, Joe." She recognized the voice of Gray Bear.

Now it was dark. She bent over with another pain. She remembered that with Grace, when the pains came this closely together it meant the baby was coming. Surely it didn't happen this suddenly! Grace had lain in labor for a very long time. Did this mean something was wrong? Was she just excited, or was something terrible going to happen?

She heard River's voice again, felt him lift her, and heard him giving orders for someone to put down a blanket. She heard the voices of other women, young women—and Mary. Hearing Mary's voice comforted her, knowing that at least River and her good friend Mary were here.

"You must keep her quiet, River, or they will find the young women," she heard Gray Wolf tell River. Then all was darkness, and the girls were whispering. Another pain came, and River held Emma close, putting a hand over her mouth.

"I am so sorry, *Agiya*," he said, squeezing tight as the scream came. "Please, you must try not to cry out."

The pain left her and she laid her head back in the crook of River's arm, panting from the strain and shivering from the cold. "I can't . . . help it," she squeaked. "How can I . . . not scream . . . the pain . . . River, the baby is coming! It's coming soon! It's not like with Grace. It won't . . . take very long. River, it will die! It will die, and so . . . will I!"

"No! You will not die, Emma, and neither will our baby."

He sat on a blanket with Emma on his lap, his back against the dirt wall of the hole. He cursed the raiders and the darkness and the cold. How could he help her when he couldn't even see?

"Emma." It was Mary speaking. "Remember, this is your baby—yours and River's. Do you want the raiders to find River before the baby is even born? Do you want them to take River away so that he never sees his child?"

"No! No," Emma squeaked, grasping at River's jacket.

"Then you must not scream," Mary said. "If you scream, they will find all of us—take River away, hurt one of the young women—maybe take you away and kill your baby."

Mary spoke harshly but truthfully, trying to make Emma understand the importance of keeping still, while wanting to cry herself at Emma's predicament.

Another pain came, just as they heard the thundering hooves of horses. The thought that Tommy Decker might be with the raiders made Emma's pain even worse. She turned her face, burying it against River's thick fur jacket and pressing her mouth against his upper arm, biting hard on the jacket and forcing back as much of the scream as she could. It was almost totally muffled by the fur.

River reached inside her heavy jacket and rubbed her lower back with expert hands. It seemed to help the pain a little. "That's my brave, strong Emma," he said softly. *"Esaugetuh Emissee* is with us, Emma. You will be all right, and so will our baby."

The black pain ripped through her again, and she felt an odd burst and then a wetness on her bloomers. Again she muffled the scream into his fur coat.

"Try to relax, Emma," River said. "I know it is hard, *Agiya*. Breathe the way Grace did, the way the midwife told her." He held her in a half-sitting position, the position the old midwives said was best, and Emma breathed in quick pants.

"I think . . . I wet myself," she squeaked.

"Her water must have broken," Mary said, feeling very grownup for knowing so much about birthing babies. She had watched Grace's delivery and was not so sure at the moment that she wanted to marry Martin Crow after all. To marry meant to get pregnant. But then again, the sweet babies that were the result seemed worth it. "We had better take off her bloomers just in case the baby does start coming out."

"No, wait." Emma's mind swam with confusion, all reason beginning to leave her. She felt suddenly angry and contrary, and she argued about removing her bloomers. She pushed at River and told him to leave her alone, and another pain came. She started to cry out, but River quickly clamped a big hand over her mouth, firmly and forcefully, so that in her deepest moment of pain she could think of nothing but Tommy's attack on her. Tommy! Tommy had come for her, and had found her! She began fighting River so that he had to turn her back to him and keep one strong arm firmly around her chest and arms, while he kept his other hand tightly over her mouth.

"Emma, it's all right!" he whispered hoarsely. "It's me, River! Nobody is going to hurt you. And if you just relax, the baby will be all right, too."

Mary managed to get the bloomers off in the dark, then wrapped part of the blanket around Emma's legs as Emma began to relax again. Reality returned for the moment, but that was no better than her imagined danger. Reality was that she was having a baby. How many babies had her mother lost?

River's chest hurt from the effort of holding her to keep her from screaming. He realized that the screaming probably helped. A woman should be allowed to do anything she wanted in such a time, if it helped relieve the pain. He slowly took his hand from her mouth so that she could breathe in the short pants again, and with every breath she whispered, "River."

"I am right here, Emma. Soon those men will be gone and we can get you up to a bed." He heard someone above scream, and rage burned in his soul. How much longer must his people put up with such abuse?

The worst part was that he was certain it would only get worse, until all of them agreed to leave Tennessee. Perhaps every Indian from the Smokies to the Gulf of Mexico and the Atlantic would have to leave before it was done. It made no sense. They were bothering no one and they lived well.

Already there were rumors of men in government working on a federal policy that would remove all Indians east of the Mississippi River to Indian Territory. It was food for much discussion over Cherokee supper tables. How could the white men just decide what to do with people, as though they were ruling gods? This was the Indians' home. They had a right to stay here if they chose. They were industrious and bothered no one. None of them could understand the white man's thinking.

But River knew the new policy would probably become law. After all, they had already received news that a Bureau of Indian Affairs had been established, as part of the War Department. Why part of the War Department? It could only be because the government intended to remove all Indians to the west by force if necessary. And as much as the Cherokee loved these mountains, force probably would be needed.

But none of the government's decisions warranted these raids by the local whites. The men who did these things should be arrested. They had no authority, and their only motives were hatred—hatred of a people they would not even try to understand, hatred of the color of someone's skin—and a jealous desire to have the land that the Cherokee occupied. After all, that was thousands of square miles of good farm land, and a few Cherokee had even found some gold in the mountains of northern Georgia. To the white man, gold was an incentive for anything, including murder.

Now, because of the prejudice and hatred of the men outside, Emma had to lie in pain and agony, unable to have her baby in her own bed. Even though both he and Emma were white, they must suffer because they had befriended the Cherokee. He thought again about Texas, but perhaps after this last search the raiders would give up looking for him and Emma, if that was why these men had come. Besides, they were safe at least for the winter after this. His instincts told him this would be an extra-bad winter in the mountains. The white men would return to their warm homes below and wait until spring before coming back.

Gray clouds began spitting sleet as again the white men ransacked the Cherokee cabins. And again the red-haired, freckled white man was with them, his blue eyes blazing, his face slightly crooked, his fist hard when he hit a few old men in an attempt to get them to tell where River Joe and the white girl were. But again, no one in the village seemed to know anything about River Joe.

Tommy turned to Deek and the other young men he had brought with him this time. An old Cherokee man lay on the ground, bleeding badly from his mouth and a cut under one eye.

"There ain't nothin' here but a bunch of old men and useless old women," Tommy complained.

"A woman's a woman, Tommy," one of the other young men answered, eyeing Grace. "And that one there ain't so old. She's a looker."

Tommy turned and looked her over, walking closer. Grace eyed him squarely, understanding better Emma's terror of this cocky, cruel young man. He started to open her jacket.

"Go ahead, fire-hair!" she spat at him. "But you would not enjoy it much. I have just had a baby. I have always heard trash like you picked only virgins. Perhaps it is because you are so small that no other kind of woman can please you—or take pleasure in you." She sneered the words.

Tommy grasped the front of her jacket, jerking her closer, and Red Wolf stepped away from the rest of the men, wanting very much to defend his woman. But they all knew that each of these visits from the white men was designed to create a stir in the Cherokee, an effort to make them fight back, so that the government could declare war against them. Still, Red Wolf knew he could not hold himself back if Tommy hurt Grace.

One of the other white men aimed his musket at Red Wolf, while Tommy's and Grace's eyes held challengingly. Then Tommy shoved her hard, making her fall on her rump. "I got no desire for no woman who's all used up," he said disgustedly. "I reckon your husband will be lookin' for a nice, new young wife now, won't he?" He laughed and turned away. He had come here for Emma Simms, and had again come up empty-handed. His frustration and anger over that obliterated his sexual desires.

Finding Emma had become an obsession with Tommy Decker; his fantasies of finding her and raping her overwhelmed any desires for other women. It was Emma or no one.

"Let's go home and call it quits till spring, Tommy," Deek complained. "It's freezin' cold up here and now it's startin' to snow and sleet. You ain't gonna find that River Joe. Hell, he's probably run clean away from here. Maybe he's up north someplace. He's white. He can go anyplace he wants."

Tommy mounted his horse, scowling at his luck. "I told Sam Gates I'd find that girl!"

"And maybe you will. He don't care if it's now or next summer. Come on. Let's go."

"I'm for that. Let's get down where it's warmer," said

another of Tommy's men. "I'm tired of chasin' these damned Indians around. I want to go back to Knoxville and find me some good whiskey and good women—white women."

Tommy glared at Grace for a moment, then turned to his men. "There's only one white woman I got a yen for. And I'm gonna find her if I have to kill every goddamned Cherokee to get to her!"

"Now, Tommy, you know you can't go around killin' them. That just gives them more to fight with as far as their own rights. You have to hassle them," one of his men answered. "You have to knock them around a little—play with their pretty girls—get them good and mad."

Tommy moved his eyes over the group of Cherkee before him. Grace stared back at him, wondering if they would ever leave. Each moment was a risk, with Emma lying in the hole in labor. One scream and it would all be over. It seemed these white men had been here for hours, when actually it had been only about thirty minutes—thirty minutes of hell.

Tommy wondered where all the young women were, but the fact that there should have been more than this one, who had just had a baby, didn't seem to register in his mind and he turned his horse.

"Come on, let's go home," he grumbled. He heard a strange cry then, like a woman's scream, or perhaps the cry of a bobcat. It carried strangely on the cold, biting wind. Tommy held up his horse and shivered, listening intently, while Grace felt nearly faint from dread.

"Shit, Tommy, let's get the hell out of here," Deek said. "These mountains give me the jitters this time of year. You hear that bobcat? Next thing you know we'll get attacked and ate up around our campfire before we get home. Them animals do strange things in winter when food is harder to come by."

Sleet stung Tommy's face. He agreed—it was time to go home. He headed out and the others followed. As soon as they disappeared into the trees, Cherokee scouts began quietly to follow. They must make sure before the others came out of the hole that the white men were really leaving.

Emma was being lifted again, this time in a slinglike contraption, for she could not climb the flimsy ladder and River could not hang on to her and climb it at the same time. As soon as she was out of the hole, men took hold of her and hurried with her, while she kept screaming for River. She felt the warmth of her cabin then, the softness of her bed.

It was all she could think about as they laid her on it now. The mattress. They had not destroyed it this time. Once this baby was born and she was well, she and River could make love again. But no! That might mean getting pregnant again, and she never wanted to feel this pain again. Of that she was sure.

Her mind seemed to float from terror to agony to sweet love. Never had she felt so many moods—such anger and then again such wonderful love for River. River! Where was he? She cried out his name as she sensed women working over her, pulling off her clothes, wrapping something wonderfully warm around her feet.

"I am right here," she heard River say.

"You should not be in here," Grace said to him. "This is for the women."

"I am staying with her. I promised," River answered. "Besides, I am a white man, remember? I do not need to leave according to Cherokee custom if I do not choose to do so."

"You are as Cherokee as the rest of us and you know it, Joe. Don't sass me, big brother. I just got knocked on my other end protecting you."

Emma sensed the tension in the big hand that held hers. "Did one of those bastards hurt you, Grace?"

"Hush. We will talk about it later. There are certain names better left unmentioned right now. Emma seems calmer."

Someone shoved a towel under Emma's bottom, and she felt a wonderfully warm, down-filled quilt being tucked around her upper body. Someone pushed her legs apart and probed, and she screamed in pain.

"Soon, very soon," Grace said. "The head is already starting to come."

"River," Emma squeaked.

"I haven't left, *Agiya*. It will not be long now. You are doing just fine. The baby is coming."

She arched in black pain then, and a terrific tug pulled at her insides, her muscles contracting powerfully, surprising her by the way her body was ruling her now. She had no control over this. The baby was going to come out, and she had no choice but to let it happen. She bore down every time Grace told her to, yet she was not really doing it at all. It seemed as though someone else was doing it—someone with huge, strong hands was pushing at her belly and forcing the baby out.

Through it all she could hear River telling her how brave she was, how proud he was of how she had behaved in the hole, stifling her screams in spite of the pain. She was lost then in the wonder of giving birth, hardly aware of any of her surroundings or even of the pain any longer. It was as though she had momentarily left her own body and this was happening to someone else, for suddenly she felt almost nothing; and the next thing she knew a baby was crying.

"A boy! Emma, we have a son," she heard River say. She felt him close to her. "Thank you, *Agiya*. You are the most wonderful wife a man could ever ask for. He is beautiful and healthy, just like I told you he would be."

"Don't . . . let me die," she groaned.

"You are just fine, Emma. Grace says everything seems very normal."

"She doesn't really know what is going on at the moment, Joe," Grace said. "Give her a few minutes."

"How is the bleeding?" Emma heard River ask. "Her mother had a lot of problems."

"I think she is just fine. In a little while we have to push on her belly and get the afterbirth. You can help. It is important to get all of it."

"I've cut the cord, Grace." It was Mary's voice. Mary, her good friend.

"Joshua," Emma whispered.

"What?" River bent closer. "What is it, Emma?"

"I want to call him . . . Joshua. Mary and I . . . we've been reading . . . that Bible the missionaries left. I remember . . . that name in the Bible . . . and God let me have . . . a healthy son. I want . . . to call him Joshua."

"Then that is what we will call him. Joshua Rivers." She felt his big hand close around her own. "He is beautiful, Emma. Soon you will feel better and little Joshua will be feeding at your breast and you will forget all this pain."

She felt someone on the other side, and something was placed beside her. "Here is your son, Emma," Mary said tenderly.

Emma opened tired eyes and turned to look at her new son. River bent over her, pulling the blanket away so she could see better.

"Don't let him . . . get cold," she said.

"He is all right. He is close to you."

She studied the red, wrinkled infant. His eyes were closed tight, and he squirmed, tiny arms and legs flailing. Fuzzy, sandy-colored hair sprouted from his crown, and he made a little squeaking sound.

"River! He's all there—and . . . not a mark on him," she said weakly.

"Didn't I tell you?"

"Oh, River! We . . . have a son! Just look at him!"

Tears stung her eyes at the realization that she really had done it. She was still alive, and the baby was alive and healthy.

River kissed her cheek. "I have never been so happy in my whole life, Emma," he said softly, "in spite of the damned raid."

She turned to look into his eyes. "We have to protect him. Don't ever let anybody hurt him, River."

He put a big hand to her face. "No one will ever hurt him."

"Or take him away from me? Don't let anybody take him away, River."

"No one will take him away. Rest now, Emma. Hold Joshua close and get some sleep."

"Help me feed him, River. He's starting to cry."

He helped her turn up on her side, pushing quilts behind her back. He pulled down the quilt that covered her so that her breasts were exposed, then helped her position the baby so he could find his nourishment.

"Oh, River, this is the happiest day of my life," Emma said softly. "I never..." The tears wanted to come again and she sniffed and swallowed. "I never dreamed something this wonderful could happen to me." She smiled as her son nuzzled her. "You're right, River. I'm already forgetting the pain." She looked up at him then. "I want more, River. Now that I know I can do it, I want more."

He grinned, bending closer and watching his new son feed at his woman's breast. "I have no doubt there will be more, *Agiya*." He kissed her cheek. "Many more."

◊ *Chapter 16* ◊

"I think perhaps our old enemy the Creek will become a friend in times of common troubles," Red Wolf said to River Joe.

Emma looked up from kneading her bread, surprised at the remark. River and Red Wolf sat near the stone fireplace in Emma and River's cabin, smoking pipes. It had been a long, cold winter for Tennessee. Soon spring would come, and already the others spoke of moving the entire village when going on the spring hunt, for now the raiders knew where they were and would probably return when the weather warmed.

Emma struggled with mixed emotions. This had been her first home. She did not want to leave it.

"What did the messenger have to say?" River asked Red Wolf. "Did the federal government pass that law on Indian removal?"

Red Wolf nodded. "That is not the worst. The Creek in Georgia signed a treaty giving all Creek lands to the United States and agreeing to leave by the autumn of next year."

River lowered his pipe. "I can't believe it! Why did they do that?"

"They love this land as much as we. It was their chief who signed the treaty. Most of the Creek disagreed with it, and the messenger says they rose up and killed their chief,

calling him a traitor. So now the government has a treaty
they will claim is good. They will use it to start forcing the
Creek into Indian Territory, even though they do not want to
go. This destroys our own cause, Joe. It can only mean more
trouble for the Cherokee."

River stared at the flames of the crackling fire. "It also
means more raiding. Now the whites think they have a hold.
It is a bad thing, dividing the people. The white men are
good at doing that. They know it makes us weaker. If they
have split up the Creek, they will try it with the Cherokee.
They will give us even more trouble so that more of the
Cherokee will want to leave and will try to talk the rest into
going. That means quarrels and perhaps signing a useless
treaty like the Creek did. All the government needs is that
damned piece of paper."

"John Ross will not let it happen."

"I am not so sure he can stop it, Red Wolf. Maybe he
would never sign or never leave, but what if others decide to
go, like with the Creek? Already more have left."

Red Wolf sighed. "That place called Texas. If we had to
leave, do you think it would be better than the land the
government has set aside for the Indians?"

River shook his head. "I do not know, Red Wolf. I do not
know much more about that place than you, but I have heard
more because I have been around the whites. They say it is
very hot in the summer—a lot hotter than these mountains."
He met Red Wolf's eyes. "You thinking of going there?"

Red Wolf studied his pipe absently. "No. Not really. The
only way I will leave these mountains is if the government
soldiers come and drag me out."

River felt a chill at the words. Joshua began to cry, and
River got up from his chair, going over to lift the boy from
his wooden cradle. "Our son is hungry, Emma," he said,
glad to change the subject. But it hung there in their minds,
and both Emma and River felt the same dread of what the
future held.

"Do you think he'll come back?" Emma asked, wiping her hands and coming to take the baby.

How many times she had asked the question, she wasn't sure. Tommy Decker had come twice. He would probably come again. The strain of knowing that Tommy Decker was out there somewhere showed in the circles under Emma's eyes.

River handed the baby to her. "He probably will. But we will not be here."

Her eyes teared. "I don't want to leave my house, River."

"We have no choice. I will build you another house, just as nice."

She held her three-month-old son close, bouncing him lightly to make him stop crying. "Can we take the mattress?"

He grinned, loving her more every day for her sweet innocence that came through at stressful moments and warmed his heart. "Of course we can take the mattress." He leaned closer. "It will give us something to use along the way—better than the hard ground, don't you think?"

"Oh, River, don't tease!"

She walked around to the other side of the bed to open her dress and feed Joshua so that her back would be to Red Wolf. River grinned and shook his head. Cherokee women thought nothing of feeding their children in front of others. But the white blood in Emma made her too bashful to feed Joshua in front of Red Wolf.

He wondered how it was that a man could want a woman more every day instead of less. The first time they had made love after the baby was born felt wonderful. She had worried that having the baby had done something terrible to her so that River would no longer enjoy lying with her.

"How do you think it is that most couples have several children?" he had teased her. "There is only one way to make that happen, you know, and if the man did not enjoy it, he would not be able to keep planting that seed, now, would he?"

To him it was all better than ever, for now she was not just his wife but the mother of his son. Joshua was bright-eyed and alert, and he ate so much that Emma swore the boy was sure to turn out as tall and broad as his father. Never in his life had River been as proud of anything as he was of his son. He would die for Joshua, kill for him! Joshua and Emma Rivers were more precious than gold, the most important human beings in all the world.

He cursed the thought of having to pull up stakes and make Emma leave the only real home she had ever known, dragging little Joshua into the elements and exposing him to all the dangers of a migration. But the boy was sturdy, and with his mother's good milk and gentle love he would be all right. River was determined that nothing bad would happen to his new and wonderful family.

He turned to Red Wolf. "When should we leave?"

"When the moon is full again, perhaps twelve, fourteen sunrises. Then we must go." He looked up at River. "Of course, you will not go down this spring to take skins again, will you?"

Emma turned her head, always afraid that River would go to Knoxville and try to find Tommy Decker as he had threatened to do many times.

"No," River answered. "I cannot go back there. We will have to hope we find some suppliers among the whites up in this area to sell us sugar and flour and tobacco. Let's just hope this is a good hunt. We need some decent skins to trade, and many of our own people need new clothes."

Emma turned her attention back to Joshua, thanking the Maker of Breath for the little son who kept River from going after Tommy. *"Wadan,"* she whispered, using the Cherokee word for "thank you." She was beginning to feel more Cherokee than white, and as far as she was concerned, she did not care if she never returned to her white world.

* * *

The second week of May found the entire Cherokee village Emma had come to know as family camped on the side of a different mountain from the one on which they had been living the past several months. Emma had to force herself not to weep like a child when she left her little cabin. But her strength came from watching the other Cherokee women, the brave, determined look in their eyes. This was only her first time, but many of these women had done this several times. Now new trees would have to be cut. New cabins would have to be built. New gardens would have to be plowed and planted.

The moving never ended. Emma could see that now. She was almost ashamed to be white, for it was whites who made all this trouble for these good people. Mary and Grace were like the sisters Emma had never had. Grace's son was looked upon by Emma and River as a nephew, and all the family loved little Joshua as if River were their full-blooded brother.

They had not settled yet. The spot had not been chosen. Emma and River were back to living under the stars, only it was more dangerous now because there was Joshua to worry about. Emma fussed over him constantly, and River was pleased and proud of her motherly instincts and her ability to love so fiercely, in spite of her having grown up without knowing any love at all. It was as though all the love she had been denied and unable to show had welled up inside her and spilled out over her husband and son.

Before a village site was chosen, Martin Crow stepped up his courtship of Mary, and Emma sat inside Mary's tent with Grace and the two babies the night that the gossipers deliberately spread the word that Mary would set a bowl of hominy outside her tent. The three women waited, giggling like ten-year-olds as Mary prepared the thick mixture of ground corn and milk, then set a bowlful outside.

All the men sat around the campfire discussing where to

settle and pretending not to be aware of what was going on, so as not to embarrass Martin Crow. None of them seemed to notice when Martin rose from the gathering and disappeared into the darkness.

Martin was a huskily built young man of no more than five feet five inches. He was powerful in spite of his height, with broad shoulders and big hands. His face was round and happy, his smile bright, and for months he had wanted Mary so much that it disturbed his sleep. Now he headed for Mary's tent, his heart pounding, hoping she would not be teasingly cruel and refuse him permission to eat the hominy.

Inside Mary's tent the three giggling, talking women quieted when someone jiggled the bells over the entrance to the tent. Emma was feeding Joshua. She pulled a blanket over herself and waited with a smile while Mary asked who was there.

"It is I, Martin Crow," came the reply. His voice squeaked a little from nervousness, and Emma covered her mouth, struggling not to laugh.

"What do you want, Martin Crow?" Mary asked. "We are three women in here alone."

"I do not wish to come in," he answered. He cleared his throat. "I see that you have a bowl of hominy out here, and I am hungry." He hesitated a moment. "May I . . . may I eat this hominy, Mary?"

Mary deliberately waited a long time to answer, so long that Emma thought she would pass out if she had to go another moment without laughing. She didn't dare look at either Mary or Grace during the silence. Little Jonathan began to fuss and Grace held him close and patted his bottom.

"Yes, you may," Mary finally answered.

"Really? Do you mean it?"

All three women began laughing then, unable to control the urge any longer. "Yes, I mean it," Mary called out.

"Hurry and eat it before it is cold." She moved closer to the entrance, waving at Emma and Grace to keep still. "Right now it is warm, like my heart is warm for you," she said softly.

Emma sobered at the sweet words, still smiling but listening lovingly.

"And my heart is warm for you, Mary," came the voice from outside. They could hear him eating then, and moments later he scooted an empty bowl under the entrance flap of the tent. "I will build you a house as soon as we decide on a site," he said then. "We will live there together. I will be your husband, Mary, for as long as you wish to keep me."

Mary picked up the bowl and stared at it a moment. "I wish to keep you forever, Martin."

They heard his footsteps as he left, then Mary hugged Emma and Grace. "I will have a husband, too!" she exclaimed. "And soon a baby!"

They all giggled again, their giggling turning to shrieks of laughter at how long Mary had waited to answer poor, nervous Martin.

"Oh, River, it was so funny," Emma said to her husband later that night. "Martin was so nervous that his voice squeaked."

River laughed lightly, pulling her close. "You women can be pretty damned cruel, you know that?"

Emma laughed and kissed his chest, sobering then. "Did you do it that way with Yellow Sky? Did she set out a bowl of hominy for you?"

River kissed her hair, breathing deeply of its clean scent. How he loved the long, thick, golden tresses. "Yes," he answered.

"Did she say yes right away?"

He grinned, sensing her jealousy rising again. "Of course she did," he answered, moving his mouth to meet hers. He knew her jealousy would make her even more responsive, and he took advantage of the moment, reaching under her flannel gown and pushing it up to her waist, moving his hand under it to her full breasts as his tongue traced her lips and searched her mouth.

She kissed him back with equal fervor, many things bringing on a sudden urgency in her soul—her thoughts of River being with Yellow Sky—the dangers of the journey—the worry over raiders and Tommy Decker. How she loved River and this new life! She never wanted this magic to end, this wonderful happiness she had found in being a wife and a mother.

His lips moved to her neck, and he pushed the gown up over her breasts, moving down to suck lightly at the tender nipples, catching a lingering taste of sweet milk, loving her with a rush of passion at the thought of what a good mother she was to Joshua.

She grasped his head, whispering his name at the thrill of her own husband seeming to take nourishment from her breasts just as Joshua did. For River it was a different kind of nourishment, a kind of strength that he took from her yet gave back to her when he was himself inside of her, taking her life, giving life back.

He reached under her legs and pulled up her knees while he lingered at her breasts, then moved around in front of her bent legs, already naked himself. He grasped her knees and parted them, bending closer and rubbing himself against her teasingly until she cried out with her climax.

He quickly entered her then, a rush of his own powerful love for her making him push deep, groaning with ecstasy.

Everything would be so perfect, he thought, if there were not the worry over Tommy Decker. Because only Tommy and a few others, but no one of authority, had come after him, River began to wonder if he was really a wanted man in the valleys below, or if this was some kind of secret revenge. Perhaps only Tommy and the man called Sam Gates were after him. If he could just find a way to kill them...

He banished the thought for the moment. He had promised Emma not to do anything foolish, and this was not the time to think about it. But the thought of Tommy being after Emma, and of the man called Sam Gates thinking he owned her, made River take her now with hard thrusts, as though the deeper he penetrated her, the better he branded her as his own. This was his Emma, the mother of his son! No man laid claim to her but Joe Rivers!

She whimpered his name rhythmically as he grasped her hips and moved first in circles, then in even thrusts that ended in a burst of life that poured into her and left him spent. He stayed close to her for a moment longer, kissing her tenderly about the face, until Joshua started to cry.

"Oh, dear. Now another mouth to feed," she teased.

"Lie still." River sat up and picked the baby up from the deep pile of straw in which he slept. He laid the child beside Emma, and in moments the soft little mouth had found its mark. Joshua's strong, fat hands toyed with the skin of his mother's breast, pinching harmlessly as his feet kicked up in the joy of suckling. River lay back down beside her, pulling the covers up close around them. Soon all three of them were asleep.

They awakened to the sound of someone clanging the cow bell they had hung outside their tent for visitors.

"Joe, got some news," they heard Red Wolf say.

River stretched and grinned at Emma, keeping the covers over them as he answered, "What is it that is so important you have to wake me up from a good sleep?"

"It's Mary and Martin," Red Wolf answered.

River looked at Emma in surprise, and Emma looked equally surprised. "Come on in," River invited.

Emma kept her covers close and River sat up as Red Wolf

pulled back the tent flap and knelt inside. Red Wolf was a stocky, handsome man whom Emma had grown to like very much. He was a good husband to Grace, and more than a brother-in-law to River. They were close friends.

"I am sorry to wake you," he said to them both. "Grace made me come and tell you. Mary sneaked out last night. We woke up to find her gone, and Martin is gone also. Apparently they did not want to wait until we find a place to settle and he builds a cabin for her. We have much to tease them about when they return. Grace says Emma would want to know." Red Wolf grinned, and Emma laughed lightly.

"Yes, I certainly do! That must have been an awfully good bowl of hominy Mary gave Martin last night."

They all laughed then, and Red Wolf left. Emma looked at River and laughed more. "I didn't think Mary would do that!"

River grinned, resting his head in his hand. "Wouldn't you have done it for me?"

She met his eyes, deliberately scanning him like a wanton woman. "Actually, that's what I did do, isn't it? In fact, I didn't even have to offer the bowl of hominy. Come to think of it, you didn't even ask first, Joe Rivers. You just took."

A sly grin moved across his mouth. "I knew I did not have to ask."

She gasped, then pushed at him. River laughed, grabbing her arms and pulling her over underneath him, away from the sleeping baby.

"I told you to stop that night," she said with a pout.

He laughed more, pinning her arms and nibbling at her lips. "Only with words," he answered softly. "But your body and these lips were telling me to keep going."

He parted her mouth before she could reply, and his tongue probed deep while his big hands let go of her arms and moved under her bottom. He traced his fingers along deep crevices, moving then to her love nest and pushing his fingers deep inside her, making her whimper.

He released her mouth for a moment, moving to lick

gently at her neck, tracing his tongue down to her breasts. It didn't matter that they had done this only hours earlier. The morning was sweet and peaceful, and now they would all have to wait for Martin and Mary to return before going on.

River worked a wonderful magic deep inside her with his fingers as he used his tongue in circular massaging motions around her breasts. In moments she felt the wonderful pulsations that made her lose all inhibitions, made her crave the terribly intimate things he did to her.

He moved into her gently, taking her with slow, teasing movements that made her groan. She breathed deeply with the glory of it, reaching over her head and grasping at a peg in the ground, stretched out before him, her gown pushed up to her neck. He rose to his knees, drinking in her slender beauty, grasping her hips and holding her to himself, prolonging the ecstasy for several minutes before finally he was unable to hold back his pleasure.

He shuddered as his life pulsed into her.

Moments later Joshua began to fuss. Emma breathed deeply, opening her eyes, which were still glazed with passion. "I guess it's back to reality," she said softly. "Joshua needs me."

River grinned, gently rubbing her thighs. "I guess I will let him have you now." He leaned close, kissing her lightly. *"Wadan, Agiya."*

"You're very welcome, *Asgaya*."

There was no time to settle in the place they had chosen. Some trees had already been cut for houses, and a little ground had been broken. But the local whites did not want them so close, and they sent a raiding party in the early morning to let the Cherokee know they were not welcome. Because they were tired from traveling, the Cherokee did not post the normal number of scouts, and the whites caught them unprepared.

River and Emma awakened at the same time, alarmed by the sound of approaching horses. River jumped to his feet and grabbed his knife and musket.

"Get Joshua and get out of the tent!" he shouted to Emma.

Emma had no time to think, to reason what was happening. She knew only that she should obey her husband. She grabbed Joshua and ran outside in her flannel gown to see others running and screaming, while white men rode through with sabers, slashing them through tents, crashing into others with their horses and riding right over them.

Emma held Joshua close, ducking her head and running toward the woods, the sound of a horse right behind her. Her heart screamed with terror. All she could think of was Tommy. Was he with these men? Had he seen her? She heard a strange thud then just as she reached the thicker trees. She turned to see River standing near a man and horse, both of which were on the ground. River held a thick branch in his hand, his hunting knife between his teeth. He threw down the branch and took the hunting knife in hand.

"River, no!" Emma screamed. "The Cherokee will be blamed!"

He stood over the man, panting, wanting very much to get his revenge.

"If you cut him up they'll know you're up here," Emma added, not sure if it was true but hoping the words would keep him from murdering the white man. River turned and ran toward her then, pushing her and Joshua down into a ravine just a few feet away. They had made love the night before and he was still naked. He lay on top of her, watching and waiting, while they heard more screams and smelled smoke.

"River, what's happening?" Emma squeaked, holding Joshua close and petting him soothingly to keep him from crying.

"I think they were locals—just trying to scare us off. Keep still."

Her heart pounded wildly, and she wanted to scream and cry but knew she must not. She wondered frantically about the others. The waiting seemed like hours, but it was really only minutes before the sudden attack was over.

"You damned Indians find someplace else to settle," a man shouted from somewhere. "Be gone by tomorrow morning, or we'll be back!"

"Dan, Hal got hurt bad! Must have hit a tree branch," someone not far away yelled out.

Emma cringed, terrified that they would be found.

"Pick him up and let's get out of here. I don't like hangin' around too long," someone answered.

There was a commotion nearby. "Throw him over his horse. Is that damned gelding all right?"

"I think so."

Emma kept Joshua close to her breast, praying to the Maker of Breath that he would not cry. The men nearby finally left, and River carefully looked up from the ravine. Emma wanted to weep at the thought that life was such a constant terror for the Cherokee she had grown to love. There was no earthly reason for the treatment they were getting, and her heart ached with disappointment at the thought of having to move on again and pick another spot. She wondered if she would ever have a permanent home.

"Come on," River said, helping her up. "We can go back now."

"River, you're naked!"

He looked down at himself. "Give me Joshua's blanket. It is a warm morning. He will be all right."

She took the blanket from Joshua and River tied it around himself.

"River, do you think . . . I mean, that one man saw you running naked. Your bottom . . . it's whiter than the rest of you. He'll know you're white."

"Maybe not. Some Cherokee are lighter than others. And I hit him so quick he probably will not even remember."

"Do you think Tommy was with them?"

"I doubt it. These were men from some local settlement who got wind that we were settling up here. That means we

cannot trade with them. We will have to keep going awhile
yet. I am sorry, Emma."

"It's all right, as long as nobody was hurt."

He put an arm around her and led her back to camp. She
breathed a sigh of relief when she saw that their tent had
been knocked down but not burned. A few others were on
fire, which would mean more hardships, as others would
have to share what they had with those who had lost their
belongings.

She felt River's arm tighten around her and understood his
almost agonizing need for revenge. As it was painful for the
other men, it was killing him not to be able to fight back.
These were brave, strong warriors. But white men's rules
and laws kept them from doing what came naturally, left
them helpless to defend their families.

"Joe! Joe, our father is dead!" Grace came running up to
them, tears streaming down her face. "They rode through
the tent before he could get out. Joe, they rode right over
him! Gray Bear is dead!"

"Oh, my God," Emma whispered.

River left her and hurried over to the site, crying out and
going to his knees when he saw his Indian father's battered
body.

Emma felt as though someone were turning a knife in her
heart. In the few months she had been with these people,
Gray Bear had been more of a father to her than Luke had
ever been.

Grace, Red Wolf, Mary, and Martin gathered around Gray
Bear, and it hit Emma with full reality how grave the situation had become for the Cherokee. Worse, she could not get
over the horrible dread of what could happen if any of the
raiders had seen River Joe and knew who he was.

She walked closer to River, cradling Joshua, tears welling
up in her soul. She watched her husband helplessly, unsure
how to comfort him. She had never had a father she could
mourn, and it was unnerving to see a man like River Joe
weep.

She realized then what it must have been like for him when Yellow Sky died. How deeply he must have mourned her loss. Emma and Joe had had their share of sorrows, but then perhaps that was what made them stronger, and what had drawn them together in such a powerful bond.

She walked closer, kneeling beside him, hesitantly putting a hand on his shoulder. "River?"

He threw back his head, saying something in the Cherokee tongue. He turned then, embracing both Emma and Joshua.

"You and Joshua are the only thing that keep me . . . from killing all of them," he said, choking out the words. "May *Esaugetuh Emissee* give me the strength not to seek revenge."

"Oh, River, I love you," she said, not knowing what else to say to him. "You have me and Josh. It's all right, River."

"He was white! I'm tellin' you the one that hit me was white," Hal told his friends, grimacing at the painful swelling across his right shoulder and his forehead.

"Them were all Cherokee. He just knocked you silly, that's all."

"Goddammit, he was white. And I swear to God I seen a woman with gold hair runnin' in front of him."

"Gold hair!" Some of them laughed. "He really *did* knock you silly!"

"I'm tellin' the truth!"

"Hey, wait a minute," the one named Ken put in. "When I was up to the Daniels settlement last year, somebody was goin' around to some of the other settlements up this way askin' if anybody knew where the Cherokee might be nestin'—wantin' to know if anybody had seen a white man and white woman among them. I think he was from Knoxville —a redheaded guy—young. I think he was from some saloon or somethin' down to Knoxville. If Hal really did see a white woman and a white man, maybe them's the ones this redheaded fella was lookin' for."

"Well, if it was, they're long gone now," another of the raiders answered. He threw the stub of a cigar into their campfire. "I ain't gonna go chasin' around these mountains for somebody that might not even really be up there. If the redheaded guy wants to find them, that's his problem."

"I'm goin' to Knoxville at the end of summer to do some tradin'," Ken said. "I aim to look up that fella and tell him what Hal says he saw. Maybe he'll pay to know."

"Go ahead," another grumbled. "All I care about is that them damned Cherokee get the hell out of our territory. What happens to them after that ain't my problem. Let's head home come mornin'."

"I'm with you," Hal said, holding his aching head. "Whoever that white man might be, I don't aim to go at it with him again. He like to have killed me."

"We would have been better off if he had," Ken replied. "Then we could report it and declare war on them bastards."

"Thanks a lot," Hal grumbled.

"They're too damned smart to fight us back," one of the others complained. "They got some educated ones among them who are actually fightin' in the courts to be able to stay here. Can you believe it?"

"Let them fight," another growled. "It won't do them no good. If we want them out of here, we'll get them out. Ain't no courts gonna tell us otherwise. This is our land, not theirs."

"That's right," Ken said. "Let them go to Indian Territory where they belong." He took out the turban he had ripped from the head of the old man. He studied it for a moment, grinning at the memory of the Indian stumbling backward after Ken had torn the turban from his head and kicked him. He had ridden his horse over him then before he could rise.

Ken threw the turban into the fire. "I wish they'd all just burn up like that," he grumbled. "It would save us a lot of trouble."

◊ *Chapter 17* ◊

Emma sliced a loaf of bread, glancing over at River, who sat cleaning his musket near the fireplace. River had been moody and quieter since Gray Bear's death, and Emma wasn't quite sure how to tell him she was pregnant again. Maybe this was a bad time to be having another baby. Little Joshua, who sat on a blanket on the floor not far from River, was only eight months old. He played with a tin cup, banging it against a spoon.

"You want some supper, River?"

He looked up at her as though just realizing where he was. His eyes moved over her lovingly. "Not much. I am not very hungry."

"Now that's unusual for my big, strapping husband."

"Mary made me sample her apple pie when I was over there. I ate about half of it."

Emma smiled, shaking her head. It was September 1825, and they had moved still farther from their old camp and had settled among another small village of Cherokee for the winter. The group they had joined were few in number, as over half of their village had been wiped out that summer by cholera. Altogether there were about 150 people in the village.

River had quickly built a little one-room cabin and a frame for another bed, on which the handmade mattress again rested.

"Come and eat your venison, River. The bread is still warm."

He ran a rag over the barrel of his musket, then laid it aside. "What do you think about Texas, Emma? Maybe we should go."

She watched him in surprise as he came to the table. "We can't go this time of year, River. Winter will be on us soon."

"Winter isn't all that bad down below. And they say it stays mild in Texas in winter."

"They also say the weather can change real fast, just like you know it can here in Tennessee. You never know when it will turn to freezing, or when it will storm. We could run into sleet, cold rain—and you don't want to leave Mary and Grace and the others, and it might be dangerous for Josh. Besides . . . we can't go yet, in spite of all those things."

He stood near his chair. "Is that some kind of order?"

She looked down at the bread. "No. It's just common sense. If I'm to have a lot of healthy babies, I have to take care of myself, don't I?" She met his eyes then. "I'm going to have another baby, River."

She could not quite read his dark eyes as he frowned at her curiously. "You sure?"

She nodded. "At first I wasn't. I mean, it was hard to tell because I was breast-feeding and I didn't get my time for a couple months after Josh was born. But then I did, and then it stopped again, so I thought it was still because of breast-feeding. But I've felt little movements." She searched his eyes and put a hand to her stomach. "I know the feeling now. I just . . . I hope it's all right with you. It's awfully soon. Grace says it's unusual to get pregnant so soon while breast-feeding."

A slow smile moved across his lips. "Well, it wasn't all your own doing, you know. Did you think I would be angry or something?"

She smiled nervously. "I wasn't sure. You've been so distant ever since Gray Bear. . . ." She blinked back tears. "I wish you'd be my River again. Lately you seem to be here only in body, not in spirit. I'm with you and yet I miss you."

He sighed deeply, walking up to her, and pulled her into his arms. "I'm sorry, Emma." He kissed her hair. "I'm glad about the baby." He squeezed her tight, and she breathed in his sweet scent. "We both want lots of sons and daughters. And you're right. We can't go to Texas. The important thing is that you have another healthy baby."

He pulled back, bending down to meet her mouth, and she knew by his kiss that he was pleased. The kiss lingered, and she returned it with sudden passion, reaching up around his neck and feeling the quick, sweet pulsations deep inside that he always awakened in her. He left her lips and held her close, her feet off the ground.

"Oh, River, I was afraid you'd be angry. I don't know exactly why—I guess because of all our worries. But nobody came back after that raid, and Tommy Decker hasn't come back. Maybe he finally gave up, River."

He kissed her neck. "Maybe," he answered, not really believing it. He decided not to spoil her joy over the baby with his suspicions that Tommy had not given up at all. Besides, maybe she was right. Maybe things would be all right now. Perhaps he was letting his grief over Gray Bear magnify his worries. It was obvious he had already let it affect Emma. She had been suffering quietly, afraid to share even her news about another baby.

"River, I hope this will be another healthy one. I was so relieved when little Josh was born so perfect and beautiful. I can do it again, I know I can!"

"Of course you can."

She met his dark eyes, still almost overwhelmed that this man belonged to her. "Make love to me, River. You were gone so long hunting, and..." Her face began to redden. "I've missed you. Josh is playing, and the meat will keep in the roasting pot. I feel so good, being able to finally tell you—"

He cut off her words with another kiss, enjoying the

sweetness of her mouth as he felt the sudden desire at her innocent request. She was going to have another baby. His Emma was healthy and fertile and beautiful, and they were all well. He must stop worrying about what might be and think about what is. He must forget about the dead and think about the living. This woman had brought him comfort after losing Yellow Sky, and she had been a good, sweet, devoted wife. He picked her up and carried her to the bed.

Joshua watched, blinking big, brown eyes, wondering at the way his mother and father were rolling on the bed, then taking off their clothes. It made no sense to the baby, and he proceeded to put the tin cup over his mouth and nose and make noises into it.

Emma's dress was already to her waist, and River kissed wildly at her shoulders, her breasts.

"Oh, River, everything is going to be good now. You'll see," she said.

His clothes came off, and hers. He met her mouth again in a steamy kiss that was almost like another form of intercourse. She gave a little push, rolling over so that River was on his back, and now she was the master, kissing back with near wantonness, her cascading golden hair caressing his shoulders and face. She left his lips, her cheeks crimson with a mixture of embarrassment and wicked desire.

"I want to try it, River—what you told me about once. I want to try it before I get too big with this baby."

He moved a hand over her full breasts, then both hands down over her waist and to her thighs. "I would love you to try it, *Agiya*."

He kept a gentle hold on her thighs as she scooted down. She took her hand and caressed her man, guiding him into her depths as she settled over him. She gasped at the glory of it, rocking gently as he pushed with her.

"River! River," she whispered, the thrill of being so brazen bringing out her wildest passions. He was her grand stallion, and she rode him in splendid ecstasy as his big hands caressed her thighs, grasping at her bottom, moving up to squeeze her breasts gently.

He drank in her beauty, the cascading waves about her shoulders, the golden hair of her love nest, the wonder of how he fitted into her. After several minutes he felt her throbbing climax. She came down over his chest and he rolled her over, pushing into her then with his own wild desires, now the master.

For several minutes they moved in sweet rhythm, until his life spilled into her.

Joshua threw the tin cup he was playing with, then stared at it a moment, his lips puckering. Perhaps if he cried his mama would go and get it for him, and he wouldn't have to go to the trouble of crawling after it. Tears of frustration welled up in his big, brown eyes, then he opened his mouth and let out the noise that sometimes made his mother come to him to see what was wrong.

"What's wrong with Josh?" Emma asked, breathing deeply as River moved off of her.

River sat up and gauged the situation. "He threw his cup aside and now he's mad about it."

Emma laughed as Joshua looked up at her, tears rolling down his face.

"You go get your own cup," River said to the boy. "The men in this family do things for themselves." He got up and walked over to the cup. "Come on. Come and get your cup. Use those fat little legs, Joshua Rivers."

Joshua sat there sniffling, his lower lip still hanging out. He looked from his mother to his father, then back to his mother.

"Do what papa says," Emma said. She got up from the bed and went to the washbasin.

Joshua stared after her a moment, then looked back at his grinning father. "Come on. Come get the cup."

The boy's tears subsided, and he suddenly grinned, rolling onto his hands and knees and scrambling after his toy.

* * *

Tommy sat down with two beers, shoving one in front of the man who had sought him out. "This better be worth a beer," he said.

"Might be worth more than that. I'd go for a ten-dollar gold piece."

"First I have to know if it's worth it."

The man took a swallow of beer. "My name is Ken Daisy. I'm from a settlement way up in the mountains. I just come in to Knoxville to sell some farm goods and such—come every year at the end of the farm season."

"Yeah, yeah. So what?"

Ken swallowed more of the brew, burping and wiping foam from his lip. "So last year on my way back home I saw you at the Daniels settlement and remembered you was lookin' for a white man and white woman who might be livin' among the Cherokee. I decided to hit every saloon in Knoxville this trip to see if I could find you. I thought I remembered you sayin' you worked at some saloon here. You still lookin' for a white man and white woman?"

Tommy's eyes glittered excitedly. "You've seen them? Did the girl have blond hair?"

Ken frowned. "Why are you lookin' for them?"

"That's my business. I asked if you saw them."

"Last spring. Wasn't me that seen them. It was my friend Hal. We was part of a raidin' party that went after some wanderin' Cherokee who was fixin' to settle not far from our farms. We didn't like that, so we decided to pay them a visit and put a scare into them, know what I mean?"

"I know." Tommy grinned. "I've been on plenty of raids like that myself."

"Well, anyway, one of the Indian men, he turned and walloped my friend Hal with a big limb, or board or somethin'—knocked him *and* his horse down. We turned them Cherokee out early in the mornin' while they was still asleep. This Indian, he came runnin' out of his tent stark naked. And Hal swears his ass was as white as yours and mine. And he also swears that the woman runnin' ahead of him and carryin' a baby had hair gold as cornsilk.''

Tommy's fists clenched. It was all he could do to keep from making a scene right there in front of everyone, so great was his rage. River Joe! River Joe running naked out of a tent with Emma! That meant only one thing. And Emma had even been carrying a baby! His jealousy made him feel sick. He spoke through clenched teeth.

"This happened last spring and you're just now comin' to tell me?" he growled in a near whisper. "God only knows where they would be by now!"

Ken shrugged. "How was I to know how important it was? At least you know they've been seen. Ain't that worth somethin' to you?"

Tommy's blue eyes were so full of hatred that Ken felt uncomfortable. Tommy rose. "Wait here," he hissed. He stormed to a door at the back of the saloon, going through it and closing it. Behind the door, Tommy moved across the hall and into Sam Gates's office.

Gates looked up at him from his desk. "You could have knocked first."

"I'm sorry, Mr. Gates. But there's a man outside from up in the mountains—says a friend of his seen a white man and a white woman with blond hair among some Cherokee they chased away from their farms last spring." He walked closer as Gates's irritation turned to interest. "It's her, Mr. Gates. I know it's her! She was runnin' carryin' a baby—and the man who ran out with her was stark naked—his butt as white as ours! It's that River Joe, I'm sure of it! And the woman was Emma. He's been havin' at her all this time— your property! That man is up there rapin' over what's yours. Now we know them Cherokee was lyin'. They *are* up there after all! You have to let me go look for them again, Mr. Gates!"

"They could be anyplace by now," Gates answered. His

dark eyes sparkled with cunning plans, and he rose from his desk, shoving his hands into the pockets of his well-tailored pants. "That little bitch is going to pay." He stepped closer to Tommy, meeting the young man's eyes squarely. "Pretty soon it will be winter up there again. Let them think no one knows. Give them some time to relax and be off guard. If this River Joe is as smart as you say, he'll still be suspicious —still be watching. Let them think you're never coming back. Wait till next spring. Then you'll have the whole summer to search. I'll pay for all your supplies and any extra men you want to take along."

"I'll need plenty. If I can find them this time, I'll surround the village. If I have enough men along, we can threaten to kill every baby and whip and rape every young girl there if they don't turn over River Joe and Emma Simms. I'll find out where this guy seen them, and we'll start our hunt from there." He took a deep, excited breath. "I'll get them this time, Mr. Gates. And with enough men along, there won't be anything that River Joe can do to defend him or his slut. I'll make sure the man dies, and I'll be bringin' Miss Emma Simms back to you."

"See that you do, or you'll be out a job. I've only kept you on here because you know the girl and are probably the only one who *can* find her for me. So far you have failed both times you tried."

"I'll bring that girl back, and I'll be collectin' the money you promised. But if I find her, I want your promise that I can do what I want with her on the way back."

Sam Gates grinned. "She's already been spoiled. Whatever you do to her makes no difference to me now. Just don't leave any scars on her. She might be valuable still as a pretty thing for my customers—or I might even be able to sell her, or use her at my coal mine."

Tommy's eyes shone with vengeance. "Don't worry. I won't leave any scars—at least not the kind you can see." He grinned, but Sam Gates's dark eyes showed no humor.

"When I'm through with her, her scars might be visible,"

the man growled. "But if she gets that kind of scars, I want to be the one who gives them to her."

Tommy grinned more, finding pleasure in the remark. He had worked for Sam Gates long enough to know how cruel the man could be to some of his women, especially those who would not cooperate. Emma Simms would most certainly not cooperate. Tommy only hoped he could be a witness to her suffering.

Rachael Mary Rivers was born in March 1826. This time the birth was surprisingly easy, and afterward River Joe downed a great deal of whiskey to celebrate, something he rarely allowed himself to do. But the birth of a healthy daughter with no problems for his wife was something to celebrate.

Emma had thought her greatest joy had come when Joshua was born. But now she had two babies. Fourteen-month-old Joshua seemed huge compared to the tiny newborn daughter in her arms, and for the first few weeks Joshua constantly hung on to his mother and tried to crawl into her lap whenever she held and nursed Rachael.

Both River and Emma were beside themselves with happiness. Every night Emma thanked the Maker of Breath for her beautiful children and her precious husband. All her life she had been afraid of having babies, and now here she was with two of her own, a strong son and a beautiful little girl with blue eyes and hair so light it was almost white.

Watching River hold his new daughter was a sight to behold, for at first she seemed to fit in one hand. Joshua was even more jealous when his father held the baby than when his mother did, and he always seemed to fall down and hurt himself or use some other ploy to divert his father's attention from Rachael.

Spring moved into early summer, and life was good. There had been no more raids, and with the birth of Rachael,

River seemed to be fully himself again, his moodiness leaving him. July came, warm and bright, and Emma knew she wanted to stay there forever, high in the mountains, living among the Cherokee who had become her family.

"You have made him such a happy man," Grace told Emma as they walked with Mary through the woods searching for fresh *anuh,* as the Cherokee called strawberries. "I hope to be with child again soon. Jonathan is already eighteen months. You are so lucky that in that length of time, you have had two children. I envy you."

"River says the children come from the Maker of Breath. He will bring you another when the time is right, Grace," Emma answered.

Three-month-old Rachael rode strapped to her mother's back while Joshua and Jonathan toddled behind the woman. Red Wolf and Martin had gone off hunting, and River Joe walked a short distance from the women, guarding them from whatever might be lurking in the forest beyond the village, be it man or beast.

"*Esaugetuh Emissee* has decided the time is right for me," Mary said then.

Emma and Grace stopped walking and stared at Mary. "Mary!" Emma exclaimed. "You are going to have a baby?"

The young girl smiled and nodded. "It is about time. I am almost eighteen summers like you Emma. And you already have two babies. Here I am with none. Martin is so excited."

They all squealed with delight, hugging together.

"You are supposed to be hunting strawberries," River called out to them. "What is going on over there?"

"Do not tell him," Mary pleaded with Emma. "I do not want to tell my brother. It is better that Martin tells him. It makes my face get all red and hot."

They laughed again, separating and looking for more berries. Joshua and Jonathan lagged behind, doing their own exploring, then suddenly separating, Jonathan running toward his mother and Joshua chasing a butterfly.

"Joshua, stay with mama," Emma called after him.

He ran wild and free, already displaying his father's traits, already big for his age. Emma called after him again, then called to River to go after him. "I can't run with Rachael on my back," she yelled.

River grinned, his smile quickly fading when Joshua seemed to disappear. "Joshua! Wait for papa," he called, breaking into a run. His heart pounded and Emma froze in place when they all heard a growl.

"Joshua!" Emma whispered. She turned and headed toward where River was running, and Grace and Mary followed, Grace grabbing up Jonathan.

"Stay back!" River shouted. He stood on a bank, looking down where Joshua had fallen over to a flat piece of ground that lay in front of a cave entrance. A pair of bear cubs played near the entrance, and a huge brown mother bear came lumbering out of the cave, rising on her hind feet and growling at Joshua, who was crying from his fall and trying to get up. "Stay still, Joshua!" River yelled. But the words were to no avail. Joshua cried harder, standing up then and picking up little rocks to throw at the big mother bear. His movements only angered her more.

River raised his musket and took careful aim. Fire spat from the end of the rifle barrel as River fired, and the cubs ran off. The mother bear tumbled backward, but to River's horror she rose again. Wounded and angry, she headed for Joshua.

River could hardly believe his shot had not killed the bear. There was no time to reload. He threw down the musket and jumped over the bank, positioning himself between the bear and Joshua.

"River!" Emma screamed. She moved closer as vicious growls increased. Her heart beat with wild fury as she heard her son's crying and the horrible snarling of the bear. She reached the edge of the bank and screamed for Joshua to stay still, then stood in helpless horror as River and the bear rolled together on the ground.

"River! Somebody help him!" Emma screamed.

"Oh, my God!" Mary whimpered, she and Grace moving beside Emma.

Joshua stood crying in terror while great claws dug into his father's neck and chest. River scrambled desperately to get his knife out of its sheath. The bear tumbled him onto his back, and he felt his own warm blood soaking his clothes. Life and energy oozed out of him along with his blood, as he finally found his knife and used what strength remained to sink the big blade into the bear's side.

He stabbed at the animal over and over, wondering which one of them would finally die first. He didn't care if it was he who died, as long as he kept the animal from Joshua until someone else came.

The bear tumbled off him at last, kicking wildly while odd growls of pain came from her throat. The kicking slowed, and she finally quieted, the life leaving her massive body.

Emma stared in horror at River, who was covered with blood. She told herself not to panic. River and Joshua both might need her. River rolled to his knees, then managed to get to his feet. He started to walk to Joshua, then collapsed.

"River!" Emma screamed.

He lay quietly, his knife near his right hand. He made no response when Joshua toddled over to him crying. The boy bent down to touch his father, trying to make him wake up.

"Oh, God, River!" Emma groaned.

"Watch Jonathan," Grace said to Emma. "I will go down to be with Joshua." She grasped Emma's arms. "You stay right here with Rachael and Jonathan. Do not try to go down." She looked at Mary. "Go and get some help!" she ordered her sister. "And get Peter."

Grace turned to climb down, and already some men were coming, having heard River's gunshot and the women's screams and the growling bear. They carried muskets and knives, but they were not needed now. Grace grabbed Joshua close, then knelt over River.

"Joe?" She touched his shoulder, leaning closer.

"Joshua," he groaned.

"Joshua is all right, Joe. We will get you some help." She looked up at Emma. "He is alive. But he is losing much blood."

Mary came running back, and several Cherokee men climbed down the bank. In moments more came with a blanket and rigged up a sling-line device with ropes and hauled a groaning River Joe to the top of the bank, then helped Grace and Joshua to the top.

Emma felt sick at the sight of all the blood. Surely the Maker of Breath would not take her husband from her. Not now! Not River! How would she live without River?

"You must be very strong now, Emma," Grace said. She hung on to Joshua, trying to quiet him as he reached for his mother. Emma grabbed him up, in spite of the weight of Rachael on her back. She hugged her son tightly, realizing what could have happened to him if River had not reached him in time. The bear's attack would have killed little Joshua. She could only pray it would not kill her husband.

River had helped her through so much, had saved her from hell, had given her two beautiful babies and been at her side through both births. Now it was her turn to help him. She struggled against panic as she saw blood drip steadily from one of his arms that dangled over the side of the make-shift stretcher as men carried River Joe to their cabin.

"Papa hurt?" Joshua wept.

"Yes, Joshua. But he'll be all right again." She followed the man and the stretcher, realizing that she could easily follow without seeing them. All she had to do was follow the trail of blood River was leaving behind.

◇ *Chapter 18* ◇

Emma forced back the terror of realizing what life would be like without River Joe as part of it. She sat on an old blanket on the floor of their cabin, River's head in her lap. Mary and Grace worked frantically to stop the bleeding.

"Josh . . . Joshua," River mumbled.

"Joshua is all right," Emma said, bending over and kissing his forehead. How many times had she reassured him his son was fine? In his present state of mind, all he must be able to see was the bear ready to pounce on his tiny son. The thought of it made Emma shiver. Such wounds as River had now would have killed Joshua. They might also kill River, especially if they became infected.

An old woman came inside then, carrying a leather bag full of remedies for River Joe. She was Ramona, the *adawehi*, a trusted medicine woman of the village. She lived among the Cherokee with whom Emma and River and the others had settled.

"Hurry, Ramona," Grace said. River Joe was already stripped down to his loincloth, and everyone had been banished from the cabin except Emma, Mary, and Grace. Some other women looked after Joshua and Rachael, and Emma gently stroked River's forehead, bending close and telling him again that Joshua was all right.

"And you'll be all right, too, River. Ramona is here. We'll all help you."

Grace began carefully peeling pieces of rawhide out of deep gashes on River's chest, where the material had embedded when the bear ripped at it and gouged its claws into River's skin. River groaned as Ramona sat down beside him and began sorting through the remedies in her leather bag. After every piece of material that Grace pulled from River's skin a trickle of blood followed.

"We've got to stop all this bleeding," Emma insisted.

"Here. Most of it comes from here," Ramona said, taking a piece of cloth and holding it tightly against a deep puncture at River's right shoulder, near his neck. "From a tooth. Hold this tight on here, white woman, and do not let go until I say."

"A tooth!" Emma pressed her hand against the cloth, her eyes wide with dread. "It could get infected. Isn't it true that wounds from an animal's mouth usually get infected?"

"Any wound can get bad spirits." The old woman shrugged. "It is a matter of waiting. If it is full of bad spirits, we will burn them out. Now keep still while I decide which medicines will be best."

Emma pressed her lips together, wanting to scream from terror. She knew River needed her now, knew she must not lose control, but Ramona's sharp answers did not comfort her. Ramona was old and crotchety. She had no use for *Unegas,* and she tolerated River Joe only because he had been raised by the Cherokee. It was not that she hated him or Emma personally, but that she hated whites; and she constantly complained that the presence of River Joe and Emma in her people's village would only bring them trouble.

Emma was not offended by the woman's curt order. She knew Ramona, knew that the woman was ill-tempered with just about everyone. But right now she wished the old woman could be a little more understanding. Still, what mattered was that the woman was good at what she did, and Emma trusted her. She had seen Ramona save a boy from a snakebite and save a baby from a blazing fever. Ramona was all they had, and Emma kept silent as the old woman began removing strange concoctions from her bag, pouches of this, jars of that, tins of herbs.

Emma held the cloth tight on the deep puncture as Mary and Grace continued to pull material from deep gashes.

"Josh," River groaned again.

"Josh is fine, River. He's over at Rising Moon's cabin. You can see him as soon as we're through cleaning you up."

"Got . . . to see . . ."

"River, he's fine. I promise," Emma repeated. "I don't want him to see you like this—all bleeding and hurt. It would frighten him. He's all right, River." She leaned down and kissed his forehead. "I'm right here, River. Emma's here, and Joshua and Rachael are fine. Just hang on, River. You'll be all right. The bear is dead. You killed her, River. She never touched Joshua."

Suddenly River began gasping for breath and coughing, his whole body jerking oddly. He rolled over and spat up blood.

"Dear God," Emma groaned, trying to hang on to the cloth she still held pressed to the deepest wound.

"Be strong, white woman," Ramona instructed. "I have seen this before. It will pass."

The coughing finally calmed, and they rolled him onto his back again.

"I think we have most of the cloth out of the cuts, Ramona," Grace said, glancing at Emma and seeing the devastated look on her face. "He will be all right, Emma."

"We will put this mineral in warm water, then bathe the wounds," Ramona said matter-of-factly. Into a kettle hanging over the fire in the fireplace she poured a white substance and stirred until the powder dissolved.

River lay groaning, physically still for the moment. He coughed again, but this time he did not turn over and cough up blood. "Emma," he whispered.

"Yes, River. I'm right here." She put a small, gentle hand to his face. "You'll be well in no time."

"If . . . something happens . . . to me . . ."

"Nothing will happen, River."

"Got to . . . hide . . . maybe go far away. Decker might . . . come . . . nobody to help you . . ."

"He won't come now, River. He's given up," she reassured him, wishing she could be sure of it. "Look how long it's been, and we've moved around so much he'll never find us. But it doesn't matter. You'll be well soon and you'll be able to protect us."

She debated telling him that it was possible she was pregnant again. Perhaps the news would give him more incentive to hang on. But this was not the right time to add to his burdens. In his condition he would only worry. Besides, it could be false news. She had never had her time since giving birth to Rachael. The other women said she would not get pregnant as long as she was breast-feeding two babies; but it had happened to her before, and now she felt again the little flutters of life that made her wonder if she was again carrying a child.

It seemed incredible, and she realized she and River might have to abstain from making love longer than usual after the next baby was born. Cherokee women had talked about staying away from their husbands for a long time after a baby was born. Emma didn't want to stay away from River. Making love was simply too sweet, too beautiful. But they had to be practical, too.

"Too many babies too fast no good for young girl," Ramona had said when the old woman assisted with Rachael's birth.

The statement frightened Emma, who still carried memories of her mother's miscarriages and death. But her love for River was stronger than her fear of birth, and right now none of it mattered. River lay bleeding, choking on blood somewhere on the inside, perhaps dying. He might never make love to her again, never hold her again.

Ramona brought over the bucket of hot water and added some cooler water to it. She dipped a clean cloth into it and wrung it out just partially, then laid it flat over some of the deep gashes. River jumped and trembled, and Mary and Grace each took one of his hands.

"Get his right arm here good, too, Ramona," Mary said then, grimacing at all the blood there from more deep wounds. "He must have used it to push against the bear's jaws." The girl's eyes teared. "Poor Joe." She looked at Emma. "He saved Joshua's life."

Emma nodded, her eyes brimming with tears. "He saved mine, too, more than once."

She kissed his forehead, whispering gentle words of encouragement to him as Ramona methodically and painstakingly washed every wound.

"Hang on very tight now," the old woman said to them, pulling out a bottle of whiskey. "This good for dirty wounds. Sting bad. Got no choice."

She began pouring the whiskey over the open cuts, and River Joe gritted his teeth, arching up against the pain. Emma wanted to scream for him, wishing she could ease his suffering by sharing it. But there was nothing she could do but listen to his cries as the whiskey penetrated each wound.

When Ramona finished with the whiskey, River lay in a cold sweat. Ramona began applying a strange-smelling salve and River shook so violently that they all had to hang on to him until the shaking subsided. Finally when every gash had been treated, bandages were wrapped tightly around his right arm and right shoulder, under his arm, and around behind his neck and back down again, so that the deep puncture wound near his neck was covered tightly.

"Done for now," Ramona said. "I sing prayer song, burn prayer smoke. Tell men come . . . put him on bed off floor. We wait . . . watch. If bad infection come, we burn."

The old woman rose, amazingly spry for her age. She began gathering her things, then set a tin burner on a table, near the bed into which she poured a rich-smelling tobacco. She walked to the fireplace to get a stick to light the concoction while Mary ran out to get some men to lift Joe.

Emma bent closer to him then, holding his face gently

between her hands. "It's all over, River. You're going to be fine. Ramona will pray for you. We all will pray for you."

"Josh . . . want to see . . . Josh."

"I'll have Peter bring him over, but just for a minute, after we've covered you up. You'll see he's just fine, River."

She kissed him again, loving him more than ever for what he had done. This man would die, if necessary, for his children and for his Emma. Never had she felt so special, so loved, as now, realizing the lengths to which he would go for her.

Peter and others came in then, carefully lifting River and carrying him to the bed, laying him gently on it. Emma covered him with a light blanket. "Go and get Joshua," she said to Peter. "River wants to see him and be sure he's all right."

Peter nodded, hurrying out and thinking what a fine wife the white woman was making for Joe, wishing he had found the white woman himself. He returned with Josh, who was crying for his mother. Emma took the boy, hugging him tightly, the first time she had really had a chance to hug her son and appreciate the fact that he was alive.

"Josh," River groaned.

"He's right here, River," Emma answered, fighting to keep from breaking down. She sniffed, kissing Joshua over and over and holding him tightly until the boy stopped crying, then held him closer to River.

"See, River? He's all right. There isn't one mark on him, except a few scrapes from falling. See?"

River slowly opened his eyes, studying his son. With much effort he reached up, pain searing through his right arm. He touched Joshua's fat knee and managed a weak smile. "Josh."

"Papa . . . ouch," the boy sniffled.

"Yes, Papa is hurt, Joshua," Emma answered. "But he'll be just fine real soon, you'll see."

The boy reached down with a chubby hand and wrapped his fingers around one of River's. "Papa."

"You . . . be a good boy . . . go with . . . Peter," River managed to say. His dark eyes moved over the boy, then he looked at Emma. "He's all right," he said as though surprised. He closed his eyes then. "Thank God."

Emma handed the boy back to Peter, then knelt beside the bed, taking River's hand. "Now you have to be all right, River," she whispered.

"*Esaugetuh Emissee* will heal him," Grace said, coming over and putting her hands on Emma's shoulders. "Pray to the Maker of Breath, Emma. He is always with you."

"River," Emma wept. She felt his hand tighten around her own then, as though to comfort and strengthen her even in this hour when it was he who needed to be comforted. A sweet warmth moved through her, and some of the terror left her.

"Let's face it. We ain't gonna find them, Tommy," Deek complained over the campfire. He swallowed some whiskey, then slapped at a mosquito. "Let's get the hell back to Knoxville. We've been lookin' for weeks, and it's hotter than hell."

Tommy lay back against a tree trunk. "You want to go, go. But I'm not goin' back this time without Emma Simms. I don't care if I have to live up in these damned mountains for five years!"

"I think you've gone plum crazy," Deek said.

Tommy leaped forward, crouching near him and clenching his fists. "Say that again and I'll knock your teeth in, Deek Malone! What the hell kind of friend are you, anyway?"

"The kind who's thinkin' of your own good," Deek answered, rising. "Even if you do find that girl, and then if you manage to get her away from River Joe, what do you think he's gonna do? You think he's just gonna let her go without a fight? Maybe you don't mind havin' that skulkin' white Indian lookin' for you, but I don't want him after *my* hide! You heard what he done to that man up at the Gillmore settlement, and we know what he did to Hank Toole."

"Well, then, we'll just have to make sure he's *dead* when we take the girl, won't we? What's so hard about that? You just aim your goddamned musket and shoot it! The man ain't *got* an iron *gut*, you know!"

Tommy whirled, scanning the other seven men with them. At one time there had been five more, but as the search continued to be fruitless and the summer heat wore at them, they had left the search party one by one.

"How about the rest of you," Tommy sneered. "Who else is too cowardly to face River Joe?"

One man slowly rose, folding his arms. "I ain't afraid of no white Indian," he said slowly. "I'm just tired, Decker, and I got matters back at Knoxville that need tendin' to."

"Sam Gates is payin you real good, Zack."

"Sometimes good pay ain't enough. I got a woman carryin', and if I hurry I can get back before the kid is born. I told her I'd be there. I didn't know this damned trip would stretch out so long. You said it would only take us a month or less. It's been four months since we left Knoxville, and no sign of the Cherokee or that woman. I'm headin' out in the mornin'."

Tommy sniffed, showing his unconcern. "Well, you just go right ahead. The rest of us are headin' over to the next ridge. I seen smoke risin' over there yesterday—from chimneys or campfires maybe. Only folks this high up are Cherokee. Me and the rest of the men here will collect that fine reward we get when we come back with the girl. If you want to give that up, you go right ahead. Just remember Sam trusts you to keep your mouth shut. You wouldn't want your woman to know you visit Sam's women."

Zack checked his temper. He didn't like Tommy Decker. He was too cocky. "If this River Joe or Indian Joe or whatever he's called is as mean as they say, you'd best be mighty careful," the man warned.

"It's *him* that better be careful," Tommy sneered. He turned to look at Deek again. "Well? You stayin'?"

Deek sighed deeply. "Dammit, Tommy, you know I will —at least to the next ridge. But if there's nothin' there, that's it. That's as far as I go. It'll be hell findin' our way back as it is. We must be eighty, maybe a hundred miles from Knoxville."

"Once we have that girl we'll have no trouble. Just the smell of that reward money is all we need to lead us there." He punched Deek on the shoulder and laughed. "Won't Emma just die when she sees us?" His grin turned to an ugly sneer. "And won't she just *want* to die when you and the others hold her down while I have at her? Till I get inside her, that is. Then won't nobody need to hold her down. She'll be wantin' it bad enough on her own."

He laughed again, grabbing the bottle of whiskey from Deek and taking a drink.

Emma bathed River's wounds again while he lay in sweating pain. It had been over a week since his injuries, and the deep puncture wound, as Emma had feared, had become so badly infected that he could not move his right arm or shoulder, or even turn his head without almost unbearable anguish.

"You know what we have to do, River," Emma said softly. "You heard Ramona."

He swallowed. "I know," he groaned. "But... anything is better... than this. Maybe you... should leave, *Agiya*."

She sighed. "River—after all you've done for me? And sitting through two babies? I wouldn't think of leaving you. I can take it. I want to be with you." Her eyes teared. Today Ramona would burn out the infected wound. "I love you so much, River. I just want you to get well."

"I will. You'll see. Just... watching you every day... is all I need to keep me going."

She sniffed. She still had said nothing about another baby. Besides, it would be another month or two before she could be certain. She took his hand. "You're so strong and brave, River."

He managed a grin. "Just being practical. Don't want . . . to die . . . not now. Too much . . . to live for."

She leaned closer and kissed his cheek, then rose, carrying the pan of water to the table. River had been improving steadily and was sitting up and talking and eating, until the last two days, when the infection suddenly took its ugly hold and drew him back down into bed. Now he was in so much pain he couldn't eat and had scarcely slept for three nights. Emma knew his weakness came mostly from exhaustion and hunger. If they could get rid of the infection and he could get some sleep and take food, her strong, virile husband would be back on his feet in no time.

Ramona knocked at the door then. Rachael and Joshua had already been taken to Mary and Martin's cabin. Mary and Grace would not be present. This would be no job for women. It would take men to hold Joe down while Ramona singed his flesh.

Emma stared at the hot iron already glowing in the fireplace, then went to the door, her legs feeling heavy and slow. She opened it to see Ramona standing there with Peter and Martin, Red Wolf, and a fourth man—one man to hold each leg and arm. Emma felt a wave of nausea, and such terror that she wanted to scream and run away. But she fought it. River needed her. She stood aside and let them in.

The men walked to the bed, Peter nodding to River. "Hey, Joe, you ready for a little party?"

"You looking . . . to see who's . . . strongest?" River retorted.

Peter grinned. "Maybe your little brother is stronger than you think."

River smiled against his own ugly dread. "Let's hope so. I . . . have a feeling I'll put you . . . to a good test."

Peter smiled sadly while Ramona came over to inspect the

wound, which Emma had unwrapped and washed again. The old woman shook her head. "Still bad. Got no choice," she said firmly. "You ready, Joe?"

His fists clenched. "I'm ready."

The old woman nodded. "You brave man for white man . . . and strong. You be okay, Joe."

Ramona turned away and walked over to the fire. "You men . . . take his arms and legs. Give him something to bite on."

Peter handed River a piece of rawhide. "Don't grind your teeth off now, brother." He slipped it into River's mouth.

Emma came over to the bed and slipped an old piece of cloth under the injured shoulder to catch blood and pus, then moved to the other side of the bed from where Ramona would stand. She got on her knees, placing both her hands on River's left shoulder, the shoulder that already carried a scar from Hank Toole's musket shot.

Red Wolf gripped River's left arm in two places. Peter took the other arm, and the other two men each took an ankle. Ramona took the hot iron from the coals and raised it, whispering a prayer in the Cherokee tongue.

"Look toward me, River," Emma said to him.

"Can't . . . turn my head," he muttered, mouthing the words strangely while he kept the rawhide in his teeth.

She rose, bending close to him. "I love you, River. Think about me and Josh and Rachael. I might even be pregnant again. What do you think of that? That's what comes from us loving each other so much."

He searched her eyes. "Too . . . soon."

She smiled. "That's all right. We'll just be more careful after this."

The wicked rod touched him then and he stiffened, biting hard on the rawhide, jerking arms and legs but unable to get away from the horrible pain because men held him.

"River," Emma whispered, fighting back an urge to scream for him. The odor of burning flesh stung her nostrils, and she kept her hands at each side of his face, refusing to look at the smoldering wound. River shook violently as Ramona moved the rod around to burn out as much of the infection as possible and cauterize the wound properly.

"Best to only do it once and take a little longer than to go through it again," she said almost sadly as she finally removed the rod. She turned and walked back to the fireplace, replacing the rod and staring at the flames a moment before returning to River's bedside.

"It's all over now, River," Emma was saying softly. "It's done."

He lay panting, a tear running down the side of his face into his ear. But he had made no sound.

"You are brave—you and your man," Ramona said to Emma then. "I have never known such brave *Unegas.*"

Emma looked at her in surprise, and the old woman stretched out a bony hand, patting her shoulder. "He will be better now. Give him plenty whiskey. Let him go to sleep. I will leave you a special medicine. Mix it with the whiskey. He will sleep long time."

Emma nodded. "Thank you," she whispered.

"Thank *Esaugetuh Emissee.* Only He decides if a man lives or dies."

The old woman turned, and Emma looked at the others. "Thank you, all of you, for helping."

"Joe is a brother and a friend," Red Wolf answered. He gave her a supportive smile and they all quietly left. Old Ramona placed a small brown bottle on a nearby table, then smiled reassuringly at Emma before going out herself. Her smile surprised and touched Emma, boosting her confidence that River would be all right.

Tommy picked up the rock. It was important not to make any noise, so he couldn't use his gun. He realized now that he was right. If a man wanted something done well, he had to do it himself. Coming up here alone first to scout the Indian village was smart thinking. One man was hard to spot, and the only way to catch Emma was to surround the village where she might be living before they knew anyone was coming. How these people had managed to hide her and River Joe both the other times he had come, he would never understand, but they were not going to get away with it again.

The Indian scout he was watching stood with his back to Tommy. Tommy waited patiently. There could be no warning this time. If he attacked this scout in any way, the village would be alarmed, and they all might flee before Tommy could get to his men and come back again. His men waited at least two miles below, with orders to make no fires that might signal the Indians that others were present.

"What if they ain't even Indians?" Deek had complained.

"What else would live up that high, you idiot!" Tommy had snapped. "At least let me go up and find out. I don't intend to mess up this time. You want to go back, don't you?"

"Course I do."

"Then let's do this right so we can go home!"

Now the scout finally walked off, going to check another area. Tommy ducked and crawled closer. He had to see who was in the village in the clearing just beyond the trees. If it looked like the right village to attack, he would scout the entire perimeter, see where the Indian scouts stationed themselves. He and his men would take care of those scouts first. Then there would be no warning, nothing to alarm the villagers who might warn River Joe and Emma.

He crawled through a thick stand of brush, lying flat then to watch. The village was bigger than he thought it would be. But that would be no problem if they could properly surround it. He watched quietly, his eyes scanning each log-and-thatch house, searching for white skin and golden hair.

Such a woman would be easy to spot among all the dark-haired men and women.

There was an odd quietness over the village. No one was laughing or running about. Then he spotted it, the roan gelding he was sure River Joe had always ridden when he came to the settlements. He glued his eyes to the cabin in front of which the horse idly grazed. It seemed hours before the door finally opened, and then Tommy's heart almost stopped beating.

Emma! A beautiful young woman with golden hair came outside. Her hair was tied into a a tail at the base of her neck. Two Indian women came up to her and they embraced. Each Indian woman held a child, one of them just a little baby. Emma took the baby and hugged it, then took the second child, which looked like a small boy, in her other arm and hugged him, too.

Two children! They already had two children! Furious jealousy raged in Tommy Decker's soul. It was all he could do to keep from rising and going to get Emma Simms then and there, but that would be foolish. He wasn't worried about the other Cherokee, but he was worried about River Joe. Where was he? Emma seemed to be crying now, and she and the three women went back inside.

He wanted to scream, yell, laugh, jump up and down. Finally! He had finally spotted her! She really was alive and living among the Cherokee. This time he would not go back empty-handed. He would go back with Emma Simms dragging behind!

He rolled onto his back, looking around carefully. His only sure bet of defeating River Joe was surprise. If they took the village by surprise and surrounded it, he could call River Joe out and shoot him on sight. The Cherokee wouldn't do a damned thing about it. They were forbidden to fight back or to kill a white man. He almost laughed out loud at how easy it was going to be.

Tommy carefully scooted back to the thicker woods, still seeing no other scouts. He moved down past a short drop-off, landing on his feet, then took off running. There was not a moment to waste! This time he would not fail!

◇ *Chapter 19* ◇

The night was peaceful for River. Emma mixed Ramona's concoction into his whiskey, making him drink a small glass. He had slept hard all night. Emma lay beside him, memories of the past several months moving through her mind, memories of the life she had led before River Joe came to her that afternoon at the river.

How different it all was now, and how beautiful. If only it could always stay this way. But an odd anxiety had plagued her all night long. It didn't seem to have anything to do with River's physical condition. It was something more. She kept watch over him, and he seemed to be sleeping deeply and comfortably.

She checked on the children, picking up Rachael once during the night for a breast-feeding. All the while she sensed a presence, a danger that she could not explain. She put Rachael back in her cradle and walked back to Joshua, bending close and kissing his soft baby cheek.

How she loved her children! How wonderful to be able to give them the love and attention she had never received. No one was going to abuse these children, and they would never lack for love. She would make sure of that. And even though it was the Cherokee custom for an uncle to take over the raising of the children, River's white blood would not allow anyone but himself to be responsible for his son and daughter. He was the father, and he was a good father, an attentive father, who provided well for all of them in spite of the hardships under which they lived. Now she realized that if anything happened to him, her children would rely on her to carry on, to protect them, feed them, provide for them.

She squeezed River's hand and a lump rose in her throat. How would she ever go on without him? They had been together such a short time, yet he was everything to her now, her very life's blood.

She closed her eyes and fell into a restless sleep.

Emma awakened to a rapid tapping on her door. The sun had not yet risen, and she was groggy, aching from too little sleep and too much worry. She glanced at River, who still slept, then moved carefully off the bed and to the door. "Who is it?" she asked softly.

"It is I—Red Wolf. Quick. Let me in!"

Emma frowned, opening the door and gasping at the sight of blood on Red Wolf's face, streaming down from a gash on his forehead. He darted inside, looking over at River, then back at Emma. "He sleeps?"

"Yes. Red Wolf, what happened to you?"

"I come to warn you. I have seen two white men. I came across them by accident, almost stepped on them. One rose up and hit me with the butt of his rifle. When I came around, they were gone."

Emma felt the terror crawling into her heart. She reminded herself to stay calm, that she must think of the children and River. She hurried to a cupboard and took out a clean cloth, bringing it over for Red Wolf to hold against the cut on his head.

"Here, Red Wolf. You're bleeding badly. Did you get much of a look at them?"

"No. I came to tell you first because of your fear of the white men. It might only be settlers spying on us to see what we are doing—making sure they are safe. Perhaps they only struck out at me because I startled them."

He pressed the cloth to his head and Emma put a hand to her stomach, looking over at River. "We can't be sure," she said. "Perhaps the men who have been looking for me and River have finally found us. Most of the night I had the strangest feeling, as if somebody is watching me." She looked back at Red Wolf. "We should have dug another hiding place. But it's been so long. We thought maybe they had given up."

Her breathing quickened as she realized the gravity of the situation. "There might not be a lot of time, Red Wolf. If you saw men nearby, perhaps more will come soon. Perhaps they have already surrounded us. If it's . . . if it's Tommy Decker—" She could hardly make herself say the hated name. "He'll be more determined than ever this time."

She swallowed back an urge to scream. Tommy Decker! It couldn't be! Surely the Maker of Breath would not do this to her.

"Emma, you must hide."

She shook her head. "No. If they have been spying then they already know I am here. They would tear this whole village apart looking for me, maybe hurt or kill some of your people I can't let that happen."

She began pacing, trying to think quickly. "Right now we have to think of River," she said then, stepping closer. "If it's Tommy and he finds River in this condition, unable to defend himself, he'll kill him in cold blood. He's mean enough to do it. If I am going to save River and my babies and save others from being hurt, then I must give myself over to them, if they come here asking for me."

"You cannot do that!" His eyes moved over her. "They will hurt you badly. You have said so yourself. Your greatest fear has been that this man named Tommy will come for you."

"I know. But . . . River . . . he can't defend himself right now. He's depending on me to defend him, just as he risked his life to defend me at times. I can't ask any of you to do it. You can't fight back, Red Wolf. And I will not be responsible for any of you getting hurt, or for River getting killed!"

She opened the door and peered out. Dawn was breaking. "We have to be ready. I want you to go to the others and spread the word quickly and quietly that River is dead—tell everyone out there that they must stick to that story. Tell them in the Cherokee tongue, so that if any white men are out there listening, they will not understand. They must understand that they all have to tell the same story and make the white men believe it. In River's condition—" She fought a building panic. "He can't help me! The only way he *can* help me is to stay alive and come for me! I know these men. They won't kill me. They want me for . . . other reasons."

She did not bother with details, nor did she dare to think about them. The horror of it began to grip her and she struggled to stay in control, reminding herself that she had to think of River and the children right now. "I can bear it as long as I know River is alive and can come for me when he's well." Her eyes teared. "And he *will* come for me! I know he will!"

"What will you do? How will you convince them about Joe?"

"I . . ." She looked around frantically at River. Tommy would kill him if he found him this way. "I'll find a way to hide him. Then everyone must stick to the story—that he was attacked by a bear and died of infections. We have to be very convincing, Red Wolf, or River will be killed."

"He will be very angry and crazy with grief when he finds out what you have done."

"I have no choice. I can't let them tear your houses apart again, and this time Tommy—if it is Tommy—will do more than that if he can't find me. He'll burn your homes and abuse your women. He won't give up this time because he or someone he is riding with has probably seen me."

Red Wolf took the cloth from his head, putting it into her hand and wrapping a big, dark hand around her own. "I will spread the message. And I will send Peter to help you hide Joe."

She nodded, struggling to be strong. "If I come outside, and we talk convincingly . . . I think all Tommy really wants is me. If I can get him to leave with just me, River will be safe and can heal. Then he'll come for me. Knowing that will help me survive, Red Wolf. Hurry now! There might not be much time. If we're lucky, this will all be for nothing. But I have this terrible fear that Tommy Decker has found me."

He nodded, studying her admiringly for a moment before hurrying outside. Emma quickly shut the door and bolted it. Tommy Decker! She wanted to scream for River to wake up and help her. But River could not help her this time. And Tommy must not know that River was in such a helpless condition.

She would rather die than see or be touched by Tommy Decker again! But River was more important even than her own horrors. She hurried to the bed. There might not be time to wait for Peter. She had to protect River. She didn't want to hurt him, but at the moment she had no choice. She prayed to the Maker of Breath for help as she eased her arms under his torso and gently pulled. He was much too big and heavy for her. She whimpered in desperation, praying again for help. She eased one arm under his neck and moved the other arm around the front of him, grasping him under the left shoulder. Again she pulled, this time half-lifting, half-dragging his torso until she got him over the edge of the bed.

River groaned lightly but was so sedated that he was barely aware of what she was doing. She was grateful now to Ramona for the powerful concoction the woman had given River to drink. She stood up and grasped River's ankles, lowering his legs to the floor. Acting quickly could be vital now. The sun was rising!

She grabbed up some quilts and covered River fully, tucking the large, handmade blanket under him for softness and making sure he was completely warm and covered. She placed another blanket under his head, then pulled and yanked at the big, wooden bed so that River lay hidden beneath it.

She hurriedly replaced and mussed up another quilt, making sure the bed looked as though she had been sleeping in it in case men came inside the cabin. Now she could only pray that if they did look inside the cabin they would not see River Joe and would then believe the story she would tell them. Her faithful Cherokee family and friends would have to help with the story.

She straightened and stared at the empty bed, feeling devastation sweep over her. "Oh, River," she whispered. "What if . . . I never see you again." She backed away, the agony and horror of what could be lurking in the shadows beyond the trees beginning to erode her sanity.

Again she reminded herself to remain calm and rational. She must force herself to bear whatever Tommy Decker did to her, for it could mean saving River's life and possibly her children's lives. That was all that mattered.

She went to her children, kissing them, touching them, struggling against screams and tears. She told herself that maybe the men lurking outside didn't mean any real harm. Maybe they really were just local settlers. If so, they had no reason to harass these Cherokee. The Indians had done nothing illegal, and they had made no moves against any whites in the area. They had gone out of their way to stay away from the whites and their farms and to lead their own quiet, peaceful life. Why didn't the settlers just leave them alone?

"Babies. My babies," she whispered.

If it was Tommy Decker out there, she must do whatever he said just to get him away—away from River! Away from her babies! And then somehow, somehow River would come for her. That hope would be her sustaining strength. She walked around the bed and knelt down, reaching under and touching him. She knew that if he were well and awake, he would never let Tommy Decker touch her. But for now...

"Oh, River," she wept, putting her head down on the edge of the bed. "River! River! Thank God you're asleep and don't know. Thank God for Ramona's potion. Maybe sleep will save your life."

If only the danger lurking outside were a bobcat or a bear —anything but Tommy Decker!

Someone tapped quietly on the door then. "Emma. It is I—Peter."

She hurried to the door, just as the sound of war whoops and hard-riding horses could be heard circling the village. Emma let Peter inside.

"They come!" he said, looking at the bed. "Where is Joe?"

"Under the bed," Emma answered, grabbing his arm. "Peter, you have to help me! They have to think River is dead or they'll kill him while he lies helpless! You have to give me over to them—tell them you took me for your woman and you don't want me anymore!"

"What! What are you saying?"

"I am saying that the only chance for Mary and Grace and all of you that I love, and the only chance for River to stay alive, is for all of you to give me over gladly. We have to convince them that River is dead and you took me after he died, but you don't want me anymore."

"No. I cannot do that to Joe's woman."

She grasped his arms, as men rode in circles now behind the cabins, carrying lit torches, laughing and shouting. "Peter, please! Those men have probably already killed or badly wounded the Cherokee scouts. They mean business this time, Peter, if Tommy Decker is with them. Please, please don't make me feel responsible for Mary being raped or one of you being killed—or for them finding and murdering River! The only way they'll not harm you is if you don't put up any fight for me. Please, Peter! Red Wolf is telling the others that they must stick with our story that

River is dead. That's the only thing that will save his life, Peter, and maybe Rachael and Joshua's, too. If they take me away, I want my babies to stay here. I know Mary and Grace will take good care of them for me."

The young man blinked, turning away in confusion.

"Peter, there isn't time to argue. Please help me save River!"

Outside, white men were already herding the Cherokee out of their cabins, while River lay in a deep sleep under the bed. This time the attack had been well planned. The Indians had had no time to hide or run. The men with the torches were shouting for everyone to come out of their cabins and stand at the center of the village.

"Hurry it up!" someone screamed. "Get your brown asses out here! Every one of you! Every man, woman, and child, get out here! We know you can't fight back, so you better do like I say, or I'll rape every girl and kill every baby and burn every cabin in this village!"

Emma recognized Tommy Decker's voice. The months away from him had not erased the memory of it, nor the memory of the day he had attacked her. He would want a terrible revenge for what she had done to him that day.

"Get moving!" someone else shouted.

How had he found her this time? She had thought they were so well hidden. River wasn't even sure they were still in Tennessee. But it mattered little now. All that mattered was that she protect River. *Protect River.*

"You, too, Emma Simms!" came the familiar, sneering voice. "I know you're in there! Come on out, Emma, honey. Have you missed me?"

River. She would think only of River, of keeping him alive so he could come for her.

"Please, Peter," she begged with a shaking voice. "It's him. It's Tommy Decker. I recognize his voice."

He turned to face her. "Joe will hate me. He will kill me—hate all of us for letting them take you!"

"No. He'll understand. I know he will. It's the only way, Peter."

He walked closer, his eyes showing tears. "All right," he said quietly, taking her arm and leading her toward the door.

Outside, the Cherokee were gathering, most of them still in nightclothes or only half-dressed. They whispered among themselves, spreading a message Tommy Decker did not understand: "Tell them River is dead." Young girls cringed and little children cried until Tommy ordered their parents to make them shut up.

"Emma Simms!" Tommy shouted then. "I know you're here, Emma! I've already seen you. Get on out here or I'm comin' in after you!"

Mary and Grace stared at him, hating the redheaded *Unega* who had terrified Emma Simms before. Now they understood that terror. Both women felt a sickening sorrow as the door to Emma's cabin opened and Emma stepped out, wearing only a flannel gown. Peter held her arm. They approached Tommy and his men, and suddenly Peter shoved Emma so hard it surprised even Emma. She stumbled forward and fell to the ground, too numb now with a determination to save River to let the sight of Tommy Decker make her cringe and try to save herself. Too many people's lives depended on this moment.

"Do not harm us!" Peter shouted. "You have come for the white woman. Take her! I have slept with her all I want. She is of no more use to me!"

Those Cherokee who understood English looked at him in surprise, keeping quiet and realizing something planned was happening here.

Emma raised her eyes to meet Tommy Decker's cold blue ones. The sight of him made her feel faint. She concentrated on River and her babies as she got up and stood facing Tommy, her chin held high, proud of the fact that Tommy's face looked crooked and he didn't speak quite right.

"Well, now, ain't this interesting," Tommy sneered. "These people been hidin' you out all this time, and now they just hand you over like you was nothin'." He shook his head and rode closer to her. "First let me bid you my greetings, sweet Emma, and tell you how happy I am to have finally caught up with you, you Indian-lovin' bitch!" He suddenly kicked out, catching her under the chin and knocking her back to the ground.

Peter struggled to appear not to care, but Red Wolf made a move toward Tommy. The seven other men with Tommy pointed their muskets at Red Wolf.

"Stay back, brown ass!" Deek Malone ordered. "I sure would love to put a musket ball in your gut!"

Peter's head ached from the desire to kill, but he knew that neither Emma nor River would want any killings or rapes to occur because of them.

"When I'm through with you, Emma Simms, you're gonna wish to hell you would have let me have at you that day at the farm," Tommy growled.

Deek looked at him curiously, wondering what he meant.

"You and me are gonna have a good time on our way back to Knoxville," Tommy sneered, "and you'll have an even better time when you take up your proper place among the whores at the Tennessee Belle saloon. Sam Gates will show you what's expected of you, and I intend to be one of your first customers!"

Emma groaned, rolling to her knees and spitting blood, while Mary burst into tears.

"Why don't you just go away!" Mary shouted. "Leave her alone! She has done nothing to you!"

Grace grasped Mary's arm. "Be still," she said quietly, realizing it was not wise for a pretty young Cherokee girl to draw attention to herself. Martin stepped in front of his young wife, glaring at Tommy, whose eyes had moved to drink in Mary's beauty.

Tommy suddenly broke into laughter. "Don't worry, boy. I ain't gonna rape your pretty woman there. Or is she your sister?"

"She is my woman," Martin answered. "And if you touch her you will die!"

Tommy laughed again. "Well, now, I don't think you're in much of a position to tell me that, boy. But I won't do anything to her, if all of you just cooperate."

Emma managed to get to her feet then, holding her jaw and looking at Peter. "I . . . I want to stay here," she wept. "Why did you tell them . . . to take me! My babies are here. Don't let them take me!"

Peter blinked, momentarily confused. But then he realized Emma's plan.

"Now, wait just a minute here," Tommy cut in. "There's an important person missin' here and if somebody don't tell me where he is, I'm gonna take that little Cherokee girl there and let my friends take her out in the woods and show her a good time."

Martin stiffened and Mary moved closer to him, grabbing his arm.

"You all know who I mean," Tommy added. "Where is River Joe? I ain't leavin' here with his woman and him on my tail. No sir. And how come that man over there come out of her cabin with her and shoved her at me and said he's done sleepin' with her? River Joe would never allow that." He turned his eyes to Emma. "Or did that white Indian get tired of you, too?"

Real tears slid down her face. It was not hard to cry; the thought of having to go with Tommy Decker, of having to leave poor River behind, and her babies, was all she needed to bring the tears.

"River is dead," she said to Tommy, her mouth still bleeding. She spat out some blood, her jaw aching fiercely. "He was attacked by a bear. Infection killed him."

Tommy studied her hard, but he saw no hesitation in her eyes and noticed no faltering in the words. He slowly dismounted, coming closer and grasping her arms. "Come on now, Emma Simms, you can do better than that."

She felt like vomiting, being so close to him again, feeling his hands on her. How she wanted to fight back again, to fight and fight until he killed her! But no matter what he did to her, she could not fight him. She had to live, for her babies. River would come to her and she would come back to her babies. They were all that mattered—Rachael and Joshua—and the baby growing right now in her belly.

"It's true," she answered. "Ask any of them. River is dead, and Peter—that man who shoved me out of the house —he took me in. I . . . I had to sleep with him because he provided for me. That's the Cherokee way," she lied, knowing that men like Tommy Decker knew nothing about Cherokee ways. "But he doesn't really care about me. When he heard you shouting for me, he shoved me out the door because he doesn't want to get hurt over me."

He squeezed her arms painfully. "I seen you with two babies earlier. What about them?"

"They . . . they're mine . . . by River. Please don't take me away from my babies, Tommy. Peter is cruel to me, but I have to stay—because of my babies."

He snickered, looking her over. He moved one hand to grasp one of her full breasts, feeling over it, grinning, deliberately humiliating her. "I don't give a goddamn about your babies," he sneered. "Me and the rest of the boys here, we'll take care of your extra milk." He looked back at the others. "Won't we, boys?"

They all laughed. "Gladly," Deek answered, making a sucking sound.

Peter struggled desperately to appear unconcerned, but Grace and Mary both turned away, Grace putting her arm around Mary, who started to cry harder. Emma just glared at Tommy, bearing his ugly insults by glorying in the fact that she just might fool him and get him away from River. When River came for her, he would make Tommy Decker pay for his despicable actions.

Tommy jerked her closer, moving a hand to run it over her bottom. "God, girl, you sure do things to a man, even after two babies. I reckon pretty soon I'll find out if them babies got you all stretched so you ain't no fun no more. Maybe that's why the young buck there don't want you now. Is that it?"

Emma stiffened with pride. She was River Joe's woman. She would not be afraid. How many times had he told her not to be afraid of anything? Courage now could mean saving his life. "You wouldn't have been enough for me even when I was a virgin!" she sneered.

Tommy lost his smile, and those Cherokee who understood English were astonished at the bold remark, and proud of the white woman River Joe had married. She was indeed brave. Tommy grasped her long, blond hair, jerking her head back.

"You'll regret that, Emma Simms!" he hissed. "Oh, yes, there are a lot of things you'll regret."

He moved back while keeping hold of her hair, and she screamed out as he pulled her around in a quick circle, then literally tossed her, sending her scraping across the rough ground.

"Now!" he shouted. "Let's have the truth before I rape all the little girls in this village and burn every house! Where is River Joe? Somebody is lyin' here! I ain't gonna leave here with that goddamned white Indian skulkin' behind me!"

"You stupid, foolheaded, ignorant white man!" Ramona screamed at him, trotting her frail, withered body away from the others and shaking a bony finger at Tommy. "Does red hair on a white man mean he has no brains? Do you have trouble understanding your own language, *Unega?*"

"Shut up, old woman!" Tommy screamed back at her, as Emma again struggled to her feet.

"River Joe is dead," Ramona said convincingly. "Ask any of these people. I doctored him myself. I am the medicine woman for this village. White men cannot take infection like the Cherokee. River Joe was attacked by a bear and he died!"

Emma broke into tears, tears of horror that she hoped Tommy would think were tears of sorrow.

"That River Joe—he said he killed a man and stole a white girl. That stupid white girl, she liked River Joe—had his babies," Ramona went on. "She stayed here willingly. Then River Joe died—left that damned white girl with us to take care of—her and two babies. But we don't want her, understand, redheaded *Unega*? Take her! Take her away! She is just a burden. But leave her babies. They are healthy. We will raise them to be good Cherokee and to help us hunt and survive. We will make them marry into the Cherokee tribe so there is no trouble. That is what we tried to do with River Joe, but he brought this white girl to us. She is nothing but trouble."

The old woman threw up her hands, walking over and kicking dirt and stones at Emma. "With River Joe dead, we want this girl away from us!" she shrieked. "Take her and be gone! We want no trouble over a stupid white girl! We Cherokee have enough troubles!"

Tommy stared at her. Emma sat crouched and weeping—weeping with love for Ramona, who she knew was only trying to hurry Tommy along and keep him from searching the cabins. Tommy nodded slowly.

"All right, old woman. I don't think an old bitch like you would lie."

Ramona toddled back to Tommy. "I had no use for River Joe once he started going down into the valleys and running with other whites. He was not a good Cherokee after that. Then he came back with this pitiful excuse of a woman who is now a burden to us. Take her away! Go! Go! Do you think if River Joe were alive, he would just let you take her away? If he were alive he would be out here defending her. That was his nature. But none of our men is going to defend a white woman, so take her and be off with you!" The old woman's voice was amazingly strong. She then trotted away, mumbling to herself.

Tommy watched after her, then scanned the rest of the Cherokee who had gathered at his command. Yes, the old woman was right. If River Joe were alive, he would never let this happen. He walked over to Emma, jerking her up and pushing her toward his horse. "Get up there! We got us a long trip ahead of us, and an enjoyable one for all my men, you can bet on that!"

Deek snickered as Emma managed to mount Tommy's horse. Tommy mounted up behind her, pulling her gown up and tucking it under her bottom so that her legs were fully exposed for the other men.

"We got us a fine prize here, men," he said. "Sam Gates will pay you well for hangin' in there with me and helpin' me find her." He ran a hand along her inner thigh and up over her breasts. Emma stared straight ahead, refusing to look at Mary or Grace or Peter or any of the others; refusing to think about River lying under the bed, unaware of what was happening to his *Agiya;* refusing to think about her precious babies lying asleep in the cabin, unaware that their mother was leaving them, perhaps never to return.

"Let's go, men!" Tommy let out a war whoop and rode off, followed by the seven other men. Emma allowed herself to rejoice inside that at least he believed River was dead.

She had saved River and her babies! She knew Mary and Grace would take care of them. And River Joe would get well. He would get well, and he would come for her! But until then, she would have to find a way to bear the horrors of Tommy Decker, until River Joe's blade found its way into Tommy Decker's heart.

◇ *Chapter 20* ◇

The summer night was alive with tree frogs and all sorts of insects. Emma remembered other nights like this—on the trail, sleeping under the stars or in a tent. But those nights were spent with River Joe, safe, secure, loved, lying in his strong arms. But River could not help her now.

Tommy had ridden for miles, taking most of the day. All along the way he showered Emma with every insult he could think of, joking about how her breasts, full with milk, bounced with the horse's gait.

He left no doubts about what he would do with her once they made camp, and she had to be grateful to the other men for one thing—they all complained that they should cover as much ground as possible by nightfall. All of them were eager to get back to Knoxville. That kept Tommy from stopping long enough to hurt her, until now, until the night.

As she listened to them talk, Emma realized just how determined Tommy had been this time. Apparently he had been on the move since spring, constantly searching. The men often mentioned how far they had to go to get to Knoxville, and she realized with every mile they covered that if River really did die and did not come for her, she would have no idea how to get back to her babies, how to find the Cherokee again.

They were all she had now. Her babies, River, Mary, Grace, Peter, and the others. The Cherokee were her family now. Never had she known such love or such courage in a people. She felt like crying over old Ramona, who had put on such a good act. The old woman had saved River's life, Emma was sure. And poor Peter, shoving her around, pretending he didn't care.

They had all done their jobs perfectly. She smiled inwardly at the thought of how surprised and frightened Tommy would be when she finally told him the truth. And she would tell him, once they reached Knoxville. River Joe wasn't dead at all! She felt like shouting it, and she wished she could tell Tommy now, but it was too soon. She had to get a lot of time and miles between them first. River needed time to heal.

She concentrated on Rachael and Joshua and River, her beautiful family. Would she ever see them again? The possibility was shattering, but not as shattering as if Tommy had found River and the babies and killed them in cold blood. Thank God for Ramona's sharp order to leave the babies with the Cherokee. The old woman knew exactly what she was doing, exactly how to handle a man like Tommy Decker, if he could be called a man at all.

"Hold up!" Tommy shouted then, startling her from her thoughts. She had concentrated only on those she loved, and on the hope that River Joe would come for her. It was the only way she could bear the hard ride and the horrible insults and touches. She wished she could nurse her babies, for her breasts were painfully full.

Tommy's shouted halt brought her back to reality, and the discomfort returned not only to her breasts but to her aching jaw and teeth. Still, the pain was easier to bear than the terror in her heart.

Tommy was stopping to make camp for the night! How could she let him do what he surely had in mind to do without fighting him? For the sake of the children, she knew she must not fight Tommy Decker. She had to stay healthy and alive. Tommy would surely beat her without mercy if she fought him.

If only they were alone like the first time; she would find a way to fend him off just as she had then. But this time he had the advantage. He had all these other men with him to hold her down, all of them probably planning on having a turn of their own. She struggled against an urge to vomit. "Let's make camp here," Tommy ordered the others.

A few men grumbled that it was too early, but they all dismounted. Tommy jerked Emma down from his horse. He turned her, looking down at her breasts, his leering smile slightly crooked.

"You ready to feed your man, Emma?" He leaned down and growled as he nuzzled against her breasts, and she fought an urge to gouge out his eyes. She knew it was what he wanted her to do, knew his temper well enough to realize that if she hurt him, he would beat her, maybe to death, for his rage would be uncontrollable. He had vengeance on his mind, and for the moment he would take it this way, through humiliation rather than a physical beating.

He laughed, pushing her against his horse and reaching inside her flannel gown to feel her breasts, calling her a milk cow. She had no idea how she was going to live through this, and she prayed to the Maker of Breath to give her courage and help her know what to do. What hurt more than anything was for another man to touch her, and there would probably be more than one man before this ordeal was over. She wanted River Joe to be her only man. She belonged to River. He was her first man and she never wanted another to invade what belonged to River. But she didn't know how to stop what was happening. She knew only that she wanted to live, to get back to her children, to be in River's arms again. But after this, perhaps he wouldn't even want her.

Tommy straightened, keeping hold of one of her arms and studying her curiously. "How come you been so quiet?" he asked, licking his lips. "Last time I even tried to touch you, you like to killed me. Now you just stand there and do nothin'. What happened to all the fight in you, Emma

Simms? That Indian you been sleepin' with beat all the life out of you?" He snickered, suddenly appearing nervous.

She raised her eyes to meet his, suddenly losing all her fear and dread. River had told her so many times not to be afraid of anything, and suddenly she was not afraid of Tommy Decker. She saw in that quick moment a hesitation, and she realized he was more put off by her calmness than if she fought him.

Perhaps he wanted a fight. Perhaps that was what excited him and made him want her more. After all, most of the girls Tommy Decker had been with were women who didn't even want him—poor, helpless Cherokee girls, young girls he bullied or beat his way into raping.

"I don't care about anything now that River is dead," she answered him. "He was the only man I ever really wanted."

She saw the hatred and jealousy grow in Tommy's eyes. He jerked her close. "Well, he *is* dead! And now you're finally mine, at least until we get to Knoxville. You want to know what's gonna happen to you there, bitch? I'm turnin' you over to a man called Sam Gates, and I'll make a pretty penny doin' it. And when Sam gets hold of you, you'll be wishin' you was with *me!* It won't be just Tommy Decker who spreads your pretty legs and has a good ride with you. It will be a different man every night, maybe *more* than one a night!"

Emma swallowed back the black dread. Maybe River would get to her in time. This she could bear if she absolutely had to, but to do what Tommy was telling her now...

"You always thought you was too good for me, Emma Simms, keepin' yourself pure for somebody else. Maybe River Joe got you first, but that don't mean I can't have what I've been wantin' for years. And it's a good thing River Joe is dead, 'cause if he wasn't, we would have finished the job ourselves. Better yet, we would have brought him back to Knoxville for a real pretty hangin', for killin' Hank Toole. Fact is, maybe you'll hang yourself," he lied, enjoying frightening her.

Emma paled, struggling against the horror of his words. "What are you talking about?"

He grinned. "You run off with him, Emma—willingly, it looks like. That means you went along with the murder of Hank Toole."

"Hank was beating me, trying to rape me! River came and . . . I had no control over what he did."

"But you run off with him anyway. You should have stayed put, Emma. Then folks would have believed you. But now . . ." He shrugged. "We'll let Sam decide what to do with you." He enjoyed the way she trembled. Why bother telling her Nigger Jim had already been hanged for Hank's murder? Let her think the worst for now. Maybe it would make her more cooperative. "Might be you'll have to agree to be Sam's little whore. Him and me, we can keep you out of trouble, or we can hand you over for a trial and a hangin'. A trial could be messy and ugly, Emma, honey. All them questions right out in public about you and River Joe—your sex life—you bein' with the Cherokee—sleepin' with a Cherokee man who wasn't even your husband. Fact is, River Joe wasn't even your legal husband, not by white man's standards. You was just a whore for the Cherokee, Emma. White folks at a trial ain't gonna look kindly on a slut."

She checked her anger. Deek Malone stood close by, grinning. "Why don't you do what you've been wantin' to do and get it over with, Tommy?" he asked. "I want my turn."

Emma felt her stomach churning. Did Tommy mean to let every man there rape her?

"I want her to think about it awhile," Tommy answered. "She hates my guts. Now she's got to think about the fact that Tommy Decker is gonna have his turn at her, and he's gonna do everything else he can think of." He kept his eyes drilling into Emma's. "I'm gonna know you inside and out when I'm through with you," he said, leering as he moved his hands over her shoulders and breasts, down over her waist, suddenly ripping down her gown so that she stood naked in front of all of them.

"Whooee!" one of the men shouted, while others made ugly sounds and comments.

"You was right, Tommy," another said. "She's a looker all right. Hard to believe she's had a couple of kids. Ain't no woman I ever seen naked who had a couple of kids who looked like that. You make sure I'm second after you."

"Deek is second," Tommy answered, grinning at Emma the whole time. "I promised him. But you can be third, Len."

"Well, get busy then."

Tommy stared at her, still looking a little nervous over the way she just stood there staring at him. "Get the camp set up first," he answered. "Put up my tent and build a fire." He grabbed her wrists and pulled her toward a tree. She stumbled over her gown, which was caught around her feet. She fell, and he half-dragged her then.

Every bone and muscle in Emma's body ached from the long day's ride and the emotional strain of her ordeal. She prayed again for some kind of miracle that would stop all of this. Tommy tied her wrists to an overhead branch so that her arms were stretched up.

"That should hold you till I'm ready for you," he said. He stepped close to her then, grasping her bottom. "There's only one reason I ain't beatin' on you, Emma Simms. There's nothin' I'd love more than to displace that jaw like you did mine—beat you till nobody can recognize you, use you like a damned punchin' bag and keep at it till you're dead!" he hissed. "I'll never forget what you did to me. But I'm holdin' off, and only because I want the money Sam Gates will pay to get you back. I don't reckon he would like me bringin' in a corpse, or a woman so beat up she's permanently ugly from it. I've got to bring Sam Gates the pretty woman he's expectin', but I'll by-God make you pay in other ways—ways that don't show on the outside! And I'll make you wish I beat you instead!"

He left her then, and again she concentrated on River and her children while the men made camp, all of them hardly able to take their eyes off her. They all seemed eager and ready to have their turn at her, and she could not get rid of the constant nausea in her stomach.

Suddenly it hit her then—a pain deep in her belly. It crawled through her insides, hard and deep, making her grimace with a need to draw up her legs. It reminded her of the cramps she sometimes felt when it was her time of the month, only these cramps were much worse, almost like labor pains.

She could not imagine at first what it could be. Perhaps it was brought on by the long ride. It was a long time since she had ridden that far, and combined with a lack of food and water and Tommy's constant abuse, perhaps this was some kind of reaction.

She breathed easier for a moment, and then the pain hit her again, so hard that she cried out. She drew up one leg, unable to draw up both legs because then she would be hanging freely by her wrists. This pain brought tears to her eyes, and brought Tommy back over to her.

"What the hell are you yellin' about?"

"Pain . . . my stomach . . ."

Tommy scowled. "I'll give you pain in the stomach!" He punched her hard in the abdomen, and Emma screamed.

"Baby! My baby!" She knew it then, realizing with quick clarity what was causing the pain. "You'll make me lose it!"

Tommy stepped back, his eyes wide with surprise. "Baby! You slut! You pregnant by that heathen Indian?"

Emma could not answer. She gasped in black pain, the only fear she had never been able to rid herself of now gripping her. The baby! She was losing the baby! It would be like her mother—the dreaded miscarriage! Maybe she would even die!

"Please . . . let me down!" she screamed. "Let me down! The pain!"

"Like hell, slut! I can't beat you, but if I can make you suffer some other way, then I'll do it!"

Tommy turned and walked away, and Emma felt a light, warm trickle down her inner right thigh. She knew without being able to look that it was blood. She would lose this precious baby. Fear and sorrow welled up in her soul, and although she knew it was music to Tommy's ears, she could not help crying. The horrid pain came again, and she screamed with it, begging Tommy again to let her down. She needed to curl up, to be warm, to hold her belly. But no one came to help her.

Never had Emma Rivers known such devastating pain and sorrow. By the time Tommy cut her down, blood poured down her legs, and she was sure she was going to bleed to death as her mother had. Through all her ugly pain she heard Tommy and the other men cursing and fuming over the miscarriage.

"I ain't layin' with that," one man grumped. "You sure messed this one up, Tommy Decker. We would have been better off bringin' along that pretty little Cherokee girl we seen back there."

"I can't have a good time with no woman who just lost a baby, even if she's a slut like that one," another complained. "It just don't seem right."

"Shut up! All of you!" Tommy yelled.

Emma lay on a mat by the fire, curled up and groaning. Someone had finally had the decency to bring her a blanket to cover her. She felt blood everywhere, but no one attempted to clean her up. She wept deep, wrenching sobs at the memory of Tommy's ugly words when he cut her down. *"What the hell is this?"* he had said with disgust. *"Hell, she's done lost a baby, I'll bet,"* someone else had answered. *"See that? That's the beginnin's of a damned baby."*

"Jesus!" Tommy had answered.

"Throw it away, you idiot," came the other voice.

Her baby! She had lost it while hanging from the tree. Tommy had just thrown it away like a piece of garbage. It should be buried, no matter how tiny and lifeless it was, no matter if it didn't even resemble a human being yet. "River, River," she sobbed.

"Shut up over there!" Tommy yelled. "Your white buck's dead—he ain't comin' for you—so shut up! I'm still takin' you to Knoxville. And soon as you're well, I'm still takin' what's comin' to me!"

Emma curled up tighter near the fire, rocking with pain. Maybe this was best. It was highly unusual for a woman to get pregnant so quickly after giving birth, especially when she was breast-feeding. That was what the Cherokee women had told her. Perhaps the Maker of Breath had deliberately let it happen to her, knowing this moment was coming. She had prayed for a miracle, something that would keep Tommy and the others away from her. She had been given that miracle, in the form of a miscarriage.

In a way, River had helped her again, for it was his seed that had planted the child in her womb. Now she had lost it, but losing it had saved her from a multiple rape, had kept her still belonging only to River.

But the fact remained that she had lost a child. It was her baby, hers and River's. Now it was dead, and she might die herself. She was getting no medical attention. No one would even clean her up.

She heard someone walk up behind her then. "I'll stick you in a creek soon as we find one," Tommy said. "Got to wash that blood off you. By the time we get to Knoxville, you ought to be all healed up and presentable for Sam Gates. It's a damned good thing this happened now and not then."

She remained turned away, her back to him. "I'll die . . . like Mama," she mumbled.

"You better not! You'll cost me money if you die, bitch!"

"Water. I need . . . a drink of water," she groaned.

"Damn!" Tommy muttered. "What damned bad luck! You've always been bad luck for me, Emma Simms!" He left for a moment, then returned, jerking her up to a sitting position so that she cried out with pain. "Here! Here's your damned water," he grumped. He put a canteen to her lips and held it up, forcing her to drink in quick gulps.

He shoved her back down then. "What a damned mess," he fumed. "If I want my money, I got to take you back to Sam Gates in one piece, well and still lookin' good. You know what that means? It means I got to take care of you, bitch! I've got to clean up your mess and keep you fed and watered like a prized horse that's took sick! I ain't sure you're worth the bother, you know that? I ought to leave you here to die alone!"

"You better take her to Sam," Deek Malone cut in. "Damn you, Tommy Decker, we come all this way and went through all this hell to find that damned girl. Now we're gonna get that reward, or you're gonna pay with your hide. You better take care of her and keep her alive!"

Tommy swung around, fists clenched. "Who do you think you're talkin' to?"

"The dumb son-of-a-bitch who brought us up here on a wild goose chase," Deek answered boldly, tired of Tommy's bossiness. "I thought I'd get a good piece of woman out of this, and there she lays, bleedin' all over the place. It's about to make me sick!"

"Then go away someplace and puke!" Tommy sneered. "Get out of my sight before I beat the hell out of you, Deek Malone!"

After a pause, Deek finally answered, "Try it," his voice firm and sure.

There was another moment of silence. "Go to hell," Tommy replied then. "We'll settle this another time. Right now I've got to keep this bitch alive long enough to collect a reward." He spoke up louder: "Everybody turn in. We're gonna ride hard tomorrow. If we keep at it, we can be back to Knoxville in a couple of weeks."

"What about the woman?" someone asked. "She's bleedin' all over the place. How you gonna move her? She might die on you, Tommy."

"If she dies, she dies. Make up somethin' to carry her—a blanket and poles we can tie to a horse. She'll be over the heavy bleedin' soon. By the time we get to Knoxville, she should be over all of it, and we'll still have a good-lookin' woman to present to Sam."

Emma groaned at the thought of having to travel in her condition. Never had she known such pain and agony as this. Now she understood the hell her mother had gone through. She could only pray she would not die from this. River! She had to think of River. He would come for her, and she would be with her babies again, her precious Rachael and her chubby, sweet Joshua. Somehow, someday, they would all be together again. She had to believe it. She had to cling to life, for the sake of Rachael and Joshua—and River. Surely he would come, and this nightmare would be over.

She clung to thoughts that made all this bearable—the miscarriage had kept Tommy away from her; and River Joe was still alive and would come for her. All she had to do now was survive the rest of this trip. But another challenge awaited her when she arrived in Knoxville. What would Sam Gates do with her?

It was two days before River came out of his deep sleep and looked around the little cabin. He lay quietly at first, gathering his thoughts. He remembered Emma telling him she loved him, telling him it would soon be over and he would be all right. And he remembered the pain, the horrible, burning pain.

He closed his eyes against the memory, turning his head and looking toward Rachael's cradle. He realized then that he was getting better. He had turned his head and felt no pain. He stared at the cradle, finding joy in the fact that he could move his head, but seeing that the cradle was empty. Emma must be feeding the baby.

He slowly turned his head the other way, waiting for the pain to come. But there was none. He saw Grace standing over a kettle at the fireplace. Emma was not there, nor were the children.

"Grace," he muttered weakly.

She turned, wiping her hands on an apron and hurrying over to the bed. "Joe! Joe, you're finally awake. How do you feel?"

"I am not . . . sure yet." He raised his good arm and put a hand to his eyes, then ran it through his hair. "Where is Emma? Go and get her, will you? I want her to know I am awake and I can turn my head. See?" He moved his head back and forth. "I am better, Grace."

"Oh, that's wonderful, Joe!"

He met her eyes and was sure he detected tears in them. "Something wrong, Grace?"

She patted his chest. "You lie still and get your rest. I have some soup ready. Let me go and get Peter. I will be right back."

He watched her go quickly to the door. "Grace, what is it? What's wrong? Where is Emma?"

"Wait . . . just a few minutes, Joe. Everything will be all right."

He frowned, an ugly dread moving through his blood. He tried to sit up and cursed his weakness. He couldn't even raise his head off the pillow, and pain coursed through his whole right side. He was better but certainly not healed.

He looked over again at the empty cradle. Had something happened to Rachael? Joshua? Had they lied to him about Joshua being all right? This was the first time he had been fully conscious and lucid since the bear attack. Maybe his memory of Emma holding Joshua for him to see had been just an hallucination. Maybe Joshua was dead. Maybe Emma had come to help him and she was hurt, too.

But no. She had been with him when Ramona burned out the wound. He was sure of it. A thousand thoughts rushed through his mind while his heart beat harder with dread.

Finally Grace returned. Peter was with her, and Mary and Red Wolf and Martin. Old Ramona followed behind, but Emma was not there. He vaguely remembered her saying something about possibly being pregnant again, just before Ramona burned out the wound. Had she miscarried? Had she died from it? Why did they all look so solemn, and why did Mary look ready to burst into tears?

"Joe, you're better!" Mary said, hurrying to the bed. "Finally! Thank God! You are the only one who can help!"

"Hush, Mary," Grace said in a motherly fashion.

"Help what?" River's face remained grim. "What the hell is going on? Where is Emma?"

Ramona bent over him, taking the bandage from his wound and inspecting it. "Much better. The infection is leaving you, *Unega.*" She straightened. "You are a man who should hear things straight out. The others love you too much to tell you. So I will tell you, Joe. White men came. They took your Emma."

River's face darkened and his eyes blazed. "What the hell are you talking about! Where is Emma? Who took her? Did one of them have red hair?" He tried again to sit up but could not. Ramona bent over him, grasping his arms, while Mary began to cry.

"Yes. They were led by the white one with red hair—the one who calls himself Tommy. She begged us not to fight for her—to let them take her and to say you were dead. It was the only way to save your life and to keep them from harming your children. It was a smart thing your woman did, and brave. She is a white woman of courage who knows how to think. She saved your life by going with them."

River reached up with his good hand, grasping Ramona's arm almost painfully. "When? When did this happen?"

"Joe, you will hurt Ramona. She is an old woman," Grace said calmly.

Tears of anger and helplessness quickly filled River's eyes. He let go of Ramona and the old woman straightened. "Two days," she replied. "They said they will take her to Knoxville, to a white man called Sam Gates. Emma knew that if you remained alive and got well, you would go and get her. It is her only hope. It will sustain her through whatever they do to her."

River groaned with the realization of what that would be. "Emma! Emma! My God!" He rolled to his left side, trying again to sit up by using his good arm to push himself. Quickly Grace moved to force him back down. Peter moved to the other side of the bed to help.

"Be smart, white man!" Ramona barked. "Your woman needs your help. You cannot help her like this. You must heal first and be very strong. Then and only then can you go to your woman. She is smart, and she is strong and brave. She will survive until you come for her."

River lay groaning with the agony of it. Emma! Emma in the hands of Tommy Decker! Death would be better. And if he did take her all the way to Knoxville, what did Sam Gates have in store for her?

"I'll kill him! I'll kill him!" he growled through clenched teeth. "That bastard! I'll kill them all!"

"You will have to be careful, Joe," Peter said. "You will be in white man's territory. If you are caught—"

"It does not matter! If I can get her away from there it does not matter!" He breathed deeply for control, realizing that old Ramona was right. He was in no condition to go after her. "They came and took her . . . while I lay helpless like a damned coward," he groaned.

"You are no coward. Your woman knows that," Ramona said. "She knows that you are a brave man who will come for her as soon as your body allows it. The best thing you can do for her now is to lie still and heal—eat and rest, Joe. You will need your strength and cunning."

"My God, my God," he groaned. "Emma."

Mary cried harder and Peter turned away. Grace took

Mary's arms and made her stand up, leading her to the door. "Go out for a while, Mary. Your weeping does not help him, and you are with child. Go back home and rest."

The girl left, still crying.

"She was pregnant. She was pregnant," River was moaning. "What he'll do to her . . . she'll lose it. She'll be so scared . . . her mother . . . she'll die."

"She will not die," Ramona said firmly. "It was not the right time to be having another baby—bad for one so young with such a new baby already. If she was really with child and loses it, it is best, for her and the child; and it would keep that redheaded swine away from her."

"But he . . . wouldn't take care of her. It would be . . . a terrible thing for her. And her mother . . . she'll die, Ramona. She'll never carry a baby through all that . . . and a miscarriage—"

"Hush, Joe," Grace said. "You do not know what has happened. Right now you must concentrate on getting well so you can help her. They all think you are dead. You have an advantage. They will not be searching or watching for you. And if you can get her away without being seen, they will never know. That frees you, Joe. You will be free to live your life, perhaps someplace new, with Emma."

"Emma," he whispered. His whole body shook in a sob. "Emma. Don't you know . . . what he's probably done to her by now? It's what she always dreaded most. She hates Tommy Decker." He clenched his fist in desperate helplessness, feeling crazed with the inability to go to her. "My God, I slept while they came and took my wife away! How many were there?"

"Eight," Red Wolf answered. "At least that is what we counted, unless there were more back at their camp. But I think Decker used all the men he had to be sure there was no trouble. They surrounded us at dawn, killed two of our scouts and wounded the others. Someone had checked us out before that, knew where our scouts were stationed. They were smart this time, Joe. They planned this one instead of just riding in straight on and letting our scouts see them. There was no time to hide or run or plan what to do."

"It was Emma's idea," Peter said quietly then. "She hid you under the bed and said we should all say you were dead." A look of shame moved through his eyes. "We were all very convincing—so convincing they did not even search the cabins. Emma made me pretend I had taken her in after you died. I . . . I shoved her toward them, told them I was tired of her. Old Ramona told them to take her away—that she was a nuisance now that you were dead. They believed it. It was the only way we could make them leave without searching for you or maybe hurting the babies. They even had their eye on Mary for a while, but they seemed satisfied just to get Emma."

River groaned again, turning away from him and putting a hand to his head.

"It was the only way, Joe," Grace said. "Emma wanted it that way. She did not want to be responsible for what might happen if she fought it. They would have raped Mary, burned our houses. They would not have believed us and they would have searched for you. And you know yourself they would have killed you where you lay. Tommy Decker would never have let you live. He is afraid of you. And if he had killed you, there would be no one left to help Emma."

"We could see it in his eyes, Joe," Red Wolf added. "He is very much afraid of you. He was glad to hear you were dead. He said he did not want to take Emma away and worry about you being behind him."

"Well, I *will* be behind him!" River seethed. "He's going to get one hell of a surprise when he finds out River Joe is still alive!"

Ramona grinned. "I wish I could see his face when that one sees you again. It would be a fine sight."

River shuddered with the horror of it. "Bring me my children. I want to see them. I want to see that they are all right."

Grace hurried off, and River covered his face with his

hand, ashamed of the tears that came but unable to stop them. He was weak and in pain, and now he had learned that his precious Emma had been taken away, by the worst person who could have taken her.

Old Ramona bent close, grasping his wrist. "You go ahead and weep, white man. Any man would weep over such a thing, whether white or Cherokee. There is no shame in it. You weep for your woman. But when you are stronger there will be no tears. There will be only revenge!" She almost hissed the word *revenge,* and she squeezed his wrist harder.

He moved his hand to take her own, breathing deeply for control. "Do what you can, *adawehi,* to make me well quickly. I will do whatever you say."

She nodded. "That is wise. I will heal you, *Unega,* and you will get the revenge that has been denied our own men. They weep, too. For them it is worse. They are strong and healthy, and yet they cannot defend their women because of the white man's laws. If they rise up against the white men who abuse their women and their property, the white man will come and kill many and make the rest of us move to a land we despise. The white man lives by strange rules, River Joe. But you know their world. You go and break those rules. You break them, and get your woman back!"

◇ *Chapter 21* ◇

The trip took over two weeks, and Emma would never forget it. Still, at least some of it was spent in blessed semiconsciousness from loss of blood. Most of her traveling had been on a travois behind Tommy's horse, but there were few other comforts. She dreaded meeting Sam Gates, already hated him. And yet for the moment she had to be glad it was Sam Gates to whom Tommy was taking her, for Tommy apparently feared the man and knew he would get no money if he brought Sam Gates a dead or battered woman.

That was all that kept Tommy from beating her and killing her, and the miscarriage kept him from raping her. It had surprised and offended him. Tommy Decker knew only one aspect of women, and that was that they were something to be used sexually. He had never thought about or encountered all the other facets of the female sex. A bleeding woman left him confused and repulsed, and that was just fine with Emma.

Deek Malone and the other men seemed to have similar feelings. "This whole trip has been a waste," she heard Deek complain the day they were to arrive in Knoxville. "All we got is a pitiful bit of woman who's half-dead from loss of blood. It's been over two weeks, and she still can't hardly get up off that travois. Sam Gates ain't gonna want somethin' like that."

"Quit your gripin'," Tommy answered. "He asked for

Emma Simms, and that's what I'm bringin' to him. Soon as she's well, he'll see how pretty she is and he'll put her to work. And I aim to be one of her first customers. She thinks she's got no more worries about gettin' laid by Tommy Decker, but I'll be around when Sam Gates tells her she better cooperate or suffer the consequences."

"You think he'd beat her?"

"I ain't sure what he'd do. All I know is I can read a man's eyes, and behind them fancy clothes and that fake smile of his is a man who knows how to get what he wants out of people and who don't like to be crossed."

"Well, I'm for gettin' my money and headin' back up home. I ain't seen my pa in a long time, and this whole thing don't stick in my craw right, Tommy. Why don't you come home with me?"

"You kiddin'? Sam pays me good. And, like I say, soon as Emma is well, I'm gonna do every last lovin' thing there is to do to a woman and gladly pay for it just to watch the look on her face."

Emma cringed as she heard the words, wondering when the trip would be over and the constant bouncing would stop. How long would it take River to come? Was he well now, or had he died?

"There she is!" someone shouted. "It's about time!"

"Hallelujah!" someone else yelled. "Good ol' Knoxville!"

Emma felt her heart tighten, and she wished she felt better, stronger. She could barely stand up and walk. Perhaps she would be stronger if Tommy had fed and cared for her properly, but she had been handled like a sick dog. How could she face up to this Sam Gates when she felt so weak and sick?

"Let's keep goin', boys," Tommy said then. "We can be there by nightfall."

They continued to descend. Their journey had been a long one, taking most of the summer. But now the search was over. They had found their prey, pitiful and frail as she was.

Emma could think of nothing but River and the babies.

They were so far away now! Even if she could escape, how would she go about finding them, or even survive the journey all alone? It was almost as though that beautiful life had all been a dream. Now she was headed for a new life, at least until River came for her . . . if he was still alive.

"I can make it now," River said to Ramona. He paced back and forth, stretching out his arms, raising them up over his head, flexing his hands. "I am a little weak, but I will eat well all the way to Knoxville, and I will make sure I get plenty of sleep at night."

He stepped close to the old woman and she looked him over. He wore only his loincloth, and she reached up and felt around his shoulder and neck. Pink scars lingered on his chest and arms, and his right arm remained bandaged. But the infection had not returned, and there was a scabbed indentation near his neck, where Ramona had held the hot iron.

"Hmmm," she muttered. "Maybe you are right. You are thinner, Joe, but your wounds look good, and your determination to save your woman will give you the added strength you need to replace what you have lost through sickness."

River smiled, an almost wicked smile of revenge. "You are exactly right. You understand such things well, old woman."

"I have been around a long time." She patted his chest. "I have no use for white men, and especially not for white women. But you are different, Joe. You are white, but you have a Cherokee heart, and so does your woman, even though she has not been with us long."

"She was never the spoiled, pampered white woman you think they all are. Emma led a hard life before I found her," he answered. He pulled on a pair of buckskin pants and laced them halfway, then turned to face her. "What will I do if she is dead, Ramona?" His eyes teared.

"You will go on—for your children," she said firmly. "You have a son and a daughter, Joe, gifts from Emma. She loved them dearly. She would want you to go on, to take care of her babies." She walked closer, patting his arm. "Mary and Grace will continue to take care of the small ones until you return. And you *will* return, *with* your Emma." She nodded. *"Esaugetuh Emissee* will help you. There will be many prayers among all of us. His power will be with you, Joe."

He took her hand and squeezed it. "You saved my life, not just from the wound, but the day you helped convince those men that I was dead. I am in your debt, old woman."

She shook her head. "I do what the Maker of Breath would have me do. An old woman like me enjoys helping the young, strong ones." She took a deep breath and assumed her usual air of unconcern. "Get dressed and go now! Grace has packed food and supplies for you. Peter has got your horse ready. I am convinced you are strong enough." She shook a finger at him. "But do what I said. Eat well and get your rest. Better to go slower and arrive alive and well than to get sick on the trail and not be able to get to Emma. Do not let your anxiousness and your desire for revenge make you foolish!"

He nodded. "I understand. I will be careful, Ramona." He finished dressing and turned to stare at the bed, its handmade mattress covered with a handsewn quilt, both products of Emma's loving care and patience. How many sweet, passionate moments they had shared on that bed!

His whole body ached for her, longed to get her back and prove to her and to the world that she belonged to him. What had Tommy Decker and the others done to her by now? What would Sam Gates do to her? The thoughts made him want to scream, want to destroy everything in sight. Men were going to pay dearly for this! He had the advantage. They thought he was dead.

He would go first to the Tennessee Belle saloon, where Emma would most likely be by the time he reached Knoxville. His plans from there were not firm yet, but he would improvise to fit the situation. He would like to charge in and kill everyone in sight and carry her off, but he knew he would have to be more clever than that, more careful. It was best that everyone continue to think him dead. He had to find a way to get Emma out of there without anyone knowing how it happened.

"Maybe I should take you with me, old woman," he teased. "You are pretty clever."

Old Ramona laughed, shuffling toward the door. "Only in medicine and in the ways of the people," she replied. "This deed is something that calls for a strong, cunning man who knows the ways of the white man. That is where you have an advantage, Joe." She reached the door and turned to look at him. "You get her, Joe. And you kill that Tommy Decker." She pointed her finger. "Be careful, and be smart. But do not leave that white man's town without killing that redheaded bastard!"

She sniffed and went out the door. River stared after her, feeling strengthened by the old woman's words. "You can be sure I will kill him," he muttered. He sat down in a chair to pull on his knee-high moccasins. It was early. He could make a lot of miles today.

Sam Gates held up a lantern and pulled the blanket off Emma as she lay on the travois. She wore the same gown she had been wearing when Tommy had stolen her away. It was torn and dirty. He hair had not been washed, and it lay in a tousled mess around her pale face. She had lost a considerable amount of weight, and loss of blood had left her weak. Dark circles showed under her normally pretty blue eyes.

She looked up into the eyes of a very handsome older man, well dressed, his dark eyes studying her intently. She felt naked, exposed and vulnerable under his stare, and in spite of his good looks she sensed a certain danger that made her curl up defensively. This had to be Sam Gates.

"This is what I'm supposed to pay you good money for?" the man asked Tommy.

"There was a problem, Mr. Gates. When I found her, she was pregnant. I didn't know it. Some damned Indian buck had took her in and slept with her after River Joe died. Then she went and lost the baby after I took her—"

"Hold up there!" Gates snapped. "I don't like one damned thing I'm hearing, and you're throwing it all at me too fast."

They stood outside the back of the Tennessee Belle. Tommy had brought Emma in after dark so no one would see. The others with him went their way, agreeing to meet with Gates the next morning to get their pay, and agreeing to keep their mouths shut. They were all men Gates trusted, men on his payroll who had worked for him before. Only Deek and Tommy were present now.

"She's a goddamned mess," Gates complained. "You could have used a little soap and water on her, for Christ's sake! Carry her inside my office and lay her on the sofa, and tell me again what the hell happened!"

"Yes, sir."

Emma was lifted, and a moment later her eyes took in a lighted room that had walls lined with books. It smelled of leather and tobacco. Tommy and Deek laid her on a cool, leather sofa. Sam Gates stood over her then, the dark eyes again moving over her. He bent closer, pushing some of the hair back from her face.

"Don't touch me," she said in as strong a voice as she could.

His eyebrows arched and he straightened. "I'll touch whatever I want, Miss Simms. You are my property."

"I'm nobody's property."

He knelt closer, grasping her arm painfully. "I beg to differ. I paid good money for you, woman, on the information that you were a virgin and a most beautiful young lady. But a certain white Indian stole you from me and spoiled the

virgin part of it." He squinted, pulling her gown partly off
her shoulder, grinning when she jerked away from him. "But
I have a feeling that with a little healing time and a little
work, the beautiful part might be saved."

She pulled her gown back up over her shoulder, scrunch-
ing up against the back of the sofa defensively. "You don't
want me now, Mr. Gates. I know why you asked Hank Toole
to bring me to you." She put a shaking hand to her hair,
wishing she were stronger, wishing she could speak more
firmly. "But I'm not the same dumb girl you expected to get.
I've been a wife, and a mother. I've got two babies up there
in the mountains." Her eyes teared then. She hadn't wanted
to cry, but her condition had left her depressed and vulnerable. "Why don't you just let me go back," she whimpered.
"I want my babies. I don't want to be here. I'm no good to
you now."

He sighed and shook his head. "You owe me, Miss
Simms." The man rose, turning to face Tommy and Deek.
"It's true then? She's had a couple of kids?"

Tommy folded his arms. "Yeah, it's true."

Gates shook his head and walked behind his desk. "You
haven't brought me anything that's near worth what I'd pay.
I know that man who first saw her said she was running with
a baby in her arms, but I was hoping somehow it wasn't
hers, let alone the fact that she's had another. You know a
woman who has had two babies isn't the best material for
my business." He cast her a disgusted look. "Look at her!
She's thin and dirty, and now that she's been a wife and a
mother, she'll be hard to work with." His face darkened with
anger. "Take a look at her, Decker! This is what I've let you
run all over the mountains to find? This is what I'm supposed to pay you for bringing to me?"

Tommy dropped his arms, turning his hands out plead-
ingly. "Look, Mr. Gates, I guarantee you'll be pleased once
she's cleaned up and has on one of them pretty dresses and
has a fancy hairdo. Honest to God, she's the prettiest girl in
all the mountain settlements. She's just . . . she's been travel-

in' like this for over two weeks—sick. She lost a baby and bled real bad. That's why she's such a mess right now. But that can all be fixed. Let one of your girls clean her up. Give her a few days to rest up, and you'll be surprised."

"If she turns out as beautiful as you say, I most certainly *will* be surprised! But what if word gets out she's got babies? That turns men off, Tommy. Nobody wants to go upstairs and lie with a woman who's pining away for the babies she's been stolen away from. Mind you, it wouldn't bother me one damned bit, but most men don't feel right about something like that. She's a damned *mother!*" He let out a disgusted hiss, turning away for a moment. "And what's this about River Joe being dead?"

Tommy sighed, running a hand through his hair, while Deek had maneuvered his way into a chair in the corner, trying to remain inconspicuous. He didn't like or trust Sam Gates.

"When we finally found the village where she was livin', she was with a Cherokee man who had took her and her kids in after River Joe was killed by a bear. River Joe is dead, so we don't have to worry about his comin' for her or anything like that."

Emma forced herself to stay awake, to remember everything that was said. She told herself to stick to the story awhile longer. River! Surely he would come soon and take her away from here!

Sam Gates was snickering. He turned to face Tommy. "You are something else, Decker. I should have known better than to put my faith and money into an ignorant mountain jackass!"

Tommy frowned. Those were fighting words for a young man like Tommy Decker, but Sam Gates was one man his instincts told him never to hit or threaten. He stiffened at the insult, struggling against an urge to clobber Sam Gates. His face reddened slightly at the realization that Emma lay there hearing everything. "Why did you call me that, Mr. Gates? I brought her, didn't I? That was the agreement. I said I could find her, and I did."

"And you really believe that story about River Joe?"

Tommy blinked. "Sure. He wasn't around anyplace. I know him, Sam. If he was alive, he would have fought for Emma. He would have showed himself."

Gates was grinning with a hint of disgust. "I have had this River Joe described to me several times, Tommy." He reached for a cigar. "Why is it I have trouble picturing a bear getting the better of a man like that? He's a man of the mountains, good with a knife, a hunter and apparently a fighter. And I don't believe for one minute that he's dead."

Emma's heart tightened, and Tommy paled with a fear he did not want to admit. "But . . . they all said he was, Sam. He wasn't around anywhere . . . and he—"

Gates waved him off. "What if he really *was* attacked by a bear?" the man interrupted. "And what if he was only wounded?"

"I . . . I don't know what you mean . . ."

Gates put his hands on his desk and leaned closer. "I mean, Tommy, that you should have done some searching. The Cherokee raised that man, you idiot! He's like a son to them! That woman lying over there *loved* the man—more than likely enough to protect him. If he was wounded and too weak to fight, you would have killed him on the spot, right?"

Tommy swallowed again. "Well, sure I would. Wasn't no sense bringin' him back here. We done hung Nigger Jim for killin' Hank."

Emma's eyes widened. Nigger Jim! He had been accused of killing Hank! Why? Tommy had made her think everyone was convinced that River had killed the man. He had said if River was alive, he would have been brought back to be hanged; and he had said that even she could be hanged, for running off with River.

"There you are," Gates was saying. "Maybe the man was only wounded, and this woman and the Cherokee did the only thing they could think of to save his life. They convinced you he was dead. Did you search the cabins?"

Tommy's temple flexed with indignity. "No, sir."

Gates sighed deeply. "I thought not." He quietly lit his cigar while the room hung silent. Emma was amazed at Sam Gates's perceptive thinking. This was a very clever, quick-thinking man. In moments he had figured out what Tommy had not even considered. She realized then that dealing with Sam Gates would be an entirely different matter from dealing with Tommy Decker. Now Gates was puffing on the cigar. He walked from behind the desk and came toward her. "Let's have your version, Miss Simms. *Is* River Joe dead?"

Emma just stared at him, trying to think quickly. This was a man not easily fooled. For some reason he had let poor Nigger Jim be blamed for killing Hank. That left River free of the murder. And at the moment, everyone thought River was dead besides. Would it foil River's rescue attempts if these three men knew the truth? She had wanted very much to see Tommy's face when she told him River was alive, yet over the last days she had thought better of telling him. It was best for River if they were not watching for him.

"I asked you a question, Miss Simms," Gates said, interrupting her thoughts. She sensed a deep, rising anger, and he leaned closer, waving the hot end of his cigar near her face. "I am not a man to be fooled with, I assure you. Nor do I care to be lied to. I have ways of making you tell the truth, believe me. And if you want even the slimmest hope of remaining alive and seeing your babies again, you will tell me the truth, young lady. Is River Joe alive?"

The babies! Her first vow had been to survive, to get back to little Joshua and Rachael. River was surely well and stronger by now. Perhaps he was already on his way. As long as he was on his feet and moving, they could never find River Joe now unless he wanted to be found.

"Yes," she answered. "River is my husband, and he is alive." With absolute joy she watched Tommy pale and actually tremble.

"You whorin' bitch!" he hissed. He went for her, but Sam Gates reached out with an iron arm and knocked him backward, almost making him fall.

"The woman is my property," he warned. "I don't want her face messed up until I see how pretty it really is." He looked down at Emma. "Was River Joe hurt?"

In spite of her weakened condition, she cast a haughty look at Tommy, almost smiling. "Yes," she answered, more firmly this time. She moved defiant eyes to Sam Gates. "He was badly injured by a bear, just like we said. Only he didn't die. He was so weak when Tommy came that he could never have defended himself. So we convinced Tommy he was dead. I knew Tommy would kill him if he found River that way."

"God damn you, Emma Simms," Tommy growled, almost in tears. "You know what that means?"

This time Emma did smile. "I know what it means. It means you can't even think about getting a good night's sleep for the rest of your life, Tommy Decker! And I have a feeling that life will be mighty short! And when you do sleep, it will be a permanent sleep; and the last thing you'll feel is River Joe's big blade slicing through your yellow back!"

Tommy stood there shaking, fists clenched, while Sam Gates only grinned at the scene.

"Damn you! Damn you!" Tommy almost squeaked.

"I'm gettin' the hell out of here," Deek said then, rising from his chair. "I told you this whole thing was stupid, Tommy! I've listened to you long enough! I'm goin' home to my pa, and if you're smart, you'll get out of Knoxville!" He looked at Sam Gates. "I don't want no money, Mr. Gates. I won't say nothin'."

"Won't you? I don't want anyone else to know River Joe is alive, Deek. That way—" He looked deliberately at Emma. "When my men kill him, no one will know the difference. You can't kill a dead man, now, can you?"

Emma would not allow his words to make her cower.

"Your men will never find River if he doesn't want to be found," she said. "He'll find you, Mr. Gates, and if you've abused me, he'll get to you without your men ever knowing it."

She saw momentary hesitation in his eyes, a tiny hint of fear. But this was a man who always got what he wanted and was well protected in his own familiar surroundings. Here was a man who was sure that anything and anyone could be bought for the right price, and a wealthy, well-guarded man could not be harmed.

"I highly doubt that will be possible," he answered. "You can be sure, Miss Simms, or whatever you call yourself now, that the rumors about River Joe being dead will soon be true. I'll be sure to bring you his body so you can verify we have killed the right man." He looked at Deek. "You can go, Deek, but you might as well wait until morning. Take room number three upstairs. It's empty tonight."

Deek nodded, casting an accusing look at Tommy. "Thanks to you I ain't gonna have the best time of sleepin' myself for a while."

"River Joe don't know nothin' about you." Tommy turned to Emma. "It's *me* he'll be lookin' for, thanks to the bitch here!"

"Did you ever tell Deek how you got your jaw knocked out of place?" Emma asked. Her voice was weak but clear. She looked at Deek. "*I* did it, with a fence board!" she told him proudly. "Tommy thought he could get under my skirts, but he found out different!"

Sam Gates grinned more, the cigar between his teeth, and Deek stared at a reddening Tommy Decker. "So *that's* your beef! You been draggin' me all over hell lookin' for Emma just to get even! It wasn't for the money or anything else. You're just plain pissed at her! Thanks a lot, Decker! Now I might have River Joe on my ass, and all because you got whomped by a goddamned, stupid girl!"

"It wasn't that way!" Tommy started after him, but Sam Gates stepped between them, glaring at Tommy.

"Go on up to your room, Deek," he ordered without even looking at the young man.

Deek turned and left gladly, and Sam grasped Tommy by the shirt front, giving him a shove. "You just might be turning out to be more trouble than you're worth, Decker!" he snarled. "Now I'll tell you how it is! You haven't brought me a new girl to decorate my upper rooms with. You've brought me a bellyful of trouble! I've got a sick girl on my hands with a husband somewhere out there looking for her, and I'm sure he knows just where to look! That means that when this girl is ready to travel, she has to be shipped off someplace else—*away* from this saloon and this town!"

Emma's heart raced. How would River find her if she wasn't here in Knoxville! Sam Gates walked around behind his desk. "I'll have Joanna clean her up—let her rest a couple of days and fix her up and have a look at her. Then I'll decide what to do with her. I'll most likely send her to the mine. My customers here in the city are more selective, with more money to spend. I'll grant you this woman here is probably quite beautiful when she's cleaned up, but she's trouble—trouble I don't need. And she's a mother and a fighter. My customers here don't want to mess with either one."

He turned dark eyes to Emma again. "But the coal miners . . . some of them haven't been with a woman in weeks, maybe months. They don't give a damn what kind of woman she is. Throw her in a barracks with twenty men, and she'll stop fighting soon enough. It will cost them a good deal of their weekly pay, but they'll pay it, and I'll get back my investment in this whole mess."

He looked back at Tommy. "When and if this River Joe comes looking for her, she won't be here; and I and everyone else in this establishment will swear we've never seen her. That will be the end of it! You won't be anywhere around, because you will take her to the coal mine. And if you value your hide and want to see the money I've promised you, you will stay there and work in the mine for six months, and make sure Miss Emma Simms does her job right. Then, and only then, will I pay you what you think you've got coming!"

Tommy's eyes widened. "The *coal* mine! I ain't workin' in no coal mine! I did what I promised, Mr. Gates! I found the girl!"

"All you did was find me trouble! And trouble for yourself! And the only way out is for you to get rid of this girl. When River Joe comes for her, I'll be ready, and my men will take care of him. I've never seen him, but I know how he looks and how he dresses. He can't come after his wife without coming straight to the Tennessee Belle. And the minute he sets foot on this property, he's *a dead* man! This place is too well guarded for him to get two feet past the door."

"He'll be sly. He still thinks he's wanted for murder."

"He thinks all of us figure him to be dead. I let Nigger Jim hang for Hank's murder so no one would know about me buying that girl—and I thought you would kill this River Joe yourself if you ever found him, and that would be the end of it! But thanks to your bungling, the man is still alive. He isn't going to give a damn if he's wanted for murder or anything else. He'll come for his wife! But she won't be here, and my men will make sure he never leaves! The choice I'm leaving you is to take this girl to the mine and stay there yourself for six months, or die at the hands of my own men! Because I don't want to see your face for a good, long time, Decker!"

Tommy blinked in surprise. "You mean . . . you'd have your men . . . kill me?"

Gates seemed to calm again. He smiled. "Yes," he answered flatly. "That is exactly what I mean. At least if you go to the coal mine, this River Joe would never look for you there. You would be safe, from him and from me. When he comes here, my men will see that he never leaves. And I won't see your face for a long time. If everything works out, and the miners find pleasure in, uh . . ." He looked over at

Emma, a chilling gleam in his dark eyes. "In Miss Simms, and I earn back my investment, you can come back and work here for me again, and I will pay you what I promised. Are we agreed?"

Tommy turned hate-filled eyes to Emma. "Do I get to have a piece of her myself on the way to the mine?"

Gates took the cigar from his mouth. "Do whatever you want with her, as long as you don't mess up her face. I want her to look her best for the men at the mine. Now get out of my office and leave me alone with the girl."

Tommy glowered at Emma. "I told you you'd regret what you did," he sneered. He turned and went through the same door Deek had exited. Emma realized there was a saloon and a crowd of people somewhere beyond the hallway into which the door opened. She could hear muffled voices and piano music, and her stomach churned at the thought of being out there, men looking at her, some deciding to go to bed with her. That was what surely went on out there. But what worse fate lay waiting for her if River didn't come in time?

Sam Gates walked back toward her, kneeling down beside her again. He nodded. "Yes, I believe Tommy might be right. We wash that golden hair and that dirty face and put a nice, pretty dress on you—" He grinned. "My men at the mine will go crazy when they see you. You'll be a very busy lady."

She fought against a scream. "What mine? Where are you sending me?"

"I own a coal mine, Miss Simms." He rose and sat down on the edge of the sofa, putting a hand on her bottom. She tried to jerk away, but he squeezed hard, his thumb against her hip bone, causing a sharp pain that made her wince. "I told you I have ways of making you do what I want, little girl," he said. "I'll give you a couple of days to rest, and one of my girls will clean you up and I'll have a good look at you. Then I will decide what I will charge the men at the mine to take their pent-up needs out on you. And don't think you can find help from anyone in the mining town. I own the whole place. It's a company town and everyone works for me. And now you will also work for me. If you cooperate, it won't be a bad life. You will be provided with everything you need."

Emma could not imagine there could be such horrors in the world. The possibility that River might not have healed hit her then. What if he didn't come after all? Her eyes teared, and a lump rose in her throat.

"Can I . . . if I . . . do it . . . can I go back to my babies?" she asked. Oh, for the feel of River's protective arms around her! And how wonderful it would be to pick up her children, to cuddle them, kiss their fat little necks, be home again with the Cherokee.

Sam Gates stood up again, grinning with victory. "I'll make you a promise, Miss Simms. If you cooperate for the six months I'm making Tommy work there, and if I make back the investment I lost to Hank Toole in that flood, plus make a little profit, I'll let you go free. I'll even hire a man to help you find your way back to wherever your children are."

She moved her eyes to meet his dark, victorious look. "How do I know you're telling me the truth?"

"Oh, I don't lie, Miss Simms. I always say exactly what I mean." He bowed slightly. "Besides, after six months with those miners, you won't be worth much to me anymore anyway. You will have served your purpose. And, of course, your white Indian buck will be dead, so everything will be nicely settled."

She struggled against tears. "I used to think my stepfather and Tommy Decker were the meanest men I ever knew," she said. "Then I thought maybe Hank Toole was. But you're the meanest, Mr. Gates. You use people like slaves, like dogs. You're lower than the dung under a pig's hoof!"

His eyes immediately blazed and he bent down, jerking

her close, bending one arm behind her and making her cry
out. She was far too weak to fight him. "Call me what you
want, Miss Simms," he hissed. "I am indeed mean. And if
you choose to keep insulting me, you will find out just how
mean I can be!"

Her breath came in pants of pain. "I know . . . somebody
meaner," she sneered, refusing to wither and weep. "River
Joe! Someday . . . you'll find out how mean *he* can be!"

Again she saw the faint doubt in his eyes, the hint of fear.
He let go of her and left the room, returning moments later
with a huge, burly man who looked her over with no particular emotion in his eyes.

"Take her up to Joanna's room, Stu," he ordered. "Use the
back stairs. Have Joanna clean her up and give her something to put her to sleep. She needs a couple of days' rest."

"Yes, sir."

The big man came toward Emma and lifted her with ease.
He carried her out into the hallway and up a dark stairway.
He laid her on a bed, then left for a moment, returning with
a glass of something that looked like warm milk. "Drink
this," he told her. "Sam says to make you go to sleep first."

"Why?" she asked weakly. "So he can inspect me while
his whore cleans me up? So he can do what he wants with
me without my protest? Without me reminding him that if he
touches me River Joe will come and kill him?"

"Who is River Joe?"

She turned away. "Never mind. Take it away. I won't
drink it."

He came closer, and suddenly a strong hand took hold of
her face, squeezing her jaw so painfully that she was forced
to open her mouth. The milky substance was poured into it.
She struggled not to swallow, but it was impossible, and
moments later the room began to swirl around her. She
thought about River and the babies, and then all was black.

◊ *Chapter 22* ◊

Emma's heart pounded harder every time she heard footsteps outside the door of the room where she was kept. She lived with the terror of wondering if Tommy Decker or Sam Gates had come to take what he thought was due him. For four days she lay with one wrist chained to the post at the head of the brass bed. She had been bathed, her hair washed and brushed, and she wore a satin bed gown. She was allowed to do nothing but eat and sleep, and whenever she had to relieve herself, the prostitute named Joanna helped her.

Emma had been unable to strike up any kind of conversation with Joanna. She was cold and unfriendly, or at least she had seemed to be at first. But Emma soon realized that Joanna was simply afraid of Sam Gates. She was determined not to strike up a friendship with Emma Simms, and Emma was sure it was on orders from Sam. There would be no comfort or help from Joanna, whose last name Emma didn't even know.

Joanna was perhaps twenty-five, a woman who was pretty but looked as though she used to be a softer pretty. Now she had a painted look that hid what remained of the woman beneath the jewelry and makeup.

Emma had at first appealed to Joanna's womanhood, sure she could gain her sympathy by telling her about her children, that she was not here by choice, that she wanted to return to her babies. She had hoped Joanna would understand and help her escape. But the fear of what Sam Gates would do to her far outweighed any sympathy the woman might have for Emma, if, indeed, she had any feelings at all.

Why Sam Gates allowed her four days' rest instead of two, Emma was not sure. Perhaps he was confident that he didn't need to worry about River. Emma rejoiced in the delay. It would allow River more time to get to her, perhaps before she had to go to the coal mine where Sam Gates intended to send her.

Emma tried not to think about the horrors that awaited her there. She had no doubt Sam Gates had prettied her up and let her rest only to make sure she was as presentable as possible when she arrived at the mine. She was sure that very soon she would be sent away, and the only thing worse than where she was going was the realization that it would be Tommy Decker who would take her there. She was healed now. Nothing would prevent Tommy from taking what he had been wanting from her for years, and she was still too weak from her ordeal to defend herself. She could only pray that River would come before Tommy took her away.

Her eyes teared and her stomach churned at the vague memory of Sam Gates pawing over her after she had drunk the horrible liquid that made her so groggy. For hours after she drank the liquid everything that happened was like a strange nightmare. Someone had bathed her, washed her hair. There were voices, but she could not remember the words. She remembered only warm water, someone rubbing creams on her, Sam Gates's face close to hers, his hands moving over her.

Now she heard footsteps again. The door opened. It was Joanna.

"Time to go," the woman said matter-of-factly. "Tommy is waiting out back."

Emma's heart quickened. Not yet! River had not arrived yet. She couldn't leave.

"You're to get dressed now," Joanna said in her usual cool

voice. "I've already packed some clothes for you. They're on Tommy's pack horse." She came around to unlock Emma's chain. "Don't try something dumb. There are men outside the door. There is nothing you can do, so you might as well get dressed and not make a fuss."

Emma rubbed at her wrist and slowly stood up, still a little dizzy and not very strong. Joanna brought a dress over to her, and Emma grasped the woman's wrist, her eyes pleading.

"Joanna, for God's sake help me! Tell me how I can get out of this!"

The woman jerked her arm away. "You can't." Joanna's green eyes again showed fear—fear of Sam Gates, Emma was sure. "Don't fight it," she said. "Trust me that much. You don't have the slightest idea how cruel Sam can be when you fight him."

She turned away and Emma removed her gown, fighting the urge to scream and run. The babies. She constantly reminded herself that she had to survive for the babies. "Have you been there, Joanna, to the mine?"

The woman walked to a window, looking out while Emma got dressed. "I've been there," she answered finally. She turned to face Emma. "Do your duty for six months, like Sam asked. Then he'll let you go. He's a cruel man, but he doesn't lie. Whatever he says, he'll do . . . including inflicting great pain if you disobey him. So don't even think about it. And don't worry about getting pregnant from all those men. There is a doctor at the mine who will fix it so you can't get pregnant."

Emma felt her blood run cold. Not get pregnant! Her eyes widened. "You mean . . . forever?"

Joanna laughed lightly. "Of course, forever. How do you think it is I can sleep with a different man every night and not get pregnant? It's not very common, what this doctor does, but it works. It only leaves a tiny scar on your stomach—nothing to worry about."

Emma felt the panic moving through her bones, and she

fought it, afraid to put up a fight while Sam Gates was still nearby. "But . . . babies mean everything to me. I . . . I want to have more! I don't want to be fixed so I can't have babies!"

Joanna shook her head and sighed deeply. "Look, Emma, why don't you grow up and face facts? First of all, you can't get out of this, and believe me, with what Sam Gates would do to you, you don't want to try. Second, once you've served your time at the mine, no man is going to want you for a wife and mother anyway, including your husband, if by some miracle he should get past Sam Gates and find you. By the time you leave the mine, you will be glad to come back here and work for Sam. This place will seem like heaven by then. And you certainly won't be a fit mother anymore for those babies you keep blubbering about. They'll be better off left with those Cherokee women you told me would take care of them."

Emma put a hand to her stomach and sat on the bed, shaking her head. "I won't let them do that to me. I won't!"

"You've got no choice."

Emma felt a cold sweat moving over her entire body. River! He had to come soon! He had to! And until he did, she would find a way to avoid the horrors Joanna had described. If she had to die, then she would die. Even that would be better than letting some man cut her open and make her less a woman. Joanna was right: she would not be fit for River or her babies then. That left two choices. Find a way to escape, or die in the effort.

An angry pride began to well up in her soul, the same pride that had made her fight Tommy Decker and Hank Toole. She was River Joe's woman! No matter what it took, Tommy Decker would not make it all the way to the mine with her. Somehow she would get away or force him to kill her. Even if she got away and died lost in the mountains, it would be better than going to the mine and letting a strange doctor cut into her.

The door opened and Sam Gates came inside the room.

"Well, are we ready?" he asked, grinning and leering.

Emma made no reply. How she hated this man, even more than she hated Tommy Decker! How she prayed that River would kill this hideous man.

Now he moved closer, looking her over. "My, you certainly are the pretty thing Tommy said you were. And Lord knows I've seen everything there is to see."

Emma looked away, wishing she were bigger, stronger, able to kill him herself.

"You'll make a tidy sum for me at the mine, Emma," he said, "and then you'll be free to do what you want—go back to your squalling babies, or come back here and work for me. Life can be good here, can't it, Joanna?"

Joanna met his eyes, seeing the threat there. "Sure," she answered. She sauntered up to him and Sam put his arm around her. "A woman couldn't have it better," she added.

He grinned, patting her shoulder. "Well, you've done a good job with Emma here. You've finally learned to stop trying to help these girls, haven't you?"

"Yes, Sam."

Sam held her tighter, signaling her to stay put, while he began unbuttoning the back of her dress, letting it fall open to reveal the young woman's back. Emma watched curiously, her eyes widening as each button began to reveal ugly whip scars from beneath Joanna's shoulder blades down past the waistline of her bloomers.

"This is what happens to pretty girls who disobey me," Sam said to Emma, a cold threat in his voice. "A few who have disobeyed me have never lived to tell about it." He grinned again, rubbing his hand over the scars. "But Joanna understands now. She realizes I don't like hurting my girls. I just have to make sure my requests are obeyed—keeps my business running smoothly. Do you understand what I am telling you, Miss Simms?"

Emma felt sorry for Joanna, even though the woman had become so cold and unfeeling. She wondered if Joanna had also started out as an innocent from the hills.

Emma met Sam's eyes boldly, still determined to find a
way out in spite of what she had just seen. "I understand,"
she said calmly. "I understand the kind of man it takes to
beat a woman into submission. You must be very proud of
your accomplishments, Mr. Gates."

His eyes lost their humor and his smile faded. "You won't
be so haughty after you've been to the mine," he said. "And
if you're smart, you'll do everything right so you don't carry
scars forever like Joanna." He pushed Joanna away and
stepped closer, standing over Emma like a black storm
cloud. "I'll keep my word about letting you go back, but
only if you do what you are told."

He suddenly grinned again, and Emma realized he was an
unpredictable man with whom it was impossible for a
woman to reason. "And I have a feeling you'll realize by
then it's senseless to go back to your children," he said. "Or
your precious white Indian, if, indeed, he is still alive. No
one will want you except men who *buy* women! Now finish
buttoning your shoes. Tommy is waiting." He turned away.
"Oh, and by the way," he added, being deliberately casual
now, "part of cooperating with me includes accommodating
poor Tommy. Let the young man have you and get it out of
his system, will you? Don't try to escape, and don't fight
him. If you do, it will be the same as fighting me. You
already know what that will get you." He smiled and bowed,
leaving the room.

Joanna stood with her back still to Emma. "Button me up,
will you?"

Emma blinked back tears, walking over to her and buttoning the dress. "River will come, Joanna, and he'll kill Sam
Gates," she said. "Then you will be free."

Joanna turned, laughing lightly. "Honey, I stopped hoping
for that a long time ago. You might as well stop hoping, too.
Your River Joe will never get near Sam. You'll never see
River Joe again. Start getting used to it."

Emma detected a trace of tears in the young woman's
eyes. She said nothing more. She turned back and went to

the bed to put on her other shoe. There was no more time to think about Joanna or to try to help her. She had to help herself now, and start thinking about how she could get away from Tommy Decker once they were away from Knoxville.

River crouched among the trees along a ridge overlooking Knoxville. He had never been to this big city, but he had been to enough other white man's towns to know what to expect and how to behave. After all, he was white himself. As far as he knew, no one in Knoxville knew who he was. That was his only advantage, and he would have to take the chance.

He was going into white man's territory, so he would be a white man. He had carefully avoided all other settlements, until he was well away from any who might know him. Then he stopped at a small town just yesterday, posing as a white man just back from a long hunt and needing a haircut and a shave. He had spent his last dime on a new suit of clothes.

His heart pounded with anticipation. He had never been this "white." His hair was cut to collar length, and once he put on the fancy clothes he had bought, no one in Knoxville would guess he was anything but a visiting white man. He would bear no resemblance to the descriptions that applied to the one called River Joe. He could only pray to the Maker of Breath that his scheme would work—that he could walk right into the Tennessee Belle and no one would know who he was. He even practiced how to talk, carrying on conversations with his horses to practice getting a casual sound to his words, using the lazier contractions most white men used, such as *don't* instead of *do not*.

Walking into the Tennessee Belle was going to be a great risk, especially if Tommy Decker was around. But he knew of no other way to get near the people who could give him some clue to where Emma might be. If he was lucky, she would still be right there in the saloon. The thought of her being taken there brought a rage to his soul so intense that it made his head ache. He would get her out of there, and kill Sam Gates and Tommy Decker, even if it meant doing it in front of everyone and hanging for it! Getting Emma free would be worth it. All that mattered was that Emma no longer be at the mercy of such men. He didn't dare dwell on what might have happened to her by now, or he would become so enraged that he would lose all powers of reason. He must keep his wits about him.

He settled back to make camp. He had to think. He had to get ready. Even though it meant leaving Emma at the Belle for yet another day, he had to do this right, which meant waiting until the night, a more natural time for a man to enter a saloon looking for a good card game and a woman for the night.

He made a small campfire, then unloaded some of his gear, letting his horse rest. He had ridden a spotted gray gelding, bringing along a white mare as a pack horse. He had been careful not to ride a horse that might be familiar to Tommy Decker or anyone else who had ever known him.

He took his canteen and poured water into a pan over the fire. When it was heated he scrubbed his hands vigorously with soap, concentrating on the calluses. He would soak them later, for most of the night. They must be soft, like the hands of an educated gentleman, for that was how he would present himself to Sam Gates.

He sat down near the fire then, taking a mirror from his gear and looking at himself again. Never had he realized with such clarity that he really was a white man. The haircut and the mustache he had grown made him look entirely different. He doubted that even Tommy Decker would know him, especially when he put on the white man's clothes. His greatest advantage was that they all thought he was dead. They would not be watching for him.

He wondered if Emma would like him this way, if she would mind the haircut or the mustache. The thought of her wrenched at his heart. Emma! Was she even still alive? Was she suffering, praying for him to come?

"Emma," he whispered, his throat feeling tight. He closed his eyes, rising to his knees and throwing back his head. "Give me strength and wisdom, *Esaugetuh Emissee*," he prayed. He bent his head to the ground then. He would spend the rest of the day praying to the Maker of Breath, who had led him to Emma Simms. Surely God had meant for them to have a long and happy life together.

"I got three reasons for makin' sure you get to Sam's mine, Emma," Tommy said. He rode in front of her, leading her horse while Emma rode behind him, her hands tied to the pommel of her saddle.

This was their second day on the trail toward the mountain where Sam Gates's coal mine was located, a five-day ride, according to Tommy. The first day he had been almost totally silent, and that first night he had not touched her or even come near her. Emma knew he was deliberately making her wonder when he would force himself on her, letting her feel the fear and dread. And she suspected he wanted to make sure there were plenty of miles between themselves and Sam Gates before Tommy let loose his wrath on her. Emma could tell that Tommy was as scared of Sam Gates as all the other people who worked for the man were.

But now Tommy was relaxing, letting his cockiness begin to show. He was on his own, his own boss again. "For one thing," he was saying, "Sam will have me killed if I don't get you there. He already killed Deek, just for the worry that Deek would tell somebody all about this. He never did trust Deek too much."

Emma stared at him in surprise. "Sam killed Deek?"

"Sure he did. Oh, he didn't do it himself. One of his men did the job. Deek was found dead in his bed the next mornin' after that night we brought you in. Nobody had to tell

me what really happened. They said he died durin' the night
—choked on some food or somethin'. But I know what
really happened. He choked, all right, by somebody's
hands."

Emma frowned at Tommy's seeming unconcern. "Wasn't
Deek your friend? Aren't you angry with Sam?"

"Sure I am. Deek *was* my friend. But Sam pays me good
and it ain't good sense to go up against him. Deek always
was slow and stupid. He didn't know how to handle a man
like Sam. I do."

"By being his puppet?"

Tommy slowed his horse, turning to look at her. "You
watch your mouth, girl. You're gonna get your turn, you
know. And you better cooperate like Sam said, or you'll die
just like Deek did. Don't think I won't tell Sam about anything you do wrong."

She glared back at him. "You don't scare me, Tommy
Decker. And neither does Sam Gates. River will come after
both of you."

Tommy snickered. "He'll never get past Sam. I ain't worried." He turned back around. "Anyway, the second reason
is the pay I'm gonna get for takin' you to the mine, and
makin' sure you serve your six months; and the third reason
is the simple pleasure of watchin' them miners take their
turns with you. I'll tell you one thing, Emma Simms, I ain't
sure which will be more pleasurable for me—gettin' inside
you myself, or watchin' them men go at you."

Emma clung to the pommel of her saddle, determined to
keep her promise to herself to find a way to escape Tommy
Decker or die. She would not go to that mine!

"I'll try the first part tonight," Tommy said. "The time has
finally come, Emma, honey. You know, you might have
avoided all of this if you had given in to me way back when
I first wanted you. I might even have married you, and then
you never would have got sold off to Hank and got into all
this mess."

Emma felt her pride and anger rising. "It was worth it just to see your crooked jaw," she answered haughtily.

He turned to look back at her again, his blue eyes like ice. "I'll break that damned snotty pride of yours before this trip is over, Emma Simms."

"The name is Emma Rivers," she answered proudly. "I belong to River Joe and you can't change that, Tommy Decker! He'll come and show you that himself before we ever make it to that mine."

Tommy snickered, turning back around. "I'll change it plenty—tonight. Your River Joe ain't comin', Emma. When are you gonna face that fact? It's all done now. I get my turn with you, and then the miners. River Joe will die and you won't never see them little lice-ridden babies of yours again."

Emma struggled not to show her inner terror or doubts. She wouldn't let it happen! She couldn't! Somehow she had to get to Joshua and Rachael. River would want it that way. If he was dead . . . oh, God, he couldn't be dead! Surely he would still come! He would find her out here before they reached the mine.

She prayed a desperate, silent prayer to the Maker of Breath to help her find a way to keep away from Tommy. She had to think about survival. She thought of old Ramona's words—*"You are a strong and brave white woman."* She would live up to those words. After all, she was River's woman. River Joe's woman and no one else's.

They rode on silently for the next several minutes, while Emma desperately tried to think of ways to get out of her predicament. And she wondered how River could keep from being a hunted man if he did manage to kill Sam Gates and Tommy. Most people thought River was dead. If he could get rid of Sam and Tommy without being seen, he could be free! Everyone thought poor Nigger Jim was the man who had killed Hank Toole, so River was presently not a hunted man. If only there were a way she could tell him that. If he knew he was not wanted for murder, he would realize how much more important it was not to let anyone see him alive.

Poor Jim. She and River surely owed the poor black slave
something. Tommy had bragged about the whole affair. Jim
had not mentioned her being on the boat, not until one of
Sam's men had tortured the poor man into admitting what he
had seen.

Emma's heart ached to think of what Jim had been
through. He was probably afraid to tell, for fear he would
be accused of doing bad things to Emma. He must have
hoped that if everyone believed Emma was not on the
boat, nothing would happen to him; and perhaps Emma
and River could escape being hunted by Sam Gates. But
Sam had gotten the truth out of poor Jim. Emma did not
like even to think about how he had done it. Then Sam
had used Jim for a cover-up.

She understood it all now. Sam had not allowed Jim to tell
the truth to the public—that there was a white girl on
Hank's boat. He didn't want people to know he dealt in the
buying and selling of women like slaves. He had let the
people believe Jim had killed Hank in order to escape, that
Jim hoped the flood would hide his deed. Sam didn't want
Emma or River Joe brought into the picture. That way he
could kill River and capture Emma without anyone knowing
he was involved. He had allowed poor Jim to hang for Hank
Toole's murder, and, as far as anyone else was concerned,
the whole matter was finished. That left Sam free to send
men in search of Emma and River. There was no one else to
know. Tommy had already told her Luke was dead from the
flood. She felt guilty that she was almost glad about Luke. If
only the flood had killed Tommy, too. Then none of the rest
of this would have happened.

Emma smiled inwardly at the fact that Tommy had spoiled
the whole plan by not making sure River was dead. As long
as River was alive, Sam Gates could not "own" Emma
Simms free and clear. Sam could have let River and Emma
go. With Jim being hanged for Hank's murder, there was no
reason to pursue River and Emma. But now that Emma had
met Sam Gates, she understood his demented reasoning, his

unrelenting hunt for her. Sam Gates was a selfish, cruel man who did not like to be crossed or cheated; and he apparently would go to any lengths to take what he considered belonged to him and to punish anyone who went against his wishes.

That made Emma anxious for River. He would have to be so careful! Maybe Tommy was right. Maybe River would never get past Sam Gates. She could not forget the scars on Joanna's back, the terrible cold and calculating look in Sam Gates's dark eyes. It would take all of River's skill and cunning to get anywhere near Sam Gates. And if he didn't, it would be up to Emma herself to find a way to keep from being taken to the mine.

She kept telling herself to stay calm, to think rationally, to be strong at heart. Night would be upon them soon. Tommy would make camp. If she were to escape, it had to be tonight. Not only was she determined never to go to the mine; she was determined that Tommy Decker would never touch what belonged to Joe Rivers.

◊ *Chapter 23* ◊

"I think we'll make camp here," Tommy said.

The words cut into her with an ugly dread. They had ridden for hours in near silence, and Emma had found herself hoping against hope that night would never come. Tommy was his old, talkative, cocky self again, now that they were well away from Knoxville and Sam Gates. She was on her own now. River was not here to help her. She wondered how she could possibly get out of this, for she was weary and still weak, and everything ached from the long day's ride.

"You're damned lucky I got orders not to mess up your face, Emma Simms," Tommy said, "else you wouldn't be able to talk right now. I'd love to slam you with a board like you did me and permanently knock that pretty jaw out of line."

He dismounted, tying his horse and walking back to her own and untying her wrists from the pommel. "It's my turn now, Emma Simms, and I aim to take what I've had comin' to me all this time!"

Her jerked her down from her horse so hard that she fell. "You ain't gonna get out of it this time, Emma," he growled, his personality suddenly turning to its ugly side. That was what was so hard to figure with Tommy—the way he could suddenly change from almost decent to less than an animal. Emma scrambled to think how to handle him when he was like this.

"I didn't touch you till now 'cause I wanted you to think about it a good, long time," he sneered. "You knew it was comin', though, didn't you?" He laughed as he grabbed her arms and dragged her to a small tree, where he retied her wrists. He leaned closer then. "I'm gonna break you, woman. After all that's happened to you, you still got that damned pride. I can see it in your eyes. But when I'm through with you, that look will be gone! You just lay there and think about it real good while I unload the horses and make camp."

He got up and left, and Emma fought the panic that welled up in her soul. Think! She had to think! She remembered how he had almost backed off the day he took her from River when she faced him boldly and did not resist him. Perhaps her suspicion then was right—that he wanted her to fight, that it aroused him. That would be her first step. She would not fight back. If he still persisted, she had to think of a way to make him free her hands.

She lay praying the whole time Tommy unpacked his gear

and set up a tent. Dark clouds moved in to shroud an already-setting sun, and Tommy set an oil lamp inside the tent.

"I aim to see everything that's happenin'," he informed her.

He tethered the horses, then removed his weapons, coming to stand in front of her then while he removed his clothing. Apparently he was not even going to stop to eat first.

She noticed then that he seemed uncomfortable as she calmly and deliberately watched him.

"There it is again, that damned look," he said. "You ain't gonna undo me with that look, Emma, if that's what you think." He bent over and cut the ropes that held her wrists to the tree. "Come on. In the tent. It's gettin' too dark out here." He jerked her up and pushed her toward the tent. To her surprise he did not retie her hands. Apparently he trusted her fear of Sam to make her cooperate. "You remember the rules, Emma. You fight me, and Sam will make it real bad for you, leave scars on you that will never go away. He said to cooperate with me, so you better do it. If you fight me and even if you managed to run off, Sam's men would find you, and you'd wish you would have just let me have what I got comin'."

He turned her and unbuttoned her dress, yanking it down over her arms to the waist, then pulling it the rest of the way off, bloomers and all. His eyes moved over her appreciatively then, his breath quickening at the sight of her.

"Finally—you and me naked together," he said then, his voice gruff with pent-up desire. "You remember Sam Gates," he repeated. "This time you'll cooperate or feel the whip when we get to the mine. You'll be stripped down and whipped in front of all them men. Is that what you want, Emma?"

She swallowed, still struggling to think of a way out, telling herself to stay calm. "No," she answered quietly. She struggled against an urge to strike out at him. She realized she was not strong enough this time, and she had the babies and survival to think about—and River. River would come.

And she was sure her suspicions were right—that fighting Tommy would only stimulate him.

Tommy turned her and shoved her inside the tent, where the oil lamp burned brightly. Tommy pushed her down onto a bedroll, then straddled her, grinning, his face red with desire, his body actually trembling with the want of her.

She lay still as he knelt over her and kissed her hard. She had only one hope, but first she had to gain his confidence. She did not struggle against the kiss. He finally stopped, rising slightly.

"There now. You've been with a man before, so you know how much fun it is, don't you? I can see you've learned a lot, Emma Simms. You're smarter now. You might think your River Joe is comin', which he ain't. But you figure till he does, you might as well go by the rules and keep the sting of the whip off your back, huh?"

"It's not that, Tommy," she said. "I just . . . you never kissed me that way before. I've always hated you . . . and yet I . . . I've always wondered, too. Now I've got no choice and I realize . . . it's almost exciting, knowing there's nothing I can do to stop you. I'm scared of Sam, Tommy. I won't fight you, as long as you promise not to tie me or anything."

His look of surprise was almost humorous. He snickered, sitting up slightly. "You bein' straight with me?"

"I don't have any choice, Tommy. We both know that. And I'm too weak to fight you anyway."

He laughed like a surprised little boy. "By God, I think you mean it! Ol' Sam must have really put the scare in you. He sure knows how to break down the proud ones."

She put her fingers to his lips, struggling against her revulsion at touching him. "I saw Joanna's back. And now that you tell me Sam had Deek killed—" She let her eyes tear, knowing he would love to see her cry. "I have no choice. You've won, Tommy. If River was coming, he would be here by now. He must have died, or else he doesn't care anymore. Don't let Sam hurt me, Tommy, please."

Tommy just stared at her, then came down closer again,

rubbing his chest against her breasts, pressing himself against her. "This is more like it," he said. He kissed her again, a hard, cold, tasteless kiss, then suddenly jerked back, an angry sneer crossing his face.

"You bitch!" he hissed, getting off her and plopping down on the ground next to her. "I ain't used to you this way and you know it. I like some life in my women, some fight."

She sat up, wanting to laugh. It was working! "Don't you know anything about gentleness, Tommy? If you would just be good to me, we could run away together—forget about the coal mine. I won't fight you anymore, Tommy, if you'll just take me away someplace and not take me to the mine."

He studied her closely, then clenched his fists. "Sure! And have Sam Gates on our asses! He'd kill me for sure and you know it! That's what you want, ain't it? You want Sam to kill me, and then maybe you'd still find a way to get out of the whole thing. That's what I hate about women! They're schemers and liars! And they spread their legs for any man who will do what they want."

"That's not true, Tommy."

He grabbed her by the hair, jerking her close. "The hell it ain't! I got orders to take you to that mine, and that's where we're goin'! And before we get there I'm gonna get what's comin' to me!"

"Then take me!" she replied boldly, meeting his eyes squarely. "Take me and get it over with!"

He just glared at her, devastated that for some reason he could not perform in this most crucial moment. Of all the women he had been with, this was the last one he wanted to see him this way—unable to be a man for her! He shoved her hard. "Bitch! You bitch!" he screamed. "I could kill you! If it wasn't for Sam Gates—"

He sucked in his breath, his immature temper getting the better of him. "The hell with Sam Gates," he growled. He grabbed her arm, jerking her close and then bending her left arm up behind her back. "A broken arm don't leave no scars," he growled. "And that's all Sam told me—don't leave no scars. That doctor at the mine can set this arm when we get there."

She screamed with pain as he began bending it farther. His frustration over being unable to rape her vented its fury through a desire to physically hurt her some other way. In desperation Emma bit hard into his chin. He let go just slightly, and their position in the tent was awkward. Emma used the moment, catching him just slightly off-balance. She pushed him, and he fell sideways, stumbling into the oil lamp. It toppled from the crate, and with a splintering crash, burst into flames.

Tommy screamed as flames spread rapidly from the floor, along his back and legs, then quickly engulfed the nearby blankets and lapped at the walls of the tent. Tommy's body jerked oddly, and he seemed suddenly to be confused in his terror and pain.

Emma whimpered at the horrible sight and darted out of the tent, backing away, sure Tommy would come charging out at any moment wanting to kill her, but in what seemed seconds the tent was consumed in flames, and Tommy had not come out. She could hear his screams, see movement as he flailed around wildly inside the burning tent.

Tears of horror welled in her eyes as the tent collapsed. She backed away farther as the heat from the fire became too intense near her skin. She ran over to the pack horse with the sound of Tommy's almost inhuman screams ringing in her ears. Tommy Decker was getting what he deserved: the Maker of Breath had helped her again.

She forced herself not to look, told herself not to give in to the insane panic that threatened to overtake her. She had to think, to continue being logical, to survive. She tore through the supply bags on the pack horse until she found her clothing. She pulled on some bloomers, trying to keep herself going despite the sound of Tommy's screams, which were now turning to gruesome groans. She pulled out a dress and put it on.

Why didn't he die? Why didn't Tommy just die and stop

screaming? She could not find it in her heart not to wish his death. He was the cause of so much of her heartache, the cause of her suffering and being separated from her children. And if River was killed, that, too, would be Tommy's fault. If he had not taken her away in the first place, River would not have to go after her.

Her heart pounded wildly as she pulled on some shoes and found a wolfskin jacket. She refused to look toward the tent, but she heard the flames dwindling now, and Tommy's groaning had almost stopped. She moved quickly, locating bags with food in them, pulling Tommy's musket and powder from his supplies. She wanted to take a horse. That would be much easier. But a horse left big tracks and would make it easy for her to be followed. Once Sam Gates found out about this he would come for her. But maybe River would kill him before that happened. Then somehow ... somehow River would find her before she died in these mountains.

She looked up at rising peaks. Somewhere up there were the Cherokee, her friends, her family, her babies. She would get to them. She would not let these mountains defeat her. She had learned a lot when she traveled through them with River. She had even killed a wild boar! She could survive, and she would, for River would come, and they would all be together again.

She finished packing all that she could possibly carry, wishing she were stronger. As soon as she was far enough away that she thought she might be safe, she would have to take a few days to rest, to get stronger. And a little farther off, after she had gone far enough that Sam Gates's men could not find her path, she would start leaving a trail for River. Only River was a good enough tracker to find her light footsteps and other signs to follow her away from this camp. Farther ahead she would start making it easier for him, leave him clues, so that he could find her even more quickly.

"You ... bitch!" she heard Tommy mumble then.

Her blood ran cold, and finally she turned, gasping at the collapsed and still burning tent, and the blackened form of a man that lay in front of it. The only thing she recognized were the cold blue eyes, their whites seeming even whiter against his burned skin, his lips looking redder, his teeth whiter as he glared at her.

"Sam . . . will get you," he moaned. "He'll . . . burn you alive . . . like you . . . did . . . me."

His head dropped and he lay still. Even if he was not dead, he surely soon would be. She thought for one brief moment about trying to help him, the softness in her still alive, in spite of the way this man had treated her. But she had to concentrate on just one thing—survival. She had to get as much distance between this campsite and herself as possible now, in case Sam Gates did come for her. Someone might have seen the fire. Someone would come to investigate, and would then go back to Knoxville with the news. Sam would realize what had happened. She could only pray that River would get to Sam Gates before Sam Gates got to her.

She turned away from the horrible sight and hurried off, heading up. It was the only direction she knew to go. How she would ever find the Cherokee and her babies, she had no idea. But she had to try.

River walked casually into the Tennessee Belle, half-expecting to see Emma sitting at one of the tables with the gamblers, or serving them drinks. It would be like Emma to do whatever she could to survive until he came. But if she was expected to take a man upstairs, River had little doubt what her reaction would be; and he worried what would happen to her if she refused.

To his relief, but also his deepening worry, she was nowhere to be seen among the several lovelies who strutted about in dresses cut so low that a tall man could see the nipples just behind the lace that covered them.

He walked to the bar, carefully scanning the room on the way. He saw no one he knew, and he breathed a little easier. If he was recognized, he could be hanged for murder. But he was supposed to be a dead man. That was his only hope.

He felt like a rabbit walking into a mountain lion's den. But if he handled this right, he just might get away with it. A burly, hard-looking man behind the bar asked him what he wanted to drink.

"Whiskey," River answered.

He noticed four of the barmaids arguing over something then, all of them eyeing him. Apparently they were deciding which one should go up to the new man and offer her services. In his own humble nature, River underestimated his attraction for white women. To those who watched him now, the tall, well-built, well-dressed man who had just entered the Tennessee Belle was very attractive, and each of them wanted to be the one to spend the night with him.

River saw his chance to find out what he needed to know. He had no interest in the women of the Tennessee Belle, but he had to use anything he could now to find out about Emma. He didn't dare stay around Knoxville any longer than necessary. The more quickly he could learn what he needed to know, the better. He deliberately eyed all four women as he drank down some of his whiskey. Perhaps a man alone in bed with one of them could discover something.

One of them finally sauntered up to him. Her reddish hair was bundled up into big curls, and her breasts billowed over a red and silver striped dress. She smiled as she came closer, running her eyes over him appreciatively. "Hello. I'm Joanna," she said softly.

River nodded. "John Beck," he answered.

She looked at the bartender. "Give him another whiskey, Stu, on the house."

Stu looked warily at River, then got the drink. Joanna turned back to River. "You're new in Knoxville?"

"Just passing through. I'm a lawyer, from Ohio. I'm on my way to Atlanta."

"A lawyer!" She took his arm and led him to a table. "Well, now, I have always heard that lawyers are rich men."

River gave her a melting smile. "The ones who are established. I do all right. I have received a good offer from two other lawyers in Atlanta."

Stu brought over the extra drink, and he and Joanna exchanged a knowing look. Every new man was suspect. River did not miss the look, nor did he miss the fact that the big bartender walked immediately to a back door and disappeared behind it. River looked back at Joanna, again giving her a warm smile, moving his dark eyes to study her breasts. This was not his kind of game, but he would play it if it meant finding Emma.

"I've been riding a long time," he said, working on his whiskey. "A man gets hungry for company . . . and other things. I hope I am not out of line in asking you if you know a place where a man can . . . well, you know . . . find a little comfort for the night? If I offend you, I apologize."

Joanna felt a rush of desire. She didn't usually have any feelings for any of her customers, but this one was not only beautiful to look at, but soft-spoken. She sensed a quality about him, a man who would not be crude and in a hurry. If she had to take a customer tonight, maybe at least this one would not be such a hideous chore as some of the others.

"I, uh, I'm not sure," she answered, per her usual orders from Sam. All customers had to be approved by Sam Gates. "I'll ask my boss."

His eyebrows arched. "Maybe it's too offensive for you to ask. I would be glad to ask him for you."

"It's all right. You wait right here." She got up from the table and went through the same door the bartender had entered. River waited, keeping a pleasant look on his face while seething inside. Where was Emma? What had they done to her?

He breathed deeply, allowing the spirit of the Maker of Breath to fill him with the strength he would need to face Sam Gates, if this Joanna brought the man back with her. Sam Gates was surely a man of experience and cunning. He would not be easily fooled. But he didn't even think River Joe was alive; and if he did suspect, he would surely expect a long-haired, buckskin-clad man to come for him, not the mustached, neatly dressed and well-spoken white man who sat here waiting for Joanna to return.

"It could be him!" Stu was saying in Sam's office.

"Not a chance," Joanna returned. "This isn't a man who runs around the woods chasing bears and living like a heathen. He's too well spoken, and look how he's dressed."

Sam eyed them both disdainfully. "I'll go talk to him myself," he said with a note of disgust. He walked around them with deliberate authority, trying to hide his own nervousness. Joanna and Stu followed.

In the main room, two other barmaids had started talking to River, while men gambled and a man at the piano pounded out bawdy songs. Sam walked closer to River, shooing away the two women. Again a sickening dread flowed through River as he moved his eyes to meet those of the well-dressed man who stood before him. River had no doubt it was Sam Gates. He nodded.

"Sir?" He stood up and put out his hand. "You must be Joanna's 'boss,' as she put it. I'm John Beck."

Gates took his hand, and River chose to give the man a light handshake, the kind a softened city man would give. He dared not squeeze this man's hand until it broke, as he so dearly wanted to do. He felt the Maker of Breath was with him, was proud of the kindness he kept in his eyes and the warm smile he managed to display.

"Sam Gates," Sam answered, letting go of River's hand. "Joanna tells me you're just passing through on your way to Atlanta."

"Yes, sir." River looked around the room. "This is a real nice place you have here. I asked as I came through town, and everybody said this was the place for a man to come for the best whiskey in Knoxville."

Sam nodded, smiling, gauging the tall, handsome man before him. Yes, he could be the white Indian, but he seemed too well spoken, and he had every appearance of being the lawyer he said he was. His clothes were immaculate and of the latest style. His hands were clean and soft. This was not the mean, vengeful, white Indian that Tommy had described. The one called River Joe would not be able to stand and look him straight in the eye as this man was doing without giving away the anger and revenge that lay beneath the smile. Sam Gates knew his men. This surely was not the infamous River Joe.

"What do you think of having our man Jackson for president?" Sam asked, testing River's knowledge.

River folded his arms in a scholarly pose. "Well, we have a couple of years to decide, but he is certainly giving President Adams a time over states' rights. I think for states' rights alone we need to vote for Jackson. He's a firm believer in keeping the federal government out of state affairs; and even though I'm from Ohio, I don't think the federal government has a right telling the southern states that their citizens can't own slaves. I've been studying up on such things, since I'm on my way to Atlanta to set up a practice. I figure with all the arguments flying over slavery, the south is a good place to do business for the present."

Sam smiled and nodded. "I like your thinking. And I have a feeling Jackson can help us get rid of the damned Indians," he added cleverly. If this man was River Joe, he would not like such a statement. But River was ready, and his face brightened at the remark. Inwardly he thanked the Cherokee leader John Ross for keeping all of them so well informed on what was happening in the government. Because of the Cherokee fight to stay in Tennessee and Georgia, many of them, including River Joe, knew all about what was going on with the federal government. And the Cherokee were closely tied to Andrew Jackson, had fought under his leadership in the War of 1812. They knew now that Jackson would probably turn on them if he became president, knew the man's feelings about states' rights. If his intentions at the moment were to test River's knowledge of the law, Sam Gates could not have picked a better subject.

"Exactly," he answered Gates. "Dealing with Indians is as much a matter of states' rights as slavery. It's true they were here first, but we have proven that things must change in this country now. We are ordained by God, I am convinced, to build this country into the truly great and powerful nation it can be. Andrew Jackson is the man who can see that it happens."

Sam looked from River to Joanna, who stood grinning. "You see? I knew you'd like him, Sam."

Sam chuckled. "Joanna tells me you were asking about, uh, some manly comforts for the night."

River grinned. "I hope I didn't insult the lady," he answered.

Sam grinned wryly. "On the contrary. For the right price, the, uh, 'lady' can afford you those comforts right here."

River's eyebrows arched in feigned surprise, as his dark eyes moved to take an appreciative inventory of Joanna. "Well, well," he said seductively. "How lucky can a man get?" He looked back at Sam Gates. "What is the price?"

"Thirty dollars."

River grinned. "She must be very good."

"The best," Sam answered. "Young and firm."

Never had River's willpower been more tested. Again Sam Gates watched him carefully, and again he caught no sign of animosity in the tall, handsome John Beck.

"You can pay Joanna in her room," Sam said to River. "If you don't pay, I, uh, have men who will find you and make you pay. I don't mean to sound rude, Mr. Beck, but I like my customers to understand how things are here." He leaned closer. "And don't follow Joanna up right away. We don't make bold public displays of our extra activities around here, although most of my customers know what goes on. That's why they come here. My girls see that they get what they pay for."

Sam smiled almost wickedly, and River felt his chest tighten. He could see through the glittering dark eyes of Sam Gates, into the man's hideous soul. He bowed slightly. "Well, then, I should be in store for a very pleasant evening. Thank you so much, Mr. Gates."

"My pleasure, Mr. Beck. And do what you can to get Jackson elected next term, will you? He's one of our Tennessee boys, you know."

"Oh, yes, I know," River answered. He watched Gates as the man turned away, pulling a cigar from his coat pocket and lighting it, walking to another table to talk to someone else. Never had River been more glad he had paid attention to John Ross and all the news from Washington. More than that, never had he been happier to be white. For once it had helped him. Knowing both worlds could be an advantage. He had proven that tonight.

He sat back down, moving his eyes to the woman called Joanna. "I'm awfully tired," he said with a gentle grin.

She laughed lightly, bending close to him so that he could see her nipples. "Room number six," she said softly in his ear. "Wait about fifteen minutes."

She sauntered away and up the stairs. River watched, wondering if poor Emma was up there somewhere. He wanted to charge up the stairs and tear into every room until he found her, but that would only get him killed.

Instinct told him that never in his life would he have to be more careful than now. This was more dangerous than stalking a bear or trying to hide from raiders. This "civilized" territory was more dangerous than all the wild mountains through which he had traveled, and the men in this place more cunning and dangerous than the wiliest Indian or the most hateful settler. This was a place of lies and deceit and murder, and the man who owned the Tennessee Belle dealt in woman slavery.

What had Sam Gates done with Emma? Somehow he had to get that information out of the woman called Joanna.

He finished his whiskey and ordered one more. But he only toyed with it, worried that too much whiskey would dull his senses. He had to be alert this night. One way or another, Sam Gates would die before dawn! He had made it into the lion's den. Before he left, he would kill the lion.

$\Diamond$ *Chapter 24* $\Diamond$

Joanna opened the door and River entered the musky room. He felt almost dizzy at the thought of Emma in such a place. He watched Joanna approach with drinks in her hands. She had changed into a feathered robe, just thin enough for a man to make out the naked figure beneath it.

"Want another drink?" she asked, holding out the glass.

"No, thank you," he answered. "I like to be fully alert when I'm with a woman, if you know what I mean."

Joanna laughed lightly, setting the glasses aside. "I know exactly what you mean. I've had men come up here so full of booze they work the rest of the night at performing. It's absolutely humorous." She put her hands to his sides and ran them down over his hips. "I have a feeling that won't be any problem at all for a man like you."

River pulled her close, running a hand over her hips, feeling every curve through the thin robe. He did not want this hard, painted woman. But she could be his only hope for finding Emma. He met her mouth with a convincing kiss that drew forth the response he wanted. He had to soften her, had to gain her confidence. His hands detected the odd indentions on her lower back and bottom. They felt like scars, but he said nothing for the moment.

"My, my," Joanna said as he pulled away then. "This is going to be the most fun I've had in a long time." She pulled his jacket off his shoulders.

"I have to be honest with you, Joanna," he said as she threw the jacket aside. "I knew I could find what I wanted here. Someone in another saloon told me to come here if I wanted more than whiskey and cards. I just wasn't sure how easy it would be to get what I wanted. They said Sam Gates was a careful man."

He watched her eyes harden slightly. "*Careful* isn't the word for it. In fact, you're quite lucky, Mr. Beck." She pulled down his fancy suspenders and unhooked his pants, running her fingers along his legs as she pulled them down. She knew her job well, but River was too full of Emma to be affected by her skilled fingers and the light kisses she planted along his legs. "Sit down and I'll pull off your boots and these pants," she said.

"Why am I lucky?" he asked, sitting on the edge of the bed. She pulled at his high, Wellington boots, tugging one off.

"Sam thought you might be somebody else—some man he's thinking might come by here looking for him—and not for friendly purposes, if you know what I mean." She tugged on the other boot.

"I see," he answered, his heart quickening. Perhaps she would be so talkative he wouldn't have to ask too many questions on his own. "Well, I'm glad I wasn't mistaken for this other person. I might not have been able to come up here with you."

She snickered. "It would have been worse than that." She met his eyes. "You might be dead."

His eyebrows arched. "That bad, is it?"

She pulled off his pants. "Some big Indian—well, not an Indian really. A white man. But he was raised by the Indians and he looks and acts like one himself, so I'm told." She got to her knees, moving her hands along his thighs to the buttons of his knee-length cotton underwear. She began undoing the buttons, and he allowed his purely animal instincts to come forward. How was he to keep her talking if he did not convince her that his intentions were what he said they were? He gripped her hair as she toyed with him.

"This problem with the Indian—must be over a woman," he said, his voice deliberately gruff with pleasure. "That's usually what men are at odds about, either women or money."

She smiled, looking up at him. "A pretty little blond girl that both Sam and the white Indian think they own." She stood up, opening her robe. "Some say the Indian is dead, but Sam doesn't believe it, and the girl finally admitted he's still alive. Still, I don't think the Indian would come to a place like Knoxville, unless he wants to die. Sam is surrounded by good men. The Indian would never get to him."

She let her robe fall to the floor. Her body was firm and shapely, and River wondered about the scar on her belly, but again he asked no questions. Joanna smiled and knelt down again. "Stand up and I'll get rid of your underwear for you."

River rose, fighting feelings of guilt in letting his manliness show as she pulled off the underwear. For the moment he had no choice but to go along with her. She moved up his legs and thighs, kissing at him expertly. "I'll make sure you get your thirty dollars' worth," she told him, pushing at him to sit back down on the bed. She stood up again, bending forward and cradling his head against her breasts as she moved a leg to each side of him, straddling his lap and then playfully pushing him back onto the bed.

"I shouldn't have told you about the white Indian," she said. She hovered over him, brushing her breasts against his lips. "I'm talking about things that don't interest you and things I probably shouldn't be talking about at all. I don't usually do that. It's just that you're . . . I don't know . . . you make me want to talk. You're an interesting man, John Beck, and you sure are the handsomest man who ever came through Knoxville."

She sat up, rubbing against him as she began unbuttoning his shirt. River ran his hands gently along her thighs and up over her breasts.

"I don't mind," he said, hoping to keep the conversation going. "I need to talk, no matter what the subject. I'll be moving on in the morning. What happens here at the Belle doesn't make much difference to me. I've been a long time traveling, mostly alone. I need to talk." He massaged one nipple teasingly. "I must say you have my curiosity going now. Where is the pretty little blond girl? She work here now?"

Joanna snickered. "No. But in a few months she'll be wishing she did. Where she's going is a lot worse than this place."

River felt himself losing control. What had they done with Emma? "Oh?" he answered calmly. "Where is she going?"

Joanna opened his shirt, then gasped when she saw his chest. River told himself to be careful. He had forgotten about the scars. This woman could ruin everything. What had she learned about River Joe? He watched her green eyes as they moved to meet his own dark ones.

"What happened to you?" she asked him.

He put a hand to his chest. "These? I guess I should have warned you. On my way here I was attacked by a bear—almost died. I'm sorry if the scars offend you."

She watched him for what seemed an eternity, then moved off of him. "You're *him*, aren't you!" she exclaimed in a near whisper. "You're River Joe!"

He sat up, every nerve and instinct alive. "Why would you think that?" he asked cautiously.

"Emma. She said you were attacked by a bear but that you would get well and you would come for her." Her eyes widened. "My God, it's you! You really *did* come for her!"

River's hand went around her mouth and he pulled her down onto the bed, keeping a hand clamped tightly over her mouth and moving a leg over her to pin her body. "Please, do not make me hurt you. I do not want to hurt a woman, but I will do anything to get my Emma back! Promise me you will not scream."

She nodded slightly, her eyes tearing. He cautiously moved his hand slightly, keeping it against her chin. "Now you know. There is nothing I can do about it. Where is my Emma?"

A tear slipped down the side of her face. "You really did come for her!" she whispered. "I didn't think men like you really existed."

"Please help me," he said, moving his hand to her neck. He ran a thumb over her cheek. "Do not make me hurt a woman. It is not a brave thing to do. The Maker of Breath would frown upon it."

"The Maker of Breath?"

"My God. He brought me my Emma. Then she was taken from me. I have prayed very hard to the Maker of Breath to help me find her, and He has led me here to you. Surely He knows you are good somewhere deep inside and that you will help me. Where is Emma?"

She blinked, alive with emotions she had never felt before. Were there really good men in the world? She had never had the chance to find out. She suddenly realized that for the first time since pirates had sold her to Sam Gates she had a chance to get away from the man.

"First you tell me," she whispered. "Can you do it? Can you really kill Sam Gates like Emma said you could?"

His eyes glittered with vengeance. "I am already here in

his very presence. If I have come this far, I can kill him. I was raised by Indians. I can be in a room without a man knowing it."

She breathed deeply with the excitement of it. Never before had she had any kind of hope, but even though she had fought against the feelings, Emma had stirred something in her, had touched deep, womanly instincts Joanna thought had died years ago.

"Pull the blankets over us," she said. "Someone might look in. Sometimes Sam peeks at us girls to see if we're doing our job right."

He watched her cautiously as he reached for the covers. He pulled them over them both, moving on top of her, putting his big hands to either side of her face. "You will help me?"

"Only if you promise to kill Sam Gates and that I won't get in trouble. They can't know who did it, or they'll think I helped."

"They won't know. I have a plan. All I need to know is where he sleeps."

"His room is at the back of the building, upstairs. I can sneak in later and make sure the window is unlocked. No one would think anything of me going in there, and Sam trusts me. I've been with him longer than any of the others. If you're good at climbing, you can get in by working your way up the tree at the back corner of the building and moving across the little balcony to the third window from the left as you look at the building from the back. You'll be able to see once you get inside. Sam always sleeps with a lamp lit. He has a lot of enemies."

He watched her closely. "Why would you help me kill the man you work for? Is he not also your friend?"

Her eyes turned colder. "Look at my back."

He rose and she turned over for him. He touched the scars, wondering what horrible things had been done to Emma. "He did this to you?"

"One of his men, while he watched." She turned back over. "That is not the work of a friend. You probably wonder why I have never tried to escape. I did—twice—a long time ago. These scars are from one of those attempts. I don't even want to talk about what he did to me the second time. A woman soon learns not to anger Sam Gates. I've never had any hope of getting away from him—until now."

He put a hand to her hair, feeling sorry for her in spite of what she was. Joanna was astonished at the gentle touch. "What did he do to my Emma?" he asked. "Where is she?"

"A Tommy Decker brought her here. She was very sick because she had lost a baby on the way. She was very weak from loss of blood."

River closed his eyes and groaned. Joanna felt him stiffen with anger and grief.

"She's all right now but still weak," she said. "Sam let her sleep for about four days. He kept her drugged part of the time."

His eyes opened and he gripped her hair. "What did he do to her?" he asked through gritted teeth. "And Tommy! What did *he* do!"

"Tommy never got to touch her. Her miscarriage kept him away from her, so it was a blessing, in a way. But the bleeding had stopped when she arrived here. And Sam... Sam always tries the girls out himself first, if you know what I mean."

His hands gripped even tighter, pulling at her hair so that it hurt. "He raped her!" he growled.

"You're hurting me," she whimpered.

He let go of her, rolling off her and grasping a pillow, groaning into it. "I came too late," he moaned.

Joanna pulled the covers up close around them, stroking his hair. "She didn't even know it, River Joe. She was completely out from the drugs. I never told her. I could tell she would have been devastated to know. She's a good, good woman. If you do manage to get out of here and find her, don't tell her. Don't ever tell her."

River hunched into the pillow, grasping it in fists so tight that his knuckles were white. He sat up then, his back to her, making odd little gasping sounds.

"Where is she now?" he asked, his voice broken.

She touched his back, feeling sorry for him. "Sam sent her away—to his coal mine."

He threw back his head and breathed deeply for control, then turned to her, resting on one elbow. She was astonished to see tears in his eyes. She had never thought of a man crying, certainly not over a woman.

"What coal mine? Why did he send her there? Where is it?" he asked anxiously.

"It's about a five-day ride from here, up by Willow Springs. But she left only two days ago. You might be able to reach her in time." At the look in River Joe's eyes, for the first time in months, perhaps years, Joanna felt sympathy in her heart. But he had to know, for she wanted to make sure he hated Sam Gates enough to go through with killing the man. "Sam sends girls there to . . . to break them, as Sam puts it. The miners—" She lay back against a pillow. "When they're through with a woman she's ready to do whatever Sam wants her to do. She's not much good for anything else. I know. I've been there."

Their eyes held, and River's blazed with a myriad of emotions, sorrow for Joanna, agony over Emma, a need to kill Sam Gates. He struggled to remain calm. If he handled things right, he could get to Emma before she reached the mine.

"It is a terrible thing Sam Gates has done to you and others," he said. He ran a hand through his hair and wiped at his eyes. "I thank you for agreeing to help me, for not screaming out."

She smiled amost wickedly. "This is the first time I've been one step ahead of Sam Gates. I like the feeling. You fooled him, River Joe! I don't think any man has ever done that before, but you did it! You were wonderful down there."

"My God was with me. Tell me how I can find this mine."

"There is a well-traveled road that goes there. Anyone in town can tell you the main route. It's called the Gates Mining Company. But Tommy will probably stay off the road as much as possible, since Emma might draw attention."

"Tommy! Tommy Decker has taken her there?"

"Under Sam's orders. Sam was angry for how Tommy handled this whole thing, especially for not being sure you were dead. Sam bullied Emma into telling the truth about you. I think she did it because she knew by instinct that Sam would hurt her badly to make her tell, and she's right. She's a survivor, River Joe. All she talked about was getting through all of this and staying alive until you came, so she could get back to her babies. She kept saying you would come. She seemed so sure of it." She put a hand to his face. "And you did come. I think Emma is a very lucky woman. I envy her."

He took her hand and moved back on top of her in case they were being watched. Someone tapped on her door then and they both stiffened. "Everything all right in here, Joanna?"

"It's Stu, one of Sam's men," she whispered.

River kissed her and she bent her knees so they would show under the blankets. He held her tightly then as she answered. "Everything is wonderful, Stu. Go away and leave us alone."

Stu laughed lightly and they heard his retreating footsteps. Joanna studied the handsome face so close to hers, then leaned up and grasped at his mouth with her own. River answered the kiss, sensing her desperate need to be kissed warmly, gently. She pressed against him, leaving his mouth then and licking at his ear.

"Make love to me," she whispered. "Make love to me like you do to her, River Joe."

He rose up, putting a hand to the side of her face. "I

cannot. I belong to her, as she belongs to me. And I must hurry. Now that she is well, and is alone with Tommy Decker, I know what he will try to do to her. There is not much time. They have two days' start on me. I will have to ride hard to catch up before they reach the mine."

She smiled sadly. "Of course. I should have known." She rolled away from him, lying on her side, her back to him. "You'll have to stay here awhile," she told him then, a sadness in her voice. "It wouldn't look right if you left just yet. I know you're anxious to get to Emma, but if you're going to continue to fool Sam, you had better stay up here a little longer. You can always leave later and tell Sam you already paid for a hotel room before coming here. Then you can leave and sneak back into Sam's room later like I told you. You had better wait until about four in the morning."

She turned to face him, and he detected more tears in her eyes. "By the way, do you have the thirty dollars? I'll have to show it to Sam or there will be trouble."

"I have it. That is about all I have to my name, but it is worth it to be able to find Emma. This will be a good night. Sam Gates will *die* this night!"

"I hope you kill that Tommy, too. He's a cocky bastard. He was mean to Emma. She was filthy and underfed when she got here. And you're right. He'll abuse her badly on the way to the mine, unless she thinks of a way to get away from him." She smiled then. "And somehow I can't imagine your Emma letting any man touch her. I think she'd die first. I've seen a lot of women come through here, River Joe. Yours was one of the most stubborn and determined ones. I ended up kind of liking her, but I didn't dare let Sam know that." She put a hand to her head. "God knows I lost most of my ability to care about anything or anyone a long time ago."

He pulled her close. "How can I repay you for all you have told me? I came here hoping to find out about my Emma, and my God led me to you."

"The only repayment I need is for you to kill Sam Gates. Nothing could make me happier. Stu is the only one besides me and Tommy and Sam who knows you might be alive. But if you aren't seen, no one can say it was you. Stu won't even bother trying to find out who did it because he wants to take over Sam's place and his business. I've seen it in his eyes. I can handle Stu. I'll talk him out of thinking it could have been you. No one else even thinks you're alive anymore, so if you kill Tommy, too, you'll be a free man. Hank's nigger was hanged for Hank's murder after he was captured and told Sam what he saw. No one knows you killed Hank Toole."

River frowned. "The Negro who worked for Hank? They hanged him?"

"Yes. Some men found him and brought him to Sam. Sam wanted everyone to think Nigger Jim killed Hank in order to be free and run away. That way no one would know about Hank bringing Emma to him. He doesn't like people to know he deals in woman slavery. People know he has prostitutes here, but they think they're all willing, not bought and paid for, then beaten into submission. When Nigger Jim was hanged for Hank's murder, that closed the subject. That left Sam free to go after you and Emma. But now that everyone thinks Hank's murder has been solved, you're a free man, if you can get away with killing Sam and Tommy."

She grinned a little. "Tommy will be easy. Anyone can see he talks big but is a coward at heart. Sam killed Tommy's friend Deek, and no one knows Tommy was taking Emma to the mine except Stu. If Tommy's found dead in the woods, people will simply think robbers killed him. And Stu won't bother looking for Emma after that. It was Sam who was bent on keeping Emma. It makes him crazy when things don't go his way. This whole thing could have been avoided, but Sam was hell-bent on killing you for taking what he considered to be his property, and then he wanted to punish Emma for running off with you. That's why he sent her to the mine. Then he figured you'd be easy to spot if you came here looking for her, and he'd have you killed, too. If you could just kill Sam without being spotted, you would be a free man."

River's dark eyes turned cunning and vengeful. "I intend to kill Sam Gates in a way that it will not even be blamed on a man," he said.

"How in the world will you do that?"

"Do not worry. Just know that it will be done."

She smiled almost wickedly. "Yes. I guess you'll know what to do. I just wish I could be there to see it—to watch Sam Gates die." She traced light fingers over the scars on his chest. "If you can kill Sam and Tommy, we'll both be free." She met his eyes. "I wish you luck, River Joe."

She saw fiery determination in his eyes. "My God is with me. I have no doubt that Sam Gates will die this night, and that Tommy Decker will also suffer. I will get my Emma back." He put a hand to her shoulder. "And you have helped me. You will be glad for helping me, and blessed for it," he said.

She smiled at the lovely words. "Well, now, you are really something. I hope you find her, River Joe, and that she's all right and Tommy hasn't hurt her."

"When I am through he will never touch another woman, nor will Sam Gates."

She thought about the horror that would be visited upon her if this man failed, but somehow she knew in her bones he would not. In minutes she had sensed his power, his strength and will.

Emma was right. Her River Joe would be the one who would get the better of Sam Gates.

"You have to wait a little longer," she said. "Will you do something for me? You said you owe me."

He studied the painted face, thinking how much prettier it would be without all the colors that covered it. "What is it?"

"Will you . . . " She could hardly believe her own words.

"Will you just hold me? You don't have to . . . do anything. Just hold me. I haven't been held kindly since I was little— before pirates came and stole me off a beach in Virginia."

He frowned. "How old were you?"

"I was only eight."

"Eight! And they brought you here?"

"Not directly. But Sam was at a dock where pirates sold their wares. He bought me, but he was kind enough to wait until I was eleven to show me what he expected of me."

River lost any remaining doubts he might have had about deliberately murdering a man. Killing Sam Gates would be like ridding the land of a black plague.

He pulled the covers up around them and drew Joanna into his arms.

He wondered if he could really trust this woman, but then he felt her tremble, felt a wetness against his chest. He realized she was crying. Sam Gates had forced her to live in hell for years. Yes, he could trust her.

He petted Joanna's hair. Tonight Sam Gates would die, and soon Tommy Decker. He would take his vengeance and then he would take his precious Emma home.

Sam turned onto his back, stretching and snuggling down again. It was nearly three o'clock when he had gone to bed, and still he felt restless now. He couldn't stop thinking about the lawyer from Ohio.

He wished this River Joe would show himself and get it over with. Every tall, dark stranger he saw now made him nervous. He told himself he was being foolish. After all, Stu slept right outside his door, and men guarded the front and back of the saloon all night. They were all good men, and River Joe could never walk into a place like Knoxville and the Tennessee Belle, night or day, without being seen.

The description they had of the man left little doubt in Sam's mind that he would be easy to spot.

Still, maybe this River Joe was smarter than Sam thought. Emma Simms seemed to think so, but then Emma Simms was, after all, a simple mountain girl who didn't know much about the ways of men like Sam Gates. River Joe wouldn't know how to handle him either.

At least the lawyer had had his round in bed with Joanna and had left. He had paid the thirty dollars and gone to a hotel. It had all worked out, and the man was gone. At least that suspicion was done with. John Beck seemed at first to fit the description of River Joe in several ways, but a man who had been raised by Cherokee Indians and who had lived in the wilds as long as this River Joe had surely wouldn't know much about states' rights and the presidency and other important matters that ignorant backwoods people knew nothing about.

Joanna had said the man gave her quite a good time and asked no unusual questions. He could trust Joanna. She was one woman who knew the ropes, and she had long ago learned not to cross Sam Gates. Joanna wouldn't dream of trying to pull a fast one on him.

He settled in between satin sheets. If he weren't so tired he would order the new girl to be brought to him. He had just bought her that morning, a pretty little thing, an orphaned mountain girl whose neighbor figured he could make some whiskey money from selling her. The neighbor was right. She was only thirteen and a virgin. Sam would enjoy turning the shivering little thing into a woman who knew how to appreciate men. She would learn to like it soon enough.

He grinned then at the thought of Emma Simms. Tommy would have finally had his turn at her by now, and the haughty bitch would soon have any lingering pride stripped away by the miners. It served her right, especially for lying to Tommy about River Joe's being dead.

He closed his eyes, finally beginning to drift off. The pendulum of a wall clock drifted back and forth, ticking to four o'clock. The guard in the alley below Sam's window drifted off to sleep for a moment, and a shadowy figure in buckskins moved silently past him. A gunnysack hung from the intruder's arm as he deftly climbed the tree at the corner of the building, hoisting himself up with strong arms and with the agility of a man who knew the woods and shadows, a man who had spent his life hunting, stalking wary animals. Now he would stalk a wary man; he would use all his skills and instincts against the most dangerous prey of all.

The guard blinked awake then, feeling a presence but looking around and seeing nothing. Above him the shadowy figure crept silently along the balcony, to the third window.

Inside, Sam Gates had finally fallen asleep. He snored and settled even deeper into his pillow, unaware that someone crept through his window without making a sound. The intruder carefully opened the gunnysack he was carrying, grasping at something from the outside of the bag and carefully letting it come to the opening. He caught it then with one quick movement of his hand before walking on moccasined feet to Sam Gates's bed.

A quick, strong hand reached out then, a thumb pressing against Sam's Adam's apple just enough to make the man stop breathing for a moment. The strong grasp about his throat made Sam jolt awake. He tried to breathe, but something kept the breath from coming, and he could not call out.

In the light of the lamp, as he came fully awake and realized what was happening, Sam could see him—John Beck! What was happening? He looked different, wilder, meaner. He wore buckskins, and in the next moment Sam Gates found himself staring into the open, white mouth of a hissing snake. He knew in that instant his first suspicion had been right. This was River Joe!

River pressed his left hand tightly, maneuvering his thumb in such an expert way that Sam could not breathe enough to yell out. He was quickly losing strength, unable to fight back. But even if he could fight, common sense told him to lie still, for River Joe held the wiggling snake in his right hand, close to Sam's face.

"Do you know what kind of snake this is!" River sneered, his dark eyes on fire with vengeance. "Some call it a water moccasin. Others call it a cottonmouth." His voice hissed like the snake, and he moved the snake's mouth even closer, enjoying the absolute terror in Sam Gates's eyes. "Whatever it is called, it is *poisonous!*" River whispered. He smiled at the look in Sam Gates's eyes. "How does it feel, Sam Gates, to be the one who is *afraid!* The one who is threatened, tortured?"

Sam's mouth opened in an effort to yell for help, but nothing came out. The room began to swim around him as lack of air made him weaker and brought on an enveloping blackness so that all he could see was River Joe's leering face and the hissing snake.

"You will never harm another woman, Sam Gates," he heard River Joe hiss.

Again Sam tried to call out. River Joe! He was right here! Where were his own men? How had this man gotten in? Joanna! She had something to do with this.

"Tonight you *die,* Sam Gates!" he heard in a gruff whisper.

It was then Sam felt it, knew there was no hope. A horrible, piercing pain seered through his face, starting near his eye with a sickening sting. He was suddenly unable to move at all. He felt something wiggle across his face, then gasped at another quick and painful bite at his neck. It was the last thing he remembered.

Joanna woke up to a scream. She quickly put on a heavy robe, her heart racing. Sam! Was he dead? Had River Joe really done it? She hurried out into the hall, where she could hear one of the other girls screaming and weeping. She watched as more gathered, and she listened to their gasps.

"Oh, my God!" Stu said.

"What is it?" one of the girls gasped. "Look at his face!"

"I don't know. Something . . . something must have bit him," Stu answered. "Stay back."

"Oh, God, look at him!" someone else gasped.

There was a moment of footsteps, scuffling. "I don't see anything," Stu said then. Another moment of silence. "Good God, it looks like he's snake-bit."

"Is he . . . is he dead?" one of the girls asked.

"Yes. I don't believe it. I never heard a thing," Stu answered. "Get some of the other men up here and we'll search the room. Watch where you walk."

"Oh, my God. Oh, God!" one of the girls screamed, darting out of the room holding up her robe.

Joanna walked carefully to Sam's room, putting on a concerned look. "What happened?" she asked. She gasped when she saw Sam, then fought to subdue a smile. What a wonderful sight! Sam's face was purple and swollen, his eyes open and staring in death.

"Snake-bit," Stu said to her. "Be careful where you walk." He shook his head. "Can you believe it? We'll search the building. What in hell do you think could have attracted a snake to crawl all the way up here?"

"I can't imagine," Joanna answered. "Maybe mice. I told Sam just the other day I've been seeing a lot of mice."

She walked to the window and looked out toward the mountains behind town, wondering how far River Joe had ridden during the night. She felt a tightness in her throat, and a keen envy for the woman called Emma.

She turned then, hurrying down the stairs and outside toward the shed where the frightened new girl had been kept for the night. How good it would feel to free her, and how good it felt to Joanna also to be free—free at last! Sam Gates had been killed by a snake. No one would ever know about River Joe's part in an act of justice.

◇ *Chapter 25* ◇

Emma took another weary step. She had no idea where she was; she had slept that night on pine needles in the shelter of a rock formation, waking at every odd noise, fearing a bear or a bobcat might pounce on her or a snake crawl across her legs. She had been afraid to make a fire lest someone see it.

The morning sun brought warmth but did not lift her spirits. She had no idea where she was—which way to go. What if she happened to stumble upon men from the mine? How close was she? What would she tell a stranger if someone came upon her? She dared not stick to a traveled roadway, even if she happened to find one. She could not risk running into other people and having to explain. Someone might force her to return to Knoxville.

What if Sam Gates came after her? Her punishment would be great indeed. Of that she had no doubt. But surely River had been there by now. Surely Sam was dead. But what if it was River who was dead? Then all her efforts at leaving a trail for him to follow would be for nothing. All along the way she had torn lace from the fancy stitching of the dress she wore and had tied it to a bush or a branch. If River could find the burned campsite, he could follow her trail easily from there. She could only pray it would not be the wrong men who found the trail.

She kept climbing, remembering River's telling her not to be afraid of anything, telling her how strong she was, what a survivor she was. If only she were physically stronger. She had not had time to regain her stamina, and the trip to Knoxville and the strain of her terror there had drained what little energies she had left after the miscarriage.

Somehow she had to reach the Cherokee. Somehow she had to get back to her babies. This all seemed so easy when she traveled with River. Now the forest had turned into her enemy.

Night came again, and the trees turned into monsters. Their branches were huge arms ready to grab her. She imagined animals all around her, felt their eyes watching her. The forest at night was terrifying, but she feared coming upon men more than she feared coming upon an angry bear or an ornery bobcat.

Morning came again, and no one had found her. She took hope in her aloneness, in spite of her vulnerability to animals and the elements. She made little headway that morning. Every bone and muscle ached, and she was even weaker now from lack of food. She had brought along potatoes and biscuits and a small jar of jam from Tommy's supplies, but she was trying to conserve, eating just once a day.

She nibbled on wild berries whenever she found them, and her feet hurt in the fancy heeled shoes she had been given to wear. She wished she had comfortable moccasins and an Indian tunic rather than the tight-fitting cotton dress she wore, with its stays and many buttons.

The days were too warm and the nights too cool and damp. Every time she closed her eyes, images returned of Tommy and the burning tent, his blackened body, his white, staring eyes. If only River would come! But he might never come. She forced back the terror and horrible grief this thought brought her, for to live without River would not be living at all. At least if she could reach Joshua and Rachael, she would have a part of River with her forever.

The sun was setting on the fourth night since she had left Knoxville. She climbed still more, wanting to go a little farther before night came again. She left behind a carpetbag of clothes, the supplies seeming to get heavier and heavier. She kept with her only the food and the musket and powder.

She was proud of how calm she had remained, in spite of her inner terror. She had begun getting used to the darkness, the noises. She began to believe she could make it. She had to, for the sake of her babies, and to stay one step ahead of Sam Gates.

Her biggest obstacle now was her weakness and hunger. She knew it would probably take two or three weeks to reach Grace and Mary, her Cherokee family, her children, if she ever managed to find them at all. She did not have enough food along with her for so long a trek. She decided she would have to try to kill something for food. And she would rest as much as she dared to.

She could do this. She had to do it. She was River Joe's woman. She left another piece of lace tied to a bush. She would survive until River came, and he *would* come. He would find the trail she had left him and he would follow.

She heard a loud roaring noise ahead, and she headed for it curiously. This day of climbing had been very hot. If there was water up ahead, she would cool herself in it.

The roaring became louder until she reached the edge of a rocky canyon. She peered over the edge. Yes, there was water, but none that she could get to. Far below, a raging river plunged through the canyon. She remembered the night of the flood, her terror of the swirling waters. This river reminded her of the rising Hiwassee.

She had no idea what river this was, but she remembered with an aching heart how River had saved her that night, hanging on to her as they made their way across the mooring rope to shore. They had been through so much since then. That awful night had been the beginning of a whole new life for Emma Simms. If it were not for Sam Gates and Tommy Decker, she and River would still be with the Cherokee, with their babies.

Suddenly the bank on which she stood gave way. It was not rock, as she had thought, but slippery clay. Emma screamed as she felt the ground sliding beneath her. She let go of everything she was carrying to try for a handhold, but everything she touched slithered right out of her hands.

A new terror gripped her as she felt herself moving helplessly toward the raging waters. How ironic it would be if she drowned after all! Her musket went crashing down to rocks below, splintering into a useless piece of wood and metal. Part of it floated away, and her bag of black powder became a soggy mass before it sank from sight. Food tumbled from its supply bag, falling helter-skelter; then Emma's feet suddenly came to rest on flat rock that jutted out from the bank.

She stood still for a moment, telling herself to be calm. The river still roared below her, but she had not fallen into it. She looked up first, to see the top of the bank was much too high to reach. The bank leading there was nothing but smooth clay, with a few tree roots sticking out. A small root dangled nearby, and she grabbed on to it for support. She managed to stand back just a little, shivering when air hit the front of her. She was covered from her forehead to her toes with wet clay, and she shook her head to get some of it away from her eyes.

Cautiously she looked down, then groaned in agony at her situation. The river roared beneath her, with no banks on which she could stand. If she fell, the deep, violent waters would surely draw her down to a dark, cold grave. But even if there were some kind of bank along its edge, she would not be able to get to it without getting hurt, for the river was still a dizzying distance below her.

A miserable, hopeless dread crawled into her bones as she realized she could not go up or down. She looked around her feet to see that the rock on which she stood was just big enough to hold her if she should sit down. She could at least slither to a sitting position and rest. Perhaps she could think of a way out of this. But helpless fear gripped her when she realized she might not be standing on a rock at all. Perhaps this, too, was only clay! What if it gave way beneath her?

So, this was her end. After all she had survived, she would die the kind of death she feared most. She would not reach her babies. She would not see River again. She was too weak and tired to care about being brave and determined anymore. She clung to the tree root and put her head against the slippery clay and cried, using her last bit of faith in the Maker of Breath to pray that River would come and find her before she died of starvation or fell into the dark waters.

River watched the camp carefully for a moment. *Esauge-tuh Emissee* was with him, for just that morning he had found the place where Tommy and Emma must have camped their first night. He could only pray from then on that he was following Tommy's trail and not some stranger's. Sheer instinct had led him along the path it seemed logical for Tommy to take if he wanted to stay off the main road but still have a fairly easy trip. After finding that first campsite the tracking had been easy.

He had followed a trail directly to this second campsite, but something was wrong here. Three horses grazed about, one of them still carrying some gear. A cold campfire looked roughly two days old, and a tent lay in burned ruins.

River's heart beat with dread. Had there been some kind of accident? Had they been attacked by someone? Outlaws? Robbers? Had someone new carried Emma away? He pulled his musket from its boot and tied his horse and pack horse, cautiously approaching the site, watching, listening.

A little creek bubbled nearby. His dark, experienced eyes took in the entire campsite carefully, moving to the creek, where he was sure that he saw something move. He readied his musket, curling his nostrils at an odd odor as he came closer, an odor that resembled wounded or dead flesh.

He scanned the waters, his eyes widening in shock when he saw what appeared to be a human body in the water. He walked closer, his blood tingling at what looked like a horribly burned man, his skin an ugly red, some of it a hard black. The man lay in the water, apparently for relief from the burns. River felt a chill go down his spine when the man opened his eyes. Surely this horribly burned piece of flesh could not still be alive!

The man groaned. "No!" he seemed to be saying. "Riii . . . Joe!"

River bent closer, frowning, finding something familiar about the blue eyes. Not all the hair was burned off the body, and River could see that what hair was left was red. A horrible dread moved through him. "Tommy! Tommy Decker?"

"She . . . did . . . this . . . bitch!"

River lost all sympathy. Emma! She might have been burned, too! Had she set the tent on fire deliberately just to get away?

"Where's Emma!" he growled, bending even closer.

"Bastard!" Tommy moaned. "Your . . . fault . . ."

"Where is Emma! What happened to her!"

Tommy actually managed a grin. "Watched . . . Sam . . . rape her . . . good show."

River grabbed his arm, yanking it out of the water and squeezing against the burns. Tommy screamed for him to stop.

"Sam is dead!" River snarled. "Where is Emma! What happened here!"

"Lamp . . . bitch started it. Ran . . . away . . . probably lost."

River threw his arm down into the water. "How long ago?"

"Don't . . . know. . . . maybe two . . . nights . . . lost track . . . dying."

"You're dying, all right," River snarled. "Let me help you on your way!"

He could not control his anger. Tommy Decker was as worthless as Sam Gates. He had watched while Sam Gates mauled his poor Emma. And God only knew the hell he had put Emma through himself. River stood up, and with his foot pushed Tommy's head off the rock and into the creek. Tommy struggled only slightly before all movement stopped. River pressed his face under the water several seconds to be sure. There must be no remaining witnesses. He finally released the pressure. The body stayed under water and did not move.

"Now you are out of your misery."

River turned away, feeling no remorse. He searched carefully around the campsite for a sign of which way Emma had gone. All his years of tracking in these mountains paid off. He found what he was sure were the prints of someone very light. But they were over two days old. Following this trail would not be easy.

For better than two hours he studied the ground and followed what he hoped was the right trail. Then he spotted a piece of lace tied to a bush.

River grinned. She had left him a trail! He ran up to the lace, then carefully studied the woods all around, spotting another piece of lace far in the distance. At first it looked like a spot of sunshine amid moving, shadowy leaves, but his experienced eyes knew the difference. He untied the first piece so no one else would find it, then ran to the second piece, untying that one also.

Yes, his Emma was a survivor, all right! She was brave and smart and beautiful. He could almost feel her in his arms already.

Emma had no tears left, nor any strength. She had managed to lower herself to the rock, or what she hoped was a rock, where she curled up to try to rest . . . and wait.

She had made her decision. She would try to stay alive until River found her. And if it was Sam Gates who got to her first, she would jump off the rock into the raging waters below and let herself drown.

Night settled over her, and a cold dampness seeped into her bones. Bent into one position, she began to ache; but she was afraid to move for fear she would disturb the rock or the ground beneath it. There was no true sleep for her, only an occasional drifting off from pure exhaustion. Even in those brief moments of rest the roaring of the river was a constant threat in her ears, and the chill permeated her damp clothes and into every bone and muscle. Everything she had brought along for survival was gone, and she realized that even if she could make it out of this place, she would probably die from hunger and exposure.

She forced herself to think of warm, happy times—of breast-feeding her babies, of talks in front of the fire in their little cabin, of lying with River on the homemade mattress, of being one with River. She could imagine that warmth, his arms, their homemade quilt covering them, the sweetness of his kiss.

She could vividly remember that first night he had come into the shed and had claimed her as though it was the most natural thing in the world. If she died, at least she had known true love, had known the feel of a baby in her belly and in her arms, the wonder of a gentle man. She refused to think of anything else, and her thoughts drifted that way until she realized it was morning.

"Emma!"

She blinked awake. She must actually have fallen asleep, for she heard River call to her in her dreams.

"Emma!"

There it was again! Was she fully awake? She sat up, looking up but seeing no one. The voice had sounded far, far away.

"Emma! Answer me if you can!"

Her heart pounded with joy and disbelief. River! It was River. She screamed his name as loudly as her strength would allow. But she feared he would never hear her above the roar of the river. She struggled to get to her feet, her legs wobbly and stiff, everything hurting. She grabbed on to the root and screamed his name again.

"Down here! I'm down here!"

She waited for seconds that seemed like hours, watching, watching the bank above, screaming his name again. And suddenly he was there, looking down at her. He had a mustache, and his hair was cut short, but she didn't care why. It was River!

Tears welled up in her soul, and she smiled through a clay-covered face, screaming his name again. She reached for him, crying out his name again, just as the ledge under her feet gave way.

River watched in horror as the huge chunk of clay collapsed. Emma screamed as she plunged into the cold, rushing waters below.

"Emma!" River screamed. He was over the side in a moment, sitting on his rump and sliding, sliding, bouncing over cold, slippery clay, half-falling and half-hanging on to roots to break the fall somewhat. The water! How she feared deep waters! Now her head had disappeared. It seemed to take forever to get low enough to jump into the water after her.

Emma felt the sudden silence of the water. Below it the roaring stopped. There were only soft bubbling sounds. She fought the tearing current, struggled to get her head above water. Finally she reached the top, but just long enough to take another deep breath. She reached out for something, anything to hang on to.

Again her head went under, and she remembered Tommy holding her upside down under the water until she could not go another moment without a breath of air. It was the same feeling all over again. She struggled to reach the surface, but she could not get there.

Suddenly something strong grasped her about the waist. She fought at first, thinking it was Tommy trying to drown her again. But the strong hands lifted her out of the water. She gasped for breath, choking and spitting, as a strong arm came around her under the arms and pulled.

"Hang on! I see a flat piece of bank up ahead!"

River! It was his voice! Had the river flooded again? Would they make it off the *Jasmine?* Was he clinging to a rope to keep the flood waters from sweeping them away? She clung to the arm. So strong he was. She stayed still for him, felt him pulling her then, felt solid ground beneath her. They fell together onto it, panting and gasping for breath.

"Emma! My God, Emma!" She felt a big hand push her hair back from her face, felt someone pull her close in strong arms. "My precious Emma."

"River," she whispered. She leaned back, looking into his face, reaching up and touching it. "You're all right. You're alive! I knew . . . you'd . . . come. . . ."

There were tears in his eyes as he put a big hand to the side of her face and bent to kiss her forehead, then held her close again. Oh, the wonderful security of those arms! There was nothing to be afraid of now.

She felt herself being lifted in the same strong arms. "I see a way back up," he was saying. "We've got to get you out of these wet clothes."

She wrapped her arms around his neck. It was like that first night. "River . . ." she said weakly. "Sam . . . he will come after us."

"Hush. Sam Gates is dead, and so is Tommy. They will never touch you or bother you again. You belong to Joe Rivers; you always have and that's the end of it. We will not speak of them again."

She mumbled something about losing the baby, about Nigger Jim, about Tommy's burning body. Always there was a gentle but firm reply for her not to think any more about those things.

"The baby was a gift," he told her as he laid her on a blanket. "The Maker of Breath caused it to happen so that you would not be raped. I am only sorry that I was too badly hurt to help you. For this I will never forgive myself. I would die for you."

She lay peacefully, everything around her seeming like a

dream. Someone built a fire, then removed her wet clothes. Someone was washing her with heated water, then drying her and putting a warm, cotton gown on her.

"I brought some of your clothes because I knew the Maker of Breath would help me find you and you might need them," he was saying.

Warm blankets came over her, and moments later someone was lying beside her. "I will keep you warm," he said. "I have put warm rocks around your feet. Sleep, Emma. I pray you do not get sick from all of this like the first time."

"River," she whispered. She snuggled close against the powerful chest, breathing deeply of his familiar scent. At last he had found her! Again he had saved her from the terrible waters, and finally she rested again in his arms. "The babies . . ."

"The babies are fine. Mary and Grace are taking good care of them. We are free now, Emma. Soon we will be back home, and you can hold Rachael and Joshua." He kissed her hair, wanting to weep with joy. "No one will be looking for us anymore. All who know about us are dead." He thought of Joanna. She would not tell. He was glad the woman was free of Sam Gates.

Emma fell into a deep sleep, brought on by terrible exhaustion combined with the exhilarating relief of knowing she was safe now.

"My God, Emma, you gave yourself to them to save my life. I will never again let that happen. I was so afraid I had lost you forever." She heard only part of the words.

Emma awakened with a start; Tommy's face was leering at her in a dream, then Sam's. Suddenly both men burst into flames. Emma cried out, and then strong arms held her fast. Someone kissed her cheek gently.

"It is all right. You are safe now," said the voice.

Morning was breaking bright and warm. She vaguely remembered falling into the river, the cold waters, the strong hands saving her. But that had been morning, too. Had she slept all the rest of that day and all the night?

She focused her eyes on the man who held her. "River," she whispered.

He petted her hair. "You have slept a long, long time. It is good."

"River, that . . . horrible man . . . Sam . . ."

He put fingers to her lips. "I told you yesterday we will speak of it no more." She saw the intense pride and possessiveness in his eyes. "You belong to me. Nothing can ever change that." How he loved her! He had vowed he would never tell her what Sam Gates had done to her. Gates was dead and would never come into their lives again; and River knew who owned Emma Simms's heart, her body, and her soul.

Their eyes held and hers filled with tears. "That . . . that place . . . that mine . . . they said a doctor there would make it so I . . . couldn't have any more babies! I didn't go there, did I? They didn't do that to me!"

"No," he said gently. "You did not go there. You will have many more babies, Emma Rivers. And only one man will give them to you."

He met her lips gently, then pulled her into his arms, nuzzling her neck. She hugged him tightly, enjoying the wonderful, safe feeling of his strength, the glorious, familiar scent of him.

"What do you think about Texas, Emma?" he asked softly in her ear. He rose slightly, kissing her forehead. "I will always love Tennessee as my home, as the place where I found you. But we have bad memories here, and if anyone should blame me for what happened to Sam Gates—"

"River! What did you do to him? Are there men after you?"

"I do not think so. I killed him, Emma. A snake bit him, but I was the one who put it there."

She gasped. "He's dead! He's dead! And Tommy too . . . the tent caught fire. . . ."

"I know. I found his body." He would not tell her Tommy was still alive when he found him. It would bother her to know that he lay suffering for that long, for her heart was too soft, and perhaps she felt responsible. "Remember," he said gently, "we will not talk about any of these things anymore after today."

She ran her hands along his muscled arms. "I'll go to Texas if you think that's best, River. I would go anyplace with you. You know that."

He smiled softly, his eyes showing tears. "I am so glad I found you. The Maker of Breath is with us, Emma. I feel it. I will take you home and you will be with Josh and Rachael again. They will be so happy to see their mama. And then we will leave for Texas. Maybe Mary and Grace and the others will come with us." A tear slipped down his cheek and she brushed at it.

"Make love to me, River," she whispered.

"You are too weak."

"No. I need you to make love to me."

He smiled through tears, coming down to meet her mouth again, gently moving his lips to her neck, her shoulder.

She opened her eyes and saw a bird flutter by. The forest was her friend again. There was nothing to fear. She was with River Joe.

> . . . His lips warmed my own,
> And together we lay
> In the soft mountain grasses,
> Where he made me his bride.
> And our love, through all hardships,
> To the end shall abide . . .

To my readers:

I hope you will continue to follow the growth of America as I take you through its history from state to state in my "Bride" novels, coming to you in future months from Popular Library. Through these novels we will travel to Texas, Oregon, Montana, and other western states, as the American West is settled by proud, strong, and courageous people.

Feel free to write me at 6013-A Coloma North Road, Coloma, MI 49038, and I will send you a newsletter telling you about other novels I have written as well as future novels. Be sure to enclose a self-addressed, stamped envelope.

F. Rosanne Bittner